SULTAN OF DELHI

Arnab Ray is one of India's most read bloggers, known online as Greatbong. A PhD in Computer Science from State University of New York at Stony Brook, he has also written three bestselling books – *May I Hebb Your Attention Pliss*, *The Mine* and *Yatrik*. He can be found on Twitter at @greatbong.

AF519462

SULTAN OF DELHI

ASCENSION

ARNAB RAY

hachette INDIA

First published in 2016 by Hachette India
(Registered name: Hachette Book Publishing India Pvt. Ltd)
An Hachette UK company
www.hachetteindia.com

SRD

Copyright © 2016 Arnab Ray

Arnab Ray asserts the moral right to be identified
as the author of this work.

All rights reserved. No part of the publication may be reproduced, stored in a retrieval system (including but not limited to computers, disks, external drives, electronic or digital devices, e-readers, websites), or transmitted in any form or by any means (including but not limited to cyclostyling, photocopying, docutech or other reprographic reproductions, mechanical, recording, electronic, digital versions) without the prior written permission of the publisher, nor be otherwise circulated in any form of binding or cover other than that in which it is published and without a similar condition being imposed on the subsequent purchaser.

This is a work of fiction. Any resemblance to real persons, living or dead, or actual events or locales is purely coincidental.

ISBN 978-93-5195-092-9

Hachette Book Publishing India Pvt. Ltd
4th & 5th Floors, Corporate Centre,
Plot No. 94, Sector 44, Gurgaon – 122003, India

Typeset in 11.5/14.5 Arno Pro by
SÜRYA, New Delhi

Printed and bound in India
by Manipal Technologies Limited, Manipal

MIX
Paper from
responsible sources
FSC™ C104740

To Anahita

Prologue

January 1972

There were no stars in the sky. There was no moon. Just the wet cold seeping through thick cloth and bone, and the fog slowly smothering the night.

Every once in a while, a truck would grope forward over the broken road. Sometimes a long-distance bus would rumble by, but no sooner would its headlights pass than the fog would flow back denser than ever before.

Milte hain dil yahaan, milke bichadne ko ...

Kishore Kumar's voice floated from the direction of the ramshackle bamboo structure that lay fifty yards to the side of the road, perceptible through the fog only because of a Hasag lantern that was hung to its front, illuminating a sign that read 'Exide Batteries'. The small shop, one of the few that still operated on this side of the highway, sold batteries, torches, kerosene, hot tea, pakoras and, if you knew what to say and how much to pay, desi hooch. It was closed now, the coal ashed, and the front covered with tarpaulin.

But it was not empty.

On a charpoy, at the front of the shop, sat two men, one hunched slightly forward and the other leaning back and looking up at the sky, holding in his right hand a small transistor radio.

'Why don't you turn the radio off? Or at least change the channel. I hate Kishore Kumar.'

'It's my radio. It plays what I want it to.'

The first man pulled his monkey cap closer to his skull and clenched tightly the two thick shawls draped over his body.

'Tell me why you like Kishore Kumar again,' he said, tapping the ground rapidly with his feet in a desperate attempt to stay warm.

'Because he has a great voice.' In sharp contrast to his companion, the man with the transistor had on, as his shield against the numbing cold, only a flimsy grey sweater.

'Because he has a great voice? That's it? I mean that's all you can say about the *great* Kishore Kumar? A ten-year-old would give that answer! Tell me the reasons why you like him, explain it to me.'

The man with the transistor said nothing.

'Mohammed Rafi,' the first man said, 'Now... that man is God.'

The other man yawned, still looking up at the sky. 'Just because you say so.'

'No. It's not because I say so. It's because I understand. You can't hide classical training. Rafi has it. Kishore doesn't. To his credit, he knows his limits and stays within them.'

'Well, I don't care.'

'See? That's the problem with Hindustanis. They hide their ignorance with a stupid "I don't care", as if that's the honest end of all arguments. It's why Manmohan Desai makes more money than Satyajit Ray and that Babumoshai Khanna is a superstar.' The man raised his shawls in one quick motion and brought out a little silver belt-flask. 'Want some?'

The other man ignored the offer with a shake of his head.

'*Mooh mein le rahe ho kya?* You have been like this the whole night. Just a hmm or aaah.'

Arjun let out a little laugh. 'Just a fine night for listening to music,' he said, then added for emphasis, 'in silence.'

'Fine night for music? *Behenchod,* here I am freezing my testicles off and you say this is a fine night for music. How do you take this cold? Oh yes, I know what you will say…you are from Delhi and…'

'See Bangali, that's why I don't need to say anything. You complete my sentences.'

'You are right,' Bangali grumbled. 'We are a regular married couple now, I know what you will say and you know what I will say and so we both say nothing. Soon I will even start looking like you, and we will be farting in bed together.' He took a long swig from the belt-flask, as if exorcizing the horror of the thought. 'Sure you don't need this?'

'I am fine.'

Bangali took the heavy metal torch that lay to his right on the charpoy, and shone the light on his wrist. 'And now will you look at the time. It's thirty to midnight and the party still hasn't shown up.'

'They will show up,' Arjun said quietly. 'They always do.'

'Fifteen more minutes and then I am off. It's going to be an hour's walk to town if the truck doesn't get here. You realize that, don't you?'

'Well, there it is.' Arjun pointed towards the road. Sure enough, a small tempo had broken through the fog and was moving slowly towards them over the hard and rocky ground, its headlights turned off.

Bangali quickly got to his feet while Arjun remained seated, still leaning languidly backwards on the charpoy. As the tempo ground to a halt a few yards away from them, its tyres spluttering dirt and stones, Arjun said, 'You know the problem with you, Bangali? You are always too filmy.'

Bangali turned around, his hand once again snaking its way into the double-shawl.

'What? *Filmy*? What do you mean? You are the one who watches all the *bakwaas* films.'

'I do but I don't let it get to my head. I am sure you have already thought of what you are going to say to my face right before you and your friends smash it in, with a bullet from your gun or with blows from the torch.'

'Wh...'

Arjun now lay down fully on the charpoy, a smile at the corner of his thin, chapped lips.

'All this planning. All this drama. All this anticipation. But in all the excitement, you forgot to check whether your gun is loaded.'

Bangali stumbled back, whipping out a gun from under his shawl. Pointing it at Arjun, he pressed the trigger. Once. Twice. All he got was one metallic click and then another. In dismay, he looked to the right and to the left. The heavy metal torch was gone.

Four men approached Bangali in the darkness. All that one could make of them were their eyes, glowing in the black with fierce violence.

'Get him. Get him now!' Bangali yelled out, his voice cracking with panic. Arjun lay back on the charpoy as casually relaxed as before, shaking his head mockingly. The four men, their heads and mouths covered with cloth, made no move towards Arjun. Instead, they surrounded Bangali.

Bangali lunged at the one closest, swinging hard with a tightened fist. It hit the man square on the jaw, throwing his head back. Another came from the side, and he swung again but this time, the man dodged the punch, and the force of the forward thrust rendered Bangali off balance. He swore loudly and threw a solid left hook which merely grazed the man's shoulder. Then he felt an arm tightening around his neck. He tried to shoulder-throw the assailant at the back but the man knew what he was doing. He stayed as he was. Bangali was built like an ox. But so were the four men. Within a few seconds, Bangali's arms had been pinned back by practised hands. He tried to kick the crotch of the man in front but missed, and his right shoe flew away into the night, hitting the dusty ground a distance away. The man who had received the first blow to his mouth now landed his punch perfectly, straight on Bangali's lip. For a moment, the cold soaked away his pain but then it stayed heavy, as the blood dribbled down the side, warm and lucid. Then a knee slammed into his stomach, and he doubled up in pain.

Arjun Bhatia stood up to his full height, a head and more shorter than Bangali, and brushed the dust off his trousers. He held a gun in his left hand.

'Enough. *Bahut ho gaya*,' he said as the men continued scuffling. Yet another knee to the groin and several solid blows later, Bangali's struggles had been subdued, but he was still trying to break free. '*This* gun is loaded,' Arjun warned as he raised it once and then brought it back down to his side. 'Move one more time and I am going to use it.'

Bangali wheezed from the effort, out of breath, his drool now mixing with the blood on his chin. 'You are not going to kill me. I know that.'

'Sure of that, are you?'

'Yes, I am. You can't kill your friend.'

'Maybe we don't read our thoughts as well as we think.'

'And because you never kill people who know more than you. Smart people ...'

'If you are as smart as you think you are, why is it that you are staring down the end of the gun and I am the one holding the trigger?' After a pause for half a breath, Arjun continued, 'I know what you know, I always have. Sandhu and Talang want the business, and they made you an offer to split it three-ways. Provided you put a bullet in my head. Oh, I forgot. Not three-ways, but four-ways because Tripathi, the khaki-*kutta* who takes my money and still wants me dead, is also in on it.'

Bangali fell silent. He tried to shake off the hands pinning him back once again, failed, and then resigned himself to being overpowered.

'Now let me tell you what you don't know. After you were going to kill me, Tripathi had planned a little encounter for you a few miles down the road, and so the split would have become three-ways and Tripathi would get that government medal he's been after. That was the plan.'

Somewhere in the distance, a jackal howled.

'Unlike you, I am not filmy. I never was. So I am not going to stand here and tell you how exactly I know all of this. That's what the villains do, don't they? Talk and talk while the hero gets a chance to get away. *Chutiyas*. But since you and I go way back, I think I owe you a bit of... an explanation. Talang's dead, and the Nepalis have his head. *Actually* have his head. They cut his head off. Now these big boys are Sandhu's men, so that should tell you where he is now. Tripathi will get his medal, but it will be one of those died-in-the-line-of-duty-ones they give your widow on Republic Day. Though I don't know if they give you those if they find you drunk and dead in a ditch, having driven your service jeep off the road. Possibly not. Because that's how they will think he died.'

The men holding Bangali laughed.

'Which leaves you. And that's the sad part.'

'I can't die like this. Not here.'

Arjun shook his head.

'I have a wife,' Bangali pleaded. 'I have a son.'

The men laughed again, and one of them twisted Bangali's arm backward, making him scream in agony.

Arjun turned his coal-black eyes to the man holding Bangali down. 'Hurt him without reason, and the one who does gets the first bullet,' he said quietly.

The cackles of laughter died instantly. Bangali was sniffling now, his chin touching his chest in a show of contrition. 'Fifteen years we have run this business together. Fifteen years we have been friends. Doesn't that mean anything?'

'I guess it doesn't. I mean, why else would you do this to me?'

'I made a mistake.'

'Why? Why did you do it?'

'It hurt me every day. To see you as the boss and me the sidekick. Once it was the other way round, after all. I got mad. When Sandhu came to me with the offer, I said yes. You had to be killed, there was no other way. You do see that, right?'

'I do.'

'I am so sorry.'

Arjun reached out and gently tapped the side of Bangali's neck. His voice softened, 'I am sorry too. You have been a brother. Not a sidekick, not a partner, not even a friend, but a brother. I mean it. A brother. And if this was just about me, I would let you go. I would give you another chance and I know you wouldn't sell me out again.'

Arjun made a gesture with his head and one of the men hit Bangali hard on the back, making him drop to his knees. They slid on the dirt, scraping the small pebbles. He did not resist. The fight had gone out of him.

'But it's not about me. It's about *my* business. It's about *my* family. I can put up with traitors. After all, some may say, and not without reason, that I am a *gaddar* myself. But what I cannot put up with are fools. They get people killed. Fools like you. Fools who think, even after all these years of working with me, that I would not know, that I would not have seen this coming.' Arjun's finger tightened around the trigger. 'Fools who think that knowing one's limits and staying within them is foolish. Fools who don't like Kishore Kumar...'

Bangali tried to say something but he never got around to it. The bullet spoke first. Then once more.

The radio kept playing.

PART ONE

1

Arjun Bhatia hated trains. Almost every time he would get on one, it would happen – the panic attack.

His hands would turn clammy, his breathing wheezy, and his heart would start galloping like a horse on the last leg of the derby. Years ago, at the age of twenty, he had almost jumped out of a moving train when a gang of ticketless students had boarded the compartment near Patna and started rowdily shoving around the passengers.

There was always something that set off the panic attack – the brush of a stranger's forearm, a particular strain of stench, whether it be of sweat trickling down the side of a neck or of urine leaking out from the third-class compartment's latrine, the thumping of station vendors on the window, the chug-chugging of the train as it pulled into the platform, or a sudden, unscheduled stop in the dark. Whenever he travelled by train, like he was now from Delhi to Calcutta, he would book himself a seat in the AC first-class compartment, plop down on the bunk, pop in a sleeping pill and try to sleep through the entire journey. Sleeping allowed him to avoid the triggers – the people bearing down on him from all sides, treading on his toes and elbowing him in the ribs. But even then, he would sweat and toss and turn. His dreams, in fevered fits and starts, would then become little cracks for the dark terror to flow straight back in...

Lahore. Twenty-five years ago. 1947.

The Bhatias had been a big family. There was daadi, big and

loud, rolling from one side to the other as she walked like a sailor on a deck, perpetually carrying a brass plate full of home-made laddoos in her hand and bellowing 'bahu! bahu!' from the top of the stairs. There was ma, thin and fragile as though cut from fine china, tending to the army of ayahs, gardeners, cooks and cleaners, in that quiet, regal way of hers. There was papa, with his round metal glasses, thin butterfly moustache, small black topi and that slight forward stoop, walking fast towards his car or away from it, always in a hurry, his hard leather shoes cracking noisily against the gravel.

And then there were the three brothers, Ramprasad, Laxmanprasad and himself. Arjunprasad.

Shyamprasad Bhatia had named his first two sons, born two years apart, Ram and Laxman. But when the third came along, again after two years, he mixed up his epics and named him Arjun. Arjun had been sickly at birth, and then three successive years of malaria, typhoid and jaundice had made him smaller than boys his age. Ram and Laxman, in sharp contrast, could pass for Pathan boys. They were tall and strong, spending most of their time playing marbles, gili-danda and football, while Arjun, doted on by the army of ayahs, nurses, daadi and ma, would read large picture books from London, play with toy trains from France and Germany, and linger long hours in the garage with Yunus, their mechanic.

Cars were what Arjun loved the most. His father owned a Buick Roadmaster and a SS Jaguar 100. Arjun would spend his days in the garage, sitting wide-eyed with wonder among the wrenches, the screws and the bottles of grease, as Yunus explained how these marvellous machines worked.

Once, when he was nine, Iqbal Malik, his father's best friend and business partner, had taken the three boys to his estate for a week of hunting. Malik had given the airgun to Arjun, expecting him to be too weak to hold it up, let alone fire it. Arjun had proven himself true to his name, dropping one pigeon after another from the sky, too many times to put it down to beginner's luck. Ram and Laxman had watched in admiration, and perhaps even a bit of envy, and Malik had patted Arjun's back and said, 'This little one has the air of the sultans. Sultan of Delhi he will be...'

Soon after this episode, Arjun's health improved and Dr Muhammed, the family doctor, declared him fit enough to go out with his brothers in the sun. He had the best time of his life that winter. He had scaled walls, raced his brothers – and lost – saved goals, pissed into the wind, and had even gotten into a stone-throwing fight. For the first time he had felt like part of the gang, like one among the brothers. He was no longer the sickly young thing on the third floor, watching kites fly through the iron grille. He could not wait to grow up, if only to beat Ram at arm-wrestling and Laxman at marbles.

But there were other things happening, things that the ten-year-old could not fully understand, things that even the adults could not comprehend, as Arjun would find out later.

The first time they had felt the coming of the storm was during the Diwali of 1946. The war was over and Shyamprasad Bhatia's Diwali party, to which the great and the powerful were always invited, was as grand as ever – with the best kababs, Scotch and French wine, Portuguese fireworks and live music. But this time, there were no Singhanias, no Mehtas, and no Vermas. They had left for India.

At dinner the next weekend, Arjun's mother had brought up the topic of leaving, wondering aloud whether it would be wise to move to Bombay, where her sisters stayed. 'Maybe,' she had said, 'we should send the boys there for a while. The schools are better and they will have children their age to play with.'

Shyamprasad Bhatia would have none of it. He was, after all, the city's biggest cloth merchant and the president of the Merchants and Craftsmen Union, being the first brown man to be so. He and the chief of police were on first-name terms, and the governor invited him for tea. There was no way he would run away like the others, with their tails between their legs. Not from Lahore, where they had lived and made their money for generations.

'All this trouble is in passing only,' he had said, wiping the corner of his mouth with a white silk kerchief, like the pukka Britisher he was at the table. 'There will be some blood in the old city when the British leave, but they fight over everything there. Even an unpaid ten-rupee loan brings out the butcher knives in Lohari Gate.'

'But still ...' She had continued to argue.

Arjun's father had rattled the cutlery with an air of finality, 'Nothing will happen here. This is Model Town, a place for gentlemen. Not Papar Mandi.'

Model Town was truly a place for gentlemen, a garden city located six kilometres from the heart of Lahore and populated by the Hindu elite. It had clean roads, perfectly manicured lawns and high walls. To those who were used to its antiseptic life of privilege, something as improper as violence would require a no-objection certificate from the cooperative if it wanted to make its appearance there.

'But Ameena was saying that the Muslims of the League are marching in Mozang and that there are Afridi Pathans from the North who are provoking the boys and planning God knows what.'

Shyamprasad spoke slowly and in a low voice; it was what he did when his patience was being tested. 'The cheapest things in Anarkali Bazaar, they say, are rumours. Some boys with no jobs and all talk are shouting slogans and we should do what? Pack up and leave? Just based on a washerwoman's idle gossip?'

This put an end to the conversation. It was clear to all at home that the subject was no longer open to discussion among them.

Iqbal Malik would visit the Bhatia residence from time to time, for business, for gossip and for the Scotch, and the conversation would invariably veer towards the affairs of the country. Malik had been sanguine. 'Changes in *siyasat* have happened in the past, and revolutions demand blood, but life has gone on for people like us, just as it always has.' And so they had stayed, though Arjun, young as he was, could still feel his mother's immense unease. But he trusted his father. And Shyamprasad Bhatia was not worried. Not in the least.

Then Arjun had fallen sick again, with high fever and fits of vomiting. Things had become so bad that Dr Muhammed had him admitted to a nursing home, merely as a precaution – at least that's what he had told his mother. It was difficult to move around the city now that it faced regular fits of violence, so he argued that it might be better if Arjun stayed where he would get good care at a moment's notice. She agreed and Arjun was immediately shifted to a hospital.

It was on a Tuesday that everything changed.

Shyamprasad Bhatia had driven to the hospital to check on Arjun. The fever had subsided, the vomiting had stopped, and the doctor on duty had wanted him discharged the day before, what with the shortage of beds for people coming in, overflowing from the city hospital. It was prudent to save the beds for patients with serious burns, stab wounds and severe trauma. But no one could discharge Dr Gul Muhammed's patient without his consent, and that too when it was the son of Shyamprasad Bhatia.

Just when Shyamprasad was going to leave, Dr Muhammed had burst into the room in a panic and slammed the door shut. He was panting and the front of his white shirt was blackened with sweat.

'You have to leave. Now,' he gasped, holding on to Arjun's bedrail. 'They are going to kill you and your family. You have to leave the city. There is no more time.'

Shyamprasad stared as if he had seen a ghost. Arjun could see it in his face. His father did not believe him.

'Dr Muhammed, please relax.' He stretched his hand out. 'Nobody wants to kill us.'

'No, you don't understand. They do and they will.' The doctor shook away the outstretched hand, with some violence. 'There is a train leaving tonight, in a few hours. Get on it. Or there will be nothing left...'

Shyamprasad again put on that polite tone of gentle exasperation. 'I know you are worried and I am grateful for that. But I am sure the police and the army can put down a few angry young men. We stay in Model Town... they won't even...'

The doctor exploded in rage, 'You think your police will protect you? You think that just because you live in a big house with tall brick walls, that the world will pass you by? I hate to have to tell this to you but the police and the army are standing back all over town. The orders have come from above, to let things happen as they must. The Hindus must leave. Either walking or feet first.'

Arjun looked once at Dr Muhammed and then at his father. He desperately wanted to believe his father.

'Why would they want to harm us? We have never done anything to them.' Shyamprasad still seemed to believe he could reason his way out of the reality the doctor was forcing upon them.

Dr Muhammed shook his head. 'You have had your fancy parties with your white tents and your white-gloved waiters while they have gone to bed on empty stomachs. You have driven past their houses while they have begged for scraps of food you wouldn't even feed your dogs. You have refused to let them sit at your table or drink water from your glasses, because your religion makes Muslims unclean, and you ask "Why would they want to harm us?" Are you stupid? Or just blind?'

Shyamprasad was still smiling. 'You know I have never done that kind of thing. At our house...'

'You are a decent man, Bhatia sahib. But that does not matter to those on the streets. For them, you are just one thing. A Hindu. An enemy.' He slapped his forehead dramatically. 'We can keep arguing here over the whys and hows or you can save yourself and your son by catching the train.'

It was then that Arjun saw something new, something he had never seen before in his ten years – fear on his father's face. He felt faint.

'What do you mean by me and my son? I have to take my family with me.' Shyamprasad paused and asked, 'They are all okay, right?'

'I don't know. The rioters were moving towards Model Town and they had your name on the list. I would say take Arjun and leave. Your family can join you later.'

Shyamprasad had started moving now. 'I will bring them to the station in my car. Can you get in touch with Iqbal? He will know what to do, whom to talk to. The governor, I need to talk to the governor.'

Dr Muhammed lowered his voice and said, 'Do not get in touch with Iqbal Malik. He is arming the mob, I saw him on the street. Who do you think gave your name to them?'

Shyamprasad stopped, sat down on the bedside chair and held his head in his hands. 'Iqbal? He is my friend... Why?'

The doctor caught hold of his shoulders. 'There are no friends in this world. There never have been. Just people looking after themselves.' He shook him lightly. 'Now will you go or do you want to watch your son die here in front of your eyes?'

Shyamprasad rose stiffly, shuffling forward to the door. Then he turned to Arjun and said, 'Come with me. We have to go for your brothers.'

Dr Muhammed stopped him. 'There's no time to waste. You should go to the railway station straight away.'

'I can't leave my family!' Shyamprasad shouted in panic.

The doctor hesitated. 'It's too risky. But if you must go to Model Town, don't take your car. It's too fancy to pass unnoticed. My car is downstairs, it has a red cross on it. They won't stop you if you are in it. My driver knows how to get through. Don't sit at the back like you do, stay down. Don't be seen through the window. And don't take Arjun with you.'

'Not take Arjun with me? Why?'

'I will take him to Lahore Junction. It's not a long walk from here, and I know the back alleys.' He turned towards Arjun. 'Do you think you can walk with me to the station?' Arjun's tongue felt heavy, no words came out. He just nodded. He had understood what lay behind the doctor's words, that death lay in wait at Model Town. The panic in Dr Muhammed's eyes, Arjun had realized, came not from the fear of what might happen but the knowledge of what already had.

He felt weak and light-headed as they stepped out, him and Dr Muhammed, through the back door of the nursing home. The moment they were outside, Dr Muhammed whispered to him, 'If anyone stops us, I will say your name is Shabbir and that you are my nephew. Understand? You are born mute. Remember that. Do not say a word. The way you talk, it gives your religion away. And if they try to pull your shorts down to check if you are circumcised, run. Do not wait for me. Do not look for me. Do not turn back. Just run as fast as you can.'

Arjun had never been in this part of the town. If he had, he had been driven around in a car. So he had no idea where he was as they walked grimly on. They kept to the narrow streets, sometimes taking shortcuts through little private yards, climbing through holes in dirty brick walls, jumping over little ditches filled with refuse and sneaking by metal cages full of fluttering chickens. Arjun could see columns of thick black smoke belching out into the sky and once or twice, a phalanx of voices shouting slogans in the name of Allah would pass by. Dr Muhammed would then pull Arjun into a corner and they would wait for the voices to die down.

Then as they were walking down a road, Arjun saw three men in white Pathan suits coming from the other end, talking animatedly among themselves. One of them held an extinguished torch, another a long sword, the rays of the afternoon sun dancing cruelly down the sharp edge.

'Assalaam alaikum doctor sahib,' said the man with the sword, and it was then that Arjun noticed the bloodstains on the blade. It had been wiped with a cloth but the red still lingered ominously.

'Wa-alaikum salaam,' Dr Muhammed said, making a slight *adaab*. The three did the same.

'*Kya baat hai,* doctor sahib, you are wandering the streets when there is so much work to be done,' the tallest one said politely, but there was no mistaking the frostiness in his words. Then he looked down at Arjun and asked, 'Who is this boy?'

Without changing his expression, Dr Muhammed replied, 'This is Shabbir, my nephew.'

The man sat on his haunches and asked, 'Which mohalla do you stay in?'

'He can't speak. Poor boy can barely hear. He was born like that,' said Dr Muhammed, putting a protective arm around Arjun's shoulder.

The man with the extinguished torch said, 'Nephew? I never knew you had a nephew, doctor sahib. That too, a deaf mute?'

There were two side lanes, one to the left and one to the right, and if he had to run, Arjun had decided he would go left, further away from the man with the sword.

Dr Muhammed said, 'I hardly know him myself. Shabbir and his grandmother came from Amritsar on the train a few days ago. The Hindus killed his family, leaving them alive.'

The man touched Shabbir's forehead tenderly. 'Doctor sahib, he is burning with fever.'

'Yes, I know. The shock of what he has seen ... all that slaughter in front of him,' Dr Muhammed mumbled.

His suspicious frown dissolving, the man reached into the pocket of his Pathan suit and brought out a fistful of gold. Necklaces, earrings and other things Arjun could not well make out.

'Take this. It's a small price for what they took from you.' The man held the items forward, gesturing for Arjun to take them. Dr Muhammed gave Arjun an encouraging pat on his back, signalling that he should take what was being given.

Arjun knew what this was. Loot from a store these three had just robbed. Maybe that blood on the sword ... He made his hand into a begging bowl, and smiled his most grateful smile. For a second, his reflexes gave him away, manoeuvring his hands subconsciously into a namaskar, because that was what he had been taught to do whenever anyone gave him a gift. Then he pulled back, for that would definitely have given away his religion, and made a low bow instead, keeping the 'please have mercy on me I am a deaf mute' smile pasted on his mouth.

The man with the extinguished torch said, 'We should get going.'

'They have a train going out in the evening. Some *fauji*s are standing guard at the station, so we have to wait till it's on the tracks to get at the Hindus,' explained the man with the sword. The three men then walked past, leaving the two standing there, frozen for a few moments, shoulders clenched in terror. Then they looked at each other, Dr Muhammed nodding a silent 'well done', and moved forward.

Lahore Junction was pure bedlam. There were people crawling all over the platforms, like flies on a piece of jaggery. Old women barely able to move, babies strapped to their mothers, young men with bandages on their heads and lines of cloth bundles and steel trunks of various shapes and sizes. There were a few army men walking about kicking at the larger trunks, yelling at the owners, 'This can't go on the train,' while their owners argued and pleaded and fell at their feet.

Dr Muhammed thrust a bundle of currency notes into Arjun's hand. 'This and that gold should get you over the border.'

'That gold ... I can't take that. It's ...' Arjun began, reaching into the pocket of his shorts where he had stuffed the gold.

'It's yours. Don't think the owners are there to lay claim. And if it keeps you alive, it would be worth much more than it would ever be on anyone's neck.' There were tears in Dr Muhammed's eyes. 'You are a smart boy. Allah may not have given you health, but he has given you an even bigger blessing. Brains. It will keep you alive.'

Arjun looked towards his shoes, and asked the question he had been dreading to ask, 'My father isn't coming back, is he?'

'I don't think so,' the doctor said sorrowfully, then he added, 'I couldn't have stopped your father from going back home. No man can leave without trying to save his family. So I did what I could.' He swallowed hard, trying to keep his emotions on a leash. 'No matter what happens, you get on that train. Do not wait for your father. Is that understood?'

'What's the use? They will kill us later on the line. That's what those men said.'

'They will try to. They may succeed. They may fail. Stay here, though, and you are dead. For sure.'

'Is there any way I can pay you back once I reach the other side? This is a lot of money you have given me,' Arjun asked, with all the innocence of his ten years.

The doctor lifted him up in his arms and gave him a hug, his beard pricking against Arjun's cheeks. His tears now trickled down without hold.

'When you grow older, go to a dargah one day and give alms

in my name. Maybe then Allah will be able to forgive some of my sins.' He put Arjun down on the platform, turned away without another word, and vanished into the crowd.

Arjun watched him go and then sat himself down near a dirty pillar, squeezing himself on the ground between a family of five and an old man. The old man was dressed in an impeccably tailored white suit, with a red handkerchief folded out of his pocket, a matching red tie and a monocle. Seeing Arjun looking at him with mild interest, he smiled and adjusted his white hat rakishly. 'If I am going to die, I might as well die in my best,' he said. Arjun thought of telling him how much more he would stand out in a crowd in that outlandish get-up when they came for them, but thought better of it. What did it matter to him? The world was changing and silence saved lives – as it had saved his back with the three men in the Pathan suits.

Night fell and the crowd grew and so did the terror. There was no sign of the train. Arjun sat still, his vision blurring and then getting crisper with the ebb and flow of the fever. He thought of Ram and Laxman and about playing tag with them on the lawns, with him always being the *it*. He thought of the cars and their gleaming round curves. He thought of ma and daadi and the puja room up on the third floor. He thought of his father at the table reading the paper, and he thought of himself that day out in the countyside, shooting down pigeons – white fluttering wings against the bright blue sky.

They were drifting away now, the memories and the people in them, like scraps of paper in a strong breeze, and he felt, deep inside, that they would never come back.

But he was wrong.

He felt a hand on his shoulder, and it snapped him out of his half-slumber.

For there he was. His father.

The Diwali before last, Ram and Laxman had tied a roll of firecrackers to the tail of a stray dog. Arjun had tried to stop them, but they would have none of it. The poor dog had yelped and barked and run around as the two boys had laughed and clapped their hands, and Arjun had rushed to tell his mother, but he could not forget the look of stark terror that had been on the poor mutt's face. It had bothered him for nights on end.

That face.

He saw that look again today on his father's face. Arjun stood up to hold his father, whose limp body seemed to almost collapse in his arms. And then his father started bawling long and loud. People were looking at them, for even in that sea of misery, his father's sobs stood out. It was then that Arjun noticed his father's shirt was caked with grime and ash, and he understood what had happened.

'They burned down everything. Our house. Everything,' his father said, through the flood of snot and tears, 'your mother, your grandmother... they are all...'

Arjun clasped his father close to his chest. Words were superfluous.

'Ram and Laxman, I couldn't find them... maybe they took them... maybe they had mercy... I don't know... I could not find them.'

'They must have run away. Ram and Laxman are smart. They will find us, daddy. I am sure someone will help them, as Dr Muhammed has helped us.' Arjun knew this was highly unlikely. The men he had met today did not seem to be the kind who would leave a job incomplete, but he needed to get his father to stop crying, at least so that he would not attract so much attention.

And just then the train pulled into the station. Which was when the fighting started, for there were too many and there was only so much a train could take. Arjun held his father's hand and pushed and shoved through the crowd, taking blows to the chin and the head, and yet jostling through. He would not remember much of those few minutes in the years that would follow, except a fleeting image of the old man in the white suit, lying on his stomach on the platform, his right leg splayed at an angle and his temple split and bloodied, crawling like a wounded cockroach towards the train that had started to move.

Arjun did not care. All that mattered was that the train was leaving Lahore and that he and his father were on it.

They sat on the floor in the dark compartment, their breaths squeezed out by the pressure of the shoulders and arms and legs of the people all around them. Shyamprasad Bhatia sobbed for a while, he was not the only one, and then he fell quiet. Arjun sat frozen, thinking of what he could do once the rioters stopped the train and entered the compartment. Should he slide under the bodies and play dead? But they would burn the train after they had killed, so maybe he should try to make a run for it, dodge between their legs, for he was small, and try to jump out on to the side of the tracks. No. That sounded much like death too. The heavy breathing on the side of his neck told him that his father had fallen asleep, and he was glad for it for that meant his father would not see them coming when they did, or would realize it too late to feel much terror. There was a woman pressed to his right side, who kept weeping and telling her husband, 'Kill me first before they take my honour. Promise me you will.' Then she turned towards Arjun and said, 'If they kill him first, promise you will kill me before they take my honour.' Arjun said yes, even though he did not know what she meant by 'taking honour' and even though he knew that there was no way he or her husband would be able to kill her. There was nothing to kill her with.

The train clanked to a halt. It was pitch-dark outside. Arjun closed his eyes, and waited for death. A man close by said, 'Just a line-crossing. Nothing to worry about.' No one believed him.

Some prayed, some sobbed, some clung together. One second coalesced into another, like water at the tip of a tap, forming a gigantic, throbbing water drop of terror, waiting to burst the moment footsteps would be heard outside. But they never came, the men with the torches and the swords, and the train chugged forward and gathered speed into the night...

When they finally arrived in India, Arjun's fever had sweated out. The horror remained though, hidden in the recesses of his mind, and he knew, even as he walked out on to the platform, holding his father's hand, that he would never ever be rid of it.

2

IT TOOK ARJUN YEARS TO REALIZE THAT ALONG WITH THE REST of his family, he had lost his father back in the rubble of Model Town. The Shyamprasad Bhatia that had been on the train with him – eyes red with tears, lips sealed dry – had been a husk, a hollowed-out shell of what had once been a living, breathing person.

After the train journey, they had been herded together into a refugee camp near Purana Qila in Delhi, housed in massive tents. For days, Shyamprasad sat in a corner, making no attempt to get food for himself or for his son. Arjun had put this down to shock, hoping that he would come out of it. The little boy had wandered from tent to tent and kindly hands had sometimes fed him, and sometimes shooed him away. When the aid trucks came, he would stand and fight for dried chapattis and watery daal with the rest of the orphans. His father had stayed away from it all, curled up in a ball, staring into nothingness. Arjun would bring back some food, his father would refuse it for a while, mumbling incoherently to himself, but then hunger would finally get the better of him and he would gobble a bit down before pushing it away again.

Arjun had suggested going to Bombay, where his mother had wanted them to go. Her sisters were there and they were well-off enough not to begrudge two extra mouths. But his father would have none of it. He would not even write them a letter. He gave no reason for his decision, and fathers were not obliged to explain their actions to their children, no matter how devoid of reason they were. Many years later, he had tried to explain his actions, while looking vacantly out of the window of their house in Lajpat Nagar. 'They took everything from me. My money, my house, my honour. Who could I show my face to? Not to anyone I had known before, definitely not to her sisters. For what is a man without his honour? An animal.' Arjun knew what 'taking honour' meant by then and he understood why his father had done what he had, but it did not make him understand his decision any more. It was foolish, he told himself, to let pride win over prudence.

It was foolish to stay aloof as his father did.

There was a great deal of activity at the camp. Refugees were organizing themselves into militia, making speeches, knocking on doors. Grand plans were being made, of marching back to wherever they had come from to get back what was theirs. Some, the smart ones, scoured the city looking for places vacated by Muslims, so that they could set up shop. They did, in Connaught Place and in Karol Bagh and any place where people needed things to buy. Money was scarce but they borrowed and begged and sometimes they stole. They occupied plots of land and started building their little structures, hovels of bare brick and cement and asbestos roofs, and they heckled and hassled the babus to give them water and to build them roads.

And in all this, Shyamprasad Bhatia stayed away. Even when men sought him out for advice and for leadership, for he had been well known in Lahore, he had shooed them away with silence, and with waves of his hand. When he finally came out of his tent, it was because the government was clearing out the camp and they had to move. The rulers were kind to him, and a small plot of land, smaller in area than their rose garden back in Lahore, was allocated in the place then called Cheap Colony, which would over the years, come to be known as Lajpat Nagar. Even though Shyamprasad was now better than he had been at first, in that he ate by himself and would utter the occasional sentence, he never built like the rest. Here too the Bhatias were bailed out by helpful strangers who took time off from making their own houses to volunteer to help with theirs. Arjun did a lot of the work, carrying cement and bricks on his head, and learning how to lay them together and then how to install an asbestos roof. He had had a late growth spurt and at thirteen, he no longer looked small and weak. He had not had his fever and chills again, and as the years passed, he realized that what Dr Muhammed had once called a 'weak constitution', was something that he had, like his family, left behind in Lahore.

The gold and the money they had been able to bring had run out long ago. But while Arjun carried bricks and cement for others and did odd jobs for food, his father was content making daily rounds of government offices, especially the one that dealt with missing and displaced persons, filling up forms and re-filling them, looking for Ram and Laxman.

They grew apart over the years, father and son. Back in Lahore, Arjun had looked up to his father in the way that little boys do, without question. It wasn't what he would call love because they were never close, for fathers were not supposed to be friendly. They were figures of authority, and children were trained to speak quietly in their presence, not go up to their rooms when they were in the house and never to sit in their chairs or touch their desks and tables. Now thrown together by fate, he saw the man behind the father. And what he saw was not what he had expected. And then one day Arjun finally lost his temper and did what he would have thought unimaginable once.

He argued with his father.

'You have to get some work. You just have to, daddy. For my sake.' Arjun referred to his father not as papa or babuji, but as 'daddy', because that is what their Anglo-Indian governess had taught them to say. It seemed to him now rather strange but he continued, from force of habit.

'I need to find my sons.'

'I am your son too. And I am here and I am alive.' He had felt guilty being brutal with his father, but the truth had to be told.

'They are alive too. You believe that as well, you told me yourself.'

'That was years ago. I said that then because you needed to hear it. I didn't believe it then. And I believe it even less now, not after all the stories we have heard.'

'You are giving up on them? Your own blood?'

'It's better to give up on fairy tales than on responsibilities.'

His father had looked at him with disappointment.

'You have changed, Arjun.'

'You should too. If you want us to live.'

The argument ended there but Shyamprasad finally found a job. Or rather he was handed one. One of the small retail merchants from Lahore, a man by the name of Satish Malhotra who once used to supply to the Bhatias, employed him out of pity. His job was to oversee Malhotra's shop at Connaught Place while the latter opened another one closer home in Cheap Colony. So that's what Shyamprasad did: he woke up every morning, went to Connaught Place, pulled up the shutters, swept the floor, managed the front, kept the accounts and rolled down the shutters late in the evening. Then he would come back home and once again step into silence. It hurt Arjun to see his father reduced to this, but it hurt him even more that it did not seem to bother his father as much. He seemed to be strangely content serving others, and whenever Arjun brought up the subject of opening a business themselves, like everyone else was doing, his father's responses were predictable.

Where would he get the money from? These shops were all illegal and could be demolished any day. There were already too many shops.

Arjun realized soon enough that these were just excuses. His father did not want, like the other fathers there, to live. He wanted only to subsist.

As the days rolled along, and Arjun understood that his father would never be convinced to start afresh, they talked less and less, avoiding each other's gaze when they were in the same room. Once, only once, had they truly fought, with voices and tempers raised. This was in 1961. Arjun had come back after a matinee show of *Gunga Jumna*. Someone had told his father that Arjun was hanging out with the 'wrong crowd'. His father had shouted at him, and Arjun had acted the part of the contrite son for a while, but there was only so much he could take. Finally, he let it all out.

'Who are you to tell me what's wrong and what's right? Who are you to tell me *anything* for that matter? And don't give me that "I am your father" lecture. So you are. My father. But you are also a fool. A big arrogant fool. And I am sorry for being so blunt but there it is. You let daadi die, you let my brothers die, you let ma die, because you ... you would not listen to her when she told you to leave Lahore. Idle washerwoman gossip. That's what you said. Remember? The only person you listened to was Iqbal Malik – the one person you should not have listened to. You had your chance, daddy. You could have left with everyone, maybe even with our money. Then we could have had a life here, like the Singhanias and the Mehtas ... but no, no ... no ... you had to close your eyes to everything going on around you. Even after that, even after killing everyone, what did you do? You would not let us go to Bombay because, God knows, it would hurt your pride. But it didn't hurt your pride to see your son pushing bricks and cement for others or standing outside people's houses, hoping they would have mercy and give him a chapatti. No. No. Why would this hurt your pride?

I am just the son who should have died like the rest but didn't.' He stopped just to swallow back the spit. 'Even if I could forget what happened in Lahore, what did you do after? You moaned and you groaned and then you spent your time trying to find the dead. And the world passed by. People who came with us and stayed in the same filth at Purana Qila now own shops. Not one. Not two. Five. They have two-storeyed pukka houses, and don't even pretend you don't know who I am talking about. It's not that I don't love you, daddy, it's that I don't respect you. It's just that I don't respect your opinions. Because I don't respect fools. Fools are the most dangerous people in the world. They get others killed.'

Shyamprasad did not reply, and Arjun couldn't remember him saying anything after that, till a year later, he clutched his chest and slid down to the floor, sweating and out of breath. As Arjun rushed towards him and took his head in his hands, Shyamprasad said, his eyes fixed on his son's, 'I need to go to the hospital. Get Yunus to bring out the Buick. Tell your mother not to worry, there is nothing wrong with me. Just a little flutter.' As Arjun rose to call for help, Shyamprasad gripped his arm tightly with strength that far belied his wasted frame. 'Don't forget to take your tonic and your barley. You need to grow as strong as your brothers.' Then the bony fingers loosened slightly and the eyes closed. Arjun sat with his father's head on his lap for a long time, brushing the dirty white hair back from his forehead.

Lahore, he knew, was finally gone. Delhi was all that remained.

Stepping into Howrah Station, he felt like he was stepping back into time.

It was 1947 here.

All over again.

The Bangladesh war had happened a year ago. Pakistan had surrendered. Dhaka had been liberated. The government propaganda machine, that reached out to the population through newsreels compulsorily screened before every movie, had hailed it 'new India's triumph'. New Delhi had been delirious and the dailies had glowed orange, white and green with nationalistic prose. But down here at Howrah Station, closer to where the war had been fought, one could see the cost of the triumph – huddles of humanity, sleeping, defecating and reproducing on the platforms, with no place to go. In 1947, when the refugees had streamed over the eastern border, they had been swept to the side of railway tracks and roads. Yet more had come, spilling over into parks and open spaces, occupying them with plastic sheet and rope and little brick structures with tin roofs. Then 1971 happened and the final tidal wave of refugees had washed over the city, human flotsam from Dhaka and Rajshahi and Barisal, flowing into whatever cracks and crevices still remaining in this, the once-great metropolis of the east.

Calcutta always reminded Arjun Bhatia of his father post-1947, frozen in pain by the memories of a better past. Maybe that's why he hated it so much.

Arjun's thoughts were disturbed by a tug at the sleeve of his shirt. A boy, not more than ten, stood at his side, snot running down from his nose, his hair matted with dirt and mud and smoke. 'Ten paise ...' The boy touched his fingers to his lips. 'Ten paise ...' Behind him were two others, one boy and one girl, both the same age, in tattered clothes covered in days' worth of dust, their palms extended. The girl had a bruise on her left brow. Arjun reached into his shirt pocket, brought out three shiny one-rupee coins, gave them in turn to the three children, and quickly trotted down the road, because he knew that once word spread, there would be more after him.

Safely away from the train station, his thoughts turned to recent events.

Bangali, Bangali... madarchod. *Why did you have to do it?*

It had been two weeks since he had put a bullet through his head. Two weeks he had felt this hollow inside.

Nothing good ever happens to those who are fools. Nothing.

He wanted to forget, to move on as he had wanted his father to have done, to tend to the living and forget the dead. Yet Bangali's laugh still came back to him loud and thunderous, with that '*salaaaaaa bokachodaaa*' rolling off the tongue with loving relish.

Arjun had made up his mind. He was out of the business. For good. He would not run guns again. The margins were not worth it any more. There was now but one thing left, which is what he had come to Calcutta to do.

Tell Bangali's woman that her man was dead and then hand over to her Bangali's share. He could then go back to Delhi, to his wife and his children, and move forward. The books would be balanced and closed and everything would be all right.

He was wrong.

Arjun got her name from a postcard that Bangali had not lived to send. Nayantara Banerjee.

Bangali had mentioned her a few times, but he had forgotten the name, only remembered it started with N. For if he had to remember every woman that Bangali bragged about bedding, he would have little room in his brain for anything else. Bangali had never been shy of talking about his romantic escapades, particularly to Arjun, for he knew it would make Arjun feel embarrassed. So he would get into progressively gratuitous details till Arjun would say 'enough' or his ears would turn red, at which Bangali would howl with joy.

'You do not enjoy *chudai*, Arjun Bhatia-jeeee. You don't even think about it. Your *lund* is your wallet. As long as that gets big, you are happy. Live a little. *Thodi aish kar, gandu, aish kar*.'

'No thank you. You do enough *aish* for both of us.'

'*Sahi hai. Main tere liye aish karoon, tu mere liye cash karein*.' He would then break into a vulgar parody of some song and then try to plant a kiss on Arjun's cheeks and Arjun would push him away with a '*chal haat, gandu*' and Bangali would thump his thighs and laugh even louder.

But this woman had apparently been special. This Nayantara Banerjee. For some reason Arjun had never figured out why Bangali had married her. It had been five years ago, when he had given Arjun the news.

'*Kutta se ab aadmi ban raha hoon.* But no regrets. No regrets at all.' Arjun had sniggered, for seeing Bangali in love was a bit too much for him to take. That, and his Bangla-accented Hindi.

'So that means no more women?'

'Don't need any. I love her, I really do.'

Arjun had sniggered again.

'You have no idea what love is, do you?' asked Bangali in his faux-serious voice.

Of course Bangali had gone on with his philandering, though he would talk less openly about his adventures. One day, Bangali had brought a box of sweets and announced the birth of a son. This name Arjun remembered, because he had liked it.

Arijit. The conqueror of enemies.

Arjun looked at the postcard. 178 Nakul Das Lane. Yes, there it was. Nakul Das Lane was a small street, wide enough for only one cycle rickshaw to pass through and one other person. On both sides were walls, broken and wet and discoloured, plastered over with rectangles of paper, black-and-white Bengali film posters, sharing space with colour posters of Sadhana and Rajesh

Khanna, their lips coloured excessively red, and over them, pasted with naked aggression, posters of a white sickle against an even redder background. Mosquitoes swirled intermittently over the open drain that ran down one side, and refuse lay piled high on the other side, with crows feasting atop the garbage. A man with shifty eyes passed by, looking at Arjun suspiciously, and Arjun knew why. The Naxalite communists were on the run and going undercover and a stranger on the street might portend a police party coming and knocking on doors.

Since 1967, the Naxalites had been great for business. After they started targeting the police and moneylenders and landowners, the demand for guns all over North India had gone up like umbrellas during monsoon. The Naxalite leader Charu Majumdar's rhetoric of 'total revolution' was seen for what it actually meant – the total annihilation of the moneyed class. Arjun did his bit too, for one must always prime the market, paying beat reporters of small vernacular newspapers – the ones that came out from district towns, the ones people really read – to carry stories of the Chinese flooding the Naxals with guns used by the Red Army.

Panic led to profits.

Getting a legal firearm was a mess of applications and you had to prove to some government-official babu that your life was under threat and, no matter what you said, approval was mostly impossible without baksheesh. Even a little child knew that if you actually intended to use a gun it was imperative that it be unlicensed. So people who feared being robbed – rich men and jewellers and hoarders – came to the black market.

People came to Arjun Bhatia.

Bangali loved the Naxalites too and while he didn't mind the money they brought him, he claimed he admired their ideals. He enjoyed talking about politics more than he enjoyed talking about sex, and Arjun could never decide which of these two topics he hated more. Silence was usually not an effective shield against Bangali for he would scrub and rub till you reacted.

'No, I don't like the Naxals,' Arjun had said with passion. 'The people that raped my mother and killed my brothers and burned down our house did it in the name of religion. These people do it in the name of revolution.'

'The Naxals don't rape anyone, and really, have you ever read a single speech of Chairman Mao?'

'I haven't. I don't need to. All I know is that these people are jealous – jealous of those who have more and they want to take it. That's all. It's basic human nature, to possess that which we do not own. So they take. They take honour. They take possessions. They take lives. Muslims did it in Lahore, the Hindus and the Sikhs did it in Amritsar, and the Naxals now do it here. They all have their pretty words and their long speeches, but behind it all, it's the same thing.'

Bangali had squeaked and ranted in that whiny, aggrieved tone of his. But Arjun had not responded further because, like every time, Bangali had just not got the point.

178 Nakul Das Lane was an ancient two-storeyed house that seemed to be even more dilapidated than the ones on either side. The cement had peeled off in places, the exposed bricks looked brittle, and a little tree was growing out from the side, its roots clawed into the cracks in the walls. Arjun knocked on the front door, once and then again. It swung open, revealing a woman of formidable proportions, with flabby forearms, a huge circular face, a thick nose that somehow sat off-centre, and wearing an enormous red bindi on her forehead. She looked at him with undiluted hate while chewing furiously on what he supposed was paan.

'Are you Nayantara Banerjee?' asked Arjun, putting on his most official air. Old Bangali had some weird kinks if this was whom he married.

'Is this something about that no-good husband of hers? What's he done now? Got arrested?' the woman asked.

'I would prefer to talk to her, *behenji*, if that's possible,' Arjun said, keeping his eyes focused on her blue Hawaii chappals. They were enormous.

She pointed to the side of the house. 'She lives upstairs.' Then she measured him up and down and asked, 'Who are you? I haven't seen you here before. Are you police?'

'I am a friend of her husband,' Arjun said, suitably enigmatic, taking a step away to excuse himself from her presence.

'Well, you tell that friend of yours to start acting like a man. Who leaves his wife and son alone in this city and vanishes for months? *Phaltoo joto sob.*' She said some more things in Bangla but by that time the door had been slammed on Arjun's face and for that he was most grateful.

It was 12.30 in the afternoon and yet the stairs were dark and forbidding. There was a patina of dust everywhere and when one breathed in, one could feel it filling up the lungs. Why did Bangali live in a place like this, Arjun wondered. Bangali made money, and he knew exactly how much that was.

He must have blown it all on women and whisky, that fool. Can't do right by his friend, can't do right by his family. No wonder that bastard never invited me home.

The door upstairs was open, and Arjun did not know what to do. He knocked and then coughed once. No one came to the door. Then he called out, 'Is Nayantara Banerjee here?' He heard the sound of the lady downstairs talking to someone, and the drip of an open tap, and that was it. No response. He peeked in and saw that the door opened into a small room, neatly arranged as a living room, with a small table, an ashtray, a few books and two small one-seater sofas. The furniture was old and had seen better days, and the sofa cover was well-worn but there was something homely and inviting about that room, and without thinking much, he sat down on one of the sofas. Leaning forward, he looked at the books and found Marx and other red literature among some Bengali paperbacks and one large picture book on Hollywood. Too much to expect Bangali to have a *Filmfare* or something, thought Arjun, and leaned back against the sofa. His back hit something hard and he sprung forward. It was one compartment of a wooden toy train. He kept it down on the floor, and looked to the side towards the passage, and that's when she came in, blissfully unaware of his presence in the room, her head tilted to the side, rubbing a towel down over her wet hair.

It was the hair that caught Arjun's eyes first, cascading down in a stream of lustrous black to her waist, which was curved slender like an exquisitely expensive vase, the kind that used to adorn their living room back in Lahore. Then his eyes shifted up to her breasts, her wet sari clinging, outlining the contours, and he could not help notice the light image of her nipples, and he realized she was not wearing a blouse but had only her sari wrapped around, and then he saw her shoulder, bare, and the prominent collarbone, then her lips, full and voluptuous, her eyes, large and liquid and burning, with a fever whose warmth he could feel even sitting there on the sofa. Arjun felt as if he were separating into two, one wanted to stride up, unfurl her sari, and then take her, pinned to the door, and the other, while realizing the totally immoral desires of the other, wanted to bolt and run down the stairs, never to return. He tried to speak, but the words evaporated on the edge of his tongue. He had rehearsed this – how to break the news, how to put the cash in her hand, and then how to leave without answering many questions. Now he had forgotten everything, forgotten why he was here and who she was. All he wanted was her, and all he felt was shame for wanting so, for he was a married man with children, and he had never ever looked at other women in this way.

Till now.

Finally, after what seemed to be an eternity, Arjun stood up and turned his eyes downwards. 'I am sorry, I knocked and then I called out your name. But … then … I …'

She stood there, near the passage, and she made no attempt to cover herself or recoil or run to wear a blouse. 'He is dead, isn't he?' was what she said, and Arjun knew the script was more different than he could have ever imagined.

'My name is Arjun Bhatia and …' He remembered now what he had thought he would say.

'I know who you are,' she said sharply and pointed towards the wall. There was a framed picture there, and Arjun had missed it all this while. It was one they had taken years ago, at a studio in Agra, because Bangali had thought it would be a great idea. There he was, Bangali, his handsome, rugged face drawn into a movie-star smile, his muscular arm thrown casually over Arjun's shoulder. Arjun looked plain and ordinary next to him, like the hero's best friend who dies in the first reel. He felt a keen sense of defeat. He would never be Bangali. In a way, without realizing it, he had always wanted to be like him – handsome, charming, well built and well read – and yet, there he was, a face in the crowd, one among many.

There was something else now in his heart, something he had never felt before. The desire to possess that which was not his, that which was forbidden to him. He had to have her.

'If he is dead, tell me. No need to twist it around.'

'Yes, he is. I am sorry.'

She leaned back on the wall near the door, and tears welled up in her eyes. She bit her lip, looked up at the ceiling, and breathed out.

'Will you please sit here? I … I need some time to think,' she said. 'How did he die?'

'One of our boys sold out. They were waiting for him. There was ...' Before he could finish his little prepared speech, she had vanished down the passage. He sat there awkwardly, wondering what to do, leafing through the books, careful not to look at the picture on the wall. All that was going through his mind was her.

'Why is ma crying?' said a voice from the door, and Arjun turned his head to locate its source. A boy of about four years stood there. He had curly hair and large eyes like his mother's but was otherwise exactly like his father, wearing a pair of oversized khaki shorts. A flood of intense shame washed over Arjun for the thoughts that had been running through his head about the boy's mother, and for what he had done to his father.

'You must be Arijit?' Arjun asked.

'Why is ma crying? Where is baba?' the boy asked innocently, nodding in response to Arjun's questions.

Arjun had not rehearsed for this possibility. How could he explain to this small child what had happened? Did he even know what death meant?

What would have happened if he had died that night instead of Bangali? How would they have told his children? The boys, Sudheer and Mohan, were eight and five, they might have understood. Riti, his baby girl, was two. She would not.

He remembered how he had been at the age of ten. He had understood what death meant. He knew it was something that had to be taught – like counting to ten and the alphabet. And the sooner you looked at death's face, the faster you understood life.

'Beta, ask your mother. She will tell you when the time is right,' Arjun said, putting on a gentle fatherly demeanour, the one that he kept for home. Arijit ran away in the direction that his mother had gone, the patter of his feet trailing away, and Arjun sat still, holding his head in his hands.

Bangali, you should have brought me to meet your family. I might still have fallen for your wife, but I would not have been able to kill you.

A week later, Arjun was still in Calcutta.

He had run away from Nayantara's house, the piercingly sad eyes of Arijit following him as he left. But before he had left, he had written down the phone number of his hotel on a sheet of paper and kept it on the table, under the paperweight. He thought he would wait for two days for her call, and then if she didn't, he would go back to the house and leave the money there, regardless of whether she was at home or not. He of course could have avoided all this and just left the money on the table that day. But that he just could not bring himself to do. He had to try to meet her once more.

She had called that evening itself, on the day he had met her. He had told her that he wanted to go back and give her Bangali's share and that day he had forgotten to do it. She offered to meet him somewhere outside, preferably not close to where she stayed. He had suggested Mitra Cabin because that was the place where he had entertained clients before. It had an old-world charm with high ceilings, sooty fans and cheap vegetable cutlets, and most importantly for his purpose, private cabins, separated from the main area by curtains and half-walls. It gave a modicum of privacy in a city where there seemed to be so little of it.

He looked at his HMT watch. She was already thirty minutes late. *Maybe she isn't coming.* He would just have to go to her place and drop the money off. He felt it sitting heavy with guilt in his chest pocket, all the notes wrapped into a large bundle inside a white envelope. Then the curtain moved to the side, a whiff of perfume circled him, and she came in. Large sunglasses, hair tied up in a bun, wearing a white salwar kameez, tight as if it had been sewn on her body, with a fluffy, frothy dupatta covering her chest, she reminded him of Asha Parekh in *Aaya Sawan Jhoom Ke*. He loved Asha Parekh. But even she paled in front of this goddess in white.

The sight of her unsettled him. In his line of work, Arjun regularly had to deal with danger – police officers, drunk on power and cheap liquor, with a loaded gun in hand and the licence to use it without consequence; murderous thakurs and their henchmen, armed to the teeth, surrounding him from all sides; state MLAs scratching their balls and then dipping their chapatti into daal with the same hand; butchers who doubled as hired muscle, sharpening knives, the grinder whirring silver sparks, and lines of severed goat's heads, their tongues wrapped to the side, ominously staring at him with upturned dead eyes. While he knew enough to be prepared for any eventuality in negotiations, death, he knew, could come any time, from a raised voice or a change of tone to the accidental click of a gun. That is why any meeting brought with it the familiar tightening at the base of the stomach and the quickening of the pulse. He liked the feeling of fear, though, for it meant that he still loved his life.

Today he felt fear, but this was of a different kind, pleasant and yet it burned. He might be crossing a line. He might be screwing up his life. He might, as Bangali had always advised him to, be living a little.

They sat across each other for a few wordless seconds.

'So why did you want to meet me?' she asked in perfect Hindi.

'Your Hindi is much better than your husband's.'

'Is that what you came to tell me?' she asked with icy cool detachment. She was sizing him up from behind her dark sunglasses, of that Arjun was sure.

He reached into his chest pocket and brought out the envelope. 'As I said on the telephone, it is only honourable that I give his share to you.'

'You could have left the money that day. But you didn't. You wanted to meet me. Why?'

The curtains parted and a waiter, holding a stainless steel tray and dressed in a blue shirt and knee-length shorts and sporting a handlebar moustache, stood at their service.

'Something hot? Something cold?' he asked with practised eagerness, his eyes darting down to check if the couple in front of him were playing footsie below the table. That was not allowed, unless a generous tip was assured.

Arjun ordered a cup of coffee and Nayantara ordered a bottle of Coca-Cola, with a haughty 'Should be cold. Else I will send it back.'

'You have taken the news of your husband's death rather well, I see,' observed Arjun wryly, once the waiter had left.

'Yes, I have, I guess. I mean I am drinking Coca-Cola, and I don't look like I'm in mourning, and that does make me as heartless as Surpanakha.' She had caught the sarcasm in his voice well enough. 'I guess I should be banging my bangles against the wall, right, and yelling "Oh what will happen to me?" Funny, isn't it? When women cry, it's always "What will happen to me?" That's the real reason, isn't it? What will happen to *me*?' She adjusted the dupatta so that the two ends hung symmetrically from her shoulders. 'I refuse to grieve over that which I cannot change. I have too many responsibilities.'

'Very practical,' said Arjun.

'So is that why we are here, for you to shame me into more grief? Somehow I thought not.' She removed her sunglasses sharply and kept them on the table. Arjun looked into her eyes and the tone of his voice changed.

'No, that was not the reason. I agree with you, it's better to move on. The living should not suffer for the dead.' He remembered his father and then as he looked into her eyes again the memory faded away.

'So you have a son? Anyone else?'

'Only him.' She absent-mindedly fiddled with a gold ring on her finger. 'He is very special. And I am not saying that just because he is my son. He can do multiplication tables up to thirty and can read the Ramayana in Bangla, all by himself. And he is just four.' Her eyes glowed bright. 'I want him to go to St Xaviers' or Don Bosco but I can't afford that on my salary.' She regained her focus. 'I would also like to move out of that place, Babli-mashi downstairs is a dear, but the other neighbours are nasty, and that *paraa* is no place to bring up Tubai. Tubai is what I call Arijit, by the way. There are some nice places coming up at Ballygunje and I would like to move into a flat there.'

'I am afraid this money won't cover all of that.'

'Oh no. I know it won't. I am just saying that the money you are going to pay me every month should cover Tubai's fees and school costs, you know, books and uniform and pencil box and all those, and rent for a place in Ballygunje. The rest I will manage on my own.'

'What?'

'What *what*?'

'Why would I pay you every month?' asked Arjun, frowning. Somewhere along the way, this conversation had slipped from his grasp.

'You just spoke about the "honourable" thing to do. Isn't that the honourable thing to do once you kill someone's husband, that too your best friend – to at least pay some of the bills for his poor widow and son? You know, so that the living do not suffer for the dead?'

Arjun sat silent, stony-eyed, weighing his options. How much did she know? Enough to attempt a shakedown. He sure got this one wrong.

'I did not kill your husband.'

'Oh sure you did,' she said, her eyes cutting into him like a razor. 'Please stop pretending that you didn't.'

Arjun repeated firmly. 'I did not kill your husband.'

She appeared not to have heard him. 'He told me all about his arrangement with, what's his name, I have forgotten, some sardar. They were going to kill you. When he didn't come back for two weeks and you came here instead, I put two and two together. The fool must have gotten himself killed. He was never very bright.'

'So this is your attempt at a shakedown? I am afraid you aren't too bright either.'

'Oh no, no,' she said. 'I am not blackmailing you. If I was going to blackmail you, I would need some proof. I don't have any. Plus I know you have good relations with the police from here to Nepal, constable to bade sahib, everyone gives you salaam, so who would trust a word of what I say? And then if all fails, you can shoot me dead, and with corpses washing up every day, what's one more? I am not very educated, but I am not stupid. If you could knock off your best friend, who am I?'

'Then why should I pay you?'

'Do I have to spell it out? I thought men liked to say these things. *Mardaangi*. Isn't that the word you use?'

'I am not sure I follow.'

'All right then, I will spell it out for you. You pay me for sex. Sex. I am sure this is the first time you have ever heard a woman use the word. So I will say it once more. Sex. You can do whatever you want with me, and I won't say no. And if you have no idea what you want to do with me, I can tell you what you would like.'

Arjun felt hot. For a second, he wanted to rush out and breathe the air outside. His heart was beating hard at the possibility suggested and then again, he felt the strong sensation of shame.

'I am a married man.'

'That I knew from the moment you came in, the way your eyes froze on my chest. Only married men have such singular focus. Your eyes, the size of *aadhulis*, fifty-paise coins – a kid in front of a jar of peppermint lozenges.'

Just then the waiter came in carrying a tray with a teacup, a metal container full of sugar cubes and a bottle of Coca-Cola. She took the bottle, touched it to the side of her cheek, and Arjun could see the water droplets condense. She looked up at the waiter and said, 'Good. That's what I call cold.' Then she smiled and the waiter seemed to forget whatever it was he was thinking, and turned away. Then he turned again and asked, 'Shall I get you something to eat?' He started rattling off the names of items like an automatic machine gun.

'Veg pakora, chicken pakora, double egg omelette, egg roll, chicken roll, mutton roll, veg cutlet, chicken cutlet, mutton cutlet...'

Nayantara disturbed his flow and raised her finger. 'Don't you have kabiraji cutlet?' The waiter nodded. 'Then bring me one. And don't skimp on the egg. And pack one kabiraji cutlet also.' She looked at Arjun. 'What will you have?' Arjun's stomach was tying itself up into knots. Food was the last thing on his mind. 'I am good,' he murmured.

'So what will it be?' she asked once the waiter had left.

Arjun reached into his pocket for a cigarette. He had been trying to quit for some time, but today he desperately needed the nicotine. 'You can't blackmail me now because you don't have proof. Once you become my keep, which is what I think you are saying you want to be, that won't be a problem. You will then get proof. Maybe a photographer friend will take a few pictures and I get an envelope of prints in my mail. Then you shake me down for more money, else my wife sees the photos. Or worse, I will be forced to marry you – that way your son gets his share too.' He brought the cigarette out and put it to his lips. 'Seen too many people get trapped by pots of honey for me to not know how this works. Played this game too many times to not know how this all ends.'

Nayantara was observing him with an air of gentle bemusement. 'You have a high opinion of yourself to think that I would even *want* to marry you. I don't want to marry anyone.'

'But you married...'

She interrupted him. 'I married Nilendu, your Bangali, because, I don't know, I was twenty-one, a little silly and romantic. I regretted it within months. He blew his money on women and drinking while I cooked, cleaned and took care of the baby. Why? Because I was the wife and that was my lot. Well, I am over that. My son is the only person I want to take care of right now. And about blackmail, well, you just have to trust me on that. If you can't, then fine, I take my envelope, we shake hands, and that's about all the touching you are going to get.'

He flicked open his carton of 555 and turned it towards her. 'Smoke?' he asked.

She looked at the proffered cigarette. 'No, thank you. But why do you think I smoke?' She made a mock 'I am thinking' gesture. 'Oh, I get it. Because I am one of those modern women you see in Hindi movies. Like Saira Bano in *Purab aur Paschim* before she gets tamed by Manoj Kumar. Right?'

'Oh, you watch Hindi movies! Your husband used to sneer at them. Too low class.'

'My husband sneered at everything. He used to sneer at Kishore Kumar. Can you believe that?'

The reference to Kishore Kumar broke the ice between them. As she sipped her Coca-Cola and he drew on his cigarette, they started discussing movies. He loved Hindi movies and so did she and they seemed to have exactly the same opinion on things. Both of them adored Shammi Kapoor, had mixed opinions about Raj Kapoor's acting abilities, and hated Rajesh Khanna with a passion. She had seen *Gunga Jumna* thrice, he had seen it four times, and she was of the opinion that the second lead in *Anand*, this tall man with a deep voice, by the name of Amitabh Bachchan, would become a huge star one day. She hadn't seen *Anand* yet but loved the songs. The kabiraji cutlet came. He ordered a plate of vegetable pakoras. They kept talking. Arjun felt slightly drunk now, swimming in that nice warm buzz you get if you stop drinking at just the right time, when you lose your inhibitions but you are still all right. He felt like sliding across the table, shaking his head and singing 'Yahoo!' but then he chided himself for he was a married man with three children, and he was thirty-five years old.

A voice from somewhere deep down was telling Arjun that he was making a mistake, one that he would pay dearly for. But that same voice was also telling him to do unspeakable things right here, before the waiter returned with another greasy kabiraji cutlet and gave them both a don't-do-what-you-want-to-do-in-this-cabin stare. Arjun locked eyes with Nayantara and the contract was made between them, without any words, then and there, witnessed only by the lonely grey lizard that balanced itself precariously on the wall, shaking its ugly spotted tail from side to side.

3

IT WAS TWELVE AT NIGHT AND SLEEP REMAINED ELUSIVE YET again.

Arjun sat in his 'deluxe luxury' room on the second floor of Adinath Lodge, lights on, looking out through the rusty iron grille. There was not much of a view, a tree right in front of the window mercifully obscuring what would have been a panorama of slum hutments and a rickshaw stand. Somewhere in the distance, a drunk was singing an old K.L. Saigal song tunelessly. Arjun held a glass of whisky in his hand, swirling it around absent-mindedly. On the table in front of him lay his gun, his favourite, the Colt Python. He had been whirring the barrel around, greasing the bore, engaging and disengaging the safety, and now that the exercise was over, he had laid it down. Guns fascinated him, as did cars. They were similar in many ways, a good car and a good gun – gears, heat, rotation, propulsion, precision, speed – and it was because he was good with both that he got into this business.

And that's how he met Bangali. Somehow today he could not stop thinking about him.

He remembered that first day and it was funny because he had never really thought of it like that before. The first day. As if he were a woman or something. It felt kind of sentimental and silly, but then that's what happens when you are a few pegs down.

What year was that? '55? Or was it '56? Definitely after Shree 420. *Must be '56 then.*

They called him Ustaad at Sharma's garage because he was good under the hood. Arjun hated the work and he hated the name Ustaad. There was no dignity in toiling underneath someone else's car and coming out with grease and oil and soot all over your face and then let that humiliation define who you were.

'Koi kaam chota nahin hota, beta,' Devinder Sharma, used to say. Yes, if no work was too small, one wondered why he never got dirty.

But why would he? Devinder Sharma was the owner of the garage.

He was a decent man, Arjun remembered, and he used to pay a decent wage, and after years of working in construction as a boy, it was less back-breaking than lugging cement. For all his decency though, Devinder Sharma had a mouth on him, even by Delhi standards, slapping and kicking the mechanics around when it pleased him. Yet he never touched Arjun, because even though he was as poor and dirty as the others, Sharma seemed to care about the difference in pedigree between him and the rest. Which was also why Arjun was the only mechanic given the key to the cash cabinet. It had, besides currency, a shining Smith & Wesson. Once, when the other mechanics were not around, he had kept two cars running, one of which had its muffler broken and, in the din, shot two bottles he had placed at the far end... a bullseye both times. He was worried that Sharma would notice two bullets missing, but he never checked the gun cabinet nor did he ever use the gun. The local inspector was well tended to by Sharma and the criminals there knew that.

One hot June afternoon, Sharma had dropped in, which was strange, for he never came in on Fridays. What was stranger still was that he was not alone.

There were three men with him. Two of them had come in Sharma's car and the other in an expensive Ford. It was the man in the Ford, an elderly gentleman who could not have been below sixty, who caught Arjun's attention. Sharma seemed extremely eager to show him respect, walking in front with folded palms, which meant he was someone important, at least more important than the owner of two garages. Arjun found him cartoonishly funny, this old gentleman, for he seemed to have walked straight off a movie set, the perfect villain in a perfectly starched white suit, gleaming black shoes polished an hour ago it seemed, a white hat, and a cane with a big silver top.

The men with him also looked very henchmen-like. One was a tall sardar, unsmiling and stern, in a loose kurta with the sleeves rolled up – the type that lived on a diet of *badaam* sherbet and eggs, who would spend two hours in the morning pumping weights. The other was as tall and as well built but younger, closer to Arjun's age of twenty, in a light blue shirt and a spotless white dhoti. He had an easy air about him, and he smiled at Arjun as their eyes met, though Arjun did not smile back. Sharma led all three of them to the back room and then, ten minutes later, came out with quick steps. He shouted to the only other mechanic to drop the shutters and go out for an hour, then turned towards Arjun and said, 'Come inside. These gentlemen want to talk to you.'

Inside the back room were two chairs and a table and the gun-and-cash cabinet. The older gentleman was sitting with the silver cane lying across his lap while the two henchmen stood to attention on either side.

'Here he is,' said Sharma obsequiously. 'They call him Ustaad. The best mechanic in Delhi. And very sharp.'

The man with the silver cane had a deep voice. 'So Devinder was saying that you are from *the* Bhatia family of Lahore. Are you?'

Arjun nodded. Sharma added, 'The only one of the sons left.'

'You can see *tehzeeb*. You can see class,' the old man said with an expression of delight. 'Good clean blood. See how he stands with his eyes down. Respectful. I like that.'

'Smart boy, I told you, sahib,' Sharma said with a small, fearful smile. 'He knows that in Delhi, when the powerful stand in front of you, you keep your eyes down to give respect.'

'And raise your eyes only when you want to fight, isn't that so, boy?'

Arjun nodded, knowing that was what was expected of him.

The old man suddenly seemed agitated. 'You know the problem with the world today, Devinder? You can't tell the high from the low. It's not like how it used to be, when you could spot a Brahmin from a Bhangi from a mile away.'

Devinder chimed in. 'Yes, sahib.'

The old man shook his head sadly. 'Now they all wear the same clothes, eat at the same place, cut their hair the same way, travel in the same train.' He touched his finger to his nose. 'But I know. I always know. Because I can still smell blood. Bad blood. It stinks. But this boy, this boy, my nose likes.'

Arjun hated being called a boy even more than he hated being called Ustaad. But he stayed quiet – for this was a man to be feared – even Devinder seemed to be nervous, on the edge, and he could not remember having ever seen him like that.

'There are two kinds of men in this world. Those who run scared. Every breathing second. The bars of jails, khaki uniforms, funny black coats, little white topis, a bullet to the head. Everything. They are scared of everything. Then there are those who know that the law is just a fairy tale to frighten little girls, written by crooked bastards and told by bastards even more crooked, and that everything, from the lead in the bullet to the stars on the uniform, is for sale. And that the only thing to fear, as the Amreekan President Roosevelt had said, is fear itself. So my question to you, boy, is what kind of a man are you?'

Arjun looked up, and his eyes made contact with the man's.

'What's the job?'

The old man nodded his head with a smile of satisfaction and pointed his silver cane to the handsome man in the blue shirt. He reached his hand out, though there was no way to shake hands, since Arjun was near the door and he was at the other end. 'My father named me Nilendu Banerjee, but my friends just call me Bangali. And my silent friend here is Sandhu.' The muscled Sardarji kept looking straight ahead.

Funny it slipped my mind, thought Arjun, touching his head to the grille of the window, I had met Sandhu the same day I met Bangali. *How could Bangali have betrayed me for Sandhu? What could Sandhu have said that was so convincing, when that* madarchod *barely spoke a word, that would make him want to kill me? Wasn't Bangali the one who used to keep saying, 'It's less painful to get a* lund *into a* kunwaari *than a word out of Sandhu's mouth?'*

Arjun laughed a little and took another sip of whisky.

Damn. It felt like ages ago.

He remembered Bangali that first day, over-explaining in the same way that he would later the craft of Satyajit Ray and those other directors whose movies Arjun never wanted to see, what it was that Arjun was getting himself into. It was not very difficult, the business they ran. They transported arms from the Nepal border and sold them to buyers from Rajasthan down to Bengal. The consignments travelled at night and Bangali drove the delivery vehicle. Two weeks ago while in Etawah, Bangali had to drive off-road to avoid a police patrol. The vehicle had broken down in a ditch. Bangali had panicked. He could not call for help nor was there a garage nearby and even if there was one, you didn't get a stranger to play around with a car in which guns were stashed. After this incident, they realized that they needed a mechanic to ride with Bangali so that running repairs could be done if needed. The money was very generous and the work sounded exciting – for what could be a better job for Arjun than one which involved cars, guns and money?

'So, boy,' the old man had asked, 'you aren't afraid of the law are you?'

He wasn't. He wasn't afraid of the law in the same way he wasn't afraid of God. It's not that he didn't believe they existed; the law, after all, was there in the books and God was there in the temple. But when you needed them, like he had in Lahore, they never showed up. And if they didn't care for him then, why, he wasn't afraid of them now.

'No, I am not.'

And then finally, after some more small talk, the man with the silver cane had gotten up and given Devinder Sharma a fifty-rupee finder's fee, which he had accepted with the most heart-warming of toothy smiles. On the way out, the old man tapped the frame of the door with his silver-headed cane and said, 'Boy, if you ever get into trouble, remember me.' He took a dramatic pause, as if there were a camera panning to him in the room, and said, 'Jagan Seth. Jagan Seth is my name.' Arjun had almost laughed out loud. When your life becomes a Hindi movie, that's as close to perfection as you can get.

The whisky bottle was almost finished and his head was feeling woolly. The drunk who had been singing K.L. Saigal was now singing Pankaj Mullick, his slurred words becoming more and more clear as he came closer.

Bangali used to love Pankaj Mullick. He had had a nice voice too, and Arjun thought of those nights, the motion of the tempo bumping and pitching forward on the rough country road, the breeze blowing through the hair, the rumble of the motor, and Bangali humming 'Piya milan ko jaana'.

They had had a nice run, the both of them. It had not taken much for Arjun to realize that Jagan Seth was too preoccupied with women and *afeem* and the affairs of his extended family to keep much control over his business. Bangali and Sandhu were running the show, making their routes, taking delivery and getting the consignments to where they were supposed to go. But even they were so occupied by the little things, the profit they made today, the women they took to bed tonight, the *daroo* they drank this evening, and their small petty scores, to think of the big things.

The business.

But Arjun did, he always thought. Bangali fell sick with typhoid and then jaundice, and for six months Arjun was operating solo. Profits soared. Jagan Seth took away routes from Sandhu and gave them to him, making it clear to Bangali and Sandhu that Arjun had ownership. In a year, Arjun was making ten times what they had been making before. Sandhu had fumed and threatened till finally he dropped out of the arms business and went over to transporting Nepali women to brothels, a dirty job if there ever was one. After Sandhu, it was their competitors who were dropping like flies, till Arjun had a monopoly over all the arms-smuggling routes.

Never had Arjun ever felt that Bangali had resented his rise in the business, for nothing had ever changed between them. They were still friends, still brothers.

Maybe he had been wrong, he thought now as the drunk stood near his window, maybe the worm had stayed in Bangali, eating away at him as it does an apple, while he smiled and backslapped and drank and drove and argued, gouging out slowly whatever there had once been.

Why had it been him and not Bangali? Bangali had gone through college, was good-looking, personable, strong like an ox, well read, well spoken and had had a head start in the business. But he had a big flaw, and that wasn't just that he drank and went after women or got into drunken brawls. It was the fact that he was too foolish, too *filmy*. And that's why Arjun was alive while Bangali was dead, a hole in his forehead where once had been a future.

'I didn't cheat you out of your business. I was better than you. I took it,' he said out loud to no one in particular.

He believed it. He was better. Better than his father. Better than Sandhu. Better than Jagan Seth.

'Does it ever bother you,' Bangali had once asked, during one of their long journeys through the night, his words slightly slurred from the cheap country liquor, 'that what we do kills? That you and I, we put the fire to the haystack, and sell the ashes? I mean I only heard about the riots growing up in Darjeeling, but you grew up in them. Doesn't it make you feel ... I don't know ... a bit guilty?' Arjun remembered the answer he had given, for he had meant every word.

'No, it doesn't.'

Bangali had always been like that. Trying to poke and finger him every which way, get him to react.

When he was twenty-three, Devinder Sharma asked him to marry his only daughter, Preeti. Preeti was a year older than him, and she was a nice girl, homely, a few kilos more than what would be considered more than required, with a hairy upper lip she always struggled to keep under control. She would sometimes come to the garage and look at him as he worked, blushing and fluttering her eyelashes. Baljit, another worker in the garage, had a name for her. Lorry. They used to tease Arjun – 'The Lorry will run you over, Ustaad' – and he would make a face of disgust in response. Yet when the proposal came, as he had thought it would, he agreed. The dowry was fifty thousand rupees, twenty tolas of gold and a bike. Plus, Devinder didn't have any son, so that meant Arjun would inherit both the garages, small and big. This was too good an opportunity to let pass. It gave him a base in New Delhi, money to add a room and more to his house, and a safe fallback in case his business failed.

Here too Bangali had his conscientious objections.

'Does it not bother you that you are marrying for money? I know you, you won't screw around with another girl after marriage, you are such a Raja Harishchandra when it comes to sex that you didn't even screw around with girls before marriage. So don't you feel bad that she will be the only girl for you? It doesn't play on your mind, not even a bit?'

Arjun's answer had been the same.

'No, it doesn't.'

You hardly knew me, Bangali. You rode with me all those years, we drank, we fought, we killed, and you learned nothing. Absolutely nothing.

Just then, right outside the grille window, a yellow Ambassador taxi pulled up on the street below, dropping a boarder at Adinath Lodge. Arjun stood up and cried out, 'Hey taxi, you still want to take a fare?'

A voice from inside called out, 'I am done for the night.'

Arjun said, 'I will give you meter plus fifty rupees.' The driver hesitated. Arjun said, even louder, 'A hundred.'

'Where to?' the voice inside asked.

'Nakul Das Lane.'

He got out of the taxi on the main street. The last thing he wanted was the sound of the car to wake up the neighbours, for curtains to move aside and for sleepily curious people to peer out of their windows. His head swam from the Johnny Walker, and yet he walked straight, approaching 178 Nakul Das Lane with determination. He was hoping the side entrance to the house wouldn't be locked for then he would have to climb the pipe, which of course he knew he could not, not in his current state. Luckily it was not, and he crept up in the dark, careful not to rouse from slumber the rather formidable lady who slept downstairs. The door was closed this time. There was light creeping through the bottom, a small light, and he knocked lightly. She must be up, he thought.

He knocked lightly again and the door opened. Nayantara took a step back in terror, and in the light of that bulb, she looked like an exquisite deer that had wandered into its hunter's tent.

'You? Here? Now?' she stammered and took yet another step back.

'Where is your son?'

Her eyes seem to glow and wane with waves of fear. 'Please... please don't hurt him.' All the confidence of the afternoon was gone.

'Is he asleep?' Arjun asked, as his hands went behind him to shut the main door.

She nodded and clutched her sari around her shoulders, 'Yes... he is. But why are you here? Now?'

He strode forward without hesitation.

'Are you crazy? What if anyone has seen...' The words were sucked out of her mouth by Arjun's lips as he pressed them hungrily against hers, his hands curling around her waist. She leaned back from the force of his aggression, his chest pressed harshly against her breasts. She tried to speak but that just made her open her mouth wide and his tongue invaded hers. They wrestled for a while, till she had been backed against the wall. He kept kissing her, and she could taste the whisky off him, and now even her head was spinning. Then he disengaged and stepped back, and she was breathing heavy, and they kept looking straight into each other's eyes.

'Please don't wake him up,' she said. Arjun grunted, and by this time he was clutching the *anchal* and pulling at it, and she spun around gracefully, the sari running off her hips in one swirling motion, till it hung to the waist of her petticoat tenuously, and there he left it for now, admiring her in her blouse and petticoat, the sari trailing away like a lover's sigh. Her arms curled up to cover herself and then she dropped them without being told. He squeezed and mashed her breasts, not believing anything could be this perfect. Then she was twirled around again with force, her back towards him now, and even though he would never be Bangali, never have that film-star smile and those sleeve-straining muscles and that aura of overwhelming masculinity, he knew he was not weak, and he wanted her to know that.

The hooks of her blouse provided little resistance, even less her threadbare blouse, worn thin through repeated use, as he ripped it off and tossed it dramatically away. Today there was a brassiere underneath, and he saw it was also old and discoloured from repeated washing. She looked back at him in shame, but not for her nakedness.

'Please don't rip that off. I only have one more.'

He nuzzled the nape of her neck, kissing and licking the length and then biting lightly her earlobe, from where hung a simple gold hoop. Arjun whispered, 'He didn't take care of you. I will. That's my promise.' The petticoat slid noiselessly to the floor and he watched how she stepped out of it, her body lithe, like a dancer's. The panties were down in one tug and then one strap and the other, forming a silent lump on the floor. Arjun stepped back to admire Nayantara, now divested of all clothing. His eyes trailed up and down the length of her body and locked with her eyes, as she turned around with her back to the wall. He took off his shirt, and then his trousers, and then stepped forward. They stood and kissed and this time he felt her tongue too was moving while his hands glided all over, savouring every curve, every crevice, every bit of silky warm smoothness of what he knew was now his. Arjun picked her up suddenly in one swoop. She was light and she didn't resist, though she threw her legs once in the air. Her eyes went to the small broken chowki near the window that was now shut, to guide him to where she wanted for this to continue. He didn't take her there.

He lay Nayantara on Bangali's study table. It was a large wooden antique – a grand table with ornate carvings that ran down the legs. It had seen better days, and even with the varnish gone and the wood blackened through age, it was by far the most regal thing in that small room. She was put down, her breasts flattened against the wood, her rear pushed enticingly up towards Arjun. She turned her head to the side, and said, 'Please don't wake him ...' Arjun's hands went to her mouth and he said, 'He won't hear.' Then with one thrust, he was inside her. He had thought it would be painful but she was ready for him and they started moving in rhythm, slowly at first and then quickening to a steady pace. Nayantara moaned and Arjun had never heard music sweeter than that, though he stifled her sighs with his palms. As his pace quickened, her teeth bore into the flesh of his palms, biting and scraping like a needle on a record, while he tore into her, their intertwined bodies forming a closed loop of pleasure. The table creaked, and one of the socialist magazines slid to the side as he kept on, his hands now sliding down the curves of her sides. Finally, he flipped her around. Her eyes were glazed over, and she reached her arms out, held him by the neck and pulled his mouth down to her. Then it began over again. She bit her lips, trying desperately to control the pleasure she felt, and he silenced her this time with a kiss. They came, both of them, synchronized, their bodies coupled, clinging to each other as if for dear life, and Arjun finally felt what real sex was like – what Bangali used to rave and obsess about all day. He understood it now.

He was hard again within minutes. He felt scared by the madness that had taken possession of him, all of a sudden, but he didn't want to think. He pointed to the floor and then manoeuvred Nayantara into the position, on her knees, one elbow on the ground and the other arm holding on to the table's leg for support. He took her then from behind, his hands mauling her pendulous breasts as he emptied himself thoroughly inside her once again.

They lay on the floor in silence, looking at the ceiling, sweaty and tired. Arjun realized she was holding his hand and he tightened his grip around hers.

She said, in a whisper, 'You shouldn't have come here. If people find out, they will talk and I won't be able to stay here. This is Shyambazar, everyone knows everyone, and everything is everyone's business, unless you need help of course. Then no one knows you.'

Arjun wanted to reply, but he found the words wouldn't form, for inside he was still galloping, his mind out of phase with his body, his breath still coming out jagged.

'My landlord is horrible, he comes and undresses me with his eyes every time I go to pay the rent, even in front of his wife. If he finds out, God knows ...'

'Why did Bangali keep you like this?'

'Like what?'

'Like this. You know what I mean. He earned enough, I know what he made.'

'I guess his other girlfriends got the rest,' she said with a short laugh. 'When you share, it becomes less for everyone. I think they call that communism. Or socialism. I forget the difference.'

They lay still for a while, enough for Arjun to catch his breath. For a second, he thought of putting on his clothes and walking out of the door, but then he realized he didn't want to.

'I am sorry about Bangali. He left me no choice.'

He had expected anger but there was none. She said, without any rancour, 'He was always like that. A moth towards a flame. How can I blame…' – Nayantara shrugged her bare shoulders, 'the fire for his fate?'

'No, you can. Not a day passes when I don't blame myself for what I did.'

'He came to kill you himself?'

'I knew that he would. He had been talking to Sandhu, he had been talking to the Nepalis, he had been talking to the police. Behind my back. I kept hoping he wouldn't, that something would hold him back, maybe guilt, maybe fear, maybe even love. But then the gun came out and, as I said, what could I do?'

'Then don't blame yourself.'

'He was the only friend I ever had. It's just that when a part of you rots, when gangrene creeps in, you have to cut it off, even though you know you will always feel that part as if it's still there. The doctors have a nice name for it, Bangali had told me. Phantom sensations. It's like that with him now. Gone but yet there. I still feel him. And it breaks my heart.'

'Not that it helps, but yes, Nilendu used to love you a lot. You told him you were planning to leave the business. He felt betrayed.'

'I just said I was planning to leave. I was not serious about it. But yes, now I am. I am out.'

'So what will you do? Put "most famous gunrunner in India" on your résumé and apply for a railway position?' she asked with a half-smile.

'I just think of myself as a businessman. I buy things, move things, sell things. Unlike other businessmen, though, I don't care as to what those things are.'

'Guns, bombs and bullets. Why would you want to leave such a business? As long as we live, there always will be a demand for death.'

'Because I am doing small margins. Sure I make money but it's not worth the risk I take. Not any more. Especially when I am sitting on a goldmine.'

'What's that?'

'My network. Over these last fifteen years, I have built up a network. From the east to the west, policemen, politicians, booth capturers, union leaders, student leaders, businessmen, black marketers, prostitutes, blackmailers, pimps, informers, coal mafia, iron ore mafia, railway contractors. Anyone who needs a gun, and there are many of them. I know what they can do, what they can't, what they want, and what they absolutely don't want. Now I want to use this network to extend further into Delhi. For that is where the money is. I have only been scratching the surface all these years. Just the surface.'

'But if you are not selling guns, what good will a bigger network be to you?' She turned to the left, and her breast was now pressing hard against his shoulder.

'Our kings in Delhi have made rules. A lot of them. Then they have hired people to keep others from breaking these rules. Then these people made their own rules and hired more people. Rules. Rules. And more rules. So what's a poor man running a business to do? If you want to open a small factory, making, let's say, pots and pans and cookers, you would need seventy different permits from the government and from ten different departments. You want to import a machine. You need permits. You want to export to Arab countries or to America. You need permits. You want to hire people. You need permits. You need to fire people…'

'…you need permits.'

'Yes. Permit *pe* permit. *Maarne ke liye permit, jeene ke liye permit.* And what I have been talking about are just central government permits. You need state government permits, panchayat permits. Moving goods from one state to another, octroi on all of it. All this is just the law, on paper and in pen. For every rupee over the table, you put a hundred under. You need to keep the unions happy, you need to keep the local police happy, you need to keep the local MLA happy, the corporator happy, the *gram pradhan* happy, the MP happy, the ministers happy… I cannot tell you what a mess they have made of things ever since the British left. As a businessman, you could get stuck for years, being shuttled from one desk to another, dealing with strikes and arrests and raids. Or you could come to me.'

'What will you do?' she asked with wide-eyed wonder.

'I will have my settings inside every government department right up to the top, the babus and the *papaa*s and the netas and the *thulla*s. I will tell businesses where to go, whom to bribe, whom to threaten and with what, where to be hard and where to be soft. If a politician or an IAS officer or a cop needs a donation, I will make my client arrange for it. If he wants it in a suitcase, I will figure out how to get it to him. If he wants the money sent to his daughter in London in pounds, I will get it done. If he wants guns instead of money, well, I know all about that. If he wants women, well, yes, that too can be arranged. If he wants someone killed or some legs broken, I am his man. "You come to me, Mr Businessman, and I'll work and oil the system so that you do what you came to do. Make your money." Much of my network is already in place, thanks to my business. The muscle, the shooters, the goondas, the police in the states, gram panchayats, unions. I just need to build a bit more into the government departments, I am weak there. The ministers at the Centre won't be difficult because I know their men on the ground, the men who get them votes, the men who hold their balls. Within two years or perhaps three, I will be everywhere.' Then he stopped, and fumbled in the dark for her breast and gave it a squeeze. 'Or that's the plan. Let's see how things go.'

'So how did you make all of these connections? Seems to be a tough thing to do.'

'What's India?'

'A country. What else? From the Himalayas in the north to Kanyakumari in the south, from ...'

Arjun cut her short. 'Wrong.'

'Somehow I knew I would be. Please go on.'

'This country, no matter what they tell you in the newsreels before the film begins, is a patchwork of little kingdoms, of coal mafia kings and iron dons and sugar cane bosses and *lunds* with more lands than they should have. Each little kingdom makes its own laws. And each little kingdom fights. Hindus fight Muslims, the upper castes fight the lower castes, the lower castes loot them back, contractors fight for railway contracts and anyone with even a bit of ambition fights another with a bit more. There are wars going on, every day, every night, and each of these wars require what?'

'Guns.'

'For me, every war is an opportunity. Bangali was happy with things as they were, but I... I wanted to prop a crowbar into the cracks and deepen them. Make them fight more. Make them buy more. That's how you grow a business. You create the demand.'

'How do you prop a crowbar in the crack?' There was respect in that question, and Arjun felt good.

'If there were two coal dons and one of them was buying from me, I would get one of my men, as a front for me of course, to sell to the other, at a loss. He would buy a lot of guns. Then my man would want to buy more, else he would be wiped out. Then the other would want even more. Now I have two customers where earlier I had one. And their orders? *Ek se badkar ek.*'

'You must have been paying the police a lot.'

'It's a bit more complicated than that. Sure you pay them and you pay at the right places, so that the money goes up and down and all around. But it's a fool who only keeps the suitcase under the table and leaves. You have got to understand what the police want. Like everyone, they want to move up. And if you are in the police force, the further up you are, the more money you make. How do you move up? Well, you make arrests, seize goods, bust criminals. Criminals like us. So I would give them what they wanted. I would tip them off about one of my own consignments, mostly defectives, and then they would take pictures in front of the guns and those would make their way into the papers. They would be handing out medals and promotions like Diwali *mithai*s for a month after that.'

'And you would have friends in even higher places.'

'Once I even got my consignment back, they were so happy with me.'

'Did you tip them off about your rivals too?'

'You catch on.' He smiled, pleased. 'In short, I made the police my best friends. They kept tabs on my enemies, found me new customers, and listened to me. Sure there would be some hard nuts now and then that would need some cracking, like that Tripathi, but mostly it was smooth sailing. Because I kept everyone happy. Anyone with a file and a government pen to sign it. I sent sweets on Diwali, heavy gold necklaces for marriages, and *chamiya* dancers for a night out on the town for the boys. I met clients, I drank with them, I played *teen patti*, I helped people out when they needed help or put them in more trouble. I made connections. When people were needed to capture booths and rig elections, I got them the men and the weapons. My side always won. And if it didn't, well, I was on the other side too.'

'I am impressed, but can I make a few suggestions? Or do you prefer women to just smile and nod... because I can do that too.'

'No, no, go ahead, you are a smart girl. That I will not deny.'

'Let me tell you a story. My parents came from Barisal. That's now in East Pakistan... I suppose you call it Bangladesh now. My mother told me of this man in her village in Barisal. He had the biggest house, the best clothes. People came from other villages to invite him for their functions, some even called him Raja, and he always went in his horse carriage and with a whole line of people running behind like strays, holding umbrellas, wiping his seat before he sat on it, polishing his shoes. Once he died, people realized that he had no money. Absolutely none. The devil had always been flat broke. He borrowed money and then borrowed money to pay off the interest on the first and so on. People gave him money without taking any collateral from him just because of how rich he seemed to be. Surely someone who owns a horse-drawn carriage can't run away with a loan of fifty rupees. And the moral of the story is if you want to impress the big people in Delhi, if you want to rise, you need to convince them you already have.'

'I understand what you are saying.'

'No,' she said, shaking her head from side to side, 'you don't. Right now when I look at you, what do I see? A cheap watch that looks like you stole it from a corpse in a ditch, a shirt bought from the roadside, sunglasses that make you look like a tout selling tickets in black outside the theatre, and that cheap cologne I smell, I'm pretty sure it came from the same place you bought the shirt.'

Arjun was about to say that these were his best clothes but then thought better of it.

She continued, 'The 555 cigarette is good, classy, but the lighter is such that even the villain's henchman would be ashamed to bring it out in public. I know I am not an important person, but given that you were thinking of sleeping with me, you should have chosen a place better than Mitra Cabin. Not that I don't like the cutlet there. Just that Mitra Cabin is not a place to take a lady.'

'I wasn't... well...'

'Finally, don't stay in places like that hotel, what's the name of the place whose desk number you left?'

'Adinath Lodge.'

'Yes. Why would you even be there? Stay in the best places. Great Eastern or better yet, Grand. If you think it's too expensive, though I think you can afford it already, borrow money. You will make it back like this.' She snapped her fingers.

He was warm now, and he had rolled over so that he was on top of Nayantara and she had spread her legs, ever so slightly, in anticipation for what was to follow.

'Is there a place you can send Arijit, for a day or two?'

'I can keep him with his aunt, my sister at Barrackpore,' she said. 'But why?'

'You were right. No more Adinath Lodge. We will be moving into the Grand Hotel for a few days. You and me. I know a good broker, he will get you a nice place to stay once I go back to Delhi. Tomorrow though, we'll go shopping, get something nice for you and him to wear. And I need to get a new wardrobe too. You were right...'

She moved her head up slightly and kissed him, her tongue taking control.

Then they started once again.

Grand Hotel had beautiful sheets, clean and fragrant, and unlike the city, which was humid and sweaty, it was perfect inside – air-conditioned, sealed tight from the noise and the strife outside, with no nosy neighbours or lecherous landlords. This meant Nayantara and Arjun made love through the night, and through the day, moaning and groaning and shuddering and shivering, interrupted only by room service and conversation. Arjun felt like a little child let loose in a toy store. It was not just because of how lush and unbridled Nayantara was, and he could never get enough of her warmth when he was inside her, but because she was utterly charming in a way he could not yet understand. She seemed to know exactly what to say, and when to say it, and how much to flutter her eyelids or part her lips, when to smile, when to laugh, when to giggle, when to be the girl-woman, when to be the taking-control mistress, and when to be the earnest listener.

They had showered together, and then Nayantara had gone down on her knees amidst the cascade of water droplets and taken him in her mouth. Arjun had no idea how she did what she did, but all he knew was that he wanted what she just did once more. And again and again. They were lying on the bed now, their bodies still wet, a white satin sheet covering Nayantara, and her fingers running lightly over Arjun's chest.

'How did you marry him?' asked Arjun.

'I have often wondered about that myself,' Nayantara replied, her grip tightening over his chest hair.

'I meant...'

'Yes, I know what you meant. I met him at the Red Room.'

'What's that? A whorehouse?'

'A whorehouse is where truck drivers go,' she said with a sarcastic half-laugh. 'The Red Room was a real high-end place, very secret and exclusive. They used to have parties, not parties as in balloons and clowns and cakes, but theme parties.'

'So you were a whore?' The moment he said it, he realized he should not have. 'I am sorry… I didn't quite mean it that way.'

She stopped running her fingers over him. 'No, you meant it exactly that way.' Then there was an uncomfortable silence, broken only by the light hum of the air conditioner. Then she continued, 'It wasn't strictly selling your body, in the way you would call it. But yes, it was. I felt it was. We were called hostesses, and it was our job to serve the men drinks. They had different themes for the parties, Hollywood, France, the cabaret, "masqued" ball, whatever… but the excuse was just to get hostesses to show leg and a lot of breast. There were working girls there too, real ones, and they would take the men to the other rooms, but the thing with men is that once they know someone is definitely a whore, they lose interest. The fantasy is gone… you understand… don't you?'

Arjun didn't quite understand but still he nodded sagely.

'Sometimes the men would pull me by the hand and make me sit on their laps and try to touch me wherever they could. I had to smile and giggle and move away just before they started doing too much. I wanted to gouge their eyes out, but I knew I could not. They paid my bills. The worst would be the movie people, and I know you don't watch Bengali movies, or I would tell you how many of the top stars have tried the pull-on-lap trick and what they say about other actresses when they know there is no camera.'

'And Bangali wound up there?'

'Yes. He told me that it was payment for some job he had done. In lieu of cash, an invitation to a party at the Red Room.'

Arjun knew what it was. Bangali had a side business of contract kills. Arjun kept away from that for it was too risky and too, as he had once said, 'hands on'. Supplying the weapons was so much better.

'I was young and your friend was handsome. He wrote poems for me with red ink on little pieces of paper, beautiful handwriting, he followed me around, he sang for me. No one had ever done these things for me before, and every girl wants a prince on a horse and here I felt was mine.'

'It wasn't like that then, was it?'

'In fairy tales, the princess kisses the frog and it turns into a prince. In real life, the prince marries the princess and turns into a frog. So that's what became of me. No more poems, no more songs, just "How many times do I need to tell you to put less mustard in the fish?" Once sex is guaranteed it becomes as exciting as a tax letter from the corporation.'

'Surely you had options. Why there?'

'I started off as a salesgirl, an honest job. But it wasn't any different. The manager would ask me to come with him to a hotel, and since I didn't give him what he wanted, he would send me on the worst routes with the worst things to sell. He would grab me at every opportunity, and I had to tolerate some of his groping and then draw the line when he wanted more. It was then that I figured that if I was going to get felt up, I might as well make good money doing it.'

'Don't you have a family?'

'My father died during the riots in Noakhali. My mother brought me and my sister over to this side. I was three then and Tumki had just been born. Mother worked as a maid and brought us up, sent us both to schools, but she is dead now. So Tumki is all I have left. She is happily married to a very nice man and I keep her out of my colourful life. Nor would I ever ask her for money.'

'Well, good then, that you left that place after marriage,' Arjun replied. He could still feel the tension between them, like a rain-heavy grey cloud that the wind refuses to blow away. He shouldn't have brought up this topic.

'Who said I left after marriage?'

'I just assumed ... given the type of place it was ... that Nilendu ...'

She sneered. 'He didn't mind the money. He pretended he didn't know how I got it and I played along.'

Arjun fell silent again.

'Aren't you going to ask me why I left the business? You have many questions, so I suppose that's next.'

She didn't wait for Arjun to reply.

'I was raped.' Her pretty face turned ash grey. 'I suppose it could have happened any day, whisky and white powder does not really make you care for what's right and what's the law. This man just dragged me by the hair to one of the rooms, ripped off my clothes which were not much, and had his way with me. Then he put one hundred rupees on the table and walked off. We used to have one daada, whose job was to protect the girls from this kind of thing, but he did nothing. Perhaps he got a hundred too. That was when I said, no more.'

'What's his name? This man who raped you?'

'You won't know him.'

'Curious.' He kept smoking, looking at the ceiling.

She moved to the side, tightening the sheets around her.

'Pulak Ganguly. Pretty big man, his films do great business in the villages. He also has good political connections and so I knew better than to talk about it.'

'Did Bangali know?'

'I didn't tell him. He didn't like that the money stopped but he didn't tell me to go back either.' She turned over now, with her back towards Arjun.

'Would you mind if I slept a bit now? I am very tired,' she said, her lips turning into a sulk.

Arjun looked at his watch. It was ten in the morning. He wore the blue shirt and the grey trousers that they had bought from New Market a day ago, combed his hair, went downstairs and made a few calls from the lobby.

Two hours later, he was at the door of the head of the Cinema Artists Union of Bengal, the biggest and most powerful trade union in Tollygunje, which was what the Bengali film industry was known as. He looked exactly how Arjun had always seen trade unionists look – like a coir rope that had been burnt in the fire, brown, twisted, and utterly drained off all life – a big forehead and a few tufts of heavily dyed hair. He sat at a large table in the union office, and when Arjun walked in, he had the end of a pen buried inside his right ear, scooping out ear wax.

'Hey, who are you?' Basudev Haldar asked, showing a set of blackened teeth. 'And how did you get in here, you *gandu*? I don't see anyone without an appointment.' He pointed to the door. 'Out.' He raised his voice. 'Out.'

A year ago, Bangali had taken a hit job in Calcutta. Arjun did not remember much of what it had been about, except that it had been union trouble in the Bengali film industry. With the telephone calls he had just made, he now knew the details. One Basudev Haldar had put a hit on the president of the Cinema Artists Union of Bengal; Partha Chatterjee and Bangali's men had carried out the job. This Haldar was now the president of the union, the same person sitting right in front of him, tapping away the detritus from his ear canal on to the floor.

'I can leave if you want,' Arjun said with a polite smile. 'But then where I will go next? Should I go to the police and tell them where Partha Chatterjee's body is? Or should I go to the communists and tell them where Comrade Chatterjee lies? You tell me where. And I will go.'

Basudev Haldar quickly stood up, the pen dropping from his hand. He stammered, 'W... who are you?'

'Someone who knows.'

'Hey, is there anyone there... get sir here some tea and biscuits... sir, will you have *singadas*?'

Arjun waved no with his hand and sat on the chair opposite without being asked. 'No thank you, I am full.'

Haldar sat down, and leaned forward. 'Please don't say these things out loud. Even walls have ears.'

'I know. That's why I was hoping you would do me a favour. Because at least the walls of this union office won't talk. Other walls might.'

He came straight to the point. Pulak Ganguly was to be blacklisted such that no one belonging to the union could work with him again.

Haldar seemed to be having a little heart attack. He shivered visibly and then gasped, short of breath. 'How can we do that, sir? I mean... Pulak-da is such a big man... and he has so many connections. And what reason can I give? What clause can I invoke?' He was blabbering now in panic. 'One just cannot kick out a man like that, a show-cause has to be given, then he should be allowed to respond... I am sorry... how can I do that?'

Arjun sat silent, letting Haldar go on. 'Pulak-da is highly respected. He is not a clapper boy or a sound engineer that I can just sign him out on a union letterhead. He is a director of hit films. Please understand.'

'You are trying to tell me that the most powerful union boss in all of Tollygunje can't find one reason to get Pulak Ganguly blacklisted. Not one?'

Haldar's bony knuckles rapped nervously on the tabletop. 'No sir.'

'Funny. A few months ago, there was this director who was show-caused by a letter signed by you. Wasn't he? Because if what I remember is correct, he was asking some inconvenient questions about Partha Chatterjee's death, about where the union's money was vanishing to, and specifically about that house you bought in Bombay right after you became president.'

Haldar reached into his trouser pocket and took out a blue handkerchief. Even though the fan was at full speed, he was sweating.

'See that was a different thing... he was...'

'What happens to you when your comrades find out *how* you became the head of the union? What clause will they invoke then?'

'You have no proof...' Haldar wiped the side of his neck and yet the smell of sweat and talcum powder wafted through the breeze.

'Oh, I have proof. One always keeps insurance. It helps people with bad memory, remember.'

'I paid for that job... this is blackmail,' he said, biting the words through his teeth.

'Blackmail is an ugly word. In the land of Rabindranath we don't say such ugly words. We say it's just give and take. What do you call give and take in Bangla?'

'*Deowa neowa.*'

'See, everything sounds so much better in Bangla. Of course, I will owe you a big favour if you do this.'

'Even if I can get him blacklisted, he will fix it with his bosses in the government. I might end up losing my job.'

'You don't worry about that part. You just make it happen that the letter sticks good, you know the right clauses, and the right language on the letterhead. I am sure you have the old letter that you sent to that director lying about in one of those files. Use that basic structure, no?'

Haldar leaned forward even more. 'If I may ask, if you have a problem with him, why don't you... you know... do what you people do...?' He moved his index finger across his neck and made a cutting sound.

'Why bleed and then kill when you can bleed and make live?'

'He has a movie on floors now, a big-budget one that he has put his money into. If the union blacklists him, it would really, as you say, bleed him.'

Arjun kept his index finger to his neck and made the same cutting sound. 'That sounds perfect then. But it all depends on you Haldar babu.'

Basudev mumbled something half into his throat.

'Are you telling me no? In which case I will have to consider some other options. These options would just lead to a lot more bleeding, of people who don't really *have* to bleed.'

Haldar nodded his head. 'Pulak-da does have a problem. We all know it. You know, glad eye, always going after girls, he is a poet at heart after all.'

'A poet at heart.' Arjun's jaw hardened as he repeated the words slowly.

'We have had some complaints from junior artists, about you know... a little bit here and there... so far I had overlooked those complaints because Pulak-da is a big artist, very senior, but yes, I think we can consider them. We had a written complaint last month against him, some Muslim girl, sensitive angle that, communal you understand and the communists are sensitive about these things, and if I look through the files, there may be others. Also, there have been some other complaints, he once slapped a clapper boy, he makes our union members work overtime without paying, I mean one or two complaints are all right, but when you have so many...'

'As the president of the union, you have to consider them, am I right?'

'Yes, absolutely.'

Arjun stood up and Basudev Haldar did so too. 'See, I knew you were a smart man. You can think on your feet and you are... pliable... So, how long before your Pulak-da gets his letter?'

'We have to serve him a show-cause and he will have thirty days to respond, as per union rules.'

'That's fine. But I want the boycott of his movie from Monday.

Monday. And don't tell me you can't do it. I did my homework. This is exactly how you people did it for... what's his name... that director you kicked out of the union...'

'Rajat Chatterjee...' Basudev seemed very disconsolate.

'Yes. His unit caught fire, I remember. Didn't it? Burned everything down...'

'You know everything.'

'Let me put some *rosogolla* on the deal. Let there be an electric short circuit on his sets, and I will send a little something for your daughter in Bombay. That house you bought in Worli, that's in her name, right?'

'That's most kind of you but, sir, people will ask too many questions. First Rajat's unit catches fire and then a boycott and then a show-cause and now Pulak-da. It will be too much of a coincidence.'

Arjun patted Haldar lightly on his shoulder. 'Well, have you considered the possibility of other coincidences? Two successive presidents of the Cinema Artists Union of Bengal end up in the same ditch in Chetla?'

Haldar slumped into his chair, defeated. Arjun walked to the door. 'I will be in Calcutta till Wednesday. I have a lot of things to do in the city, so please don't make me come again.'

'It will be done. But if I may ask, why? Why Pulak-da? Why him? Why do you hate him this much.'

'One need not explain hate, Haldar babu. Just as one need not explain love.' And then he walked away, leaving the president of the Cinema Artists Union of Bengal breathing not even a little bit easier.

It was an hour before he got back to the Grand. He opened the door with his key and found Nayantara still under the sheets, just waking up, her arms raised above her head, yawning away the remains of her sleep. She looked at him and smiled radiantly.

'Where have you been?' she asked. 'This shade of blue really looks nice on you.'

He unbuttoned his shirt, looking at himself in the mirror.

'Oh, just went to finish some unfinished business...'

'So what happened? Did you finish it?' Her voice was still groggy.

He turned around from the mirror, his buttons now all undone, and looked at her peacefully.

'Yes, I think I did.'

There was more unfinished business for Arjun, for there was always business to finish. On the way back to New Delhi, he got down at Mughalsarai and met Yadav, Mishra, Pradhan, Gyanendra, Goyal and a few others at Hotel Bliss – the favourite haunt for whores, small businessmen and gunrunners with secrets. He made arrangements for how the operations would work after his retirement, divvying out areas to each of his men, giving them his contacts in the police and in the administration, which most of them knew anyway. Arjun knew that before long they would be fighting for turf and some of them would be dead in a few years, and a few others would go on to become MLAs and councillors, but he would have been far gone from this world by then. All he wanted from them was goodwill and they seemed happy to hear that. His orders were explicit, they were not to contact him for now, and if he needed to, he would seek them out. Arjun had decided in Calcutta itself to cut off all links with them for a year, let the weaker ones die, the stronger ones rise, and then, once the churn was done, he would reconnect with those who could benefit him in Delhi. But this he did not tell them. That would have been a foolish thing to do.

All business having been taken care of, he boarded the train again. The curse of the rail journey had been magically lifted. He didn't need sleeping pills any more. On the way, he took another decision. He was going to move out of Lajpat Nagar. Nayantara was right, a Lajpat Nagar address made him look like the successful owner of a garage. His English needed some work. For nothing gave a man more respect in independent India than talking in the language of the colonial masters. A voice came back from the past, a voice of a traitor and a murderer, but perhaps a voice of a man as smart as Arjun wanted to be.

One day, he shall be the Sultan of Delhi.

And Sultans didn't live in Lajpat Nagar. Nor for that matter did they drive an Ambassador or struggle for words in English.

When he reached home, it was late morning. Sudheer and Mohan were playing out on the streets with the neighbourhood kids. Sudheer ran towards Arjun and hugged him hard, holding on to his midriff. Arjun ruffled his hair and Sudheer asked him what he had got from Calcutta, jumping up and down. There were goodies in the trunk, Arjun assured the boy, and he could see them, but only after lunch. Then Arjun walked through the door and the maid stood aside to let him pass. Taking off his shoes, he went to the kitchen, where Preeti was standing at the gas stove. He approached her from behind, and suddenly held her by the waist and said, 'I am home.'

She turned her head, surprised, '*Kya kar rahe ho?* The servants are around.' He smiled and said, 'So?' Preeti knitted her brow, even though she was smiling now. '*Kya hua?* You seem to be in a romantic mood, mister.'

Preeti looked different, in a good way, and Arjun could not figure out what it was. 'There's a lot to talk about. We will do that at night after the children are in bed. I have some things I need to run by you.'

She moved away from the stove. 'That could be late. Riti is upstairs sleeping and she has a temperature.'

'Did you call Dr Banerjee?' Arjun asked, concerned. She nodded, and he spent some time asking her about their children.

As he was about to leave the kitchen, Preeti said as coquettishly as she possibly could, 'I have kept a *vrat* for you. So no romance this month. *Samjhe, mister*?' It was then that Arjun realized what had seemed different about her. She had done her upper lip.

Then she added, with a shake of her heavy-bangled wrist, 'We should go to see a movie tomorrow. Mrs Khanna was saying that she loved *Pakeezah*.' Arjun said yes, even though he had just seen *Pakeezah* in Calcutta with Nayantara. The pressure cooker went off with a hiss and he took the opportunity of the diversion to quickly excuse himself.

That afternoon he stood on the balcony, looking out on to the street. Though a feeling in his stomach pointed him towards Calcutta, he felt happy, in a way he had never been before, happy to be home, to be in the moment, and to be alive.

He took a long sip from the tea Preeti had made, and for once, he did not grudge the cloying sweetness of that extra spoon of sugar.

It was time to close the door to the past, to let go of it forever. Then he would be free.

4

1966

THEY RODE THROUGH THE WHEAT FIELDS OF DEORIA – BANGALI at the steering wheel and Arjun sitting in the passenger seat, one hand stuck casually outside, cutting through the breeze as their vehicle whizzed past. The side road they were on did not exist on the map, so no police patrol would be found here, which is why Arjun loved this way through the wheat fields. Not that he worried about the law. They had been paid all the way up, from the mouth to the ass, though one could never be sure of not encountering a crooked uniform, eager for a quick shakedown. Today he particularly wanted to avoid attention for they were carrying an expensive consignment of revolvers and rifles, all hidden within bushels of hay. The railway contracts were coming up for renewal, which meant that the contract *thekedaari* gangs would be fighting, raiding and counter-raiding, setting fire to each other's godowns and raining bullets on each other. There had been two main *thekedaari* gangs for years and a third was coming up and this meant business was good. Very good.

The drop point was a few hours away and they could see that a storm was coming from the way the sky had turned grey-blue at the edges. Bangali had bought a smuggled Japanese camera from Bombay and Arjun had it on his lap, inspecting this expensive contraption with more than a bit of eagerness.

'I don't care how great you think this is, but you should not have bought this camera,' said Arjun, turning it over in his hand. 'Not with how much you blew up last month.'

'You sound like you are seventy years old. Live a little, *gandu*.'

'I do live,' Arjun said with determination.

'But you don't live in the present.'

'I live for the future,' Arjun replied, turning the lens towards his face.

'See – right there is your problem. The future for you always stays in the future. It never becomes the present. That's why you will die with regrets, my friend.' Bangali reached out and slapped Arjun's shoulder. 'What if we died today? Here on the road. Right now. I would have had my camera and a house back in the hills for my mother and my whisky and so many women that the government should be taxing me for it. You? What would you have?'

'The knowledge that my son will be looked after and that my wife won't have to sell her body to bastards like you to survive.'

Bangali laughed. 'I don't know if bhabhi would be selling, but I won't be buying.' Arjun made a face of mock anger. Bangali continued, 'No disrespect. She is just like the government-issue pans they sell at ration shops, so thick at the bottom that it takes till the end of time to even boil water in it.'

Arjun shook his head. 'I should throw your camera out of the window.'

Bangali smiled apologetically. 'Don't mind me. I say these things. Even though I mean every word.' Then he laughed again, even louder than before.

When he spoke again, the mirth had gone out from Bangali's voice. 'I do have a problem with money. My father was a regular Yudhisthira when it came to cards, and Duryodhana when it came to telling the truth. The old man gambled away everything that we had, and even though I hated him for it, and still do, I think I have turned out exactly the same. A natural gambler.'

'They have gambling in Darjeeling?' Arjun asked, and was about to say something equally flippant when he realized how serious Bangali had become.

'It killed my mother every day to see him come home with nothing. They never fought. You would think she would give him hell but she never did. Shrugged and just went on cooking.' He wiped his arm on his brow carelessly. 'That's why I never want to get married. You know? Never settle down. Don't want to turn another woman into my mother. If you ever see me doing that, be a good friend and shoot me in the head, will you?'

Arjun ignored what Bangali said and stuck his neck out through the side window and yelled up towards the back of the truck, 'Eh, Chottu, you doing good up there?'

Chottu was the third wheel of their little driving party. He was sixteen. At twelve, he had run away from home because he did not want to wash clothes and clean donkeys all his life, which was all that society would allow a boy from his caste to do. Chottu's journey to freedom had ended at a ramshackle dhaba where he had survived washing dishes, serving food and, after the sun had set, servicing truckers and long-distance bus drivers with his mouth or behind. One night, a heavy-set man with an ugly scar had taken him behind the bushes and pulled a sharp cleaver on him when he tried to resist. Bangali had rescued him before the knife had sunk fully into the socket of his arm. Since then, Chottu worked with Bangali and Arjun on the truck, helping them with the loading and unloading of goods and other odd jobs. Today, he was up on the back of the truck, sitting atop the hay under the open sky, free finally from the sweat, pain and humiliation that had been his life. A few minutes ago, he had been singing 'Aaj phir jeene ki tamanna hai ...' from *Guide* in his sweet voice, but he had suddenly stopped mid-*antara* and Arjun did not know why.

It was then that Arjun saw them, standing a quarter of a kilometre ahead – five men, two with rifles pointing straight at them while two were rolling two big rocks right on to the road. The fifth was standing arms akimbo, wearing a blue-pink shirt that was dramatically thrown open down the front revealing a well-muscled chest, khaki trousers, black boots, a cheap gold-framed pair of sunglasses that would be five rupees in Lucknow but could be bargained down to two, and an elaborately twirled moustache.

'Slow down,' Arjun directed Bangali, only so that he had a few extra seconds to think.

He could see the rifles. Those were standard police-issue weapons which meant that the men with the guns were most likely policemen. Yet they were not in uniform. So this was not a raid. This was a stick-up.

The leader of the group took off his sunglasses and put them into his chest pocket. He had cruel cat's eyes, blue and still, and the arrogant air of authority that comes from having a uniform and a badge. So there were three policemen in all, with the man with cheap sunglasses the ranking officer, Arjun guessed. The two others – bare-torsoed large men, with oil glistening on their chests – carried large lathis with them, and Arjun was sure they were hired muscle.

So who were these people? Policemen moonlighting as dacoits? But that didn't sound right. All the gangs here knew better than to touch his consignments. If they did, Arjun would go after them and so would the police and, within hours, the bastards would be dead or hung by their wrists getting beaten naked in a lock-up.

Which meant that Arjun, Bangali and Chottu were in great danger.

If they were here to rob, they were also here to kill. It didn't make any sense to do one without the other.

What if we died today? Here on the road. Right now. What would you have?

He couldn't die today. There was too much of his future left.

They were only a few metres away now.

'Stop the truck. Take the pipe.' There was a broken, rusty lead pipe on the floor of the truck in the space between them.

'Shall I get my gun?' asked Bangali as he slowly applied the brakes.

'No gun,' Arjun said as he carefully pulled out his Colt from under his shirt.

The man at the centre was now raising his hands, asking them to stop.

Under his breath, Bangali protested, 'What do you mean? You are taking *your* gun out.'

'That's because I know how to use it,' Arjun said tersely.

'I can try to run them over.'

'No.' Arjun shook his hood, still staring down the road. 'We are top-heavy. Ride those rocks and we will tip over. Plus they will shoot if we don't stop. Brake,' he said loudly. 'Now!'

The truck screeched to a halt, throwing up clay and dust and pebbles, and it was still moving when the door opened to the side, and Arjun hopped down with the gun stretched out in front. Bangali followed a few seconds later from the other side, brandishing the pipe. The breeze had gathered strength, and the clouds were closing in on all sides.

Closer now, Arjun observed the men more carefully. The one in front had his thread going down his chest, and when Arjun looked to the ones with the guns, he could discern, from their up to-belly-opened shirts that they too had threads.

Brahmin dacoits? He would have time to figure that out later, he told himself.

Arjun studied the two gunmen. One was holding the rifle in the correct position, balanced lightly on the shoulder. The other was holding it wrong. When he would fire, the bullet would fly above target, because the kick of the rifle would make his arm go up.

So one expert. One novice.

The man at the centre staggered forward, his fingers now arrogantly hooked into his trousers. 'Aaah, one holds the bow and the other the club. Arjun and Bheema truly.'

Filmy, very filmy, thought Arjun.

And because he was so filmy, Arjun realized, the man's moment had just passed.

Arjun fired. The bullet went exactly where Arjun had wanted it to, burrowing into the expert shooter's right shoulder, throwing up a little cloud of blood and bone. He yelled in pain, twisted to the right and fell on the ground clutching the spot where the bullet had gone in.

Arjun could have killed the man if he had wanted to. But he knew that this was a policeman. Killing a uniform, and that too a Brahmin in these parts, was a line that could not be crossed lightly.

The man in the middle – the one with the cheap sunglasses – froze. It seemed that he had not expected Arjun to start firing without replying to his taunt.

Arjun whirled to the side and his Colt roared again. By this time, the second man, the novice, had got in his shot, but just as Arjun had expected, his rifle kicked up the moment he pulled the trigger. The rookie missed his mark. Arjun's bullet did not, searing through the fleshy part between shoulder and chest.

Perfect shots, he congratulated himself, just like those pigeons back in Lahore.

And then he heard a cry, a stifled scream of monstrous pain. It had come from behind him.

He turned around. Chottu's lifeless eyes stared back at him in deathly surprise, the bullet from the missed shot having gone clean through his forehead, from which blood streamed down in ugly criss-cross lines. While all this drama had been going on, Chottu had somehow crept from the back to the top of the truck to see what was happening. That decision had killed him.

The world seemed to go still for a fraction of a second. Then Arjun fired again, this time at one of the men with the bamboo lathis. Even though he was pretty sure that this was not a policeman, he did not shoot to kill. The man with the cheap sunglasses suddenly seemed to remember that he had a gun too and reached behind to bring it out. But he was too late on the draw. Bangali had sprung upon him with an agility that belied someone of his size. The man was no pushover himself. With a solid blow to Bangali's arm, he was able to knock the metal pipe out of his hand before they fell together on to the ground, a mass of elbows and knees and half-finished curses and dust. Bangali used his weight to knock the man on to his right, pinning his gun hand below. The man tried to free himself, only to find his arm twisted. The gun dropped from his hand and made a clattering sound as it landed on hard rock.

'Don't kill him. We need him alive!' Arjun shouted, just as Bangali brought his right fist down on to the bridge of the man's nose. The man doubled up in pain, swearing and shouting, holding the place where the bone had shifted to the side. Bangali took the leader's gun and threw it away. He then stood up and reached for the lead pipe.

Now there was only one left. The second man with the lathi. He had been hovering, not knowing what to do. Now seeing his leader lying on the ground, paralysed by pain, he finally forced himself to move, approaching Arjun gingerly, twirling his bamboo lathi, the fear plain on his face. It was not his battle any longer, but one that he was bound – perhaps because he was due payment – to finish.

Bangali grinned. 'This one's mine.'

The lathi whizzed past his head as the man struck, and Bangali, who had grown up fighting with lathis, nimbly stepped aside, throwing his head back. Arjun remembered how he had seen him years ago doing the *dhunachi* dance during Durga Puja. His movements were graceful, measured and confident. The man reversed the lathi immediately for a return blow, but Bangali knew that trick too. He waited till the last moment and dodged, the lathi cutting through the air without making contact.

'Enough fooling around. Bring him down.' Arjun knew that Bangali was now showing off.

The man grasped the lathi tightly with both hands, knitted his brow in concentration, and lunged forward. Yet again Bangali moved away, light as a cloud, but now the man's side had opened up, and Bangali swung the lead pipe, hitting him square on the ribs. The man clenched his teeth and his hand went to his side, dropping the lathi. Bangali charged leisurely forward and brought the pipe up in a smooth arc, striking him just below the jaw. The man stumbled backwards, his face now a display of blood and bone.

'Enough!' Arjun yelled.

'They killed Chottu. What are you saying? We let them go?' Bangali stood, the pipe raised above his head, poised to bring it down on the man's skull.

'I said, enough!' Arjun shouted even louder. 'Any of you so much as move this way or that, *khopdi uda doonga, madarchod.* And you know I can.' He walked forward and picked up the gun that Bangali had thrown away, the one that had belonged to the leader, who now nursed a broken nose.

Yes. It was police issue too.

Acting quickly, Arjun made all of them sit on their knees in a straight line on the road. They groaned as blood dripped down their faces and bodies, soaking through their clothes. Then Bangali brought rope from the truck and he tied their hands securely behind. The policemen all had their identity cards in their pockets, genuine with the official government seal, and Arjun looked at the leader, and then back at his card.

'So Head Constable Ramdayal Mishra, how did you know we would be here at this time?'

Ramdayal Mishra looked defiantly back, the bridge of his nose bloodied and visibly dislocated. 'Your mother told me. A noisy one, that *kutiya,* when I take her *gaand.*'

Bangali caught Mishra by the back of his collar. 'We should kill them right here.'

Mishra's eyes had a nasty glint in them and whatever pain he felt, he was brave enough not to show it. 'You know you won't. Because your friend knows you can't kill men in uniform. You kill one, and the whole force becomes your enemy. You kill a Brahmin and you are going to hell. Now are you willing to risk that?' He then turned his eyes upwards to Arjun. 'You got lucky, *behenchod*. But I am going to find you. And I am going to shoot you down like the pig you are. Remember, I am a policeman. No one messes with me.'

'Get me your camera, Bangali.'

'What?' Bangali asked. 'My camera?'

'I want everyone for a hundred villages to know the bravery of Head Constable Ramdayal Mishra and his boys. So that the next time they need a bunch of men to dance dressed as girls in red ghaghras and cholis and *payals* on their feet, they know exactly who to call for a *chamiya* dance.'

Bangali nodded his head. '*Haan, chalo. Inki izzat lootte hain.*'

Arjun kicked and punched them, keeping them on their knees while Bangali took pictures. He pocketed their identity cards and took away their service rifles and guns. Ramdayal Mishra spat at him once, the froth hitting Arjun on his shoes, and Bangali put the gun to the side of his head and let loose a volley of abuses, but all of them knew he wouldn't use it.

Finally, Arjun and Bangali brought Chottu's body down from the top of the truck and wrapped him in the blankets they carried with them for nights spent out in the open. The skies had let loose above them and large drops of rain came down hard and heavy, in wind-slanted lines, drenching them to the skin, making their shirts cling to their bodies. Blood ran out from every wound, in small rivulets into the mud, and the injured back on the road, tied up like pigs, cursed and begged for mercy.

Chottu remained silent and so did Arjun and Bangali.

The truck rumbled forward into the storm with Bangali at the wheel. 'So we just let them go? His death counts for nothing?'

'Let's just get Chottu some wood and some fire.'

'What about Ramdayal Mishra?' Bangali made no attempt to hide his anger as he drove through the storm. 'Are you going to just forgive and forget?'

Arjun had kept Chottu's head on his lap, and was wiping away the blood as best as he could with a torn towel.

'I don't forget easy, Bangali, and even when I do forget, I never forgive.'

The Senior Superintendent of Police looked down at the black-and-white pictures spread out on his table. He was trying to be as calm as possible, but Arjun could see the worry on his face.

No, Arjun thought, not worry. Fear. Which meant things were going as per plan.

The SSP knew Arjun and what he did for a living. He had been posted as the head of the police district five months ago and Arjun had sent him a welcome packet, a Samsonite full of currency notes, and then had followed it up with an expensive gold bangle and necklace set for the 'family'. So when Arjun had showed up at his office, he was obliged to grant him an audience. Arjun told him the story of what happened in the fields of Deoria as truthfully as he could, with some changes.

Like the caste of Chottu, from a barber he made him a *chamar,* the tanner. They were both Dalits, lower castes, the barber and the tanner, and the main reason for the change was that the SSP came from that caste himself.

'I can't do much about this officially. Plus Mishra-ji is quite powerful among the inspectors. Why don't you just settle with him ... you know, pay something and get him out of your hair,' the SSP said without making eye contact. 'I mean I should not be the one teaching you how to do your business.'

Arjun collected the pictures and started arranging them into a pile.

'SSP sahib, if you order me, I will settle. I honour every word you say. But my heart won't be in it. I can't let a Brahmin murder a *chamar* and get away with it, like they have for centuries. '

'I don't want those pictures in the papers. Promise me that won't happen.' The SSP was worried for a good reason. He was new to the post, but he had been there for enough time to know that Arjun paid money to the reporters of the local Hindi and Urdu newspapers, and if those pictures, of policemen bleeding and kneeling, tied like chickens at the butcher's, made it to the papers framed with headlines like 'Policemen become criminals, criminals capture policemen', his bosses would have his head on a plate. The only thing that was expected from SSPs was to keep a semblance of order in their areas. Pictures of captured policemen, high-caste Brahmins no less, would definitely establish more than an acceptable level of lawlessness, even by the standards of Uttar Pradesh. The transfer letter for the SSP would come within hours. Since the SSP was making quite a bit on the side from regular payments from the girl-runners and the liquor distillers and the railway contractors, a transfer at this time was not a pleasant possibility.

That's why Arjun had taken the photos. To keep the SSP honest.

'Of course they won't leak. I just took those pictures so that you believe what happened to us. Otherwise who trusts the word of petty crooks? I will destroy them right after I leave.'

Arjun had no intention of doing so. And the SSP was smart enough to know that. 'I know I am a small man but if I may, can I say something?' The SSP nodded.

'You are too nice a gentleman for these times. These people are animals. Just animals. The British left twenty years ago, and yet they haven't been able to let go of their old ways. You understand what I am saying?'

It was clear from his silence that he did. The SSP was among the first batch of those that had once been considered untouchables to have made it as a policeman, thanks to the policy of reservation in post-independence India. It had taken twenty years for things to change but finally they had. But those lower in the police hierarchy, those who were of higher castes, deeply resented this. They made fun of the SSP at the police chowkis, referred to him as '*chamar* sahib' behind his back. Once when the SSP had visited a chowki, the head constable, who was a Brahmin, had pointedly changed his position such that the SSP's shadow did not fall on him, for even the shadow of a Dalit was considered to be an ill omen. This act of defiance had subsequently acquired the status of a fable, told with embellishment and exaggeration at every police chowki in the state. The SSP obviously knew about this, and Arjun was sure that he had not forgotten the humiliation. And now he was going to offer the SSP a chance for revenge.

'You need to teach these animals a lesson,' Arjun said, with an animated expression of concern. 'Their time is gone, and someone has to show them that.'

'What do you want me to do?' the SSP asked hesitantly, and Arjun knew he had him exactly where he wanted.

'Nothing, sir. I will do what needs to be done. After all, he killed my friend and tried to steal from me.' Arjun fiddled with the clasp of the heavy leather bag he had on his lap. 'All I want is that you don't take this personally. There is a reason why no one touches a policeman ... every policeman then becomes your enemy. I just don't want that to happen.'

'It won't.' His jaw hardened with determination. He opened a file that lay on his desk, trying to look official. 'Be assured, their uniform won't protect them. Not any longer.'

Arjun slapped his hands on the chair handle. 'That's what I was saying, show them who they work for. Make them smell the leather of your shoe.' Arjun paused, letting the words sink in – for *chamars* used to work in tanneries with leather – before continuing. 'Food or water, we can live without. But self-respect ... that's worth killing for.'

'Leave it, enough of this horrible business,' Arjun continued. 'We should talk about better things. Your daughter's birthday is next week, isn't it?'

The SSP looked up eagerly from his file. Arjun pushed a red jewellery box across the table. 'I won't be in this area next week, so please accept this small gift for Munni.'

The SSP looked at the box and said nervously, 'There is no need for this.'

Arjun made a face. 'What sir? What need? Can't I give Munni something?'

The SSP mumbled a vague refusal as Arjun pressed the box into his hand. 'You are her father. Throw it away if you want. But you can't stop me from giving the little girl something. Please. That's my right as an uncle.'

The SSP quietly lifted the lid, looked inside, and then closed the latch. For the first time, his pudgy face betrayed happiness.

Arjun stood up and made a quick bow.

Ramdayal Mishra sat on a broken wooden chair, his arms and legs hog-tied securely with firm coir rope. There were four others in the room. There was Arjun. There was Bangali. There was a thin teenager with a faint moustache and exposed ribs standing absent-mindedly while pointing a gun at the back of Mishra's head. And then there was an old gentleman with silver Gandhi spectacles, who had on his lap a leather pouch that had been opened to reveal a set of gleaming knives. There were also cows, white, black and brown, thin, with their ribs out like the teenaged gunman, moving about the straw bed, mooing from time to time, shaking their tails to shoo away the flies that swarmed from cow to warm dung to human and back to cow again. They were in a *tabela*, somewhere far away from where the roads ended and from where the screams of humans reached only the ears of those that did not speak. Mishra's broken nose was bleeding profusely through the bandage, his nose and lips a waterfall of bright red, and yet his eyes stared defiantly back at Arjun.

'No one gets away with touching a policeman,' he snarled and a fresh stream of blood oozed out. 'No one.'

Bangali was pacing in a state of great agitation, with a handkerchief to his nose, more concerned with the smell of the pools of fresh cow dung than the man tied up in front.

'Do you hear police jeeps outside? Do you hear someone shouting into the megaphone "Come out with your hands above your head" like they do in the films? No, right?' Arjun leaned forward, getting into Mishra's face. 'It's been a week since your friends were shot down like the dogs they were, and here we are, the ones who shot them – all of us are walking about in broad daylight. If there was anyone who was hiding in a hole and had to be flushed out, it was you. Wasn't he, Bangali? Our policeman here? Mishra-ji? Hiding like a rat?'

Mishra's fellow policemen had been brought out from the government hospital, at gunpoint, taken to a ditch outside, made to kneel down and been shot there at two in the afternoon. Getting Mishra had been tougher. As soon as news about the fate of his cronies had reached him, he had fled. Arjun had to send a few more suitcases full of cash around, make some personal calls, and spread his men far and wide before they finally found Mishra in an old abandoned temple in the jungle.

Arjun lowered his voice. 'You can walk out of here with your life and all of your fingers and toes, you can walk out of here with some fingers and some toes, or you can leave without your head. The choice is yours. So let me ask you once again, how did you know we would be there? Who told you?'

'Your mother, *jab main uski gaand maar raha tha. Sooar ki tarah chillati hai, saali budiya.* But I already told you that day, didn't I?'

Arjun gestured to the old man. Within minutes, the struggling Mishra's hands had been placed on a slab of stone and the old man had brought out a large steel butcher knife with a curved handle from his leather pouch. He raised it in one swift motion and was just about to bring it down on Mishra's forefinger when Mishra burst out, 'I want money. Twenty thousand. Give it to me and let me go and I will tell you everything.'

Bangali exploded, 'Cut off all his fingers. Now. And his balls while you are at it.'

Arjun raised his hand, asking the old man to stop. 'Twenty thousand it is then.'

'What?' Bangali yelled. 'We are going to pay *him* twenty thousand? I am telling you *unke ande se* omelette *banake usi ko khilate hain*.'

Ignoring Bangali's outburst, Arjun kept looking at Ramdayal Mishra, while he gestured for the other two men to leave the room. They seemed only too glad to go out and get some fresh air.

Mishra seemed to hesitate, struggling to form the words.

'I know you didn't come to take the guns,' Arjun said. 'You came to kill us. Someone put out a job in my name and you took it. Of course you would have taken the guns, but that wasn't really why you were there.'

'You have this all figured out, I see.'

'I know who sent you. But still, I would like to hear the name from your lips.'

The man stayed quiet, and one could see that he was fighting with himself.

'Come on, out with it,' Arjun urged. 'The smell is killing me.'

Mishra finally made his decision.

'Sandhu. He told me to do it.'

'Just Sandhu?' Arjun asked.

'Well, it was Jagan Seth who wanted you dead, and Sandhu was looking for a good man.'

Arjun heard Bangali gasp audibly.

'So you work with Sandhu?' asked Arjun.

Mishra nodded. 'I provide him police protection when he moves *randis* over the border.' He leered through the blood. 'He lets me break a few in too. The *asli chiknis*.'

'I don't believe the *madarchod*,' Bangali said. 'He could be... trying to get us to fight among each other.'

'No, he is right,' said Arjun with a tinge of sadness. 'Only Jagan Seth knew we were passing a consignment at the time. It could only have come from him. I knew it all along, I just wanted to be sure.'

'But why? Why him? He brought us into this business. He is like a father to us. Okay, I know you are going to say I am talking filmy. But consider this. He owns this business, we make money for him. Why would he want to kill the ducks that lay the golden eggs?'

'Because he doesn't own the business any more. We do. We own the routes, we own the customers, we own the MLAs, we own the police, we own everything that's worth owning. And what does he have? The trucks? His silly silver stick? For that he takes away most of our profits. This couldn't have gone on.'

Bangali still could not believe it. 'But...'

'Jagan Seth is smart. Sure he looks and talks like K.N. Singh from the movies, but a stupid man would never have gotten to where he is. He knows he serves no purpose and he knows we will realize that, if we haven't done so already. So he did what anyone with half a brain would do. He struck first. Sandhu would get the business, and you and I would be killed in that field. And Sandhu, being Sandhu, would be easier to control. Not a bad plan.'

Bangali seemed disconsolate. 'I know he is a *chutiya*, I know that, but he was always... like a father. I just can't... just can't put this...'

'There you go again. All filmy. There is no father, no brother, just people doing their business. It's not personal, never is.'

'So now what?' asked Bangali.

'Now the loop closes.'

'What the hell is that supposed to mean? The loop closes?'

'We make sure that Chottu's soul rests in peace.'

Arjun brought his gun out from his trousers, turned around and pointed it at Mishra.

'But... but you promised...' Mishra screamed, eyes open wide in anticipation of what was to come. He strained his body forward against his restraints and Arjun held his pose, letting the terror of impending death sink in before the bullet did.

Then he fired.

Mishra's head jerked backwards, his jaw swung open, and then when his head flopped forward on to his chest, there was a fiery hole right between his eyes. Just like there had been in Chottu.

'Yes, I know I promised,' a fierce fire glowed in Arjun's eyes. 'I lied.'

Bangali looked at the dead man and then back at Arjun.

'I thought this was business. Nothing personal,' Bangali said with a knowing smile.

'I lied.'

'What do you mean, we aren't here to kill him?' Bangali looked at Arjun with disbelief. 'Then why, *behenchod*, have we been scoping out Sandhu since yesterday? And don't tell me you are here to buy cows, please don't tell me that.'

They were at Sonepur, the field in front of them dotted with tents of various colours and sizes, some flat and spread out, some thin and high. Milling all around, with their smell and their sounds, were the animals, also of various colours and sizes – cows quietly grazing; goats in long obedient lines; camels on their haunches, gazing calmly around; elephants curling their trunks upwards.

And then there were the humans outnumbering them all, a wild assortment of turbans, dhotis, lungis, long sticks, some out for a bargain, some out to sell, and most just to gape in awe, like they had for centuries from the times of Chandragupta Maurya.

It was the largest animal fair in the country; some said it was the largest in the world – and Arjun and Bangali had been camping here since Thursday, out on Sandhu's trail. He loved to buy exotic animals, and when the sun set that's when the people dealing in animals of the illegal kind did their trade, near tents that only those in the know would come to find, and Arjun's source had told him that Sandhu was in the market for a leopard.

'What kind of a person buys a leopard?' Arjun had asked, feeling hot and sweaty under the red turban swirled around his head.

'The kind that is going to die soon,' Bangali had replied. But now, just now, he had been told that Sandhu was not going to die.

'We don't kill him unless he does something really stupid,' Arjun muttered while keeping his eyes on Sandhu, who stood a hundred yards away near a rickety refreshment trolley. Then Arjun asked, absent-mindedly, 'What kind of person has an ice-lolly when it's so cold outside? I suppose the same kind that keeps a leopard at home.'

'Why? Why are we not killing him?' Arjun could sense the rage growing inside Bangali, and that is why he had not told him so far. Bangali had a way of letting his heart get the better of him and acting drunk without having touched a drop. But now was the time to make the move and Bangali had to be told.

'Because fighting is bad for business. Sandhu has his powerful friends, and if we drop him here, there will be a war. I don't want that.'

'So we are here to roll our pyjamas down and spread our *gaand* for him? Just because his friends are going to get hard? What's wrong with you?'

'We are here to talk. And I am pretty sure Sandhu is here for that reason too.' He turned towards Bangali. 'The bastard knows we are somewhere nearby. He is waiting for us to show ourselves.'

A small line of baby goats moved past them, the bells tied to their necks ringing together in a little symphony of death, for that was where they were heading.

'Goats for sale. The best prices. Lovely, tender goats,' the man herding them cried in a cheerful sing-song.

'I don't think he knows we are here,' Bangali said. 'Look at the *gandu*. He is standing, sucking a lolly like a little kid, without any guards anywhere. Let's do it. Put a gun to his back, take him some place, and knife him to death.'

Arjun did not reply, but kept watching the goats jingle by.

'Did you hear what I just said?'

'He has men. Two of them. See that moustache with the blue turban, staring at the udders of that cow. Him. And that man over there, with the beard, in the white shirt, the one who looks like he has not taken a bath since Independence. He has told them to stay back so that we do not get scared away, but the moment we approach, they will come.'

'Well, we have our own men too. So why are we afraid?' Bangali paused and then asked, 'But how do you know those are his men? I don't think they are, none of them are even looking in his direction.'

'They were both there last night at the *nautch* tent. Keeping their distance from Sandhu just like they are today.' One of the traditions at Sonepur were the huge *nautch* tents, where women danced on bamboo stages to live music from films, and this year the new song 'Jhumka gira re' had been very popular, before crowds of sweaty, drunk men shouting obscenities, the only wild animals at Sonepur who walked without a leash or a master.

'These two were in that *nautch* tent to watch breasts swing.

Just like hundreds of others. How does that make them his bodyguards?'

'Because they weren't looking at the girls. They were looking at the crowd, and sometimes at Sandhu.'

The man selling goats was now level with Sandhu, and Sandhu bent down to pet a goat. They had started talking, discussing prices.

Bangali said, 'Maybe they like men. Maybe they were looking at Sandhu's *gaand*. I don't know. But that doesn't make them security.'

'Men who like men won't buy tickets to see women dance. If they want to see men, well, they can stand outside here like us. Watching men.' Arjun smiled. 'Plus both are carrying guns.'

'So what do we do?' Bangali sounded less sure of himself now.

Arjun tightened his shawl around himself. His hand gripped tightly his pistol, hidden inside.

'We walk towards him. And let me do the talking. Understand? You just keep a watch on those two.'

'What about our men? They are around here too, tailing Sandhu.'

'I have told them about Sandhu's bodyguards. They've got them covered.'

'So why am I here? What am I supposed to do?'

Arjun had started walking towards Sandhu. 'You are going to stay calm. You are not going to kill anyone. You are not going to break any bones.'

Bangali grumbled, 'As if I was the one who shot that inspector,' as he started walked along.

Despite the cold, Arjun could feel a bead of sweat slide down his back. His pace quickened. The goat seller was still standing, trying to convince Sandhu to make a purchase, while he stuck to whatever it was he had offered for the goat.

Now Sandhu had seen them. He turned his head to the right towards white-shirt and then to the left towards blue-turban. They started closing the gap.

Bangali muttered under his breath, 'You were right. Those two are his paid dogs.'

They were getting close. Sandhu once again turned his head to the right and to the left, noiselessly ordering his men to hurry up. Taking advantage of that momentary distraction, the goat seller stepped to the side of Sandhu and pressed a gun to his waist. His guards had stopped moving because other men blocked their path now, men with intent, Arjun's men.

Bangali muttered, 'Isn't that lovely?'

They were in front of Sandhu. Despite that thick beard and the impassive face, his eyes betrayed fear.

'We are here to talk,' said Arjun.

'If you wanted an ice-lolly, you just had to ask.' Sandhu was eyeing his surroundings, looking for a way out. There was none. 'Why have a gun at my side and another pointed at me through the shawl if you just want to talk?'

'You were expecting me, weren't you?'

'The boys say you have a liking for elephants. Since you married one, I suppose I would expect you to be at Sonepur looking for a mistress,' Sandhu quipped.

'As I said, we are here to talk,' Arjun said. 'And I know you want to talk too. You don't want a fight. Neither do I. We are businessmen, you and I.'

'Kings fight. Businessmen deal' Sandhu said morosely, looking around, and seeing Arjun's men everywhere.

'Why? Why did you do it?' Arjun asked.

Sandhu shrugged. 'It wasn't my idea. It was Jagan Seth's. I just made the connection to Mishra.' He cast a sideways glance at the man who still held the gun to his side. 'He was a powerful man, that Mishra. Heard you made boti kabab out of him.'

Boti kabab was slang for cutting up a corpse into small pieces and then burning them with acid.

'I know it wasn't your idea.' Arjun still kept his gun pointed from below the shawl. 'That's why I don't want to make this personal. I want to propose a truce. Between you and me.'

'A truce can't be made at the end of guns.'

'How about over dinner? You choose where.'

'Why not here? Say what you want. And put down the guns.'

'It's the smell of all these animals. Doesn't help me think, doesn't let me talk.'

Seeing Sandhu still deliberating, Arjun said, 'You want out of this mess as much as I do. It's not like we will be stroking each other's *lunds* tomorrow, but we do need to have some sort of understanding. Unless we both want to settle it as kings, right here and right now.'

Sandhu nodded. The numbers did not make sense. He was overwhelmed. He dropped the ice-lolly which had melted away, and stomped on the stick with his foot. 'Friendly Hotel. It's about half an hour's walk. That okay with you two?'

Bangali looked at Arjun once before breaking his silence. 'I heard that the mutton curry at Friendly Hotel is good.' He bent down and patted the goat just like Sandhu had been doing before they came. 'Seeing that you were in the mood for goat today...' and then he thrust his pelvis forward.

'As a sign of good faith, I will let you keep the gun that you have. I will also keep mine. Bangali is unarmed,' Arjun said for Sandhu's benefit.

Bangali was enjoying this. 'What good is a gun when you can't bring it out the moment a beautiful goat walks past?'

Arjun gestured to Bangali to stop. This was going to be a simple business meeting, not a playground rock-fight. But then someone still did need to lay down the law.

'Don't try anything funny on the way or at the hotel,' Arjun said sombrely. 'Because if you do, it won't be mutton curry for dinner. It will be boti kabab.'

5

WHEN DECEMBER BEGINS, IT STARTS GETTING COLD IN DELHI. IT sits down on you, like a cold wet fog of pain, early in the morning and late at night, making your joints tingle and creak, if you are the kind that has arthritis.

Jagan Seth was that kind.

He was pushing seventy, and he hated winter, for the allopathy and the copper bracelet and the homoeopathy globules that made no difference. This particular winter he had hated more, because he had given Sandhu a job to do and the idiot had goofed it up, that useless moron. Maybe he should have asked Arjun to kill Sandhu, not that it would have solved his problem, but at least Arjun would have done the job right. Now Arjun and that insufferable Nilendu were still alive, though Sandhu had sworn on his mother's head only yesterday that both of them would be dead by this week. Everything had been planned perfectly this time and Sandhu was going to do the job himself.

Let's see how that plays out, Jagan Seth thought.

But right now, as the car sped towards one of his 'other' houses, he felt a strangely comforting feeling of warmth, soothing in a way no balm could ever be.

Sandhu had brought a new girl for him today, after more than six months.

Sandhu transported hundreds of women every year, the old man thought to himself, and yet he can get only one every year that catches my fancy. The *madarchod.*

After all, his requirements were simple. Sixteen, not a day older. Beautiful. Perfect skin. But most importantly, untouched by another human hand.

Flowers. He loved flowers. And nowadays it seemed like flowers didn't come easy even in a garden.

He closed his eyes and leaned back into the seat, strumming his fingers over the silver cane, sinking into memories of days gone by. The screams. The cries for mercy. The stifled sobs. The glassy stare of acceptance. The head turned to the side. The feel of smooth skin, of his saliva slobbering all over their face, mixing with their tears, salty. The tightness, what in the world could be more comforting, what indeed could be more beautiful, not seen, not heard but felt, just felt.

And then, just when everything had cooled down, he would turn them around. Like a stained bedsheet.

How many had he taken? Sixty, seventy, a hundred? How did it matter? It was all one experience really, a single string of pleasure on which all these flowers had been strung. And tonight he would add another to his garland.

How would she be? He could only imagine. Jagan Seth reached to the side and there on the seat was a garland of rajanigandha flowers.

Mala was Sandhu's main madam. She would have been to his house earlier in the evening, setting it all up in the way he liked it. First he would have a meal, pure vegetarian. Then two glasses of almond milk for stamina. He had never needed tablets or herbs to make himself powerful. Not when he was twenty-five and not now. Clean thinking. High living. That's what the British used to teach in their schools. And he had lived that lesson.

He thought again about Mala. Mala was a most efficient lady, about his age, and knew exactly what Jagan Seth wanted. The girl would be dressed in a red wedding sari and Mala knew exactly how to make a girl look demure, innocent and yet lush. She also personally looked after the other arrangements, including his bed which would be flowered up like it was the night of marriage, garlands hanging from the posts and roses thrown on the fresh sheets, for he wanted the experience to be special for the girl too. After all, losing one's virginity was something to remember.

The woman who had worked in the house before Mala had been a scatterbrain. It was on her watch that that horrible thing had happened. After his young virgin's wedding night, rather than lying peacefully with Jagan, as the others did, this girl had gone up to the roof, because that blasted woman had forgotten to lock the door to the stairs, and flung herself down. Worse, she hadn't even had the good sense to die, just gotten herself bent and broken and made a mess of the flower grove. God had been kind that this was during the crazy days of 1948 or else there would have been a lot of trouble with the police. They all knew what went on here but this would have been a bit much for even them to ignore. Not that it would really have mattered, except that he would have had to pay through his nose to make the stink go away.

Then Mala had come along, after which there had been no accidents.

The gates rolled open and Jagan Seth's car drove in on to the gravel. He looked at his watch. Nine o'clock. It was going to be a long night.

The driver opened the door and stepped aside. He was a new guy, sharp and well heeled, definitely of good birth. He never allowed any of those lower castes to get anywhere close to the house, unless it was to tend the garden or to clean, though it had become increasingly difficult to maintain that discipline.

Bad blood. He could smell it. This boy smelled clean.

One of the guards ran over, and he couldn't remember having seen him before. Sandhu kept changing men, so that was nothing odd.

'What's your name?' he asked the guard.

'Goyal.'

Goyal escorted Jagan Seth up to the main entrance and to the living room.

'Where is Mala?'

Goyal seemed nervous. 'She is upstairs, getting the girl ready.'

Jagan Seth knitted his brow. He did not like people being tardy. So *un*-British. He was already here and on time, and the girl was still getting ready. It sounded too much like his real wife, always getting ready, and *she* had been dead for twenty years and thank God for that. He patted his silver-headed stick on the marble table.

'Well, get my food, boy. Or is that also not ready?'

'It's coming. I will send word immediately.' Then he stepped out of the house and closed the main door behind him. Jagan Seth heard the key in the lock turn as Goyal exited.

'Hey you, why did you lock it?' Jagan Seth called out to Goyal.

At the same moment, he saw two shadows fall across the wall of the living room. He turned his head to the side towards the passage, expecting Mala and his food. She was not there.

Standing in front of him was Nilendu. And with a gun in hand, Arjun.

Jagan Seth scrambled up and made for the door but Nilendu was on to him in a flash. Stepping behind him, he pulled his arms back with a light crunch, and the old man howled in pain.

'The more you struggle, the more it will hurt.' Arjun's voice was soft yet deadly.

Jagan Seth knew that struggling got you hurt. He had said that so many times to the girls here, so many times that he himself had forgotten.

'We are going to go upstairs to your bedroom. We are going to go real slow and easy and no one gets hurt.'

'What do you want?' Jagan Seth spat out in disgust. 'And where is Mala? Where is Sandhu?'

'Mala has gone home and Sandhu has given you up.' Arjun pointed towards the staircase with his gun and Jagan Seth noticed it was fitted with a silencer. 'Which means Nilendu and I are your entertainment for the night.'

It was then that Jagan Seth realized one more thing. Both Arjun and Nilendu were wearing gloves.

It was cold in New Delhi in December. But not that cold.

First Jagan Seth shouted. Then he swore. Then he threatened. Then he wept. Then he offered money. Then he begged. Then he broke into a fit of coughing. Then he shouted and the cycle repeated itself. Twice.

Finally, all his energy spent, he sat weeping on the chair, hands tied behind, drool sliding down the side of his mouth.

Bangali stood at the window, right behind Jagan Seth. Arjun sat on the magnificent four-poster bed wearing an expression of tired boredom, the gun pointed at their prisoner, looking around from time to time to the pictures of naked white women on the walls. Neither of them had spoken a word since they had brought Jagan Seth to his bedroom. It was their absolute silence – their total lack of desire to engage with him in any way – that seemed to have petrified Jagan Seth more than anything.

'My sons will rape your wife and sell her to a *kotha*.'

'I will give you half of what I have. No, I will give you all of it.'

'It was all Sandhu's idea.'

'Please, you are like my sons.'

'I brought you into this business.'

'I will do anything you want.'

'I will rub my nose on the ground in front of you.'

'My sons will slit the neck of your child.'

Nothing Jagan Seth said seemed to provoke the two, who sat looking at him with stony-eyed impassiveness. When Jagan Seth had seemed to have run out of threats and promises, Arjun finally broke his silence.

'Are you done?' he said quietly.

Jagan Seth rolled his eyes in the way he used to do when he was angry, but now it just made him look like a scared clown.

'No, I am not done, you little rats. Release me this moment, I demand it.'

Arjun brought out a rag from his pocket and said, 'Fine, then.'

Seeing the rag, Jagan Seth screamed and started pleading for mercy, not knowing what Arjun planned to do. Arjun merely stood up, tied the rag securely around Jagan Seth's mouth and then returned to the bed.

'Now listen to me carefully. Very carefully, to each and every word I am going to say. I don't want you to reply, not that you can, but I want you to hear. Understand? Nod your head if you have understood.'

Jagan Seth nodded his head slowly.

'Very good.' Arjun leaned forward, making full eye contact. 'The most important thing in life for me is family. They are why I live. They are why I can die. You tried to take away my family from me. If I had died there that day, I would have never been able to know whether my second would be a son or a daughter, nor would I ever burst crackers on Diwali with Sudheer, nor would I grow old and see them get married, and then get to play with my grandchildren.'

Bangali interrupted, 'Bhabhi is pregnant?'

Arjun nodded.

'When were you going to tell me?'

'Can we have this conversation later?'

'No. It's not as if he is going anywhere. When have we stopped telling each other things like this?'

Arjun ignored Bangali's interruption and turned to Jagan Seth again. 'You understand what I am saying? That's what you were taking from me. Not my life. But my family. And I will never forgive anyone who does that. Never. So save your breath asking for your life. You have little of it left.'

More tears rolled down Jagan Seth's wrinkled cheeks, soaking into the rag. He tried to say something but it just became a muffled blot of sound.

'I am going to give you a choice though. Listen to this carefully for I will say it only once.'

Arjun raised his forefinger. 'We can, of course, kill you. Now if I am in a good mood, and I can't say I am right now, it could be as simple as shooting you here.' He took the gun and placed it against Jagan Seth's forehead. The old man's eyes grew wide with terror. Then he closed them, expecting the shot. But none came.

'It sounds painless but it's not. A close shot often does not kill, merely scoops out skull and brain and you need a second and sometimes even a third to complete the job. As I said, I would shoot you if I were in a good mood. Which I am definitely not.'

Arjun brought the gun down and placed it on his lap.

'We could definitely stab you to death, and I know you have stabbed people before, so you know how that works. But what I really, *really* want to do is to take you to the roof of this house and throw you down on to that flower bed of yours. I heard a girl once did that to herself here. Jumped down from that roof to end her life. But she didn't die. So maybe you won't either, in which case Bangali and I would have to lift you from there and throw you down again. Hopefully that would do it. You know like Akbar and ... Bairam Khan?'

Bangali corrected, 'Adham Khan.'

'Anyway, you get the picture. Now the problem with spilling your blood, besides the fact that it's awfully messy, is that your sons and your sons-in-law would come to know that you have been murdered. They might figure out it's me, despite being the idiots that they are. They would then come after their father's murderer, for that's what good sons do in Hindi films. If they do, Jagan Seth, I *will* wipe them out. Your sons *will* be dead. Your daughters *will* be widows. I can write this down on a piece of paper and sign it. And you know I have the balls. That's why you set me up for a quiet, sneaky kill.'

Arjun stopped for a second and collected his thoughts.

'I will be honest. I don't like the idea of slaughter. Not because I particularly care for your sons or your daughters, but because I am a businessman. When I am killing, I am not making any money. That's bad for my business. That's bad for my family.'

Arjun raised two fingers. 'Option number two. You kill yourself. You write a note here, and I have the pen and the paper, and those ceiling beams and these bedsheets would do nicely for a simple hanging. That way your sons and your sons-in-law will weep a bit, have a nice big funeral, then put large rajanigandha garlands around your picture – now you do like rajanigandha garlands I have heard – the sons get their inheritance, and everyone is happy. They don't come after me and I don't have to waste my time and bullets putting them all in the morgue.

'Know this. You *will* die tonight, Jagan Seth. No matter what you do, no matter which way the wind blows, it ends with cotton balls inside your nose. There is no getting around that. Now I am going to give you five minutes to make up your mind. If you do not take option two by the time it's 10.30 by my watch, then I will kill you. I will be in a wretched, nasty mood and that makes me very creative. So think, think hard.'

Silence surrounded them again, disturbed only by Jagan Seth's heavy breathing through the rag. He finally nodded his head and said something. Bangali took the rag off. He pleaded again, offered more money, and promised to write this house in Arjun's son's name. Arjun signalled to Bangali and he tied the rag around Jagan Seth once again.

'It's twenty-six after ten. You have four more minutes,' was all Arjun said, pointing to his watch ominously.

Jagan Seth needed only two. When the rag was taken off, he tried to compose himself for a while, choking back the tears and snot. Then putting on a mask of courage, he said, 'You have to untie my hands if you want me to write.'

A minute later, Arjun stood with the gun at Jagan Seth's head. His right hand was untied and a fountain pen put in it.

'What do you want me to write?' he asked.

'Bangali, tell him what to write,' Arjun instructed. 'I told you to have something in mind.'

Bangali said with prepared confidence, 'Write – "Life is beautiful. But dear sons and daughters, anything that begins must end. What then could be better than to end my life on a lovely night like ..."'

Arjun made a face. 'What? Is this a poem by Rabindranath Thakur? Lovely night? Life is beautiful? Does anyone write suicide notes like this?'

'Well, you tell him what to write then. It's not as if I have been writing suicide letters all my life,' Bangali replied.

Arjun grumbled. 'One simple thing I tell you to do. And you can't even do that.'

Then he turned towards Jagan Seth. 'Just write – "I am sorry. My blessings to all. Be happy." Write it in your best handwriting, don't scribble ... yes, that's perfect. Now sign. Good.' Bangali was still grumbling. He did not like the wording of the note. It was too prosaic for his taste.

Jagan Seth's hands were tied up again. Bangali made the noose, hung it from the beam above, tested it once and then signalled to Arjun. The rag was removed.

Jagan Seth tried to say something and then thought better of it.

'Please, some dignity, please,' was all that gurgled out of his throat.

Jagan Seth stood on the chair and placed the noose around his neck. He breathed hard and then he prayed. Arjun and Bangali stood watching. Then he clenched his shoulders and kicked the chair. The noose tightened, his eyes bulged and he gasped for air. Which is when Arjun slid gracefully down to the ground, sat on his knees, and raised his gloved hand to support the heel of Jagan Seth's shoe.

'What are you doing?' Bangali asked in utter shock. 'Let him die.'

Jagan Seth kicked his feet wildly trying to get away from Arjun, flapping like a fish caught at the end of the hook. But Arjun kept his hand at his heel. Jagan Seth's stomach voided itself and the stench filled the room. His eyes were almost popping out of their sockets now, the face had turned blue-green, and yet life seemed to not leave him. Then finally, Arjun let his heel go and he jerked once, then he swung for a few seconds like a pendulum, and finally went still.

'Why... what was that for?' Bangali could scarcely believe what Arjun had done. Arjun's eyes had that glint he had seen in that cowshed, the silver edge of an ice-cold dagger. It scared Bangali.

Arjun stood now, arms crossed, looking up at Jagan Seth's dead body.

'Some say that when you die, what you feel in those final moments, is what you carry into your afterlife. If you were happy and at peace, then that's how you will be for all time to come. Now I am pretty sure that's all a fairy tale, but still, one never knows.'

'It's because of those girls, isn't it... the ones he... you wanted him to...'

Arjun kept looking up. 'I remember the first time I met him and what he had said then. Low-caste people all around and the bad blood they reeked of... The *behenchod* never realized that it was himself he smelled – the only blood that ever stank was his.'

He turned towards Bangali and his eyes were glinting again.

'Time to close the loop,' Bangali said, and they both started cleaning up.

'And here you keep telling me not to blow money on cameras and watches.' Bangali looked at the bundle of notes that Arjun held in his right hand, rolled tight and held in place with a rubber band. 'I can't believe you are going to give all of this away.'

Arjun moved slowly down the steps of Jama Masjid, looking to the left and then to the right at the line of men sitting below.

'It's not charity,' Arjun said, 'it's the interest on a loan. The principal I will never be able to touch.'

'I know. I know. Someone saved your life in Lahore and this is your payback. But it is insane.'

Arjun bent down and put a fifty-rupee note on the white cloth that was stretched out. Behind that cloth, on the ancient steps, sat an ancient man with a weather-beaten face and glasses thicker than the bottom of a bottle.

'Ever heard of the great king Harshavardhana?' Bangali asked. 'He gave everything he had away, at Prayaga. Took off his clothes and gave those away too. Don't do that please, don't let me see you naked.'

The old man reached out his frail hand, took the note and held it up towards the fading light to check whether it was real. He could scarcely believe what he held in his hand. A crinkle-free note fresh from the bank.

Arjun did an *adaab*. By now the other beggars had noticed the largesse of Arjun's donation. Those who could move were inching closer and those who couldn't, the ones with stumps for legs and those that did not have them, sat expectantly.

Bangali continued, 'I get it. You are the good man. You give to the poor. You screw one woman. You live for your children. But why, oh why, do you have to give so much away? Couldn't you make your divinity a bit low budget?'

Arjun moved reverentially from beggar to beggar, dropping notes into outstretched palms and beat-up tin bowls and dirty blankets, always with a polite smile and an *adaab*. Soon the bundle of notes ran out. The news had spread. Arjun reached into his long white Afghan kurta to pull out another bundle. Bangali rolled his eyes.

'To think I always give *chaar anna* to any beggar and then say "please forgive me".'

This went on till Arjun had very little left in his kurta pocket, just one note or perhaps two. Satisfied with the donation, they both hurried away from the masjid because more beggers would be coming. In the old city of Delhi, good tidings move even faster than bad, and one did not want to see despair when one had seen so much light, even if it had been just a little flicker.

'I am not a good man nor do I want to prove that to anyone, certainly not to myself,' Arjun said after they had walked for a few minutes. 'I don't know what the word "good" means. Nor do I care, frankly. Good is like God. I would like to believe there is good in this world, just as there is God, but beyond temples and books, where is God? Where is good?'

'Now you are the one talking like a communist. Remember, I am the Bangali here. You the Hindustani, you don't get to doubt the existence of God.'

Arjun smiled. 'I try not to. I really do. But I wonder. Does God care? Even if he is up there? Did you see those people there, blind, abandoned, no legs, wounds, boils, sores? You think anyone cares? God or man? And if neither God cares nor man, what is good then? And what is God?'

Bangali took out two cigarettes from his pocket and offered one to Arjun. 'Someone is very philosophical today.' Arjun took it and then they stopped as Bangali fished out his fancy new gold lighter, which he had bought from the smuggler's market in Bombay, where he had been told that this was of Swiss make. 'So, Arjun, tell me,' Bangali asked, 'what do you believe in?'

'What I told Jagan Seth,' he said, lighting up a cigarette. 'Family. My family. That's where my world ends. That's where it starts. I will do whatever is in my power to protect them. And if anyone tries to do them harm, I will finish him. Without exception. This is all I know. All I can truly believe in.'

'So why didn't you kill Sandhu?'

'Because killing that bastard would put my family in more danger than letting him go.'

'You made Jagan Seth suffer like a mad dog and you killed the policeman. Was that only for your family?'

'I didn't say everything I do is for my family. I mean I am smoking... this is definitely not for them, I am talking to you, that is definitely not for them.' Arjun stayed silent for a minute, standing and smoking. Kites flitted above, scraps of colour floating in the breeze, framed by the reddish-orange twilight.

'I know what I sell kills people. Some of them I know deserve to die, and many who do not. So sometimes, I want to... I don't know...'

'Care? And by caring you want to be good?'

Arjun nodded his head. 'You were right. We are talking philosophy. Next thing you know, I am singing Rabindrasangeet and understanding Satyajit Ray.' He smiled but Bangali still looked serious.

'Can I ask you something? Honestly?'

'Sure.'

'If I ever betray you, would you kill me? I know if *you* betrayed me, I would never be able to pull the trigger. Never. I used to believe you wouldn't either, but the way I saw you, the way your eyes went all crazy when you killed those people, you seemed ... I don't know... so different. And somehow I was not so sure if this is the Arjun I grew up with.'

'Those were not my friends.'

'I know that. But still, would you kill me? Ever?' Bangali asked, almost sadly.

Arjun looked at his cigarette intently. 'If you are my best friend, you should know me better than anyone else in the world. Right?'

'Of course.'

'Well, if you do, then you would know that *I would know* before you betray me that you are going to. I always move a few steps ahead of the world. It's how I stay alive. So if you decide to sell me out, you must have thought, "I am one up on Arjun". The moment that thought crosses your head, my friend, you would have done something very, very foolish.' Arjun took a long puff, the end glowed red. 'And you also know that I cannot tolerate fools. Traitors, yes. Bastards, yes. But not fools. For fools get people killed without even wanting to.'

'Maybe a fool then, but I would still be your friend. Your best friend.'

'No. You would no longer be a friend. I mean, if you don't know the first thing about me, that I cannot be fooled, then how can you be my friend?'

'You are an arrogant *madarchod,* aren't you?' Bangali said, and there was spite in his voice. 'You think you are so smart, and I am so stupid.'

'No. I don't think you are stupid. Not at all. If I did, we would not be in business together. But tell me, why this sudden strange talk of betraying me?'

'Well, figure it out, you *chutiya,* you know everything. Read my mind.'

Bangali dropped his half-finished cigarette on the road and stepped on it with his shoe.

'*Ma chudaaye yeh sab*. I am going to have my family. My own family. So I don't have to come to beg you to be my friend.'

'I thought you wanted me to shoot you in the head if you ever got married,' Arjun said, trying to lighten things up. 'Though that's a great idea. You are never really a man till you have a family.'

'I will. I will have children. And I will have a beautiful wife and I won't marry a truck to get a garage. But of course I am foolish and you are the smart one.'

'Aww, come on.' Arjun tapped Bangali on the shoulder. 'You miss the point. I never said you are stupid. I never think that. You are the guy who reads all those big books, knows English so well, watches Italian movies at film clubs and buys Cuban cigars. All I said was if and only if you thought you could get away with putting a knife in my back, then that would mean you didn't know the first thing about me. Simple.'

Bangali still sulked. 'Well, I have not told you this. But I am in love.'

'And how many times have you fallen in love this year already?'

'This is different. It's serious. Someone I think I want to settle down with. You didn't know that, did you, all-knowing genius?'

'Settling down? Do you even know what that means?'

'Better than you ever will, *madarchod*.'

'What's the lucky girl's name?'

'None of your business.' He pushed Arjun lightly by the shoulder. 'You stay in your little cave with your lioness and your cubs and pee all around and roar "Don't get near my family."'

'What's her name? At least that you can tell me.'

'No, I am not going to.'

'I know you want to. Otherwise you would not have brought it up.' Arjun pointed towards a dhaba. 'Dinner? I am buying. Come on.' Arjun fished out a few crumpled notes from his pocket and rustled them in his fingers. 'See, there is always some for friends.'

Bangali said, 'Chicken jahangari. Two plates for me. And a full tandoori chicken. I am not sharing. But really, where is this smug superiority of yours coming from?'

'Smug superiority? Me? Aren't you the one who calls me a low-culture Hindustani with no understanding of good things?'

'But you fell asleep during *Apur Sansar* and you think Kishore Kumar has a better voice than Mohammed Rafi. What else can I say?'

The sun had by now dipped behind the massive dome of Jama Masjid. Matia Mahal was an ocean of humanity, rickshaws and handcarts fighting for space. The evening air hung heavy with a haze of kabab smoke. Women bargained. Bearded shopkeepers held their own. There was sweating and swearing and raised tempers all around and yet a quiet sense of contentment held dominion, a sensation not dissimilar to the comforting satisfaction of a good meal sinking down into the base of the stomach.

The two friends walked on, still arguing animatedly, into Gali Kababian, their voices blending steadily into the symphony of Delhi.

Part Two

6

1975

'REQUESTING ALL FIRST-CLASS PASSENGERS TO BOARD INDIAN Airlines flight IA 360 with service to Calcutta.'

Arjun Bhatia was happy. The purchase order from the ministry of defence had been executed. A consortium of Israeli arms manufacturers, through front companies in Russia, had won a huge order for military equipment. He had brokered the partnership, got the tender rewritten for his clients, taken it through the ministries, and wiped his tracks. He was going to be rich, not that he was not already, but a payday of ten crore was not something that happened every Tuesday. Put this with the petrochemical approval and he was looking at more money this year than he could have imagined.

And it was not even July.

He adjusted his Aviator glasses slightly as he passed the air hostess, and gave her a smile of acknowledgement.

'Please proceed, Mr Bhatia.' She handed him back his ticket and the gentle whiff of perfume that wafted through the air as she did so reminded him of Nayantara. He would be with her in a few hours, and the expectation of her gentle ministrations already made him hard.

'Would you like a newspaper?' the air hostess asked, pointing to the rack of dailies kept to the left. Arjun shook his head but glanced at the headlines as she passed by, and they were all reporting things he had known a week ago.

Delhi had fallen easily, easier than he could have dreamt it would. Within just a few years of leaving gun smuggling, he had a network in Delhi, he understood the people, and he knew all their secrets.

'What kind of secrets?' Nayantara had asked him the last time he had been in Calcutta, during a lull in their lovemaking session.

'The ones they keep in the bird's belly,' he had said, his hands running over her impossibly flat stomach, before curling around the bottom of one of her heavy breasts and lifting it up for his descending mouth, 'as they say in the fairy tales, the life of the demon.'

'Well, tell me a few. The juicy ones.'

He had. Stories of blackmail, double-dealing and strategically applied muscle. She had listened wide-eyed and when he had finished, he was ready again.

Arjun sank back contentedly into his seat in the aircraft, and stretched his legs forward, mightily pleased with the legroom, himself and the world.

Then a voice inside his head whispered, 'Remember what mummy used to say. Pride comes before a fall.' Which is when he tried to sober down, to reflect on his failures.

Namely his marriage. He would leave for work early morning before Preeti had woken up. Since they had an army of servants and guards and gardeners and ayahs for their bungalow in Defence Colony, there was little for her to do at home. So she read the film glossies, or left for the parlour or shopping or went to kitty parties or hosted them herself. It was not that Arjun and she did not talk, they did from time to time, but it was the same kind of conversation he had with that old man he would run into during his morning walk – desultory, polite and without passion – one in which his feet started moving before the words were finished. He could never talk about his business, nor about sex nor about politics and what she said he simply nodded to – religious *vrats*, neighbourhood gossip and the latest developments in the lives of Rajesh Khanna and Raj Kapoor.

The only real topic of conversation they had together was about their children. And it was precisely there that their placid life of comforting acceptance had started fraying at the seams.

Sudheer, the eldest, was eleven and Arjun was worried for him. His report card was more red than blue and only the fact that Arjun was the school's biggest donor had kept the boy from being held back a year. Whenever the topic of Sudheer's academic progress or the lack of it came up, Preeti's response would be simple and consistent.

'Why does he need to study? That's for middle-class people.'

'He needs discipline,' Arjun would protest.

'Discipline? Why? Don't you love your son?'

He had hired a private tutor. Then he got an Anglo-Indian governess to teach him English and play the piano, just like he used to have in Lahore. But there was little they could do because Sudheer would just run away. Preeti indulged his anarchy every step of the way, loading him with the best toys, the best clothes and a whole lot of chocolates and laddoos and ice cream.

It had already left a mark. Sudheer was obese, extrusions of lard squelching out from neck and stomach, making him look years older.

'I am worried about Sudheer's health. He is too fat for his age.'

'He likes to eat. Why do you have a problem with that? It's not that you cannot afford it.'

'That's not the point,' he had said, clenching his fists in frustration. 'Have you looked at him? He wheezes after walking up one flight of stairs. He can't run from here to the gate without gasping for air and holding his sides. You don't see the problem?'

'Why does he have to run? He has made the ayah's son his permanent runner, he even runs his runs for him in cricket.'

Arjun had said it slowly, 'And you *still* don't see the problem?'

'Don't you love your son?'

The final straw had been the cat. The ayah's son who did the running for him had gotten Sudheer run out in a match. Sudheer had slapped him hard, sending the poor kid flying into the dirt. The boy had called him a fat pig and then run away, and Sudheer was smart enough not to give chase. A day later, that boy's cat was found dead in the shrubbery. Someone had broken its legs, all four of them, and then smashed the head in with a blunt object. The ayah had gone to Preeti first to complain and then to Arjun.

Arjun had summoned Sudheer and he had confessed to having done it.

That evening was the first time that Preeti had raised her voice in all their years of marriage.

'The ayah has to go. She just has to.'

'But Sudheer killed her son's cat.'

'So what? It's a cat. They work for us. For that ayah's boy's cat, you even slapped our son.'

'Your son killed a cat. He is lucky he got only a slap.'

'Don't you love your son?'

Arjun had given the ayah five hundred rupees and asked her to leave, not because he believed that was the right thing to do but because that would give him peace at home and time to think. He made a decision. Sudheer had to go to boarding school. And since he was sending him, he might as well have Mohan go there too.

Mohan was not like Sudheer. One would not even know if he was in the house. Reed-thin, with sharp, somewhat feminine features that reminded Arjun of his own mother, he had mastered the art of staying invisible, usually up in his room, solving jigsaw puzzles and reading books. Again, unlike his brother, his teachers at school liked him, because he did what he was told and did not make a peep.

Arjun was worried about Mohan too. In a way, he understood Sudheer. Mohan was a riddle. When the boys were together with their cousins, all from Preeti's side of the family, Sudheer would be the leader of the group – bullying, shouting, fighting and laughing. Mohan would slip away quietly either to his jigsaw puzzles or make one up himself by tearing leaves or flowers, and then trying to reassemble them by matching edges.

He had asked Mohan one day why he never seemed to want to make friends.

'Papa, they all talk too much.'

'Why don't you play cricket or football or badminton with the rest of the boys?'

'I play cricket. Sometimes.'

'Sudheer says you are very good at batting and fielding. But you don't like cricket much, do you?'

'No, I don't. It's okay I guess.'

'Well, what do you like then? Besides jigsaw puzzles and books?'

'When I figure it out, papa, I will tell you.'

They had to be sent somewhere else, both of them – one so that he could keep himself in and the other so that he could let himself go.

When he had told Preeti his decision, she had not taken it well. She had wept and then called her mother whom Arjun positively detested and not just because of the old-person smell she gave off. She had come immediately and both of them had tried to wear Arjun down, each in their own way. Arjun had tried to explain, as best he could, that this was the best course of action for the boys. The school he would be sending them to in Dehra Dun was the very best, and there they would have round-the-clock care.

'I know why you are sending them away,' Preeti had said, through intense sniffles.

'Please tell me why.'

'Because all important people send their sons there. So now you can get to know their fathers. This is all your way of getting influence. Now you have started using your own sons for business.' Preeti shook her bangles dramatically, and her mother had looked on in that stern disapproving way of hers.

'I am doing this for you,' Arjun had said equally dramatically. '*We are not middle class*. Isn't that what you like to say? Well, here you are. This is where rich kids go.'

'But…' Preeti had faltered and Arjun had congratulated himself for turning her own words against her.

He pressed home his advantage. 'The sons of today's kings will be the kings of tomorrow. That's how Delhi works. Our sons will be there, growing up with other princes. Isn't that better than keeping them here, where they grow up playing with the gardener and the ayah's son?'

His mother-in-law had said, with her dragon breath of paan and *zarda*, 'But *beta*, if you send those two away, how can Preeti live?'

Arjun had half a mind to say, 'Well, I am sure between the kitty parties and Mrs Khanna's charity balls and special issues of *Filmfare*, your daughter will live.' But he hadn't survived this long without knowing when to hold fire. So he let it pass.

'Riti will be here,' he had said, as a means of reminding Preeti that they had a daughter also.

Riti was his youngest, all of five. Curly hair, a brilliant smile and the ability to fill a room with her presence, she was the bright sunshine in Arjun's life. The only time he really enjoyed being at home was with Riti on his lap, flipping through a picturebook, with her looking at his face and then back to the page and then once again at his face. They had their little games, and their own little language of nods and whistles, and they would spend hours drawing pictures together, and prancing about on the lawn behind, early in the morning, before the others had woken up. There was no way he was going to send her away, though in a little corner of his mind he felt he should, maybe in a few years.

'Don't you dare even think of sending her away. Ever,' Preeti had said with emotion. 'She will be here till she goes away to her in-laws.'

Her mother had interrupted, 'Why would Arjun send her away? He should know that a girl's place is in the house. First at her parents'. Then at her husband's. And then with her son.'

Arjun was going to say, 'Then what is your mother doing here?' but once again prudence won. He shook his head and walked away, as Preeti came remonstrating to her mother, 'Just because of a cat. Just because of one little cat.'

And that was that. The boys would go to boarding school. Sudheer had cried for days and Preeti had not helped matters any by saying, 'Don't look at me. It is your papa's decision.'

Mohan had said nothing but one evening he had come up to Arjun's office, in his long shorts and suspenders.

'Why are we going to boarding school?'

Arjun went through the whole little speech – of making them men, of the opportunities that the school would provide, of the importance of a British education and of being with people like themselves. Mohan had listened patiently, even though they had been through it all once before.

'I don't want to go.'

'Why? I thought you said people here talk too much.'

He had looked at his feet and fidgeted with the suspenders.

'They might talk even more there.' Then he had turned around, his head still bent forward, and shuffled sadly away. Arjun had called out to him but Mohan had kept going, down the stairs, pretending not to hear, his steps becoming increasingly quick. Arjun had thought of going down to search for him but then thought better of it.

Now, as the plane was about to take off, he wondered if he had taken the correct decision. Had Preeti been right? Was he indeed using his sons as pawns in the big game? Had his real interest been in meeting the ministers and the IAS and IPS guys who sent their sons there too? Not that he would not use the opportunity if it presented itself, for it would be foolish not to, but no, that was not the reason he had decided to take this step. Sudheer and Mohan had to grow up to be 'someone' and that school in Dehra Dun would give them the substance and training they required, but more importantly, it would give them pedigree.

Pedigree. The only currency they accepted in Delhi. Not talent, not intelligence. Just who you knew and what they could do for you.

Arjun glanced impatiently at his Rolex. Just a few more hours. Just a few more hours before Calcutta.

And Nayantara.

7

ARIJIT WAS IN HIS OWN UNIVERSE. SITTING ON THE GROUND cross-legged, in a pair of khaki shorts two sizes too big, he was assembling a transistor radio, his hands a blur of movement, while humming a song which Arjun had guessed must be Rabindrasangeet for he was, after all, Bangali's son. He could hardly believe this was possible, a disassembly and a faster assembly, and yet there Arijit was, tightening the cover with a screwdriver. He turned the knob and the transistor radio crackled to life, followed by the familiar voice of the All India Radio announcer.

Arjun clapped.

'See, uncle, I said I can do it in ten minutes.' His smile was an exact replica of Bangali's, and Arjun felt that familiar lump in his throat every time he saw it.

'Very impressive. Who taught you this?' Arjun took the transistor in his hand, almost trying to convince himself that it was not a trick. A seven-year-old had actually done this.

'Subayu-da.' His eyes lit up with a spark that reminded Arjun of Nayantara. 'He is an engineer. He is my friend.' The last sentence Arijit said with some pride.

'How many times did he show you this?'

'Twice. I picked it up the first time. The second was just to confirm.' Then he added, 'I understand some of it too. The principles. Subayu-da explained it to me.'

'So can you teach me?' asked Arjun. 'I would love to learn.'

Arijit flicked up an eyebrow. 'If I teach you, what will you give me?'

Arjun thought for a second. 'Anything you want. Swiss chocolates. American toys. Anything.'

Arijit grimaced. 'No. Not those. I want to learn how to repair cars.'

Arjun looked at him for a while. 'Who told you I know how to repair cars?'

'Ma said you are very good. That when you were my age you used to repair foreign cars.'

Arjun scuffled Arijit's hair. 'Quite a bit older. But tell me why not a nice remote-controlled toy car?'

Arijit shook his head wisely. 'No, uncle. Things get lost. They break, they grow old. But when you learn something, it stays.'

Arjun nodded. It had taken him years to learn this. And yet this little boy...

Nayantara broke his reverie, entering the room holding a tray with two cups of tea and an assortment of biscuits. They were at her home now, so she wore her sari demurely wrapped around herself, and yet the moment she came in, Arjun was instantly transported to that feeling of 'I must have her'. He felt guilty immediately because Arijit was there. She seemed to have caught his glance and, putting the tray down on the coffee table, she said, 'Tubai, your friends are downstairs playing badminton. Why don't you join them?'

He said eagerly, 'I was showing uncle my transistor trick. Can I show him my magic now?'

'No, not now. Later. Go down and play.'

He rushed out, jumping over the threshold, towards the stairs, with Nayantara calling out, 'Wear your shoes. And don't take them off once you are down there. I can't be cleaning up after your dirty feet.'

Arijit's 'yes ma' was lost as he ran down the stairs eagerly, the patter of his feet trailing away.

'I wish you would not look at me that way when he is around,' Nayantara said while stirring the tea.

'I ... I couldn't control my eyes ... anyway, he is too young to understand,' Arjun said apologetically.

'Maybe on this. But Arijit is wise beyond his years. His teacher had him tested. Some IQ test or something she said. It was off the charts. Anyway, I am worried about him.'

'Why?' Arjun took the cup in his hand. 'I am worried about my sons. For good reasons. Because one is stupid and the other ... well, I don't know what he is. Why should you be worried for Arijit?'

'Because people talk. They ask him who you are. He says "uncle". The older boys smile. He repeats you are his uncle and doesn't understand why they are smiling or what they are trying to tell him. But he will. Any day now.'

Arjun took a sip and then put the cup on the saucer. Nayantara hated wet marks on the coffee table.

'I thought you wanted to come to this place because rich people don't talk.'

'Yes, call me naïve.' Nayantara leaned forward and Arjun tried to look away from the hint of cleavage. 'Now I see that people talk everywhere. Even here on Ballygunje Circular Road.'

'As bad as your old place?'

'Just that the neighbours won't knock on my door and ask me to leave. You think a woman who says she is a widow and yet keeps herself dolled up, who does not have a husband but is still rich enough to live in a place like this, and who has a gentleman who does not look Bengali visiting her once in a while, yet her son calls him "uncle", is not suspicious? That it would pass notice?'

Nayantara and her son lived in one of Calcutta's most posh localities, in a new block of ten-storey buildings on Ballygunje Circular Road, the housing complex of choice of the top executives of the city's private companies. Arjun didn't quite like coming here, instead preferring to have Nayantara over at Grand Hotel, where he could do what he wanted with her without her fretting over 'Tubai will hear'. But the ayah for Arijit had decided to skip out of town right when Arjun was in it, which meant the Grand was out for now.

'Who is this Subayu-da whom Arijit was speaking of?'

'Do I have to tell you?' Nayantara asked, and Arjun looked up to see the hint of a smile on her lips.

'I guess I have to, since I am your paid keep,' Nayantara said and there was no malice in her voice. ' He is Mr Chatterjee's son. They live upstairs. Smart boy with radios and those things and Tubai simply adores him, though I know perfectly well why he hangs around Arijit, because I can feel his eyes burn into my behind the moment I turn around. Not smart in that way. His father is smarter though. When he watches, he doesn't make it so obvious.' She bit into the thin arrowroot biscuit nimbly.

'Wait, didn't your last landlord look at you in that bad way too?'

'Yes, he did.'

'Now father. Son. Who in Calcutta doesn't look at you in a bad way?'

'Jealous?' she asked with a naughty arch of an eyebrow, and he knew she was watching him with those probing eyes of hers. He continued to look down into the cup. 'Come on now, he is just a boy. And you know I like men. The rough types. The one with the loaded guns. Not scrawny engineering college kids with their heads in their books and their hands inside their shorts. Nor their father with bellies and a visiting card that says "Assistant Director, Labour Relations".'

'I don't think that's right,' he said, trying hard to hide his irritation. He heard Nayantara giggle. 'Why would you let this Subayu chap come here when you know his motives are not honourable, unless you like the attention?'

'Oh ho. What an honourable man we have here. You can watch my behind too if you want now. I won't mind.'

'I thought you didn't like doing it here, in your house.'

'Tubai won't be back for an hour, at least.' She had gotten up from the sofa, closed the main door with a firm click, and was moving towards him slowly. He was sitting with his back against the wall, reclining on the divan and watching her movements. Her walk was now maddeningly sensuous, that exquisitely curved waist tracing lines through the air, challenging him to get up and pin her to the wall.

He stayed in his place. He had to appear to make it difficult for her. For hadn't she denied it to him when he had already been here for a day?

'No, let's wait till we can get to the hotel.'

'Aww, come on.' She sat demurely next to him now. 'Don't tell me you don't want to. Even Subayu has some sense of shame. You are shameless.' She moved her mouth to the side of his neck, snaked her tongue out and traced a line slowly down. He shivered. His hands reached for her breasts from below and they were just as familiarly full as he had remembered them. He kneaded and pushed them together, and then attacked her lips with his tongue.

She whispered, between kisses, 'No need to go inside to the bedroom. Let's do it here.'

They did, moaning and squealing gently with pleasure.

It was an almost an hour before they got their breath back. Arjun realized that the transistor had been on all this time. The musical programme had been interrupted by an announcement.

The prime minister had declared a state of Emergency.

Nayantara buttoned up her blouse and draped the sari tightly over her chest.

'Is this bad news?' she asked, concern in her voice.

He nodded gravely, 'things are going to change now, and change ... change is never good for business.'

Without danger, Bangali used to say, one becomes like a lion in a zoo – the anger is gone and so is the hunger as you sit on your haunches and children throw peanuts at you all day long, growling from time to time from force of habit. Now that he no longer ran guns, Arjun had sometimes felt like that zoo-kept lion, well fed and satisfied. This business – of wheeling and dealing through the corridors of Delhi – required smarts, a nose for opportunity and the courage to go all in, but there was never a sense that you were in any kind of harm, the adrenaline never flowed, the stomach never tightened, and you became fat and lazy.

Well, here it was again.

Danger.

And somehow now that it was right there in front of him, he did not quite jump at it as he had thought he would. For the first time in his life, he had not seen the danger coming. For the first time in his life, he had not been prepared. Not for Emergency, which had now been going on for three months, and definitely not for this man.

It had all started with a phone call. His secretary Marie D'Souza, a free-spirited Goan girl with a nice telephone voice and an air of quiet efficiency, had transferred the call to his office.

There was a lady calling on behalf of her boss to fix an appointment. When she mentioned his name, Arjun immediately sat up in his chair.

Ranvijay Pratap Singh.

It was a name he had heard many times before. But not by the full appellation. Simply RP. The initials were enough.

RP's father, Jayant Pratap, had practised criminal law at the Supreme Court. He was known for being a ruthless trial lawyer and for his connections with those with *khaandaani* or family wealth, rulers of princely states and old business families. He controlled the sluice gates of campaign cash, so come election season, politicians of all sizes and shapes would sit with begging bowls at his durbar on Aurangzeb Road. Jayant Pratap had died of a heartattack in '68, and the rumour was that his heart had given way when he was planting the flag in one of his innumerable conquests. Then the empire had passed on to his eldest son.

Ranvijay Pratap Singh. RP.

And now RP wanted to meet him.

Arjun had wanted an appointment for Tuesday but the voice at the other end of the line insisted that it be tomorrow. Delhi was as stratified as it had been during the time of the Mughals and RP, very obviously, expected his pedigree to be respected, and so their meeting had to be at his convenience. Arjun had half a mind to tell the secretary that it had to be next week or not at all. Strength had to be met with strength, such was the way of the city, but he decided to give RP some ground, figuring something big might be around the corner.

He was wrong. And he was right.

Aurangzeb Road was the address of choice for the well-connected Delhi insider, known for its gulmohur-tree-lined sidewalks and iron gates and high walls that protected the massive bungalows. It was in a neighbourhood referred to as Lutyens Delhi, as much a community of genteel well-heeled men and women who met over glasses of champagne and laughed at the foibles of the masses they ruled or commiserated over their backwardness, as it was a metaphor for the power centre within the power centre of Delhi. And there Arjun found himself, being driven through the enormous gates, past the guards, and having his driver park the car on the gravel.

A guard dressed in a smart white uniform led Arjun to what he figured was RP's late father's chambers, a cavernous room full of large-backed leather chairs, framed photos of JP with prime ministers and presidents, and floor-to-ceiling glass cases packed with red and black legal tomes. He took a seat in front of the large mahogany table and waited. And waited. Not that he was surprised, for it was just like Delhi to keep those that are less important waiting, for nothing shows power more than the ability to waste someone else's time.

An hour late for his appointment, Ranvijay Pratap ambled in. The name might have been regal and the slow walk of arrogance even more so, but RP looked like no king. He was a small man, five feet and a little more, with an ordinary face sought to be made extraordinary through a rather grand moustache, an expensive Nehru jacket with gold buttons and gold-framed round glasses. His eyes were hard, cruel and smoky like a cat's, reminding Arjun for a second of the eyes of the inspector who killed Chottu all those years ago.

'You are lucky I am not my father.' RP leaned back into his large leather chair. 'If you had remained sitting when he came into the room, it would have been the end of our meeting. Which would also mean the end of you.'

'Well, if your secretary had told me that I would have to stand up, I would have done that.'

'Aah, spunk. I like that in a man. There is a Yiddish word for it. Chutzpah.' He cracked the knuckles of his right hand absent-mindedly. 'I assume that you already know who I am and what I do. You would be a fool not to and I know you are no fool. You obviously don't know what Yiddish is, but you do know how to win contracts for the Israelis.'

This was exactly what Arjun had thought the meeting was about. In the battle for the military equipment purchase, he had, without really knowing it, hurt RP. He couldn't but help feel a little bit of pride.

RP massaged each joint of his left hand, slowly and with deliberation. 'Bhatia, I am a peaceful man, I don't like to fight, especially when there is so much around for so few of us. As long as you would have stayed in your little box somewhere, I would have let you be. But now you want to play with the big boys and you don't just want to play, you want to try to take their toys away. That I can't let you do. Not in this town. Not in my playground.'

Arjun had been threatened before. Many times and by many powerful people. A direct threat from a man this high in the food chain meant he had drawn blood. The first thing you should do when threatened, Arjun had learned over the years, is to make a counter-threat, but it should sound exactly the opposite.

'I am sure if we make a sincere attempt, we can stay out of each other's corners. I think that would be in both of our interests.'

JP lifted a paperweight from the table and started spinning it casually. 'I agree. But what about the disrespect?'

'Disrespect?' asked Arjun, knowing that they were moving to the second round of the dance.

'The way you talk, the way you sit, the way you look at me as if we are equals, the way you didn't get up when I entered the room, the way you didn't even bother to find out who was behind the French. Disrespect is the only word I can use. You are an upstart, and I don't like upstarts. People far bigger than you have sat on the floor here with their heads down and their hands folded. That's the kind of respect my name commands. You need to show me that respect, and as I see you are not going to give it on your own, I will take it from you.' He raised his finger and said, 'A few months ago, the country was going to the dogs. But now with the Emergency, things are as they should have been, the way my father always wanted. The country is now in the hands of good men. Now good men finally have the power to put the black marketeers into jail and hang the hoarders by their balls. No *dalal* reporters to get you sympathy, and no commie whores running about crying human rights. No evidence, no charge sheet, no witnesses. Just phone calls. One call from me, Bhatia, and we throw you in under MISA. If you continue to show me disrespect, then that's exactly what's going to happen. Hard labour in Tihar, your house and your cash seized, your family on the roads. If you think I am making this up, think of this. The princes could not keep their purses, national netas could not keep their behinds out of jail and, as we speak, the Bombay mafia are weaving chairs while wearing black-and-white uniforms. And you ... you are just a little gunrunner who has had a good run of luck.'

RP pointed to the big black phone in front of him.

'But I don't want to make that call. I don't want you in jail. Instead I want there to be peace. Now I am sure you are thinking, if this man could really do what he says he can, why hasn't he? Why is he offering me a way out? You would be right to wonder why. There is something you have that I want, and because you have that, you get to sit in that seat. Now I am going to ask you a question. If you lie to me, I will take it as more disrespect because I know part of the answer. So here it is. Do you know where the Raja of Pratapgarh – and I know you know which Pratapgarh I am talking about – buried his family treasure?'

This Arjun had not anticipated. This question, of all the things in the world. No. He hadn't seen it coming.

RP was right, Arjun knew that. With the Emergency, if someone as powerful as RP took a personal interest in his ruin, there was little Arjun could do. The Maintenance of Internal Security Act, or MISA as it was known, allowed people to be thrown into jail without formal charges and for the authorities to search and seize without warrant. The newspapers had been blacked out, the government controlled the airwaves, and spies and turncoats were everywhere. Arjun's money and his contacts could not save him, not from this and not now.

And this man wanted the Pratapgarh treasure.

Arjun had heard hushed whispers, that with the Emergency ongoing they, whoever 'they' were was never made clear, were going for the hoards of jewels, gold, silver, cash and diamonds that kings of erstwhile princely states, small and large, had hidden away from the eyes of the government. Long cavalcades of vehicles, or so the whispers went, were moving seized wealth away to where no one knew.

The Raja of Pratapgarh was the king of a small princely state, one of the hundreds that had been assimilated into India after independence. He had a taste for the latest guns and many years ago Arjun had been one of his suppliers, and they had struck up a friendship. One day, he had called Arjun up into the old music room at his home, and there between fits of coughing and pulls on the hookah, had told him about a problem of his. His estranged son, the Raja had come to learn, was planning to run away with the family treasure. The Raja was sure that his son was close to figuring out where it was hidden and that he had to move it some place safe. Since he did not know who among his own men could be trusted, he wanted Arjun and Bangali to arrange for the transport of the treasure to a place in the woods, and bury it in the backyard of an old abandoned temple. Arjun had not wanted the job, but since the Raja was an old customer and a good man, Arjun had gotten five trusted men to move the treasure. He had thought it would be a small amount, made to appear more important than it was by the paranoia of an old man whose glory days had passed him by.

He was wrong.

There were ten huge chests full of gold and diamonds and ancient treasures, and they had buried the stash where the Raja had asked them to. As Bangali found out later, the Raja's ancestors had been dacoit kings and all the gold in the trunks was stolen loot, handed down the ages. Moving the treasure away may have secured its safety but could not save the Raja. One day, for no reason, he 'fell' from the third floor balcony.

And now, with Emergency in place, the son of the Raja had gotten in touch with RP to retrieve his inheritance. Yes, thought Arjun, that is how it would have happened. He paused to consider his options and came to the realization that he had none.

He bowed his head humbly, 'Yes, I know where it is buried.'

'Good,' RP said, a smile of contentment creeping over his face. 'Dubey will call you tomorrow. You will tell him where the treasure is buried. Then you will go with him and dig it out. If you try to act uppity, Dubey will bury you. Or I will.'

Arjun nodded. He was overpowered. There was nothing he could do. The conversation continued for some time. Or rather RP spoke, and Arjun listened. From now on, whenever he wanted to do business with anyone, he would have to give Dubey all the details. If RP wanted to do the deal, he would take it. If RP felt like it, he would give Arjun a baksheesh, as he put it, else nothing.

If RP had his hands full with business, Arjun could do the job but whatever he made, fifty per cent would go to RP. 'Consider it *jiziya*, this being Aurangzeb Road,' he had said with a slight smile and a gentle shake of his head, as if satisfied with having come up with the observation.

Arjun bowed and nodded. Inside though, he burned with helpless rage. This man was razing to the ground his little kingdom.

'Yes, I understand, RP sir,' Arjun said, bottling it up inside, putting the emphasis on sir.

RP recognized the effort and laughed viciously. Pointing to a giant portrait of his father, he said, 'He had this saying. If a dog acts too much like his master, neuter it.' He made a little snipping action with his fingers. 'Now that I have done the job on you, you have started giving me respect. See. You are learning. Next time you might even be sitting on the ground when I come in.' He banged the paperweight on the tabletop, made an imperious gesture of dismissal and Arjun walked slowly out.

8

OVER THE YEARS, THEIR LOVEMAKING HAD SETTLED INTO the rhythm of comforting familiarity. Not that the lushness of Nayantara's body ever ceased to amaze Arjun and he was sure she had become even more beautiful as time had passed, but the violence and abruptness of their initial frenzied couplings had been replaced by an intimate harmony, the knowledge of when to play what note and in what scale. They talked a lot, and Arjun remembered their walks in the parks, going to the cinema together and having *jhalmuri* on the streets afterwards with more fondness than the sex, even though he still looked forward to their overnight sojourns at the Grand Hotel with the same urgency.

But this time it had been different. He had not talked much

during dinner, even though Nayantara tried several times to initiate conversation, instead choosing to play idly with the fork and knife, making circles in his plate of food. After that, he had taken Nayantara into the bedroom where he had pinned her to the bed with his arm, divested her of her sari in one fluid but violent motion, popped her expensive blouse hooks down the back, making them fly in every direction, before yanking her bra off with nothing that could be called gentleness. Then he pulled off the pins securing the bun on her head and, holding her hair, he turned her head and kissed her, but with none of the understanding softness that she had become used to. He then proceeded to have her every way, ploughing into her with controlled violence, and today there was no banter, no pause, no interruption, only guttaral commands like 'kneel' or 'spread them' or 'turn around' and Nayantara doing all that he asked, without protest or question. When he was spent, he let Nayantara lie on the bed alone and sat on the couch, looking up aimlessly at the ceiling.

'Did that get it out of your system?' she asked.

He sat silently for a while and she began picking up her clothes or whatever was left of them, when he suddenly said, 'Thank you. I needed this.'

'You want to talk about it?'

He hesitated but then started to vent.

He told her about the meeting with RP. How he had met with Dubey the next day and then a week later he had accompanied him and his men to Pratapgarh. Dubey had put him to work along with the hired hands, and Arjun knew RP had asked for that, to show him his place. Nearing forty, he was still reasonably fit, but he was not used to labour any more, and certainly not the heavy shovelling kind. He sweated and panted, wiping the sweat from his brow, but soldiered on in the sun, determined not to show any weakness.

On the way back, Dubey had said, between the periodic rolling down of the car window and spitting out of betel juice on to the country road, 'Before I became RP sahib's right hand, I used to be a pimp. All of my best girls went to his father. He was the kind of man who liked to live like a king – wanted new girls for his harem every Friday, and fond of good music and art too. Anyway, there was this old saying I would tell the girls, and they used it in that new film, whose name I can't remember now. The saying was, "As long as your feet move, you stay alive." Of course in their case it was more like as long as your legs spread, you stay alive.'

He had cackled in delight. 'You seem like a good man so my advice to you would be one thing. Be useful to RP sahib. Make money for him. Make more money for him. The moment you stop doing that, he will come for your money, your house, and whatever else you have stuffed in your pockets. RP sahib is very ruthless and he has no mercy. His father was more a romantic, you see, Urdu poetry and pretty women. RP sahib reads only James Hadley Chase and lacks that, what do you call it, old-world large-heartedness. You have not given him respect, and he's going to take you for it. So my advice, keep your ass lubed up and warm, cause if you don't give him a happy time, he is going to kill you, dry you up and then shove his *lund* into your eye sockets. You are not a man to him. You are just a hole.'

Over the next two months, Arjun had had to surrender all his important clients to RP, leaving him with almost nothing. Staying in business made no sense. Almost everything he made would be taken away by RP but stay he had to, lest he no longer remained useful. Whether he accepted it or not, Dubey was right. His only way of staying out of jail was by making money for RP like a whore does for her pimp. He felt emasculated, as if his cock had been snipped from between his legs, and today taking Nayantara in the way he did, made him feel like a man again, at least within the confines of an expensive hotel room.

'I am worried for you. I have never seen you look like this.'

Arjun had never seen himself look like this either. Ever since RP had taken away his business, he had had a lot of time on his hands. The boys had been packed off to boarding school, Riti stayed surrounded by ayahs, and Preeti was either going to a kitty party or returning from one. Arjun would retreat to his room upstairs and lock the door. Never more than an occasional drinker, he had taken to drinking quite regularly. The evenings when he was not at the office trying to make money for RP would be spent in a daze of drink, trying to drown the sensation of impotence, but it never really went away. He had gained weight, he knew that, and the fact that his eyes had puffed up and that he had an ugly stubble made him look every bit the wreck that he was.

He had told Nayantara everything. Not just what had happened with RP but how he felt, how he had spent the last few months. He felt naked as he was opening up to her. She listened patiently, with very little interruption, staying on the far side of the bed, not asking him to join her as she would have done on other days, allowing him the comfort of his own space. When he had finished, she asked, 'So you will give up? Just like that?'

He did not reply.

'You came to this country with nothing. Do you remember?'

'Of course I do.'

'And you did this. All of this. You didn't give up, did you, not ever. So why now?'

Arjun slapped his palm on the handle of the couch. 'You don't understand, Nayantara. I can't kill him. I can't do anything to him, he has me in a chokehold, thanks to this Emergency.'

'So you are giving up.'

'I am not. I just don't know what to do. I never saw this coming, and that makes me mad. I ... I don't know how I could not have ...'

'What's this obsession with "I never saw this coming"? You

may be smart, but you are no parrot pulling cards. The big things in life blindside us, whether it be love or death, and there is no use later shaking your hands and saying, oh no, I didn't see it coming.'

Arjun held his head in his hands and sat quietly.

Nayantara continued, 'He is no God. He is just a kid with a big daddy. He's done nothing in life except live off his father. And you ... you have fought all your life, yourself, with your own hands.'

'But you don't understand ...'

'No, I don't. I don't understand your accepting defeat like this ... but then I have never claimed to be smart.'

'It's the Emergency, it's MISA. It's ...'

'Yes, I know. You told me. But the Emergency is not going to last. Neither will those who brought it in. There is a lot this country will put up with, but it won't put up with their tongues being nailed to the top of their mouths. Sure, trains run on time, rice is cheap in the market because the black marketeers have been put out of business, but then there are rumours of the government doing things to people, cutting off their cocks.'

'They don't cut off their cocks. It's called sterilization and doctors do it.'

'Whatever. Same thing. You can't do that. You can't have people looking over their shoulders, you can't have brother rat out brother. This can't last. And when the system goes belly-up, you have to be ready. That's when your RP will be at his weakest.'

Arjun laughed. 'Hah. I have to be ready. Easy to say that.'

Nayantara pursed her lips into a straight line. 'You say you feel as if he has made you become less of a man. I don't think he has. You have done this to yourself. Being a man isn't to walk around with guns or knock someone's teeth out or do a *randi* in the *gaand*.'

'I am sorry if ...'

Nayantara did not stop for the interruption. 'I know that's what people think being a man is. But being a man is something else. It's to take whatever God throws at you, dust yourself up and keep walking. He will strike you down again, and you will get up again. And the last one standing – he has won.'

'That's all very fine but real life doesn't work like that.'

'I am not saying what you have to do is easy. It is not supposed to be. You want to rule India and yet you expect it to be simple. How can it be?' She was making her hair back into a bun, the sari now thrown in one fold over her breasts. 'God gave you something he hasn't given other people. Brains. Now I know it's not the kind of brains my husband had. His was the college professor kind of head. That's why he is dead.'

Arjun was going to say something but stopped.

'You will figure it out. I know you will.' She walked up to him, one round of cloth draped around her naked body, and bent down, holding his hands in hers. 'As a matter of fact, I think you already know what is to be done. You are just afraid of taking that first step, because the path is so long and difficult.'

He looked up at her and Nayantara realized this was the most vulnerable she had ever seen Arjun.

'I am afraid.'

'You have never been afraid before.'

'I know.'

'But then why now? Why now after all these years?'

'That time you are talking about, I was young. I was reckless. I was arrogant. Was I brave? I suppose I was. Not because I had courage but because there was nothing to be afraid of. What did I have to lose? My life? It was worthless anyway.'

'And now?'

'Now I have a family. I have things I value. Things that it would hurt me to lose. And most important…' Arjun tapped his head with his index finger. 'I think more. I worry more. I hesitate. I know I can make mistakes. I know that there are bigger fish in the pond.

I know luck won't be with me all the way. I am forty and I have become soft.' He paused and collected his words. 'You are right. I am afraid of taking that first step. I fear the path. I fear the pain of walking it. I fear I will fall and I will die but before that I will see everything I love wither away and that terrifies me so much that I can't move.'

'If what you told me about RP is right, you have no choice. Move or he will cut you down as you stand.'

Arjun turned away, looking up at the ceiling. Nayantara gave him a while to be alone with his thoughts. Bathed and refreshed and in a new set of clothes that clung to her body the way she knew Arjun liked it, she sat on the armrest of his couch.

'Now you listen to me, Mr Arjun Bhatia.' She leaned forward and hugged him close. 'Call your travel agent right now and cancel tomorrow's flight back to Delhi. Then you will go to a barber and get a shave. Then you will bring your bags to my place.' Arjun started to say something but she put a finger to his lips. 'I don't want to hear a word. And no more drinking. Not a drop. This week is the last seven days you are going to have to feel sorry for yourself or afraid or lazy or whatever it is that is keeping you from bringing this man down. Tell yourself that. Then after seven days are over, you leave for Delhi and you will go to war and you will take back from RP what belongs to you. Are we clear?'

He turned to the side, tipped his head back such that their eyes met, and clutched her arm tightly to himself.

'Uncle, are you all right?' A small head peeked out from behind the frame of the wooden door, eyes sparkling, its owner wearing a white vest and blue shorts. He had been told not to disturb his uncle, but now that Nayantara had left for a while for the vegetable market and was not expected back for at least an hour, Arijit had tippy-toed to the guest room.

Arjun asked him to come in. 'Why do you think I am not all right?'

Arijit walked towards the bed tentatively. 'You have not asked me about the transistor even once. You haven't even asked to see my magic tricks. So I was wondering...'

'I just have a lot of things on my mind.'

'What are they?' Arijit sat at the farthest corner of the bed. 'I shouldn't be here. Ma will be angry.'

'Don't worry, I won't tell.' Arjun smiled.

'So what are you thinking?'

'Oh, nothing special. Some things I have to do.'

Out of the blue, Arijit asked, 'Do you miss my father?'

Arjun didn't know what to say. He had no idea what Nayantara had told Arijit about Bangali. The little boy seemed to understand his hesitation.

'It's okay, you can tell me,' he said almost conspiratorially. 'I know he is dead. Ma tells me baba is missing. She is silly, she does not know that it hurts me more to believe that baba is alive and does not once come back to see me.' He looked up and said, 'Ma told me you were his best friend. Do you miss him?'

He didn't need to lie. 'Not a day goes by when I don't.'

'Ma cries at night sometimes, when you are not here. It must be worse for her than it is for me.'

'Why must it be worse for her?'

'Because I don't have any memories of baba. She does. That's what makes you sad, isn't it? Memories. I feel sad for Kaloo because I remember him.'

'Who is Kaloo?'

'The stray dog that sometimes sneaked in through the gate downstairs.' Arijit picked up a badminton racquet whose handle was sticking out from below the bed. 'A bus ran over him.' He banged the side of the racket on the floor with violence. 'Just like that. He was dead.'

'Your father loved you a lot,' Arjun said, remembering Bangali's last moments those years ago, knees in the dust, gun to his head, pleading to be let go. He had never heard him talk about his son before that, not at least with any kind of special fondness. Maybe he did not care. Maybe he did. He would never know the truth. But then again, the truth is never what really happens. The truth is what we choose to believe.

'How will I know if he did? He is dead,' Arijit said again and his lips trembled but his eyes remained as dry as before.

'This might be a little too heavy...'

'Like Rabindrasangeet?'

Arjun couldn't help but smile. 'Yes. But then seeing how smart a little boy you are, I think you will understand.'

Arjun reached out and held the small wrist. 'We all die. Your father. Me. Kaloo. Everything that's come into this world goes there.' He pointed to the sky. 'That's why the time we get in between is all the more precious. If we lived forever, time would be cheap.'

Arijit nodded. 'Right. Otherwise ma would never say, "Tubai, don't waste my time."'

'Exactly. That's why it's important what we do in the time we have, the stories we write with our lives.'

Arijit lifted an eyebrow. 'Stories? But you find them in books.'

'Only some.' Arjun wagged his finger. 'The big stories, the exciting stories, they are what we write every day. Our own stories. You don't read these stories from the pages of a book, you live them. That's what makes them so amazing. I know your father's story. And his story has you in it.'

Arijit's face lit up. 'Tell me some stories about baba.'

Arjun paused for a while. He was never much of a teller of stories. Fairy tales to Riti at bedtime he could manage, ghosts and goblins and princes and princesses, none of them made any sense anyway, he just started and then when her eyes closed, he would tuck her in and quietly sneak away. But reality, with the bad parts chopped out and then sprinkled with imagination and fitted with a halo for a little kid without a father, that was hard.

But he wanted to do it. For Arijit's sake.

So he started. Some of what he said happened. Some didn't. Soon he was on his own, spinning one story after another – the sparkle in Arijit's eyes was all the encouragement he needed to go on, for if this bright kid believed the stuff he was making up, he was doing all right. Then after some time, what would comfortably be more than an hour, they both heard the sound of the key turning in the lock outside. Arijit looked at Arjun with alarm, put his finger on his lips, and ran away out of the room, a spring in his step, dropping the badminton racquet where it had been.

Arjun's mind was made up. He was not going to let his story be told to his children by someone else.

He would live not through others' words, but his own.

He was going to go to war.

'Why are you doing this? Why?' The surprise in Arjun's voice had now been replaced by fierce exasperation. 'I don't know why I told you anything about the money. One should never tell women anything.'

Nayantara smiled indulgently, sliced a piece of the kabiraji cutlet off with her knife, and scooped it into her mouth elegantly with the fork. Arjun had an early morning flight back to Delhi the next day and Nayantara had suggested they have dinner at Mitra Cabin, the little place they had had their first dinner together, unchanged through these years with its small private cabins, age-old walls with peeling plaster of paris, ancient soot-clad fans, food that left little ringlets of oil on the plate long after it had vanished, and officious waiters smelling of deep-fried pakoras.

Arjun explained, a hint of desperation in his voice, 'When I said money was going to be tight, I never meant that I would be sleeping on the street. The house will stay, at the least the one we live in. I will sell the foreign car but we will still have the Ambassador. I will keep my family, perhaps not in the way they are used to, but still in a way that is more than good, and if I can do all that, I sure can look after you and Arijit.'

Nayantara stopped chewing, and said, 'It was here in this place that I made a deal.'

'And your point is?'

'I am freeing you from it.'

'Aren't we getting just a bit filmy? I am telling you I will have the money.'

Nayantara's eyes, large and placid, remained as calm as ever. Arjun's steadily rising voice and his clenching of his fork seemed to have no effect on her.

'Every little bit helps.'

'What am I telling you? I have the money.'

'I know what you spend on us isn't a little bit. I made sure that it was not. Anyway, it's not about money. It's about your family. I want you to keep them close. Bring the boys back from their boarding school, keep them around, talk to your wife, make your marriage work.' A piece of the kobiraji cutlet dropped off from the end of her fork on to her plate and she picked it with a quick stab. 'It's you who says that the only thing that matters in life is family.'

'Yes, I do. What about it?'

'Well, now don't just say it, show it. You have to know what you are fighting for, or you will never win.'

'But ... but you are like my family too. I have never thought of you and Arijit to be different.'

She did not reply. They sat in silence for a minute till Arjun finally said, 'Something else is the matter, isn't it?'

'It's over.'

'What?'

She went back to her cutlet.

'Look at me.' Arjun reached out across the table and held her hand firmly. 'What's over? What are you saying?'

'When I came here to Mitra Cabin all those years ago, I was scared. Very scared. You wouldn't have made that out from the way I talked, all forward and confident, but I was shaking all over inside. I was desperate then, I had a son and no money, and nothing to sell except myself, even if it was to the man who I knew had killed my husband. I knew I could get a job but I also knew that sooner or later it would come to that only. Me in exchange of security. I figured it was better to give myself to you than to a stranger though God knows why I thought of you as not a stranger, since I had met you for only five minutes before.'

'Why are you saying all this? What's going on?'

'But it's wrong, Arjun. All these years it has always been wrong. I was sleeping with a married man for money. I tried to put that simple fact out of my head, in the same way I guess you put what people do with the guns they buy from you out of your head, but I really could not. I was scared that God would punish me, punish us, for our sins. Maybe he already has.'

'And you realize it's a sin right about the time I get kicked in the teeth? Is there someone else now? Or do you think I can no longer keep you?' Arjun's voice stayed icy cold and Nayantara's hands felt colder still.

Nayantara smiled, and this time there was a wan sadness to it. 'See that's the thing. I don't want to be your keep. I don't want to be anyone's keep. I want to live my life as a person. I want to be me. Nayantara. Not the moll. Not the little escape on the side. Just a woman. Just a mother.'

'If you want, I can marry you. I know of people with two

wives. I can do that. Is that what you want? Recognition of our relationship?'

Nayantara shook her head firmly, biting her lip with determination. 'No. Never. I do not want to be your wife. Not your second, not your first. Remember that day you had asked me if that was what my game was, whether it was to trick you into marriage? I said no, and I meant it.'

'*Ab bas bhi karo yaar.*' Arjun slammed his palms on the table, making the crockery jangle. 'Will you stop talking about what I said years ago? I didn't know you then, I know you now.' He leaned forward, and said the words very slowly, with more passion than he thought he had. 'What do you want me to do? To go down on my knees?'

'No.'

'Well, what can I say? I need you more than ever. You are the only person I have in my life.'

'No, I am not. That's exactly why I need to go. I am just a hobby, an expensive one at that, and you have to put your hobbies on hold for now.'

'You know how happy my marriage is.'

'Whose fault is that? It's not your wife's. It's yours and it's mine.' She adjusted a strand of hair from her forehead. 'A wife can never compete with the other woman. I know. I was someone's wife once.'

The waiter gently lifted the curtain and peeked in and his stern expression told Arjun to keep his voice and the cutlery banging down. Arjun reached into his pocket, took out a fifty-rupee note and banged it down on the table and gestured to the waiter to leave. He promptly took it and backed out.

'It's because your whole attention is on coming to Calcutta that you can never enjoy being in Delhi. That's why your marriage is in such a mess. That's why you never saw RP coming. That's why all of these things happened. My husband ... he did the same thing. And see what happened to him.'

'You are saying RP is God's revenge because I am not a faithful married man?'

Nayantara opened her mouth to say something, stopped, thought for a second and then continued. 'Love your wife, take care of her, make your marriage work. Beat that bastard RP to the ground. I know you will do it. I just know it.'

'Why are you doing all this? Just before I am leaving, all this? We had one week and you never said anything.'

'Because I didn't want this conversation to ruin everything. I wanted to take care of you, in the best way I could, not at the Grand but in my own place, not as a keep but as a friend. I don't know if you care any more, but this was the best week of my life. Me and you. Friends.'

'You really are serious about breaking this off?'

'I am. Very serious.'

'Can I call? Can we just meet if I am in Calcutta? I promise I won't take you to the Grand, since you seem to hate that so much.'

'I am going to leave the city. I hope I can trust you not to come looking for me or to put one of your men on my tail.'

'Why are you running from me?'

'It's not going to work for either of us otherwise.'

'How will you survive?' asked Arjun, his voice breaking a bit.

'You have been generous enough. I have some money now. I am thinking of starting a Rabindrasangeet school. Plus I am good with a sewing machine.' She patted Arjun's hand. 'If I were very principled I would have given back the jewellery you bought for me. But I am not that much of a Harishchandra. So don't worry. I do know how to look after myself.'

Arjun pushed away his plate. 'You take me for a fool? You are dumping me because you think I won't have money. You think

I am going to lose.' Arjun could now barely bring the words out, he was so angry. 'You think I am not man enough. Don't I know? You are just moving on to a new target.'

Arjun stood up and walked out in a huff, slamming more notes on the fake-silver plate that had the bill, not noticing that Nayantara had taken out her handkerchief to quietly daub away the tears at the corners of her eyes.

9

ONCE BACK IN DELHI, ARJUN FOCUSED ALL HIS ENERGY ON restructuring his finances. There was no way around it – he would have to sell off most of what he had. The problem was that it would be impossible to hide all this selling from Preeti.

Of course, Arjun did not plan to tell her about RP because she would not understand. It was worse to consider a scenario where she might actually understand, and that scared him even more. Maybe like Nayantara, she too would see him for what he was right now, less of a man, unable to provide for his family in the way that he always had. She knew her husband had never been an upright law-abiding citizen but had never quizzed him on the details, what exactly it was that he did or where he went. As long as there was money to do the things she wanted, servants available to dust and clean, ayahs available to look after the children, cooks and gardeners to make sure that the dinner table and the garden looked straight out of high-living glossies, she had been happy to keep herself occupied elsewhere. The silent provider and the unquestioning housewife, this was the contract on which their marriage had stood for all these years, and now Arjun was going to have to change the terms.

He broke the news to her gently, a few days after coming back from Calcutta, just before they were going to bed. As usual, she was at the dressing table, rubbing moisturizing lotion on her arms and shoulders as she did every night before settling down with a film glossy. He had avoided making eye contact throughout the uncomfortable conversation, sparing as many details as he possibly could. With the Emergency and the police becoming more and more aggressive, business was becoming tough. She had thought it was just idle complaining, the kind that husbands do at the end of a long day. It had taken him some time to make her understand the gravity of the situation. The houses he had bought for Sudheer and Mohan were going to have to be sold, and the one he had been thinking of buying for Riti, well, that was no longer going to happen. Not for now, anyway. The foreign car would have to go and so would much of the hired help. He could see the alarm in Preeti's eyes though she did remain calm, at least by her standards. 'How did things get so bad so fast?' she asked several times in different ways. He shrugged the question away with an evasive 'times are bad'. Then he had brought up bringing Sudheer and Mohan back from boarding school. He had thought Preeti would be the happiest about this.

To his surprise, this was where she protested the most. The boys had settled in their boarding schools, she insisted, and bringing them back would disrupt their lives all over again. Arjun wished he could tell Preeti the real reason he wanted the boys back. It wasn't just the money. He was afraid for their security. If things went south, and RP made his move, he would come after Arjun's family and if the boys were in Dehra Dun, Arjun would have no control over their movements. It was better for them to stay in their walled house, be schooled for a year or two at home by tutors for they were never going to be geniuses anyway, and he would invest in a good set of security guards, not the kind that walked around with a wooden stick and slept on duty after having opium, but those with licensed firearms and training. Yes, it would cost him but the most important thing he needed right now was peace at home, to know that his family was well guarded, and that if RP truly came after him with the full force of his power, they would stand a chance.

Arjun tried his best but he just could not get through to his wife and she started crying. She offered to sell her jewellery in order to keep the boys in school, but Arjun assured her that that would not be needed. Then she asked him, 'If business is bad, are you going to be staying home now?' He said he would not be, as a matter of fact he would be gone for long stretches of time. 'Why?' she asked and Arjun wondered when she had last questioned his decision on anything. 'I have to get our business back on track, that's why, and I can't do that sitting at home,' had been his reply and then he had rolled over, turning his back to her, which, in the house of Bhatias, meant that the conversation was officially over. But not today.

'Are we in some kind of danger?' she asked.

He grunted back a 'no', desperately trying to fall asleep but there was no mistaking the frosty resolve that seemed to envelop him on his own bed.

'It's that woman, isn't it?'

'What woman?' His stomach felt heavy and a dull pain throbbed at the base of his spine, the kind of sensation he had not felt before, at least not in his own bedroom.

'The woman from Calcutta. The one *jisse tum chodne jaate ho*. And have been doing for years.'

Arjun had never heard his wife use the Hindi word for 'fuck'. It was not the kind of word he had ever expected her to use, 'romantic' being her euphemism for anything carnal. But that was the least of his surprises for now. Preeti knew about Nayantara and Arjun figured it would be useless to deny or pretend.

'No, it isn't her.'

'Of course it is her. She is blackmailing you now, isn't she, that *randi*? I knew this was going to happen. I knew it.' She patted her forehead theatrically, her bangles clanging together. 'She found out how much money you have come into, and you are too big a fool to understand how women work, and now she is squeezing the lemon to see how much she can juice out. Tell me ... tell me that's the truth ... and I can deal with her. Who does the *kutiya* think she is going to blackmail you with? Me? Well, tell her that I know.'

'Trust me,' he said, and knew immediately that the word trust sounded strange right now. 'It's not her. Anyway, that's over.' They were right next to each other on the bed but yet the distance between them felt like Delhi and Lahore.

There was sadness in her voice now. And hurt. 'I have known for a long time. She made you feel good, much more than I could ever hope to.'

'It's not like ...' Arjun tried to interject.

'No, don't deny that. I could see the difference between when you left the house for her and when you left the house for everything else. You would dress better, you would put on your duty-free perfume, and you would come back happy.'

'How did you know?'

'You forget who gives your jackets and your clothes to the washerman, and who cleans out your pockets and arranges the notes in your wallet. Ticket stubs from Calcutta, for a movie you told me you had not seen. Receipts for saris I never got. Once a picture of her too.' She stopped, choked up and then said, 'She is very beautiful.'

First RP, now Preeti. Maybe he wasn't as smart as he thought he was nor was he as careful. Maybe that was the lesson for him in all this. Maybe Nayantara had been right. He had lost his game.

'It's not her,' he said, trying to maintain the impassive demeanour he thought Preeti had always associated him with.

'Then what is it? What is it that needs you to sell our houses, our cars and bring my boys back from boarding if it's not for that *randi*?'

Arjun reached out to the side table for the glass, took a big gulp of water and began. He needed Preeti on his side and she deserved the truth. He outlined his operations in Delhi, how he made money, and who RP was. He did not tell her about the buried gold and how he was made to dig it out and how much of his business he had had to cede to RP. But by the time he had finished, Preeti looked frightened. 'Let's leave everything and buy back my father's garage. You are good with cars, and our sons will learn on the job. We can make a lot of money.'

Arjun touched her comfortingly on the nape of her neck and, to his relief, she did not shake him off.

'We can't hide. We can't run. And we shouldn't.'

'But why?' she pleaded. 'Why can't you just let go? That's why you came to Delhi, you told me. Because it was too risky, running guns. Now if this place is even worse, even more dangerous, why would you even want to stay here?'

Arjun had thought about this many times before. Why? Why was he doing this? He knew the answer now and so it rolled off his tongue smoothly.

'I don't know what I told you but I didn't leave the gunrunning business just because it was too dangerous. I quit once I knew I could make more money taking less risks. I didn't run, Preeti, I climbed. I have climbed all my life. And I am going to be damned if I let some *madarchod* with nothing but a big name kick me down from that ladder. If I run today, if I climb down a rung, I will run all my life, I will slip down to the bottom and I will break. I will be your husband but I won't be the Arjun you married. Do you want that?'

She looked up at him and shook her head.

'Then I want you to help me. I need all of you, the boys, Riti, all of you together here.'

He felt her breath on him, heavy and tense.

'Things won't be easy and we both know that. But it's only when things get difficult do we truly become a family.'

Arjun felt her head on his shoulder and the wetness dripping down on to his kurta. They were not tears of anger or sadness, but of something else that he supposed existed in other marriages but that he had never really found in his.

And it felt strangely comforting.

* * *

The first phase of any war is reconnaissance.

Arjun had to know RP. He had to know everything about him, who he slept with, whose ass he kissed in the government and who kissed his, who paid his bills and where he parked his money.

A man could spend a lifetime trying to dig up all the dirt and still come up with his face black but with nothing in hand.

Or he could go to Abdul Ismail.

Arjun had met Abdul Ismail during the Israeli arms deal. Arjun had been working on breaking in a few officers in the army by digging up dirt about past procurements. Someone had suggested Abdul Ismail, who went by the somewhat strange alias of Aladdin Investigation Agency. It was, as Abdul Ismail had told Arjun the first day they had met, not the kind of agency that spies on spouses, or invoices for taxi fare and refreshments. Their price was in lakhs, sometimes in crores, based on the target and the value of the information and if he couldn't get the information asked for, he refunded the money.

Abdul Ismail had never had to give a single refund. The intel he had provided had been rock-solid. Arjun had come to admire not only Ismail's efficiency but also the man. He spoke very little, never talked about himself, and never bullshitted. In that respect, he was unlike every other guy in New Delhi.

Arjun had once heard a story about Ismail from one of the Israelis. He had been an officer of the Indian military intelligence, the very best. They had sent him undercover in Karachi during the '65 war when he was captured by the Pakistanis. The Rangers had gone to work on him with a knife and saw. The Indian government had rewarded his bravery by putting him under investigation when he returned and though his court martial never proved anything, the suspicion that he had given Pakistanis information to secure his release never went away. He got a dishonourable discharge and no pension. Arjun didn't know how much of this to believe, because people loved to make up stories in this town, but it did explain Ismail's glass eye, the deep knife scars that he tried to hide behind a dense beard, and the stump where his left hand would have been.

The Aladdin Investigation Agency had no address. The only way to get in touch with Ismail was to call a certain restaurant at Parathewali Gali and ask for a thousand aloo parathas. Within an hour, Ismail would call back and fix a meeting point. Arjun knew, the moment his fingers rotated the dial, that he would be selling his houses just to pay the genies at Aladdin.

But then no war is fought without casualties.

The first file that Ismail produced was the dossier on RP. Much of the gossip surrounding RP and his father was indeed true. The son had inherited his father's taste in women, though perhaps not his boundless energy for new conquests. He had married into a big industrial family, and had a boy Mohan's age. He had a sister and two older brothers, both men dead, one of malaria in '66 and the other in a car accident shortly after. Ismail had been intelligent enough to explore the angle that RP may have wasted them, but the police reports looked clean and the deaths checked out as natural. On the social front, RP was part of Delhi's young brat pack, hanging around at posh nightclubs in Delhi and sometimes in London and Paris with his friends. This Arjun already knew but what he did not know was that RP did cocaine and his father had sent him to a rehabilitation centre in the Swiss Alps for a few months. He had stayed off the habit till his father died but was now into it again with the enthusiasm of a recovering addict. His great public passion was cricket, being one of the bosses at the Delhi board for cricket, and apparently he would make it a point to attend every Test match held at Lord's.

A few weeks after delivering the personal file, Ismail gave him the bigger file – the one with information about RP's contacts in the administration, his businesses and his investments. The file wasn't really one file. It was eight boxes full of material. Liquor licences, mining rights, real estate, textile and automotive plants, three different chit funds, and stakes in almost everything that would make money. RP seemed to have his claws everywhere.

Now that he knew where to look, it was time for Arjun to start the second phase of the war.

The first part of that was the feint. He handed over whatever clients he had remaining to RP and made sure that Dubey knew he was not taking on anyone new. He had to let them believe he had been broken, and since Dubey never called, at least that part had been accomplished.

Then the journey began.

Over the next few months Arjun travelled all over India. He went back to his old friends from from his gunrunning days. A few of them were not very happy to see him but most were. He used them to reach out further into RP's interests. He understood how liquor licences were handed out, how government quota obligations for mining licences worked and how they were gained, which automotive plant produced parts that were exported to which country, loopholes in export licences, which imports RP's textile plants depended on, what kind of environmental clearances were needed to take protection away from forest land, how the value of RP's real estate holdings doubled every two years and which land assessors, local politicians and police and bureaucrats RP kept in his pocket. He consulted lawyers, slipped hundred-rupee notes into the pockets of peons, left cash-filled envelopes with desk clerks, supplied prostitutes to government inspectors and made hefty contributions to unions and politicians.

Arjun's savings were all gone. Soon he was borrowing money, and a lot of it. It came with high interest, either rupees or in promises of privileges moving forward, but it was almost always given without collateral because Arjun's word had weight. In all these years, he had always delivered on his promises and those around him seemed to believe that he would this time too, even though Arjun sometimes felt he could not. He was taking on too much too fast and the only way out was not to think – not to think of what would happen if he were to fail.

For the better part of the year, this went on. Life was as tough as it had ever been. To save money, he travelled second class in trains, stayed at the cheapest of dumps, and some nights he would be so tired that he would just lie down under a balcony on the open pavement and go to sleep. His love handles were gone and though Preeti would be very concerned about how his trousers were swimming about his waist and how his cheeks had lost their pink sheen, he felt more energized than he had ever been since he moved to Delhi. Riti was growing up fast, Sudheer and Mohan stayed close together, Preeti had taken control of the house, and the few days he would be at home, it finally felt like home. They would sit together for dinner in the evenings, in the afternoons he would join the boys in a game of cricket, and once in a while he and Preeti would go out to catch the latest Hindi release.

They were just another family.

He should have been happy. He wanted to believe that he

was and yet he knew he was not. Whether it be in a dark theatre watching Amitabh Bachchan dispatching the baddies or bowling underarm to Mohan during afternoon cricket games, he could only think of her. The music of her voice, the touch of her hair, the weight of her body on his chest, the arch of her back, scraps of conversations, the taste of the *dhokar dalna* during lunch – he wanted to forget it all, but he could not.

Where was she? How was she doing? Did she have enough money for herself and Arijit? Had she found someone else?

And would he ever see her again?

She was the blade. She was also the balm. And nothing, right or wrong, would ever change that.

One day, he was walking down a narrow grey street on a cold evening in November. He was near Jharia, one of the little coal dumps, which seemed to lie forever in the darkness, asthmatic with dust and despair. He had been travelling and meeting people through days and nights, catching an hour's sleep on a platform or leaning against the cold steel wall of a train, and he knew he just had to lie down or else he would collapse. Yet he could not for he had in his briefcase about twenty-five thousand in cash and valuables that he had to hand over to a government assessor within an hour. Clutching his shawl tightly around himself he stumbled forward through the dense fog.

Then it happened. Two men came out from nowhere, or was it three, because Arjun did not know, for they were just shadows and one heavy breath of country liquor. A strong hand snatched his briefcase away and as he reached out to grab it back, something heavy cracked into the base of his skull. His legs gave way and he fell back. From force of habit, he reached for his gun but he no longer carried it, and in any case it would have been useless now. Lying face up on the road, he saw the men half-walking and half-running away into the fog with the briefcase.

The searing pain radiating from the back of his head focused his thoughts for a moment. These were not RP's men, for if this had been a hit, he would be dead. They were local, someone had informed them he was carrying twenty-five thousand in his briefcase, and that could only be the government assessor. Nothing would come of going to the police, for they would merely squeeze him for more money and throw him in jail after that, for some of the money would have reached them too. He tried to get up and he realized his head was stuck to the gravel, glued to it by the blood and what he figured was his own splattered flesh. Now he felt thankful, for with the money gone, he could sleep here and bleed out, and he no longer cared what became of him. His eyes became heavy with fatigue, he breathed heavily, a strange sensation of languid peace creeping upward from his legs.

Maybe it was all over. Maybe this was the end.

He was never going to see them again. The broken mango-wood bat. The dressing table. The wall clock. That frightful crockery Preeti insisted on keeping in the display case.

Preeti, Sudheer, Mohan, Riti. They were never going to see him.

Pity he had no money to leave behind, just debts to last a lifetime and then several.

In that twilight between life and death, regret and despair, he could have sworn – though in the years to come he would never tell anyone for no one would believe him – that he had felt a presence. He knew who it was though he could not see her, for she was not really there. Nor was it her voice for it came from inside him, the voice from Mitra Cabin and Grand Hotel and every perfect moment he could ever remember, and it said, in tones that cut soothingly through the pain, 'Hold on, Arjun. Hold on.'

And he did.

'Now we have to let your father sleep,' said Preeti as she folded the clothes, freshly returned by the dhobi. She began putting them into the large steel almirah one by one, the large bunch of keys that lay tied to the end of her *anchal* making a slight jingling sound. 'We don't want him to fall sick again, now, do we?'

'It's fine, she can stay,' said Arjun, putting a protective arm around Riti, who sat next to him on the bed, her little legs tucked in behind her, mouth and lips smeared with chocolate, brown splotches on her knees and on the freshly washed bedsheet, though it was obvious from Preeti's relaxed smile that she had not seen the last part yet. Riti stuck out her tongue, coated brown as well, rebelliously at Preeti and said 'see', before throwing a scrap of golden wrapping paper at her mother.

Arjun's wounds had healed but even five months after the attack, he still had occasional episodes of blurred vision, which Dr Banerjee had put down to the effects of the head trauma. He had not stopped travelling even with his head bandaged up, and nothing serious had happened to him on the road. It was only after the bandage had been removed and he was at home that one day he had had a blackout and rolled down to the bottom of the stairs. Fortunately the damage had not been much, just a twisted ankle and a hairline fracture on his toe, but after that Preeti had kept a strict curfew on his movements outside the walls of their home.

It didn't matter though. He didn't need to travel any more. All arrows had been fired and his quiver was now truly empty. Today he would know for sure if they had hit their mark.

For today was the day they were going to announce the results of the elections.

The twentieth day of March 1977.

The Emergency was officially over. The country had gone to the ballot and the counting of votes had begun. Arjun was sure that people were tired of being in a dictatorship. Or were they? Maybe the country preferred trains running on time, black marketers and mafia men in jail, and the order that the fear of the state had brought. One could never be sure.

The voice on the radio droned on joylessly. Only a few constituencies had been reporting so far, and it would not be till hours later that the real leads would start coming in. Till that happened, there was only Riti and her wide-eyed wonder about the world to make Arjun believe that there was still something worth looking for in it.

'I hate the elections,' grumbled Preeti.

Arjun smiled. 'Yes. Because they cancelled the radio plays today.' Preeti was addicted to them, the trembling voices, the theatrics and the ominous music.

'No. I hate them because of what it has done to you.' She closed the almirah and joined Arjun and Riti on the bed. 'Promise me when this is over we will start a garage.'

Arjun didn't have the heart to tell her that all their savings were gone and, if he lost this battle against RP, it would be a thousand years before he would have the capital to start anything again. He didn't want to think of defeat, but think he did, every second, unless there was Riti or one of the boys keeping him busy.

Unlike Riti though, the boys only kept him occupied when they got into trouble. Sudheer was thirteen but looked eighteen, folds of fat below his chin, a rolling gait from his thighs brushing against each other, and a stomach that seemed to expand even more every time Arjun saw him. Puberty had hit him bad, leaving behind a thin trace of a moustache, and a raspy, complaining voice. He spent most of his days playing cricket and hanging out with a group of boys that Arjun knew were no good, but since he had been away from home for stretches there was little he could do about it.

Then there had been that incident sometime around

September the year before – Arjun was trying to find his gold Rolex. After months of searching and asking around, he had finally found a buyer for that watch. Not that people didn't want good foreign watches, it was just that, now with the Emergency, they didn't want anything that would attract attention. The income tax people had eyes and ears everywhere and it took only a jealous relative or a neighbour to write a letter and they would swoop down like hungry hawks. This buyer, though, was in a fix. His daughter's wedding was in a week and the groom had made yet another demand at the very last minute, and any Punjabi with knowledge of how the world worked knew what could happen if the in-laws of the groom felt slighted. He needed a second-hand Rolex in good enough condition that it could be passed off as new, and there was a shop in Connaught Place which would take care of the packaging and the polishing to make it look as if it had come fresh from Switzerland. Which meant Arjun could finally make this sale.

He had opened his steel almirah and the little vault inside to find that the Rolex was gone. His first instinct had been to suspect the servants but they had let all of them go, and he had definitely seen the Rolex the last time he had looked for it. Someone had stolen the watch within the last two weeks. Preeti flashed through his mind and then he felt guilty for it could not be her, but then that left only two suspects. Sudheer and Mohan.

Mohan was a quiet child. He went to school at the right time and came back on time, and his report card was satisfactory without being spectacular. Once home, he spent most of his time sketching or reading or solving the jigsaw puzzles he had from his childhood, again and again and once again, talking in monosyllables or slight nods of the head. Sudheer would drag Mohan along to neighbourhood cricket games with him from time to time, and, having played with the boys, Arjun knew that

Mohan was quite a good player. But cricket didn't interest him nor did any other sport. Arjun had tried once or twice to get him to open up and Arjun himself knew he had not tried hard enough, because he had too many things on his mind, more important than the moods of a difficult eleven-year-old.

In this case though, Mohan was not the problem. He would not steal. He had no reason to. Which only left one other person.

Arjun caught hold of Mohan when he knew that Sudheer would not be at home. That's something he had learned from the business – always question them separately. Mohan denied having taken the watch. Arjun had been expecting that to be the case. Then Arjun asked if he knew who had taken it. Mohan shuffled unsteadily on his feet, looked at one toe and then the other, but refused to answer. But by then Arjun knew for sure who it was.

Sudheer came home at seven, a bat balanced proudly on his shoulder. Preeti had gone to the temple for her evening *aarti,* and this Arjun knew was good, because that meant she would not come in the middle of what he had planned.

Arjun asked Sudheer to come up to his room. After he came up the stairs, with a quizzical expression on his face, the first thing Arjun did was lock the door.

'Did you take my watch?'

Sudheer first pretended not to have understood. Arjun repeated the question calmly. He shrugged his shoulders and said 'Your watch? I don't know what you are ...'

He never finished. Arjun's extended palm made contact with Sudheer's cheek, with a light thwack.

'Did you take my watch?'

Arjun thought he would feel bad for he had never hit any of his children before. But he did not.

Tears welled up immediately in Sudheer's eyes, but he still shook his head.

Arjun brought his hand back in the opposite direction, this time hitting the boy's cheek with his knuckles.

'Did you take my watch?' he asked again, his voice steel in its coolness.

The tears were flowing freely down Sudheer's cheeks. 'Yes, I did. I did.' He crossed his arms over his chest and he stood in a gesture of defiance. 'Yes, I took the watch and I sold it.'

Arjun dropped to his knees in front of Sudheer and asked, still as calm and collected as before, 'Why? Why did you sell it?'

'I won't tell,' he said, sniffling, the snot now flowing down in two tiny streams from his nostrils.

Arjun's hand shot out again and this time the slap was harder, the sound echoing through the house, the impact of the hit making Sudheer's knees buckle for a second.

'Why did you sell it? Who did you sell it to? Sudheer, we can make this easy for both of us if you just start talking.' Arjun had said this to many people over the course of the years, in dark sweaty rooms, but he never thought he would have to say it to his son.

'Why does it matter to you?' Sudheer tried to wipe away the snot and the tears with his forearm. 'You would have sold it anyway. That's what you do. Sell our stuff. Sell our car. Sell our house. That's all you do.'

Arjun let Sudheer continue, as he always did those who had started singing.

'You let the servants go and the driver go. You took us out of boarding and put us in a school where beggars and drivers send their children. I took the watch and played cards with it.'

Arjun put his hand encouragingly on Sudheer's shoulder. 'Cards? You mean *matka*?'

He nodded. 'I usually win. But that day... my luck was bad.'

'Who else was with you?'

'Praveen, Babul and Pappu.' Arjun made a mental note of the

names. He asked Sudheer more questions – where he had gone, how many times he frequented *matka* dens and who would take him there. Sudheer poured the answers out, reassured by his father's soothingly calm voice. Once Arjun knew he had got all he could get out of Sudheer, he stood up and let the truth sink in.

His son had given away a watch worth a fortune for a game of roadside *matka*. He thought of it for a second, and then for a second more, and then he looked into Sudheer's eyes. There was fear in his son's eyes, definitely, but that was the fear of a slap. There was no fear of his father, no respect, no feeling of awe, no shame, not even a glint of recognition of what he had done. Just more of feeling sorry and more of complaining.

Something snapped inside Arjun.

Preeti had just opened the main gate when she heard the sounds from downstairs. Dropping the *aarti* plate with a loud clang, she ran up the stairs, shouting Sudheer's name. The door was locked. She banged against the door again and again, crying out for Arjun and then for Sudheer, and when Arjun finally opened the door, she rushed to the corner where Sudheer had crawled to, shaking in terror, and took his head in her arms.

'What have you done to him?' she screamed at Arjun, running her hands over Sudheer's cheeks, red and burning from the stings of the slaps that had rained on him. 'How could you? He is just a baby.'

'How could I?' Arjun asked, standing with his hands on his waist. 'Indeed. How could I? Your *laadla* is a thief, smart enough to get at your keys,' he said, pointing to the keys tied around a knot at the end of her *anchal*, 'to open the almirah and sell my Rolex. Your baby. Yes. Indeed. *Jab main khoon paseena ek kar raha hoon*, trying to find every paisa I can from anywhere, your little *laadla* has just blown away lakhs of *my money* because he wanted to show his no-good friends what a hero he was in playing *matka*.'

'So what? So he made a little mistake! He is your son.'

'A little mistake? Is this a little mistake? Your son is growing up to be a thief and a gambler and soon the cops will be doing much worse to him. *Likhke deta hoon main* ...' Arjun pointed his finger aggressively at Sudheer. 'If I ever catch you with those boys again, and I mean ever, I will flay the skin off your bones. If you steal from me, I will call the police on you. Believe me.' He had stormed out of the room downstairs, and as he had walked by, he saw Mohan looking at him, silently, and he turned to him and said, 'Let that be a lesson to you too. I let you go this time but the next time I see you lying or covering up for your brother, things won't go as well for you.' Riti had fortunately slept through all this, for she was sick, and for that Arjun was thankful.

Sudheer had howled for hours, not because he was hurt – for Arjun had been careful to keep the slaps to his fleshy parts, of which he had a lot – but because he was scared out of his wits. At night, Preeti had argued with Arjun, something which she rarely did, and Arjun had tried to impress on her the need for discipline. Though she never did say it directly, Arjun knew what she was trying to say in different ways: 'But you are a thief and a crook too!' He had stayed awake that night, wondering if Sudheer had deserved the beating he got or had it been because Arjun was angry that his son did not respect him. He had himself not respected his father because he had always been weak and powerless, and that was exactly what his sons thought of him too.

Less of a man. Less of a father.

And if today on result day the cards fell against him, he would be on the streets. And so would they.

Preeti's pressure on his arm brought him back to the present. 'We will go back to the garage, right? Promise me. Please.'

Arjun rose from the bed, shaking off Preeti's grip. Going back was not something he wanted to even think about. Pulling on his brown, road-worn slippers, he said, 'I am going to CP. It will be quicker than this blasted radio.' They had constructed giant election-result boards at Connaught Place and Arjun wanted to be there when the results started going up. When and if defeat came, he did not want to be around his wife and children.

'What do you mean?' Preeti said with concern. 'You can barely walk. What if you fall out there in the middle of so many people? They will walk right over you.'

Arjun reached for the shirt and trousers that lay carelessly thrown on the back of the wooden chair, 'Don't worry, I won't fall.'

'If you fall today, you won't be able to get up.' Preeti refused to let go of his wrist.

'I know. I know that very well.'

'We always have the garage.'

But Arjun did not hear her; he was walking quickly down the stairs.

Preeti waited. And waited. Riti went to sleep. Then so did the boys. She sat at the dining table with Arjun's food, warmed it twice and then put it away. The clock struck twelve. She looked at the telephone on the glass table. But then who could she call at this hour? What would she tell them? At one, she went out, stood at the gate for what seemed to be an eternity but it could not have been more than half an hour and then walked a few minutes out to the main street and stood beneath the streetlight, looking down the empty road, praying. Finally, drained out, she went home and dropped off to sleep on the couch.

When she woke it was to a gentle shaking of her shoulder. Arjun was standing there, his face close to hers. She looked into his eyes for he was so close, and the exhaustion and fear and the anger and the pain she had seen there all these years was gone.

He said, his voice low with excitement, 'I was right. I was right all along.'

'W... what happened? Where were you? I was so worried.' All these years he had been out, she had never felt she had lost him as much as she had these last few hours.

'It doesn't matter where I was. What matters is that I am back. And I am never going away again.'

'Who won?' Preeti asked, remembering where he had gone and why.

'I did.'

10

1978

ARJUN PICKED HIS BATTLES VERY CAREFULLY AND THIS ONE he was definitely going to sit out. Preeti wanted the new office at Jor Bagh to be straight out of the pages of one of the lifestyle magazines she was so fond of reading and after what the family had gone through over the last few years, he did not have the heart to say no. He would have liked to have stately old wooden furniture and ornate couches like the ones they had had in his father's office in Lahore but when the professional designer had pointed to various glossy things printed in glossy brochures and used words like 'decor' and 'ambience' with exaggerated flourishes of the hand, he had nodded his head. He kept nodding when Preeti had asked if he approved of the design and nodded some more when paying the bills. He was not happy with the number of zeroes on the invoices or the diffused blue lights or the strange-shaped tables or the uncomfortably square chairs or even the designer, who was a woman but dressed like a man or was it the other way round, and, most of all, by the fact that two months after they had moved into his new office they were still working on it, installing a new glass wall one day and fixtures from Italy the next. All of these distractions were getting in the way of his work. There was, after all, a lot of work. Business was great, Bhatia Consultants was signing more clients than he could handle, government tenders were being written and granted in the rooms around, forty people were already working for him – clerks and lawyers and managers – and it seemed like he had outgrown his office even before the workmen had stopped drilling.

But today he was not thinking of the furniture or the representative of the biggest French arms supplier whom he had met last night or the profusion of money plants that made him feel as if he was sitting in a jungle. He was thinking of RP. For there he was, right in front of him, leaning forward, almost as if he were about to jump across the table and strangle him.

'Shall we talk straight, man to man?' RP asked. 'Or shall we dance around trees?'

'Let's talk,' said Arjun, getting the image of Randhir Kapoor from *Jawani Diwani* out of his mind. 'No dancing for me. My knees aren't what they used to be.'

It was the first time they were in the same room since that first meeting. RP still had that menacing stare and that haughty, superior way of talking and that suit that made him look more impressive than he was, but everything else had changed.

It had started changing the day the election results had been declared. Every politician, big or small, whom Arjun had bankrolled over the last year, each and every one of them, had won in their respective parties and states. The victors had started pouring into Delhi by the afternoon, wearing little white topis and dhotis, quickly starched for the big occasion, with their handlers, and brothers-in-law, to stake their claims and say salaam to the man behind them. The elections had churned the earth and turned up into the light a new breed with new dreams and insatiable greed. New connections had to be made, new alliances to be forged, new territories had to be divvied up and there was only one man in Delhi they knew who could broker it all – the new spider at the centre of the web.

Arjun Bhatia.

With his men installed firmly in Delhi, Arjun had launched his attack. He had waited for RP to import machinery from Germany, and then just before RP was going to begin production, he got the ministry to increase the import duty on every key raw material that the process at the plant needed, some becoming more expensive by as much as five times. RP not only lost everything he had invested in the plant but his partners had, within days, discreetly sent out feelers to Arjun for protection.

That had just been the start.

RP's family had controlled the liquor business in and around Delhi for decades. So Arjun got his ministers to pass a prohibition law. He then made some calls and within hours, all RP's registered shops had been shuttered and padlocked. On cue, bootleg liquor started flowing in from Haryana and Uttar Pradesh, where Arjun and his politicians had bought out all the suppliers.

All over the country, the assault had continued on RP. Coal inspectors suddenly woke up to the fact that RP's clients were under-reporting the production of coal to the government. Investigations immediately followed and the results were almost as if Arjun had written them himself. Environmental clearances for the hotels RP had stakes in were withdrawn. Adulteration was discovered in the petrol that was pumped out from his petrol pumps. The railway contractors who owed allegiance to RP lost their contracts. RP's textile mills were found to be using machinery that had been imported illegally, his bottling plants were locked down after they were found to be dumping dangerous chemicals into the water, and all his real estate projects in Delhi and Bombay and Madras ran into serious roadblocks. RP had tried to fight back, but Arjun had burned every escape route that he could have taken and finally, when Arjun had managed to cancel RP's membership to the Delhi cricket club, RP had swallowed his pride to seek an audience with Arjun.

Of course he had summoned Arjun, because RP never went below his station in life, but Arjun had made it very clear that if he wanted to talk, it had to be at his place and at his convenience. He had come with two bodyguards, which amused Arjun for that showed RP was shaken, so shaken that he feared that Arjun would kill him. Arjun knew he could not, for RP, even down and out and with blood flowing out everywhere, was still a force. But RP himself was not confident of where he was, which meant the war was almost won.

Now Arjun had to get through this meeting.

'I know you must have spent a lot already, Bhatia, and only God knows how you got that amount of money, but you and I both know it's a battle you can't finish. Not with me.'

Arjun simply smiled.

'Fortune is a fickle whore,' RP said slowly in his impeccable accent. 'Right now she is in your bed and I know you are feeling all warm and cocky but she will come back to me. You can be sure of that. And when she does, I am going to get to work on you.' He paused, adjusted his Nehru jacket, and continued, 'You are a sly little fox and I didn't take you seriously. That was my mistake but I won't make that mistake again.'

Arjun leaned back casually into his chair, ignoring how uncomfortable it felt against his lower back. 'But you are making a mistake again. Here you are sitting in my office, your bodyguards are standing outside on the footpath surrounded by my men and you are threatening me here with ... with what? With the future? *Yeh madarchod-behenchod ka sheher hai, angrezi gaali se kisko darwayenge?*

'What do you want?' asked RP. 'What do you really want?'

'Aah, now we are talking business. You are right. I do want something.'

'Revenge?'

'Oh no. Not revenge. If I wanted revenge, I would have made you sit for an hour waiting for me, then if you had not stood up when I came in, I would have made you sit on the ground, or perhaps made you hold your ears and stand on one leg. No, I don't want revenge. Because it's bad business.'

'Then what?'

'I want your friendship.'

Right then Marie, his secretary, entered with two cups of coffee on a silver tray, and cast a nervous glance at RP and then at her boss. The tension was plain on her face. She knew who he was.

'So this is your way of making friendship? By trying to run me out of my businesses?'

'What can I do? Sly fox *jo hoon*.'

Marie had kept the tray on the table and RP bent forward, letting the steam flow over his face. 'Aah, good Columbian. I kind of figured you to be the instant coffee type.'

'I am,' said Arjun agreeably. 'This is something I had been saving specially for you. I know you like this particular blend.' RP glanced sideways at Marie, but did not reach for any of the cups.

Arjun realized that RP was worried there would be poison in his coffee. He was more scared than Arjun had originally thought.

'So yes, friendship. Why do you think, after all that you have done, that I would consider being friends with you?'

Arjun gave Marie a slight sideways glance. She got the message and left quickly. 'Because that is your only way out right now.'

RP drawled slowly, 'As I said, you are taking your good fortune a bit too seriously.'

'And you are taking your smarts a bit too seriously. I know

everything about you, where you keep your money, which apartments are bought in the name of your dog, and which in the name of your Belgian girlfriend and which in the name of your wife's brother, and yes, I know even the brand of coffee you like. Right now, you may feel you still have something to fall back on, but I have you surrounded.'

'If you could have finished me off, you would have done so already. No one gives an enemy a breath of air is what my father used to say.' RP kept looking intently at the wisps of smoke snaking up from the coffee. 'I call your bluff.'

'Well, then, you can walk out.' Arjun took a sip of the coffee. It was too bitter and strong for his liking. He wanted to spit it out but held it in. 'Trust me, a part of me wants you to walk out because, I swear to God, I am in the mood for blood. You stole from me, and you treated me like a *bhikhari* and I don't want to stop until you are begging on the streets yourself. But this would be, as you once told me yourself, bad business. Fighting is always bad business. And I would not underestimate you. You still have power in this city and a big name. I don't feel it's worth my time to destroy all that, that is, unless you force me to. It would be better if we join hands, become partners and not allow a third person to come and take away everything, like the British did two hundred years ago. I remember you once saying that the city is big enough for both of us, and why not keep it that way?'

RP did not move but clutched the handle of his chair tightly. Whether it was anger or the hardness of the seat, Arjun could not determine.

Arjun continued, 'Consider all that has happened as my way of getting your attention. You see, years ago, you thought I was a pushover, a second-rate heartland *gunda* with guns and a bad dressing sense, and I have hopefully proven to you that I am not.'

RP nodded. 'No, you are not. You are good. Damn good.'

'Thank you, coming from you that means a lot.'

'It was Dubey, wasn't it?' asked RP, finally reaching for the handle of the cup. 'He sold out to you, didn't he?'

He had. It had not taken much for Arjun to turn him. While Ismail had been a big help, RP's destruction would not have happened without Dubey's knowledge of his master's dirty little secrets.

'You should have paid him a bit more. He was always complaining of how stingy you were.'

RP gave a shrug of defeat. 'Or perhaps not let him know so much. But then, what's past is past.'

'Indeed. The past is better forgotten.'

'Give me Dubey.'

'What makes you think I have him?'

'Because now that I think of it, I haven't seen that rat for a while. So he must be hiding somewhere. Give me that swine, I will make him answer for what's happened, and you and I can move along as friends.'

Arjun sat quietly, the coffee circling his mouth. It didn't seem as strong now – as a matter of fact, it had a rather pleasant, blunt aftertaste.

RP understood the silence. 'Aaah, I get it. Dubey came to know a bit too much about you too. So you have already taken care of him. Fine.'

He was right. Dubey was the kind of man you didn't trust. But that was not the only reason he was dead. Dubey had made it personal. He had made Arjun dig and then had spat at him while he was doing so. Now he was in a ditch in his own little hole. Somewhere.

'So let's make a more pleasant offer,' RP said, leaning back and pointing to the door. 'Send your secretary for a night to my farmhouse, you know that cute girl with the nice...' – and RP curved his palm to indicate her behind – 'who came in just now.'

Arjun took another long sip while RP went on smiling. 'That's the way my father used to do business. Seal the deal with a laddoo, if you know what I mean.'

'You talk about your father a lot.'

'That I do. Daddy was a great man.'

Arjun kept his cup down sharply on the table and stood up. 'I am sure he must have been. But right now, *main tera baap hoon*.'

RP sat stunned by Arjun's sharp change of tone. No one talked to Ranvijay Pratap like that, no one had had the balls to.

Till today.

He started to say something but Arjun lifted his finger and he stopped, his mouth still open.

'Go home. Take a shower. Think about what I said. If you want to continue to go on about how great a man your daddy was because he used to treat people like the soles of his shoes ... well ... that's your choice. If you want to show me disrespect, by showing my people disrespect, like you just did, that's your choice too. But know what will happen if you do.'

RP was breathing hard, gasping for words.

'There is only one law in this town from now on. Be my friend and I will shake your hand. Be my enemy and I will twist it clean off. *Aur jab haath nahin rahega na, RP sahib, na kha sakoge, na dho sakoge, na hila sakoge*. Now, if you'll excuse me, I have important people to attend to. The door is straight down the hall, and then take a turn to the right.'

The following Tuesday, a card was delivered to Arjun's office, with an original painting by one of India's rising artists along with a hamper of expensive sweets and dry fruits.

It was an invitation to RP's sister's wedding.

For Arjun Bhatia and family.

Part Three

11

1993

Arjun Bhatia hated turbans, and he hated them even more when they came in shocking pink. Right now, he was putting as much time as he could between him and the turban. Not that he could push it off forever. Preeti would send him further summons, and then he would have to walk from the rear wing of his house through the long passage, over to the front and then again to the main lawn, smile, do namastes, shake hands, be polite and hospitable, while his hair, or whatever was left of it, would mat wet with sweat underneath that heavy pink turban. At least that Punjabi DJ from London, with the Jamaican extensions in his hair, would not be blasting away the peace of his lawns as he had yesterday and the day before.

Thank goodness for small mercies.

'It's bass, papa, not thump-thump-thump and you feel the rhythm here, in your heart,' Riti had said in that American accent of hers which made Arjun so proud. She had been in 'the foreign' for ten years now and people said, hearing her talk, that she did not sound like an Indian.

'There is no melody, no peace in this, not like Rafi ... and even Kishore. It's too loud and it's too crude.' He had little patience for what passed for music today. He had heard that new song on television, the one that everyone was talking about that asked 'Choli ke peeche kya hai?' and while Arjun considered himself permissive for his age, his ears had turned red at the innuendo and he had thumbed the remote with violence.

Crude. Yes. He liked that word. Much of today's world could be described by that. And loud.

It definitely described the two men in front of him right now. Father and son. Crude and loud.

The father. Manoj Karnik. He had started out as a small-time union leader, picketing locked gates, pumping fists and waving banners. Arjun had seen his potential back in '76, when they had first met and talked, over paneer parathas and tea, and then his rise up the ladder had traced the phenomenal arc of Arjun's own ascension. The reed-thin man with a broken chin, a mild stutter and a dirty-grey white shirt, was now, more than fifteen years later, obscenely obese, a cabinet minister, a real estate baron, sugar mill king, and the proud owner of bank accounts from Switzerland to Cayman Islands. Legs splayed at an angle on the couch, in inappropriately tight trousers he seemed to have outgrown in the past hour, generously flashing his gutkha-stained teeth in a parody of a smile, Manoj Karnik brought to Arjun's mind the image of a huge toad, waiting to flick out its wet tongue at any opportunity flying about.

The son. Rishi Karnik. Slick hair pushed back, a cloud of Clive Christian perfume, gym muscles straining against a tight shirt, three buttons undone to display a large gold cross nestling in the foliage of chest hair, he had tried to break into Bollywood as an action star, but after three flops, had gone into the safer business of being a cricket bookie, running a network that ran through Pakistan and Dubai. He was part of Sudheer and Mohan's group and the only reason he was here, rather than outside on the lawns with the rest of the gang, was because what they were discussing concerned his future.

It was not particularly polite to be holed up in a room on the day of your son's engagement ceremony, pink turban or not, when guests had already arrived. Arjun knew that, and in a previous life, he would have been at the gate, greeting the new arrivals and shaking hands. But if he had learned one lesson it was that humility was a weakness in the city, and the bigger the asshole the more people knelt to kiss it. He had earned his reputation well over the years and it behove well for him to come outside at the very last minute, and acknowledge the most important with a word and the less important with a glance. Not that he minded doing business, but the Manoj Karnik problem seemed neverending, with the man refusing to see reason, getting on his nerves. And so this session was needed, father, son and himself, all in the same room.

Vantor, the American energy company, was setting up one of its mega power plants in Karnik's state. One of its conditions of investment was a financial guarantee from the state government. If Vantor made a profit, it would take the cash. All of it. But if they lost money, the state government would have to reimburse the loss with its own tax-earned revenue. The whole arrangement sounded unfair to Arjun. But then the more unfair a deal, Arjun had understood over the years, the better chance it had of going through. Vantor had approached Arjun to oil the deal through the pipes of the government, which had required, among other things, passing a bill that allowed foreign investment in power. Once that had been done, Arjun had introduced Vantor to Karnik. His party ruled the state with an absolute majority and it seemed like there would have been little problem getting the required green light.

Except there had been. The chief minister, Raman Kulkarni, once a Karnik loyalist, had gone rogue. Not without reason though. Kulkarni was on the payroll of the biggest industrialist family of the country, the Mehtas. They had their own plans for setting up a mega power plant and the last thing they wanted was Vantor in their backyard. As if being allied with the enemy was not bad enough, there was bad blood between Raman Kulkarni's son and Rishi Karnik. Raman Kulkarni's son was a major Bollywood financier. His movies were doing considerably better than Rishi Karnik's ever had, and to make matters worse, Rishi's actress-girlfriend had slept with Raman Kulkarni's son for a role in his upcoming movie and that had made it all very personal.

Arjun had a solution to all this, one that he was absolutely sure would work. Raman Kulkarni no longer wanted to be the chief minister, Delhi was where his eyes were. So Arjun would make him a central minister through the nominated Rajya Sabha route. A Karnik rubber-stamp loyalist would be made the chief minister, who would then sign on the Vantor dotted line. The kickback that was being paid by Vantor to Karnik would be split 70–30 with Raman Kulkarni. The Mehtas, who happened to be Arjun's clients, would be provided preferential shares in the Indian subsidiary that Vantor would set up and Sudheer, Arjun's eldest, would sit on the board of directors. That way everyone would be happy.

The only problem was that the Karniks refused to negotiate with the Kulkarnis.

'I understand what you are saying, Arjun ji, but what to do? Respect is everything. And Kulkarni disrespected me.' Manoj Karnik rubbed the side of his cheek contemplatively. 'After what he did, go behind our backs to the Mehtas, I thought he would at least have the decency to come crawling to us begging for forgiveness. I mean what was he before I gave him his throne? Just a ...' Manoj Karnik was going to use an expletive, but then looked at Arjun, who was frowning in anticipation, and thought better of it.

Rishi piped in, 'Uncle, I have talked about this to Sudheer and Mohan. We have a plan. I have some friends in Dubai. They specialize in giving special treatment to movie producers that don't play nice. They can make some calls, and we can get a shooter over from Uttar Pradesh, and maybe that son-of-a-bitch Raman would see reason then. We won't kill his son, just break a few bones. It would serve him right.'

Arjun sank back into his seat, shook his head disapprovingly, and lowered his voice when he spoke. Those who had known him for years, like Manoj Karnik, knew exactly what that lowered tone meant.

'Beta, you are my son's friend, so allow me the privilege of dispensing some advice. First of all, I don't know what happened between Kulkarni' s son and your girlfriend, nor am I particularly interested. All I can say is that your girlfriend has every right to be with whom she pleases and for whatever reason she wants and if you take that as an insult to your manhood, to the extent that you would consider calling in a shooter, and in the process putting at risk a deal worth crores, then you are, forgive my words, a fool.'

'But uncle, I did not say murder. I said...'

'It's bad manners to interrupt when elders are speaking.' Arjun smiled a most unfriendly smile. 'Second, my sons – and forgive me for I have indulged them a bit more than I should have, and you can thank your aunt for that – are not really the people you should be taking advice from. Maybe advice on movies, perfumes, sports cars, fashion... but not these things. Not yet, anyway.' He then turned his eyes towards the father. 'It's only out of respect for our relationship that I am sitting here, getting late for Sudheer's engagement ceremony and earning the anger of my wife, trying to convince you of what I think is good for everyone. If you believe you want to handle it your own way, then go ahead. But I will warn you what's going to happen if shots are fired. The Mehtas will come after you with everything they have, and both of us know what they have.'

'I will expect you to manage the Mehtas,' said Manoj Karnik. 'You do their business for them, they listen to what you say. And I have no problem reaching a deal with the Mehtas. They are good people. Just not Kulkarni.'

'But why should I manage the Mehtas? If people do not respect my advice, why should I help them out? Respect is everything, were you not saying that a while ago?'

Arjun stood up, brushing the side of his waist. 'It is said that friendships, like apples and medicine, have expiry dates. I don't like to believe that, but lately I seem to be getting too old to understand the world. But please forget all this unpleasantness on such a nice day. I hope you will be staying for dinner and to bless the happy couple.'

Manoj Karnik controlled over thirty MPs in the Lok Sabha and a state and crores of rupees and acres of land. But even after all this, he knew that once Arjun withdrew his friendship, it would be days before he would be done wiping his own blood off from the floor. He looked at his son. Rishi was staring at the marble floor, not making eye contact. Because both of them, the father and the son, knew the rule of the town, they had seen it enforced all these years.

Be my friend and I will shake your hand. Be my enemy and I will twist it clean off.

The conversation wrapped up in five minutes. Things would be as Arjun wanted.

Except, of course, the pink turban.

'A little to the side, please, yes sir, yes, turned to the side like this.'

The pink turban was proving to be a bigger steam bowl than he had thought it to be. There were the photographers and the men with the video cameras, shining their big hot lights on him and then there were the yards of cable snaking around, and they had already tripped a cabinet minister as he had come to pose with Arjun. Everyone wanted to have a picture taken with him, judges to generals to cabinet secretaries to ministers, for proximity with Arjun Bhatia, even if it was 'in the same photo frame', was cold, hard currency in the corridors of Delhi. Which meant Arjun Bhatia was posing almost every minute. Sometimes strangers would put their arms around him a bit too familiarly, drawing him close by the shoulder, and there had been times, in other parties, when he had asked the cameraman to not take a picture. But today was his son's engagement ceremony, today these were all his guests, and today he could not say no. So there he was, flashing smiles into the camera, the warmth of the smile in direct proportion to how comfortable he was with having his photograph taken with the man next to him.

But this frame was going to be special.

For he had his two sons on either side.

Mohan on his left. Sudheer on his right.

'Where is Riti?' Arjun asked Sudheer. 'I haven't seen her all evening.'

Sudheer brushed away some crumbs of food from his royal-blue sherwani. 'I haven't seen her either. Have you seen her, Mohan?'

Mohan shook his head.

'To the front, yes... say cheese.'

Arjun placed his arms around the shoulders of his two boys and looked ahead, straight into the camera.

It was a beautiful October evening. The day had been hot for this time of the year, but now there was a cool breeze blowing across the lawns, caressing away the dry heat with the fragrance of flowers. There were close to five hundred people on the guest list, and yet they seemed to be dwarfed by the sheer expanse of the impeccably manicured lawns, criss-crossed by gravel paths where not even a little pebble was out of place, and a swimming pool, illuminated bluish-green from inside, that had been been installed a few months ago by a design firm from France, so grand that it had led to the Bhatia residence making it to the cover of *Good Living* magazine, published from New York. The guests were milling around in small clumps in front of the enormous stage that had been constructed for the couple. There had been dancing on the stage yesterday and the day before, a concert by two of Bollywood's biggest playback singers on Tuesday and, right after the engagement ceremony today, there was going to be a qawwali concert by Fatah Ali Shah and his troupe, especially flown in from Lahore for the evening.

Arjun craned his neck to see if he could find Riti in the crowd. He had wanted her to be in this picture. But the flash of the cameras was blinding. He knew he could not afford to look distracted, not here, not now, for his every action, every smile, every snub, every frown ended up being dissected in the gossip circles of Lutyens, and Arjun knew that only too well.

He wrapped his hands around his eldest's head and gave him a kiss on his forehead.

A smattering of applause and more flashes of cameras followed. On cue, Sudheer bent down, which for him took some effort, bouncing against the tyres of fat that ringed his waist, and got about knee length before Arjun terminated the attempt at a pranam, and gave him an embrace, a pat on the back and smoothened his hair. Sudheer then turned to the right to bend down again for his mother and Preeti's spontaneous show of emotion, Arjun knew, was genuine. Unlike his. But he joined in the applause as was expected of him.

'I don't know why you don't like your sons, I mean they are your sons ...' he remembered Preeti having said so many times.

'That's not true. I love my sons more than my life,' he would say, knowing that was perhaps not the whole truth. 'It's because I love them that I want the best. I just don't think Sudheer and Mohan are doing the best they can for themselves, that's all.'

'Not doing the best they can?' Preeti would ask. 'Sudheer runs companies, has his own foreign car dealership, he owns so many foreign cars. His friends are all important people. How many twenty-five-year-olds do you know who have achieved this much? And what about Mohan? He is two years younger, and even he has his own companies. He also has his foreign car, the import-export garment business is doing very well, you told me that yourself. Boys their age are standing in line at government offices to get jobs paying five thousand a month and look at our sons. Yet you ...'

Arjun could not tell Preeti that the companies his sons ran were fronts for money laundering, the directorships in companies they had were because that was the payment for Arjun's services. Nor did he want to remind their mother that each of their 'foreign' cars were paid for by him and that Mohan's export-import business, which Preeti was the most proud of because their son would be seen in the Milan fashion show, was how some Italian clients, whose investments he looked after in India, channelled their payments through to Arjun.

So all he said was, 'First of all, Sudheer is not twenty-five, he is going to be thirty in a year. And the thing is that they don't take responsibility. That's the problem. They behave like teenagers, partying and racing their cars and God knows what else.'

'And you know what your problem is? You don't appreciate what God has given us. Look at Mrs Lakhotia's sons, and yes, those Kanal twins, they are at each other's throats. And look at our sons. They call them Ram and Laxman for a good reason. Or will you deny that too?'

'Yes, they love each other and that's all very good but ...' Arjun accepted that the brothers loved each other, though comparing Sudheer to Ram and Mohan to Laxman seemed blasphemous. However, they did get along much better than other brothers with a lot of money and power between them, despite the fact that they were so different from each other.

Two hundred and fifty pounds of lard and body hair with a fondness for tandoori chicken and Jack on the Rocks, Sudheer had a loud voice and an even louder laugh. The nickname 'Big Bear' was well earned and not just for his size. When in the grip of rage, he would make a grizzly baulk. Once, a bartender had refused to serve him any more whisky because he was falling off his chair and in a rage, Sudheer had proceeded to trash the whole bar, smashing all the glassware, leaving the bartender and anyone foolish enough to get in his way, spitting teeth and wiping away blood. Another time, at a traffic signal, a beggar had asked him for money and he had been too busy eating to notice, only for the beggar to scratch the side of his Mercedes with a bottle cap. Sudheer had gotten out of the car and had then, in broad daylight, pounded the beggar into submission. When other beggars had rushed to help, he had brought out his gun and waved it around, and all this when he was not even drunk. He was free with his money, and that was why he had such a crowd of hangers-on. The Big Bear farts cash was what they said in Delhi and people got rich just by walking behind him and cleaning the seat before he sat on it. Known as a soft touch, anyone with a hard-luck story had a good chance of leaving with a lot if they managed to make the Big Bear sentimental, particularly after he had downed a few.

Mohan was the exact opposite. Thin, and handsome in a slightly chocolate boy way, he barely spoke and when he did, you could barely hear what he said. If Sudheer was bright colours, with clothes that were flashy and tight, and nearly always sweaty and smelly, Mohan was Bond himself, never a hair out of place or an untidy fold. He hardly ever laughed, and the best one could get out of him was a sideways grin, here one moment and gone the next. Mohan trailed Sudheer like a shadow, always in his party on their nights about town, but he never drank. They called him 'Milk Moustache' for that, and also for his well-known fondness for women with ample breasts. He was obsessed with them, and by porn in general, of which he had an apartment-full. His Panchsheel flat was stuffed with VHS tapes and toys and contraptions from Japan to Germany, that required infinite imagination and flexibility. Besides that, he had many other lonely passions, jigsaw puzzles, dominoes, stamps, coins and the newest Japanese swords. Unlike Sudheer, he had no propensity for charity nor did he have any real friends, and the only emotion he ever showed was absolute devotion to his brother.

Preeti would continue, 'They enjoy themselves and why does that bother you? They are young, they can afford it, and if they don't enjoy themselves now when they are young, when will they?'

'The problem is that they only enjoy. Sudheer's mind is busy thinking about what he's going to eat next. Mohan, God knows what.'

This was when Preeti would start to get angry. 'But you don't give them any responsibilities. You don't let them handle the business. You put more faith in outsiders than in your own blood.'

Arjun knew these were Sudheer's words. He complained to his mother. Often and loud.

'They are afraid of you. Both of them. They are afraid because they respect you and you don't seem to even acknowledge that ... how good they are as sons.'

Arjun had a different explanation for their respect. They knew where the money came from and they knew the Golden Rule: 'He who has the money makes the rules.' Of course, Arjun was careful not to say that to their mother. Instead he would say weakly, 'Their time will come. I mean everything I have will be theirs', hoping that Preeti would change the topic.

She didn't usually.

'You don't like them because they didn't have a rough life like you had.'

'No, it's not...'

But then she would not be stopped.

'No that *is* the reason. You believe everyone needs to have a hard life. You would have been happy if they had been doctors or engineers or I don't know what else... but you want them to suffer, to travel by DTC bus, to get pushed around...'

'People learn through hard times. Not if everything is given to them on a plate. And I don't know what gave you the idea that professionally qualified men, doctors and engineers suffer.'

Preeti had developed quite a little temper as she had grown old. That and a prominent limp, which she had refused to get treated with a knee replacement. She would say, loudly now, 'My sons are born to be kings. Sure, they are not perfect, but when you have diamond rings, who cares if they are a bit bent here or there.'

This was when Arjun would throw his hands up and walk away. But Preeti needed to get the last cut in.

'What about Riti? What about all the money this family has put into her? In Switzerland and then the US and for how many years, ten or is it twelve, and it's not cheap. Private school and then college. All in dollars. What has she done with all that? Does she do anything? And yet you can see nothing wrong in her.'

She was right. Riti was different. Riti resembled Arjun's mother, the same aquiline, almost fragile beauty, with gently forgiving eyes. She had spent most of her adult life in Europe and the US, first at a private school in Lausanne, then in Massachusetts, then at a woman's Catholic college near San Francisco and was now majoring in theatre and film studies from NYU.

'Riti is getting a degree. An American degree,' Arjun would say sternly. 'It requires brains. If your sons had wanted to go to the US to study, I would have had no problems in paying for that. But they want to go to Vegas and Monte Carlo and Paris and Milan with their friends. And it's not that I haven't paid for that too.'

'But why bother? Why bother with all this fancy education and all when Riti is going to get married and go to someone else's house? Why spend all this money on top of how much we will spend on her wedding?'

Arjun always ended the conversation here. He refused to argue over Riti.

It was Preeti who had fixed the match for Sudheer. Nimmi Ahuja, the only daughter of British steel magnate Praveen Ahuja. Arjun had found Nimmi Ahuja a decent enough girl, and Preeti could not stop talking about Nimmi's milk-white skin and the old-world Indian values the Ahujas had instilled in her despite her foreign upbringing. Sudheer had agreed to the marriage because it allowed him to do what he had been wanting to for a long time – move out of his father's mansion to the new place that Arjun was building in Fatehpur Beri, and even more importantly, take a seat among his father's inner circle of advisers. Arjun had agreed, albeit reluctantly, to his son's involvement in his business. But then, like the story of the camel that starts off with the nose and ends up ejecting the bedouin from the tent, Sudheer had insisted on Mohan being allowed 'in' too. Arjun had resisted but had finally given in to that too. At least one brother spoke for the other and there was much to be said for that. As they stood, the two brothers and Arjun, on the stage with the cameras clicking away, the tension of that reluctance still hung around them like a cloud.

Arjun was brought back to the present by a gentle hand on his back. It was the father of the would-be bride, Praveen Ahuja, and in his hand was a mic that he was extending towards Arjun.

'Everyone wants a speech ... come on ... something.'

Arjun was not prepared to give a speech. He looked to the left. There was Preeti beaming conspiratorially along with Nimmi. Then Sudheer said, 'Come on, papa, please, don't say no today,' and suddenly, for a fleeting second, he felt a tenderness for his son.

Arjun took the mic, patted it with his index finger to see if it was live, and then began.

'I am not too good with words and I also know that, standing between my son and his engagement ceremony, how eager he must be for me to finish.' He paused to let the polite laughter subside. 'So I will be very brief. When I came to this country with nothing, if someone had told me I would be here in my own home, with my family and friends, celebrating the engagement of my son this way, I would have perhaps uttered an obscenity and told that person to shove off.' There was more laughter. 'I am where I am today only by the grace of God. I have had the best of friends and the best of family and here, tonight, as Sudheer and Nimmi embark on a journey together, I ask God to watch over them as he has watched over me, to bless them with the same kind of family and friends as he has blessed me with.'

Arjun's voice choked a little, just for a moment. He was thinking of other people, his best friends, the ones he would never see again, and wondered whether his love had been a blessing or a curse. Then he resumed.

'Nimmi, look after my son. He eats too much, and watches way too many films.' More laughter and even Sudheer let out his belly laugh. 'And Sudheer, I am not going to give you any advice because it's your day and you deserve a break. But tomorrow, I am going to start shouting at you again.' Sudheer laughed some more and reached his arms out. This time Arjun hugged him closer.

Preeti's voice came back to him. 'They just want your approval. They live for a kind word from you.'

'Now my friends, I ask for my wife to please preside over the exchange of rings.' Arjun stepped to the side as Preeti proudly took centre stage and the cameras flashed in unison.

He looked at the dais and then at the crowd. Where was Riti? Why would she not be here on the dais? What could have been so important...

Suddenly he caught sight of her. She was standing behind the main crowd. There was someone with her. A man. Riti's eyes met his and she immediately moved awkwardly and Arjun was quick enough to understand that this man had been holding her hand.

Once the ceremony was over and the stage cleared for the concert, Arjun moved to the place where he had seen Riti and the man but they were no longer there. The servants were arranging the chairs now and people were taking their seats, which left Arjun the freedom to move about without being ambushed by photo-seekers. It took five minutes before he found Riti again.

He was about to admonish her for not being on the stage when something about her expression made him stop. She looked flustered, her cheeks had taken the colour of the pink lehnga she was wearing. Arjun could not remember having seen her as unsure as she seemed right now.

'What's the matter?' he asked, frowning slightly.

'Papa, I want you to meet someone. Someone I have been wanting you to meet for a long time.'

So that's it, thought Arjun. My little daughter has brought a boyfriend. He could not help but stifle a smile. So that's why she looked so flushed.

He looked to the right. The man, who had been standing in shadow, stepped out.

It was then that Arjun felt it. A hammer to the heart, a wobbling of his knees. All at the same time.

There was Bangali, exactly as he remembered him. Except it was also Nayantara, the way he could never forget her.

'Let me introduce you, papa. This is Dr Arijit Banerjee and this is...'

The man extended his hand and smiled politely.

'How are you, uncle?'

I have to tell papa first. He will make the others understand.

Riti had told herself this many times over the last few months. If she told anyone else in the family, it would be a disaster.

If ma got wind of this, she would, of course, weep her eyes out, rush over to the temple, and then after all that drama, she would truss her up like a chicken and get her married off. It's something ma had wanted to do ever since Riti turned eighteen, because according to her 'a daughter is a responsibility you hold for another family'. She had made no secret of her not liking Riti staying alone in the United States, or doing theatre with strange men, and if she had gotten any hint of what had been going on, she would immediately have gotten her husband's men to pick Riti up, pack her off in a plane mid-term, and bring her to Delhi where she would have been passed on to that lurking 'another family'. It would have been the diamond merchant's son from San Francisco, Sushant or Prashant, Riti could never quite remember what his name was or perhaps even Sudheer's pervy brother-in-law, now that he was running the steel mills in Milwaukee.

One would normally be expected to confide in their brothers or sisters. But she could not tell Sudheer. Because Sudheer would tell their mother. She could also not tell Mohan. Because Mohan would tell Sudheer and then Sudheer would tell their mother.

Things would escalate rapidly after that.

Papa, though, would understand. Every time ma had brought up marriage, which was more or less every time they had all been in a room together, he had shot it down. Two years ago, Riti had come back for the summer break and she was showing pictures of New York to Sudheer and Mohan and ma, and one came out in which she was wearing a skirt that was on the shorter side. Sudheer had said, in a tone that was less brother and more father, 'Is this why we have sent you abroad? To wear such clothes? Have some thought of our reputation…' Ma was just going to take the ball and run with it when papa, who had been reading the newspapers with what seemed to be intense concentration, looked up and said, 'Sudheer, I am glad to hear you are so concerned about our family's reputation. Seeing you behave as you do, I would never have thought that possible.' Ma had tried to say something in support of her dearest son but papa's silence had made her stop, and Sudheer was, from that day, too scared to comment on Riti's pictures even when their father was not around. There had been this incident, she knew, when she was very little, when papa had flown off his handle and after that her brother had never hid the fact that he was afraid of him. Riti had once asked Mohan what had happened, and all he said was 'none of your business'. She remembered what Yadav uncle, who looked after the security of her papa and their family, had once said, 'Why blame Sudheer? The whole country fears your father. Even the prime minister shakes in his shoes if he frowns.' Maybe Yadav uncle had been exaggerating – after all, he did like to talk big – but even the little time she had spent in India had made her realize that very important people talked respectfully in her father's presence, with their eyes lowered and their voices down.

Yet Riti had never been afraid of her father. She had always looked forward to his visits to New York. Sometimes he came with the rest of the family, and sometimes alone, though she preferred the times he was alone. Ma could be so overbearing at times, openly resentful of her African American friends or anyone she felt looked weird, which included people who had piercings or tattoos or men with Mohicans and black eyeshadow, to the point where Riti would be embarrassed to be with her. And, to be honest, neither her mother nor her brothers were particularly interested in what she was doing. Ma would spend most of her time shopping on Fifth Avenue, while the brothers would be out on their own, possibly scoping out the delights on 42nd Street or a luxury limo out to Atlantic City. Only her father would sit down and ask her about her life. She had gone to Broadway productions with him, explained to him the nuances of set design and lighting, and though she was sure that her father did not understand much of what she said, he never seemed disinterested or even politely detached. Her father was great with her friends; he would take them out to nice restaurants in New York and be charming and engaging. The best memories of course were when they were alone. The last time he had visited, en route from Toronto in the summer, Riti and her father had walked around Central Park. For some reason, he had become very nostalgic, and told her stories of Lahore and of Delhi before she was born, of politicians and men in power and how he kept them in line, which made Riti feel privileged for she was sure he never discussed these things with anyone else, at least not in the family. She had been nervous all that afternoon, hiding her secret, and she had come close, once or twice, to even telling her father about Arijit, but something had held her back. She knew what it was, the fear of losing that perfect day.

'I want you to settle down here in the States, bring up your family here. Else your US accent will go waste,' he had said with a glint in his eye, while digging into a banana split. Ma had made it impossible to have sweets back in India, what with the doctor having diagnosed him with diabetes, and he more than made up for it outside the country.

'Why is everyone in such a hurry to get me married? And why should I live forever in the States? Don't you want me back, papa?' Riti had asked, even though she also did not want to go back to India, but still hearing her father say this made her a bit sad.

The vanilla rolling down the side of his lips, he had suddenly becoming serious. 'No, I don't.'

'Why, you don't love me any more?'

'I do love you. But love is not just about drawing in and clinging on. That's being selfish. It's about wanting the best for someone, even if that best entails being away from each other.'

She had wanted to argue but then again, she did not want to lose that perfect day.

But now, back in India for her brother's wedding, she had to tell her father. She had to.

She was going to settle down. In India. With Arijit.

She reached out and held Arijit's right hand, and he looked at her calmly, smiling reassuringly. If he was nervous, he was not showing it. Her papa had the mic now, his arm thrown lovingly around Sudheer, and he was saying something she heard but did not register. Standing in the shadows, away from the rest of the family on the stage, she already felt detached, as if watching them all from afar.

'You sure you don't want to join them up there?' Arijit asked softly, lowering his head, as he did to cover their difference in height.

She shook her head, still looking straight up at her family.

Would papa like Arijit? She was sure that ma would not. If Arijit's father had a diamond business or was the chief defence secretary, she may have been happy. But his father was dead and his mother taught Rabindrasangeet for a living in Calcutta.

Arijit was not the type who would make it to Sudheer and Mohan's circle of rich *baba log* friends. He didn't care for gratuitous acts of macho Punjabisms, like drinking till he puked or peeing from the roof down on to the garden below, which meant Sudheer would have nothing to do with him. Neither was he into race cars or clubs or Scotch or other things that rich men did and that meant Mohan would smirk silently at him, with that superior half-smile of his. In any case, it didn't matter. Like ma, they would hate Arijit without even trying to get to know him, because it had been her choice and good girls who give a damn for their family's honour didn't make choices, unless it was something like which shoes go well with today's dress.

But what about papa? In many ways, both the men were similar, strong, gentle, loving, sensitive and always in control of themselves. That was probably one of the reasons she had fallen in love with him. Despite all they said about likes repelling, they would warm up to each other, that's what she had told herself. Also papa loved educated people, if there was something that he respected, it was a big degree. In that, there could conceivably be no one more impressive than Arijit. Being a tenured professor at MIT by twenty-five was impressive, even by papa's high standards.

Yet there was a problem, a problem that kept eating away at her the more she came to know Arijit, a problem that she was afraid would get between him and her papa, if not now then some day.

Arijit was an idealist. He made no compromises. And papa, well, he, and that much Riti knew, sold compromises for a living.

It was because of Arijit that they were going to have to come back to India. It was because of him that she was going to have to break papa's decades-old dream. She could hear ma telling papa, 'You should have enrolled her in Lady Augustine's down the road. At least then she would have grown up proper and we wouldn't have spent a fortune on her education.'

Riti had never been the type to fall in love easily. Sure, there had been the odd crush once in a while. Back in Switzerland, there had been her Apollo-like Greek god of a gym teacher, straight out of the pages of a romance novel, and then in freshman year, her mentor in Greek drama class, married and stern with silver-brown hair, whose interest in her she could never fathom, purely professional conscientiousness or something else. But all these had been the silent gaze-from-afar, tiny flutterings of the heart, not to be acted upon or even spoken of. She knew she was not ravishingly beautiful, but she was pretty, and she knew enough about dress and make-up and hairstyles and what to say and how to say it to be – to use a word that ma loved to use – 'presentable'. She knew she attracted male attention whenever she was out with friends, or in class, or during her drama presentations, but this she waved away as more interest in the aura of affluence she gave off, even by Manhattan standards, than in her as a person. Whatever may have been the reason, she never reciprocated whenever anyone expressed interest in her. Any attempts to get her phone number or ask her out were met with polite yet firm brush-offs. Her best friend, Sally, whose father was a senator, used to affectionately call her a 'frigid bitch', and she had wondered if there was some truth in that. But no, the real reason she held herself back was because she did not want to betray her father's trust in her. She did not want ma to say 'See, that's why girls should stay at home.' She did not want another lecture on family honour from Sudheer or for Mohan to shake his head in silent disapproval. So, without taking a conscious decision to do so, she had been waiting for ma to fix her match, and avoiding any complication on the way to that inevitability.

Then, and she still remembered the exact date, this man had walked into a performance of *Our Town*. Her progressive professor had been keen on colour-blind casting and so she had been cast as Emily. She had not been at her best that evening, and had been trying to leave quietly after her performance without being noticed, when there he was, standing near the exit. There was another man with him, an Indian, but that man had stood back while he had walked ahead to shake her hand. She had to stop because he was physically in her way. He had started to say something and then she had brushed past, with a smile and a nod, not really in the mood to talk. The next show, which was on the weekend after, he was there again, this time alone, and once again he had stood at the gate. This one had gone considerably better and Riti had been in a better mood. When he said, 'This was a much better performance,' she had suddenly asked with a cocky arch of her eyebrow, and that was so unlike her, to speak to a stranger in this tone, 'Really? How was this better than my last one? Explain.' She knew it had been much better, but she did not expect a random Indian guy, with a rather unfashionable jacket and eight-dollar-KMart jeans, to be able to understand the difference. In the next five minutes or so, the stranger had precisely described the differences between her performance this week and last, picking up on every nuance with the quiet confidence of a professor of drama, so much so that Riti immediately started feeling guilty for her arrogant presumption, to compensate which, when he asked her out for coffee, she did not give an excuse and rush away. His name was Arijit Banerjee, and he was a professor at MIT. He was visiting Columbia for a project, and, while in the city, had been making rounds of non-Broadway theatrical performances. He was interested in theatre, that was fairly obvious, but also films, Spanish poetry, and when she had asked what it was he taught at MIT, he had said, 'solid state physics'. It was a fascinating evening, followed by a few more. She had introduced him to Sally, her roommate, and Sally had said, after he had left, 'What a dreamboat. If you are not going to be fucking Che Guevara there, which I am sure you aren't, can you please leave him for me?'

A dreamboat, of that Riti was not sure. He was handsome, though. Lean, wiry, tall, and the unkempt hair and beard together with the large poet's eyes, liquid and tranquil, made him look somewhat like Che, and the fact that he spouted Brecht and Georges Lefebvre made the connect with the Argentine revolutionary even more authentic. Being her father's daughter, she had discreetly put a call through to the physics department of MIT to confirm whether Arijit Banerjee actually was a professor there, for he seemed way too young for the qualification, and his story had checked out. After a few Broadway shows, a few walks through Central Park, a few street plays in Greenwich village and a drive out to Princeton, she realized she was falling for him, and she rationalized it always as 'papa will like him'. Settling down in the US with a professor from MIT, surely he would not mind.

Of course, she had not told Arijit how she felt. Firstly, good girls didn't fall in love with strange men and even if they did, they waited for the man to make the first move. He had gone back to Boston and she had gone back to her life, though she found herself flubbing her lines more than she should, and waiting, with more anticipation than she had felt for anything in her life, for the phone by her bed to ring. She thought he would propose some day, maybe on his knees with a diamond ring from Tiffany's right below the huge Christmas tree at Rockefeller Square, or maybe during the dropping of the ball at Times Square or maybe he would wait for her to be in Boston, perhaps near the Wharf, to a Spanish poem from the sixteenth century. She waited and she dreamed.

Till one day she opened her apartment to find him already there. The apartment complex had just installed new security systems and her first reaction had been, 'How did you get in?' She could immediately see Arijit was nervous, his eyes flickering from one corner of the room to the other, as if searching for something. 'I am sorry, Riti, but I have to leave.'

'Where? And how did you get in, this place just had...'

'New security systems. I know. Very simple to break through really, takes two minutes.'

She kept her shopping bags from Macy's on the table with a dull thud. Now she was worried.

'You broke in? What's wrong? What's happened? And where are you going to go?'

'Back home. India. They have asked me to leave... leave this country... I have two days.'

She had walked up to him, and despite herself, she wrapped her arms around him.

'Who are they? Please tell me what's happened.'

He didn't. He just kept looking out pensively through the window. 'I will understand and respect whatever decision you take,' Arijit had said, pale like a yellow leaf in autumn, holding on by its last fibre in the face of a stiff October breeze. He was avoiding eye contact, looking out at the tourists walking past down below, clutching shopping bags and coffee cups and their overcoats tightly, for it was cold in that cruel New York city way, and the chill had seeped into her Manhattan apartment, heated as well as any ten-thousand-dollar a month pad in the Upper East Side would be.

'Do you want to break up? Is that what this is all about?' she had asked, praying that the answer he gave would be the one she had wanted to hear.

'No, I don't. I want you to come with me to India. '

'Why?'

'You know why.'

'If I am going to make my family angry, if I am going to walk away from all this, the least I can expect would be to hear it from your mouth. No?'

'Because I love you.'

This was not the way she had thought things would go. This was not the proposal she had dreamed of.

'Arijit, you have to tell me what's happened.'

'I would ... rather not.'

'If you can't trust me ...' She left the rest unsaid.

It took him some time to tell her. That's when she came to know that Arijit had another life, a life that went beyond solid state physics and drama and film, one that she had never known of till now, a life that had gotten him into trouble.

A lot of trouble.

As the snow started falling softly outside, settling slowly down on the sidewalks and on the streets and the shoulders of black trenchcoats and red scarves, she poured two cups of coffee and pushed one towards Arijit. There was a choice for her now, him or her papa, a choice she knew she had made by the time she held him by his shoulder and leaned into him for a kiss, feeling his rough weather-chapped lips, bitter with coffee, with the softness of her tongue.

But now, as she saw her father walking towards her, she was scared about the choice she had made. She felt afraid of her father for the first time in her life.

Maybe he will not make others understand. Maybe he will not even understand himself.

Arjun looked tiredly at the piles of paper strewn in front of him on the table, pushing back with his fingers whatever was left of his hair. Abdul Ismail, that indefatigable procurer of information, had been as thorough as always.

This was a lot to digest. At fifteen, Arijit had won a scholarship to go to the US. He graduated at seventeen, had a doctorate by twenty and went on to be a professor at MIT. 'That's the best place in the world,' Ismail had told him, and he had no reason to doubt he was right because that's also what Riti had said. There was a list of his patents, and cuttings of his awards, all very impressive, and his mind went back to that little boy taking apart and assembling a radio, all those years ago.

Why had this happened?

Luck? Bad luck?

Luck is what men say when they are too stupid to understand the connection.

This was too much to have been done without design, for two people in the world to meet like this, and as he looked over to the other pile on his table, he was even surer that it was not.

It had been five months since Arijit had come back to India for good. That's when it had started – labour troubles, newspapers carrying stories not in the interests of Arjun's clients, inspectors getting tough, one in Madhya Pradesh, a few in Bihar and Uttar Pradesh, and even at the new petrochemical plant in Gujarat. It was not that these little things didn't happen all the time in the kind of business he was in, not even that any of them had caused him much damage. Just the timing of it all, and the critical mass of the incidents, had seemed to be too much to blame on coincidence. He had bled RP slowly once and he could damn well tell if someone was doing the same to him. Of course, he had no way to be sure for now. There was no evidence linking any of this to Bangali's son.

Maybe I am being paranoid. Maybe I am finding order where none exists.

'How are you, uncle?'

Arjun could not forget that smile. There had been something there that was not quite politeness, it was like the edge of a sharp knife, flashed quietly and then put away in the pocket, a challenge, deliberate and well thought out.

'How are you, uncle?'

He wanted him to know that he knew.

Or maybe I am being paranoid.

Of course Arijit knew who he was, he was not that young that he would not remember his face. Had he figured everything out or had Nayantara told him?

It didn't matter. He had revenge on his mind.

I am being paranoid.

He had played his moves well, the boy. He hadn't told Riti

anything about how he was connected to this family. That was his bargaining chip, the little tick-tick bomb in his pocket that he had kept to keep Arjun in line. Of course he had no proof, but that was the thing about love.

Trust.

Arjun thought about his daughter, the conversation they had after everyone had left, out on the lawn, because he had not wanted anyone else in the family to know. He had pretended to be very angry by her supposed betrayal, using that word 'trust' and 'break' several times, till she had cried. She was in love, of that Arjun was sure, and he knew what dangerous things that little word made people do. He had made her confess to everything, when they had met, and how, and how long this had gone on, making little mental notes in his mind as to the things he would tell Ismail to check up on.

Then she told him why he had been deported from America. It was an amazing story, which he realized would have perhaps been more amazing if he had understood everything about it. Computers. He had a vague idea what they were. A year ago he had worked with a few American companies bidding to computerize national banks, and that's when he had come to know what they were. But he had not warmed to the business of computers, because the margins were not enough to retain his interest. Mohan, though, had been particularly keen on computers and felt that 'infotech', which is what he called computers, had a future, so Arjun had let him spend his energy on it, if only because it would keep him out of his hair.

But what Riti had told him went beyond anything he had known about computers. Apparently, the Americans kept their big secrets in computers which were connected through phone lines and could talk to each other like people. Arijit was, and this Preeti had explained to him, like an expert cat burglar who could break into computers and telephone systems. He had broken into the computer network of the CIA and the US Army, and had stolen loads of information that he had planned to publish in a magazine he and some of his friends ran. It would be the embarrassment of the century for the US government. But the FBI had a mole in the magazine and the agents had come for him in Boston within hours of his getting the information and they had shoved him into a black van and driven away. In the story Riti had told Arjun, the Americans had asked Arijit to tell them how he did it and then to work for the government in secret, and only if he did this, his life would continue as it had. Else he was to leave the country in two days and never come back. Her man had not compromised, Riti had said with stars in her eyes, and Arjun had shaken his head in disbelief. This was too fantastic to be true.

Since the eighties, one of Arjun's biggest clients had been the CIA. The Americans knew that Arjun Bhatia ran the best illicit money laundering network in this part of the world, and so he managed for them an intricate web of front companies and offshore accounts and money channels to move money to Afghanistan and Pakistan for the fight against the Russians. He kept the Americans informed on KGB moves in the corridors of Delhi, reminded ministers encashing cheques signed by the 'Great Big Imperialist' to go easy on the Israel-and-Coke-Pepsi-bashing rhetoric from time to time, and during critical votes in the UN, he would make some personal calls to diplomats. Over the years, Arjun Bhatia had done enough for the Americans to be considered a 'Class A strategic asset' at Quantico. And he just called in a big favour.

The contact had met him at the bakery of Le Meredien and Riti's story had, to Arjun's surprise, checked out.

'An anarchist,' the contact had said in a thick accent Arjun had difficulty understanding. 'Your friend here belongs to a network of anarchists.'

'What's that?' Arjun had asked, because he had never heard that English word before.

'To put it as simply as I can, he wants to break down the system. For him democracy, capitalism, communism – they're all the same. They are all systems. So he wants a state with no laws anywhere. A whole world that's like Delhi traffic.'

Arjun laughed politely for the big white man had made a joke.

'The bastard really got behind our defences. The stuff he stole even the KGB haven't been able to get at, and they have been trying. For years. He was going to break into the trading system on Wall Street next. If he had been able to go through with that... shit, say hello to the fan.'

'If he was that bad, why did you let him go? Don't tell me the CIA has a conscience.'

'Killing him would have been easy, I guess. If it was me I would have done that. We fuck up too many times trying to sleep with the snake. Nicaragua. Cuba. Too long a list. But what would I know? The suits back in Quantico believe that the good doctor is about ten years ahead of the NSA. They might not value his life any more than I do but they have put a big tag on his brains. If he cannot be worked on now, that doesn't mean he can't be a few years down the line. So it would be better that he's sent back to India, where he will not have the tech to go after our computer networks, at least for some time. Let him play around here, and then maybe with the weather and the traffic and no *Melrose Place* on TV, he will want to come back to America. Then we will talk again.'

They had given Arjun the tapes of Arijit's interrogation and he had gone through them twice already.

'The world needs to know about your financing of dictators all over the world and your citizens need to know where their money goes.' Arijit's words had a slight Bangali accent.

'Lay off the bullshit,' the American voice said and there was someone else mumbling, whose words Arjun could not catch. 'Just answer the questions, governor. We got time.'

'No, agent,' Arijit said. 'You've got no time. A few years and what I just did would be like a little paper cut.'

'Tough talk. Tough talk. I will see how much of the tough talk stays when we put you into federal.'

'You are not going to put me in jail or you would have done so already. You won't kill me or you would have done that by now also. We both know what you want, so why don't you lay off the good-cop bad-cop routine? I watch Hollywood too.'

They must have had him in a dark room with a light on his face. Maybe even with his hands cuffed. He must have been terrified, and yet he had not broken down, instead keeping a quiet confidence in his voice. Somehow, and he did not know why, he was filled with a sensation of slow dread.

I am being paranoid. He is just a kid, and you are…

He remembered Riti crying as she had told him about Arijit while he had kept his voice firm and authoritative. 'It's not going to be easy explaining this to your mother and brothers and you know that. You going and falling in love like this, and not telling us, and we have a match fixed, and oh, this is all such a mess. I need time, you understand that?'

She had nodded her head.

'For now, you are going back to the US, you are not talking to anyone about this, and you are not coming back till I tell you to.'

'But…' she had started to say and he had put a hand on her shoulder. 'Finish your studies and if it is meant to be, he will be here.'

Riti had been in Delhi for two more days, which she spent mostly at home and then she had been made to board the flight back to New York. What she didn't know was that two of Arjun's best men had also gotten on to the flight to keep an eye on her and that she had men tailing her in New York, in case Arijit was stupid enough to try to get back to the US.

But how long would that last? He could hear Arijit's voice in his ears.

'You've got no time.'

Sooner or later, this whole affair would need to be resolved one way or the other. Trying to reason with his daughter was impossible.

Should he deal with Arijit directly?

No, he could not. For one, he was not sure whether Arijit was actually attacking him. He needed to be sure about it. If indeed he was attacking him, he might be working with someone and he needed to know who that was.

He thought about it once again. No, he was not as scared of Arijit as a person, as he was afraid that in trying to deal with him, he might lose the love of his daughter.

There was too much emotion here. And emotion, he knew, always led to foolishness.

And fools ... they die.

After sitting quietly for a few minutes and staring at the ceiling, he picked up the phone, and with his heart beating harder than it had in years, mumbled into the mouthpiece.

'First class return to Calcutta, please.'

The rain came down in gun-barrel straight lines, exploding on the sidewalk and on the walls in little sprays of violence, beating down on the roof of the taxi, and on the glass window.

'We are here,' the Sardarji said gruffly, half turning towards the back seat. This was the second time he had said the words, and yet his passenger sat, silent, looking out at the house to the right.

It was a small one-storeyed building, freshly whitewashed walls turning blue with the damp of the rains, with piles of wet sand and cement and a broken shovel lying to the side near the open iron gate. Arjun had never been to this part of the city, and yet he felt he had been here before, so comfortingly familiar was everything.

The driver reached back and gently shook Arjun by his shoulder. 'Oye, look at the meter.'

So accustomed had Arjun become to being driven around in his fleet of foreign cars back in Delhi, that he had almost forgotten that as opposed to a well-heeled chauffeur, a taxi driver did not automatically step out, open the door, and stand to attention whenever the engine came to a stop. With a mild, apologetic chuckle, Arjun shoved a wad of notes into the Sardarji's hand and stepped out.

He immediately realized that he had also forgotten to bring an umbrella. The rain lashed down so hard that Arjun wanted to bend forward and rush towards the gate. Then he heard her voice. She was singing. It was a Bengali song the words of which he did not understand, but it was beautiful and sad, and he stopped to listen, turning his face to the grey sky and letting the water rush over. The shirt clung to his body, the hair to his scalp, and he was back, it was '72 again, and for a second, all was washed away, all that had come to pass, and that second became another, and yet he stood in the rains, looking up at the wet crow pecking away at a tendril of rubbish. Then her song finished, and there was just the rain. So he took a few steps, raised the latch of the gate, and used it to knock on the door of the house, his heart now in steady resonance with the rhythm of the water.

The door opened. There she stood, her hand holding on to the side of the frame, lit from behind by the light. They said not a word, for there was nothing to be said, till the silence was broken by the distant rumbling of thunder. As calmly as if Arjun had gone out to get a cigarette without an umbrella and had been caught in the rain,

Nayantara motioned him inside. 'The bathroom is to the left. Take the white towel.' He followed noiselessly, dried his hair, feeling still strangely at home, and again when her arm materialized, laying a white shirt on the towel handle, he changed into it without a word, walked out and sat down in the living room. This was a new place, not as posh as the Ballygunje Circular Road apartment nor as dingy as the Nakul Das one, but still clean, airy and nicely maintained. On the wall was a framed picture of Bangali, a fresh tuberose garland around it and a half-burnt agarbatti stuck to the side, his face frozen forever in the way that Arjun would remember him, never to grow old, never to change. He looked around: the old picture of him and Bangali that had once adorned the living room was gone. On the cupboard stood three framed pictures of Arijit, one accepting an award from the American president, the second from when he was much younger, with a hint of a moustache and wearing a school uniform, standing with his mother who was holding a trophy. The third picture was taken in Times Square in New York city – Arijit in a long trenchcoat with his arm thrown casually around Riti's shoulder.

'How have you been?' Nayantara placed the tray with tea and biscuits on the coffee table. Arjun turned to look at her and noticed the change; she was not the way she used to be, not the same as she had been etched into his memory. She was still a strikingly beautiful woman, the kind that would make heads turn, and yet she looked pale and broken. There were purplish-black circles under her eyes, and her hair, once a waterfall of dense black, had thinned away to scrawny streaks of grey and white.

'You have lost a lot of weight. Are you all right?' Arjun asked. She sat down on the sofa opposite, looking back at him with eyes that were as piercing as ever. 'It's not a bad thing at our age to lose the baggage of our past.'

'That's right. Look at me,' Arjun pointed to his waist. 'I am carrying enough baggage for the both of us.'

Yet he wondered.

There was something not right, though knowing Nayantara, having deflected the question once, it was not going to be possible to make her give him a straight answer.

At least not right now.

'I knew you were coming some day,' she said quietly, stirring his tea, 'and not just because of the two men who have been keeping watch outside since Monday.'

She was right, Arjun had been having the house watched. He did not want to run into Arijit. Only when his men had reported Arijit getting on the train to Delhi had Arjun boarded the plane for Calcutta.

'So you know why I am here.'

'I think I do, but still, tell me.' She reached forward to give Arjun his cup, and he could not but notice that her hands shook involuntarily.

'Are you all right?' he asked again, and then waited for an answer. Realizing that none was forthcoming, he began.

'This thing has got to stop. There is no future for it, it's not going to happen.'

She arched her eyebrow in the way Arjun remembered she used to, and with a smile at the corner of her lips, said, 'Isn't that what I said fifteen-odd years ago?'

He took the proffered cup with a shrug of exhaustion. 'You know what I mean.'

'Why do you think I can stop them?' She glanced towards the picture of Arijit and Riti. 'Your children must be very well behaved, if you believe that children care for what their parents say, on things that matter anyway.' Her fingers, still shaking slightly, went to the lid of the tin can that held the biscuits. 'By the way, have you told Riti to stop? Did she agree?'

'My children listen to me, maybe not always from the goodness of their heart but definitely from fear.'

'So it's simple. Tell Riti to stop.'

'I have sent her away to the US, and told her not to come back till I have talked to everyone regarding this.'

'Lying to her is not really the same as asking her to stop, is it?'

'I can handle her, when the time comes. But if your son is determined to keep this going, it will be difficult.'

'You have a problem with love? Or just my family?' Nayantara asked, and there was no mistaking the sharpness in her tone.

'Not with love. Just revenge.' Arjun reached forward for the biscuits, and dipped them into the tea. He realized he had not done this for years, watching the arrowroot biscuit melt to softness. 'How much have you told Arijit about us? And about his father?'

'I have not told him anything. But I would not be surprised if he has figured things out.' She coughed once – a dry, deep painful cough. 'As you may have understood, my son is no ordinary man.'

'Did he tell you why he had to leave America?'

'Arijit got into some trouble with the government.'

'He didn't tell you, did he? Why *exactly*?' Arjun then proceeded to explain as best he could, what the Americans had told him. Nayantara listened silently and, so far as Arjun could tell, with a bit of motherly pride. Once that story was finished, Arjun told her his own suspicions about Arijit, that he had been going after his business interests systematically since the time that he had been in India.

'So you see this is not about love. It's him paying me back. Now your son is free to attack my businesses and I am not here to ask you to spare me from that. But not my daughter, not her, he has no right to bring her into any of this.'

'It doesn't add up, nothing of what you told me adds up. If Tubai wants to go after you, why did he try to steal the secrets of the Americans? It's only once they made him leave that he has started – and I have only your word for this – attacking you.'

'America was a testing ground for Arijit,' said Arjun, 'in the way South Africa was for Gandhi. They removed him from a train also, didn't they, and wasn't that how it all started?'

Nayantara smiled wryly, rolling her eyes at the comparison. 'You do think highly of Tubai to compare him to Gandhi. And here I keep telling myself that I am too blinded by my love for him.'

'India is where he has always wanted to be, his target has always been this,' Arjun pointed slowly to his own forehead.

'The problem with you is that you feel you know everything.' Another attack of coughing made her double over, but then she tapped her chest once, and continued. 'I don't doubt you are a smart man but I know Tubai, in the way a mother knows her son.' Nayantara's voice tightened with emotion. 'Tubai sees only injustice, and wherever he sees that, he fights it. He goes for the biggest targets, because he does not know fear, nor for that matter, good sense. There, he had America. Here, you.'

Arjun started to say something but Nayantara raised her hand slightly and Arjun stopped.

'Though I may seem silly and foolish, hear me out. I don't deny he has been targeting your business. But it's not because of what you did in the past, but what you have become now. It won't be just you he will go after, he will go for everyone that he believes is like you. The oppressors, the corrupt, the puppet-masters in the shadows.'

'Puppet-masters who stay in the shadows? You seem to know a lot about me.'

'I know you just a bit less than I know Tubai. But that still counts for a lot.' Once again she coughed, and this time, her voice came out broken. 'I don't know what you do now, I stay in my little corner of the world. But you once told me where you wanted to be. Remember?'

'Yes, I do.'

'I *always* believed you would succeed. I guess you have made it, haven't you?'

'I have. I suppose. And you are right. I am the bad man. I always will be. But that still ...'

'And that's why he will fight you.' The lightning flashed from outside, illuminating the side of Nayantara's face in a moment of blue. 'It's not personal, Arjun, it never is with him. He is against the system, and you ... you are the system.'

'I get your point. But I am here to talk about Riti, I keep telling you that ...'

'That's love.'

'It can't be. It just can't be.'

'Tubai loves the world. When he was in high school, he used to give his tiffin to the guard's son, every day, without telling me. He stole some of the jewellery you had given me to help a stranger have a kidney operation. Whatever money he makes even now, he gives most of it away. It sounds strange, and to use a favourite word of yours, filmy, but that's Tubai for you. A man like him, he does not manipulate a girl to settle scores with her father, he just does not.'

'Now you are making him out to be Gandhi,' sneered Arjun.

'He is not like you and me. Nor is he like his father.' Her eyes lit up with pride. 'Tubai is special, in every sense of the word.'

'But then Gandhiji should listen to you, shouldn't he? If he loves the world, why not just let my daughter go?'

'But why should I tell him to let her go? Why should I tell my son to not follow his heart, to not love the woman he loves? You and I have lived our lives on our own terms, done whatever we wanted to, not cared for society nor for anyone else. Then what right do we have to tell our children to do differently?'

'You don't understand ...'

'No, I do. I know why you are here. You are here to save Tubai's life, to give me a chance to change what will be his future, the chance you wish you had given me for my husband.'

'That's not what I...'

'But that is the truth. I know it.' Her voice faltered and Arjun saw her hand shake again. 'Tubai is going to die. I know that I will have to live with it, as I have lived with the death of my husband. And, if that was not bad enough, I will know that it would be the same man who will have pulled the trigger both the times, the same man I have...' She looked up at him and sighed. 'It will break my heart, and the thing about hearts is that they break again and again, but still I don't care, I will never ask Tubai to stop.'

'Why would you not tell him then, knowing what can happen?'

'Because...' Her voice was now choked with tears. 'Because what Tubai is doing is right. I will not tell him to stop caring for people. I will not tell him to stop standing up against injustice. And God is my witness, I will not tell him to stop loving the woman he loves. If he is going to die, let him die in his own dream, than live in the nightmare men like you have made.'

They sat quietly, save the sound of the rain, and of Nayantara's heavy breathing, and the occasional car splashing down the road. Arjun slumped forward, burying his face into his hands, till Nayantara spoke.

'Can I get you something to eat? Maybe another cup of tea?'

He reached out and held a bangled arm. For a moment, Arjun felt whole again.

'You are not well, are you?'

'If the question is "am I dying?", the answer is no. I am not Meena Kumari, and this story isn't written by Guru Dutt.'

'I can find out, so please don't lie.'

She did not reply, and Arjun gently let go of her arm.

He stood up, feeling as if he had suddenly aged twenty years. There were so many things he wanted to say to her that he knew that if he started, he would never leave.

'I ought to get going. I think it's just drizzling outside, and if I don't get going now, I will get caught if it gets worse.'

'I have an umbrella. I can take you to the taxi stand.'

'Like Raj Kapoor and Nargis?' he asked, raising his hand and hunching forward in the manner of Raj Kapoor, and she laughed, with a slight sniffle.

'No, I will manage,' he said. 'I saw where the stand is.'

She followed him to the door.

'Oh wait.' He suddenly remembered. 'My shirt. I should change…'

'No, it's still very wet. Wear that. It's yours.'

'I don't think Arijit will like me wearing his shirt.'

'It is *yours*. It had somehow stayed with me and good thing I never threw it away.'

'And now I am leaving behind another… for the next rainy day.'

They were outside near the gate now, the drizzle had reduced to a few random cold drops, and for a moment, all Arjun wanted to do was to hold Nayantara in an embrace, but he knew he could not, not ever again. Instead he said, 'That song you were singing just before I came in was beautiful. I don't think I have ever heard you sing that before.'

'Milon hobe koto deene, amar moner manushero sone?'

'What does it mean?'

'How many days do I wait for the person I love?'

'An eternity I guess.' He smiled sadly.

Nayantara nodded. 'And yet we must not stop loving for he is already there. In our hearts.'

'I think you should go in now,' he said, gently placing his hand on Nayantara's shoulder. 'We don't want to make that cough any worse.'

She stopped but made no move to go back. He wanted to say so much, a hundred and then a thousand words fought their way from his heart right to the tip of his tongue, and in the end, the ones that won were just these.

'I am sorry. I am so sorry for everything.'

Nayantara said something but Arjun never heard it. He had started walking away.

12

NAYAK NAHIN... KHALNAYAK HOON MAIN.

The remixed version of the song from *Khalnayak* reverberated from the party downstairs, thumping the walls and bleeding into the room.

'That song, uff that song.' Mohan squinted, sniffed in the white powder, and murmured, 'I wish I could take a grenade launcher, and blast their faces off, like Tony Montana.'

They were in one of the second floor rooms of Rishi Karnik's sprawling Mehrauli farmhouse and the party was on in full swing. It was by invitation only and a ring of bodyguards stood outside the gates with guns to keep out the riff-raff so that cricketers, *baba log*, bureaucrats, models and wannabe starlets could rub shoulders and other body parts away from prying eyes.

'Who's Tony Montana?' asked Rishi Karnik.

'Only a *choot* of a particular *aukaat* would ever ask that question,' Mohan grunted back.

Rishi Karnik shrugged.

'Tony Montana is the *baap* of all your Bachchans and Dutts. But as I said, it's beyond your *aukaat*. Because all Indians can do is lift scenes straight off *Scarface*.' Mohan was normally quiet, but Hindi film music and cocaine combined was one of the few things that made him lose his composure.

Sudheer was sprawled out on the large black sofa, his legs skewed at an angle, head thrown back, shirt buttons open to the summit of his large hairy belly. '*Madarchod, yahaan humaara gaand chodi ja rahi hai,* and all my little brother can give a fuck about is the music downstairs and some *firang* flick.'

It had happened very fast. All the newspapers in Delhi had received, right in time to make the Monday papers, identical brown packages. In each of them were tapes, transcripts and photocopied documents. On the tapes were conversations, one a call from Arjun to the energy secretary asking why certain regulations still had not been written the way Arjun had asked for, another from Manoj Karnik to Arjun with choice expletives directed at the Mehtas, and another from Manoj Karnik to the energy secretary asking for the transfer of a stubborn bureaucrat in the environmental clearance office. Apart from this, there were numerous conversations among Vantor officials about money transfers to political parties and incriminating internal memos of Vantor, referencing the calls. In all, there was enough material in the packages to blow the government sky-high. None of the papers had carried it all – the editors knew better than to get on the wrong side of Arjun Bhatia – but still enough had leaked out to be of embarrassment to the principals involved. Even then it would have been fine, had not the same set of tapes and documents been sent to the offices of some anti-Vantor lawmakers on Capitol Hill. The lawmakers raised questions about the business practices of Vantor in foreign markets, specifically whether they were violating US law on kickbacks. Within twelve days, Vantor held a press conference where they announced that market conditions were not aligned with investing in India and that they would be looking at other emerging markets like Brazil.

'Someone has gotten into the phone system,' Vinod Khandelwal had said in the emergency meeting at Arjun's house. 'We have no idea how they did it. The level of sophistication suggests a foreign government, maybe Russians, maybe the Chinese, but I don't see what angle they could have in targeting us.' Vinod Khandelwal was in charge of Arjun's energy and pharma operations and was considered the smartest guy among Arjun's inner circle, a slightly stooped man, whose English accent had given him the nickname 'Amreekan'. Arjun had said nothing, just sat quietly glum, and Sudheer and Mohan had both been surprised by how powerless he had looked, as voices were raised and accusations exchanged at the meeting. After the outsiders had left, Arjun had made a few calls to smoothen some tempers in the ministry, and his tone and demeanour, the last few weeks, had been of a man on the defensive. His sons had never quite seen him like this.

Rishi slapped Sudheer on the back chummily. 'We are not getting fucked in the ass. We got him, man. Now we do the butt-fucking.'

On the glass table in front of them, near the lines of white powder and glasses of Jack Daniels, were two photos and a few sheets of paper.

'He looks like a homo,' said Sudheer, picking up one of the photos, '*Chikna chora hai*. I think he might enjoy the butt-fucking.'

Mohan looked cagey. 'You sure that's him?'

Rishi nodded. 'As sure as I know you are your papa's son.'

Rishi had got hold of the memos that had been sent to the newspapers. They had a Delhi postmark. The memos had then been sent to a lab in Japan for analysis. Only one brand of photocopiers made those kinds of grabber marks and used that kind of toner. Rishi's men had worked with the police to scope out Xerox shops in and around Delhi, concentrating their line of questioning on the few that had that brand of photocopiers. It took them five days to locate the shop. The man who had come to make the photocopies was identified easily enough by the shop owner, he had even gone to his house to deliver some of the copies. Within a day, Rishi had his picture.

'How did he do all this?' asked Mohan. 'Do your men know that? How did he manage to listen to and record all our calls?'

'From what I know, he is a shadow, this chap. Attends union meetings but isn't a part of any. Does some work in the slums around the Yamuna, *gaand-maaro-ing* builders and other kinds of commie mischief. He maintains that address in Noida, stays alone, doesn't seem to have family here.'

'*Wohi toh uski gaand se nikaalenge.* How did he get into the phone lines? Who is he working for? What's his game?' said Sudheer, opening and closing his eyes rapidly.

Rishi opened the bottle of Jack Daniels and poured himself a peg, the liquid gurgling over the ice. 'That's what I want to know too. *Chikna chora* here definitely isn't acting alone. There is someone with his cock inside him, and I suspect it's Kulkarnis. This has his cumstains all over it.' He took a photo from the table, and tapped its edge. 'We need to make this guy sing, sing like Lata Mangeshkar.'

'Maybe we should ask papa about this, maybe we just let him know,' Mohan said, putting his finger on his nose and inhaling.

There was silence for a moment, with only the sound of music filtering through and nothing else.

It was broken by a blur of motion – Sudheer took his glass and flung it. It flew through the air, a good foot away from Mohan's head, and exploded on the wall, leaving in its wake a stain of whisky and broken glass all over the floor. '*Madarchod,* how many times do I have to tell you? We do this ourselves. You hear? No running to papa, with our tails between our legs.'

Mohan looked strangely collected, in spite of the glass that had just zipped by his head and his brother's violent outburst. He just adjusted his jacket and leaned back on to the couch.

Sudheer was still bellowing at the top of his voice. 'This is exactly why papa does not take us seriously. He treats us like little boys whose balls haven't fallen. Well, I say, we show papa we are made men now. We go and we do what needs to be done and we do it ourselves. Yeah. Ourselves, *behenchod.*'

'When papa wants us to show a bit more initiative, I am not sure he wants us to deal with things as big as this.'

'*Jaa apna lund hilaa jaake madarchod.* I am going to do this, with or without you.'

'It's one thing to be high here and talk big, another thing to actually go and do it.'

Rishi sauntered up and held Mohan in a mock chokehold. 'Oh relax, you two *choot*s are going to have a bad trip tonight the way you are fighting. And oh, by the way, I think that fat fuck of your brother is right for once.'

'Yeah?' asked Mohan, his voice still devoid of all emotion. 'Says who? The bookie son-of-a-bitch.'

'Hold on, *madarchod.* I just saved your family's *gaand.* Remember who found this man out, don't you forget that, *baawade.* What's the matter, Mohan boy? I thought you were the brains of the family. 'Cause right now it seems to me that your brother has the big stomach as well as the big brains. *Chikna chora* is a danger, a danger to me and my papa, true, but a bigger danger to you. If he can get into...'

'I am not saying he is not a danger. As a matter of fact, I am saying he is such a big danger we should tell papa.' Mohan looked at his brother and then at Rishi, hoping one of them would see reason. 'We don't know who is holding his pyjama strings, and the last thing I want to see happen is – we rush in, the cord drops, and there staring at us in the face is a big flopping cock we can't handle.'

Sudheer was about to say something and Rishi gestured for him to stop.

'Mohan, my dad, he is a mean *madarchod.* I am telling you. A mean, mean *madarchod.* He has killed people and he has watched people bleed out like pigs. And though he won't say it aloud, even he is afraid of Arjun uncle.'

'Yeah, he should be,' Mohan said. 'My papa keeps a line of your papas as *randis*. That's why.'

'Be that as it may,' Rishi continued, 'the real reason is because my papa knows a few of your papa's old friends. Arjun uncle has killed more people than *tum dono ne randi chodi hai,* and I know that's a high number.'

'Tell me something I don't know,' Mohan said, smoothing back his hair.

'And these people your father killed and tortured were *madarchods* too, *not chikna choras* like this fag with John Lennon glasses. The city fears your father, and it's not just because he gets things done. It's because he knows what to do when things don't get done.'

'And your point is?' Mohan asked.

'Your father did not ask anyone's permission before doing what he did. He did not run screaming to his father. That's why he is a legend and you two will end up as *baba log.* That is if you keep up with this whole *permission* thing. Your father won't tell you "beta, go and do this". No. He expects you to handle shit. On your own.' Rishi got up and perched himself on the arm of Mohan's couch.

'Let me tell you a little story about your father.'

'Spare me,' said Mohan.

Rishi ignored him, papa told me this when he was drunk, so I am pretty sure it's true. Everything he says sober is a lie of course. Anyways, back in the '60s, when he was still running guns, Arjun uncle put his best friend and business partner into the ground. Took him to a wheat field, and, boom, shot him in his head. Didn't even bat an eyelid. What do you think he would do if he was in your place today?'

'I have heard that,' Mohan muttered. 'Everyone has fucking heard that.'

'Leave it, Rishi.' Sudheer seemed to find his voice again. 'If little brother is wetting his diapers at the thought of a little blood, you and I will do it. We get a crew, and we make *keema* out of him.'

The track had changed to Dr Alban's 'It's My Life' and Mohan looked into his empty glass morosely. 'If we are going to do this, why do it ourselves? I am sure Rishi has men who are better at getting information out of people than we are. That encounter guy from Punjab... what's his name?'

Sudheer bellowed, 'I am sure Rishi also has men with bigger cocks than you have. So are you going to let them screw your wife? I should have hit you with that glass, I really should have.' He tried to get up, tottered, and slumped back on to the couch. 'Didn't you just hear what Rishi said?'

'I did.'

'So? Did papa send someone else to clean his shit up? No. He did it himself. 'Cause it's personal. Revenge is personal. Like a fuck. If you are a man, you stand up, you look the bitch in the eye, and you pull the trigger, and you don't stop going in and out till the eyes close and the bitch feels it, feels it enough to know she shouldn't have messed with you.'

'So you are going to shoot him? I mean that dialogue you gave is all *chawanni-phenk*, but can you do it? Pull the trigger on *chikna chora*'s face? 'Cause face it, you are no papa.'

'And you are?'

'I never said I am. That's why I said, let the professionals do it.'

Rishi slapped Mohan's shoulder. 'Look, there are going to be no bullets. Sure, we will have guns, but that's just to get the guy to talk. We will slap him around a bit, I mean look at him, he is going to be crawling on his knees in no time, and if he tries to be Amitabh Bachchan or something, we put him in our jeep, drive out somewhere lonely, and there I have my men work on him. He is going to sing sooner or later. And I agree with Sudheer, we do this whole thing ourselves. No need to tell Arjun uncle or involve his men. Come on, it will be fun.'

Sudheer roared and punched his fists in the air. 'Yeah, guns. I am going to carry my Beretta.' He made shooting sounds and growled, mock Clint Eastwood, 'Do I feel lucky? Punk? Fuck it, I need another whisky.'

Mohan murmured, 'It's "do you feel lucky?"', and stood up, adjusting his jacket. 'Since I suppose this has all been planned and settled and nothing I say is going to matter, I think I should go downstairs and ask the DJ to change the track.'

Rishi looked at his watch, 'And finally little boy Mohan's cock has come to the party.' He grinned conspiratorially at Sudheer. 'I was wondering what was up with Mr Milk Moustache here, sitting and sulking like a girl on her monthlies when there is wet, needy, paid-for pussy downstairs.'

'Aren't you coming down, Rishi?' asked Mohan. 'I mean this is *your* party.'

'I will join you in a bit,' he said, pointing towards the door. 'Pick someone up for me, please. You know the kind I like.'

'Yeah, hijras. Cock for when he is sober, hole for when he is wasted,' Sudheer wheezed, bloodshot eyes half-closed. 'And I need more whisky. *Madarchod*, how many times do I have to ask? The bottle's done here.'

Mohan walked down the stairs briskly. Rishi got up, closed the door, and then sat down on the single-seater where Mohan had been sitting, right opposite Sudheer.

'There's something I wanted to tell you. Just you alone. I would normally not have any problems saying things in front of Mohan, but you are my friend, and he is, well, just my friend's kid brother. And he lacks courage, so he needs a little *garmi* to rile him up. Which I just gave him a nice blast of. But with you ... with you I can be honest.'

'Tell me, but you have got to promise me to send someone here with another bottle.'

'I will. But first I want you to listen to me carefully. You are not going to like what I have to say.'

'I don't care. Just get me another bottle.'

'Things are looking bad for Arjun uncle after what happened with Vantor,' Rishi said slowly. 'I mean people are talking, you know how they talk. They are wondering whether he can push such big deals any more, whether age has made him lose that edge, you know how batsmen lose their timing and hand–eye coordination. Like that. And well, don't get angry, they are also saying that you two aren't really up to take over from the old man. They are saying Arjun uncle is not as strong as he was because he has to take care of you two.'

'Don't you think I already know that? They think of me as a fat retard and my brother as the thin shadow. Why am I saying "they"? Even my papa thinks that.'

'That's why this is important. You have got to take control. *We* have got to take control. You and me, we can do this. Mohan is a nice kid, but *woh bahut* easy *patloon geela kar deta hai yaar*, and still thinks he can get by, clutching his father's coat-tails. You and I ...'

'I know what you are trying to say. We have to take control. Since papa won't give me control ...'

'You need to take it yourself. You need to find out who did this, and why, and you need to resolve it. Arjun uncle, I don't think he can do it any more.'

'And then every *madarchod* in Lutyens can stuff their whispers down their throats. God, I hate this city.' Sudheer had suddenly started crying, big drops of tears rolling down his pudgy cheeks in a steady torrent.

'Are you all right, man?'

'No, I am not. I am not all right.' Sudheer rubbed his eyes with the palms of his hand, and all that did was make his drunken eyes even more red. 'All my life, I have been trying to make my papa take me seriously, to make him know I am worthy of being called his son. He treats me like I am some exotic pet he bought from Madagascar, he puts me in a gold cage, he gives me food when I want it, and lets me walk around, but he never…you know… treats me like a human being. I got married, and I have my own home, and I don't have to see him every day, but I can still feel him, you know, looking down at me from above, disapproving of everything I say and I do. He trusts strangers, he asks counsel from outsiders, and when it comes to his own son…' Sudheer made a face, mimicking Arjun's voice, '*Why don't you run over and see what your mother is doing?*'

'Come on, it's not as bad as that,' Rishi said, trying to be comforting. 'You have your own companies, you got your Mercedes and your Audis and I heard you are getting a Jaguar, and people in Delhi know that, that you are someone. See what I was trying to say was…'

'You don't have to piss it down. I know. Even my wife knows.'

'What do you mean?'

'She knows I am not my own man. I can feel it, the way she talks, the way she orders me around, even the way she fucks, it's like when she is with me she is watching news on Doordarshan, gets it over with and watches *Superhit Muqabla*. I know I am no Sean Connery, but still the way she makes me feel…'

'She is a rich NRI bitch, and you know how stuck up that kind is. And face it, you are not the prince young girls dream of while diddling themselves at night.'

They sat wordlessly for a while, till finally Rishi said, fiddling with the large gold chain that hung from his neck, 'Why don't I send someone over with the whisky? I know just the girl to lift your spirits – Mona will make you feel like a rock star, guaranteed.'

'Just get me him,' he said, pointing to the picture of Arijit on the table, 'and everything will be all right.'

Five-foot two with a moustache that covered his upper lip like camouflage and a squeaky voice that gave him the nickname 'Chuha', though he always claimed it was because he could infiltrate enemy hideouts like a rodent, Charanjeet Singh had once been a senior inspector with the Punjab police. At the height of the Khalistani insurgency, he had notched up 106 'encounters', five bravery medals, two exit wounds, one in his shoulder and another in his thigh, and one guest appearance as himself in a Punjabi film. On unpaid suspension for the last two years, he was facing a departmental enquiry for being a contract killer. He still ran that business but now out of uniform, though recently he had had little cause to use his gun. His new specialization was gathering information from men reluctant to give it, for which he had perfected several painful methods.

'Rule number one,' he said, with breath that smelled of stale cigarette smoke, as they sat packed together in the back of a jeep. '*Tera baap Patiala ka maharaja ho ya teri maa Shah Jahan ki rakhel, mujhe kuch farak naheen padta*. As long as you are with me, you are going to listen to everything I say.' Chuha paused for effect. 'I mean everything. I will say it again. I don't care who your father is, or how much you are paying me. Once we go in, I am the boss. Now, are we okay with that?'

He looked first at Rishi. Rishi nodded. Then he looked towards Mohan. Mohan saluted, 'Yes sir.'

Sudheer did not make eye contact.

'*Aye, motay*, ate your own ears?'

Sudheer opened his mouth but before he could talk, Rishi said, with a nervous shake of his head. 'Yes, he understands.'

'Are you his mouth, Rishi ji?' Chuha asked. 'I don't think so. *Motay* may have eaten his ears, but he can move his mouth, or else he wouldn't have become this *motay. Kyon, motay, galat kaha*?'

Sudheer's face turned red, and he sweated in a suppressed anger, for no one spoke to him like this. But he knew better than to make Chuha angry.

'I understand.'

'Good, and now I want all of you to hand me your hardware.'

'No way,' said Sudheer, clutching his Beretta tight. 'No way am I giving you my gun.'

'I am not taking away your gun, *wahan jaake jee bharke hilana*,' said Chuha, trying to be agreeable. 'I just want the bullets, that's all.'

Sudheer turned towards Rishi. 'You said we could bring our guns.' There was a rising panic in his voice. 'My brother and I are not going there without our guns. Definitely not.'

Chuha smiled politely. 'I am the only one who is going to go in loaded. *Kyunki*,' he pulled out a gun from the holster under his jacket, '*mujhe ise chalana aata hai*. If there is one thing I have learned in all these years, it's that guns in the hands of people who have never used them is like cars being driven by women.'

'Well, you are wrong. I have fired my Beretta on a range and so has my brother. That too in America. Both of us are licensed to carry guns.'

'Tell me how I know *ki iss business main abhi bhi tumhara nath nahin utara*. Ask me how?'

No one replied.

Chuha repeated, 'Ask me no? How? *Poocho poocho*.'

'How?' asked Rishi.

'Because only *chutiya*s bring licensed firearms to an operation like this. Rule number two. Never bring a gun that can be traced to you if you have any intention of using it.'

'Wait,' said Mohan, nervously chewing gum. 'Who said we

have any intention of using it?' His eyes darted from Chuha to Rishi and back to Chuha. 'I thought your man checked out that chap. He said this was safe.'

Chuha had sent his man half an hour ago, pretending to be a salesman of water purifiers. Arijit had opened the door and had spent two minutes politely expressing his absolute disinterest in installing the latest German ultraviolet technology-using water purification solution, time enough for Chuha's man to take a discreet look inside. He had reported that the living room had very little furniture, just two chairs and a table, but it had a lot of books and loads of equipment, wires and batteries and circuit boards and that Arijit looked to be the only one in the house.

Chuha took out a packet of paan masala from the pocket of his safari suit. 'This happened ten years, yes, sounds about right, ten years ago. It was my first day out on a questioning. My very first day. There was a village, ten kilometres from Amritsar, where one of our informants had been found dead in a field, and so three of us went to the house of the man we suspected of having done the killing, *naam bhi yaad hai,* Simranjeet Singh. So this is a small house with a courtyard in front, and when we walk in, the only living being there, besides two big dogs, is this old lady. Wrinkled and bent over with glasses like the bottom of a bottle. She says Simranjeet and his father are both out with the tractor. Jaspreet was just made inspector and his blood was all warm with his new uniform, and he says, "*Ae budiya, charpoy nikaal. Aaj jamke behenchod ki khatirdaari karenge.*" She goes into the house, and when she comes out, the *chudail* is holding an AK-47. Jaspreet dies first, and then the other man whose name I have forgotten flies back, dead before his body touches the ground. There is blood everywhere, the dogs are howling, *aur meri to* pant *geeli ho gayi. Pehla din, behenchod. Pehla din.* Then the *chudail* turns towards me, and I don't know if she realizes that I am a virgin and even a policewala should not die before he has tasted a woman, or whether the shock of killing two men had just set in, but she hesitates, just for a second, and that's when I fire, right between the eyes. That was my first encounter, and within two hours, I had made my second and third, near the tractor, five really, if you count the two dogs, but that's not the reason I told you the story. Why did I tell you the story then? *Poocho poocho.*'

'That there is nothing such as "safe",' said Mohan.

'Precisely.'

'So you are saying your man has no idea whether Arijit has a gun or not. Those wires and batteries he says he saw could well be a bomb,' Mohan said. 'And this kind of *chutiyapa* is what we are paying you for.'

'Well, I will tell you what you are paying me for.' He angled his head back and started tapping the paan masala into his mouth. 'You are paying me for an experience. Now I don't know what this *haraami* did to piss you off, I guess he must have overtaken your car, or maybe tried to talk to your girlfriend, or spat on your shoe. Don't know, must be something. You want revenge. You could have just hired me to rough that *haraami* up, but no, you guys want to be heroes. After all, *thoda* danger *chahiye na lund ko khada karne ke liye*? I understand that. Even after all these years, I get hard before the rush. But you three don't really want to die, do you? And that's why I am here, to make sure you have the same number of holes in your body going in and getting out. For that you should not be firing bullets, should it – and I am not saying it will – come to that. Because if you do, what will happen is that you will hit everything but the target – the walls, the chair, and what is most likely, yourselves.'

'For a mouse, you sure talk good,' said Sudheer, to which Chuha nodded before he reached out his hand for the guns. In one minute, the magazines of all the guns were emptied and he handed them back to the respective owners. 'For the last time, this is how it's going to happen. I am going to knock on the door, the *haraami* is going to open it, I am going to barge through and pin him to the ground. Rishi ji enters first, and then you two. Close the door immediately. I will put a hold on the guy and tape his mouth shut, Rishi ji you put the blanket on his head, and then we walk him out to the jeep. My man will keep the engine running. *Andar-bahar do minute mein*. If someone comes in, *raaste ke Mahatma,* I am going to wave my ID, and say I am special branch, and this is a wanted terrorist. Since I will have my gun out, no one is going to look closely and see that the ID has expired. None of you will talk once outside the house, none of you will make eye contact with anyone outside and, this is the most important, none of you will have your guns out. Now, *acche bacche,* can I have a "yes", all together?'

Things started out according to plan. They walked behind Chuha and he knocked on the door. The moment it opened, everything happened very fast, Chuha shoulder-butted the man inside so that he fell back, his glasses flying across the room. Rishi, Sudheer and Mohan glided smoothly in, with Mohan slamming the door shut. So quick was Chuha in rolling the duct tape over his victim's mouth that Arijit did not even have the time to scream. The only sound after the slamming of the door was the dull thud of Arijit's body hitting the ground. Arijit swung his arms trying to get a punch on to Chuha's face, but Chuha dodged it with practised ease. Then with the skill of a butcher tying the legs of a chicken together, he had Arijit's wrists bound with rope, and flipped him over on his stomach. On cue, Sudheer dramatically brought out his Beretta, and then, standing over Arijit, his legs on either side of the fallen body, he pressed the barrel to the back of Arijit's head.

He had rehearsed this line for the past three days, and it came out just right, '*Chal behenchod, ab gaana shuru kar*.'

Just then, from the corner of his eye, he caught the shadow of another person standing in the doorway leading away from the living room. All the others seemed to see this at exactly the same time, turning their heads in unison. Chuha reacted first, whisking out his gun and whirling it in a smooth half-arc to fix it on the target when the person spoke.

'Sudheer? Mohan? What ... ?'

For there in the doorway, wearing a long white T-shirt that said 'MIT' and knee-length shorts, her hair messy and her lipstick smudged, stood Riti.

For a moment, everyone in the room froze.

Then Sudheer charged, like a bull out of the pen, but not before his heavy shoe had thudded into the small of Arijit's back. Riti ran towards Arijit, who lay doubled up in pain from the blow, screaming into the duct tape covering his mouth. She never reached him. Sudheer got to her just as she neared Arijit and he yanked her back by her hair, throwing her off balance. Her body went parallel to the ground, her legs flying up as she fell as Sudheer loosened his grip on her hair. The back of her head hit the edge of the table on the way down and Sudheer was left standing with a few strands of her hair in his hand. Rishi had by then rushed forward and was holding Sudheer back by the shoulders. '*Randi*,' he bellowed. 'This is why we sent you to the US? Our family, our honour ...' He shrugged his shoulder to shake Rishi off and charged again towards Riti, who lay motionless on the floor, when he felt the bore of a gun pressed against the back of his skull.

'*Motay, ek* inch *aur hila na to peeche teesri aankh bana doonga*,' Chuha whispered slowly. '*Ma kasam*.'

Riti was unconscious, a thin trail of blood seeping out from where her head had hit the table. Arijit screamed into the tape and then started crawling on his stomach, towards where Riti lay. Mohan bent down over her, his voice full of fear. 'What did you do? She is...'

Sudheer kept his voice low, 'I give a shit if she is dead.'

Rishi turned towards Chuha whose gun had stayed level with the back of Sudheer's head. 'Why did your man not tell us there was someone else in the house?'

He did not meet Rishi's glare. 'Take three steps back, *motay,* and sit on that chair unless you want to join *damaadji* on the ground.'

Sudheer did not argue with the only loaded gun in the room, stepping quietly back. Barely able to get the words out, from the exertion of it all, he breathed hard. 'Whatever Rishi is paying, I will pay you ten times more. Just give me your gun. Now.'

'Motay, utna paisa diya toh main tujhe apni biwi ko bhi ungli karne doonga,' Chuha said with a deadpan expression. *'Par* trigger *pe ungli daalne nahin doonga.* We are in a lot of trouble now, so don't make it worse.'

Mohan was still doubled over Riti, gently moving her head, 'Riti, Riti, wake up.'

'What now?' asked Rishi, gliding his fingers through his hair, the big gold chain dangling out over his unbuttoned shirt. 'What do we do now?'

'Exactly what we said we would,' Sudheer said, now finding some of his breath and courage once more, 'except now we have to take Riti to that safe house along with this *behenchod.*'

'Behenchod sahi, par behen to teri chodi hai.' Chuha smiled. 'But no. I am not taking your sister to my safe house. My Jat friends may not be able to control themselves once they see this fine little bird. No, your sister goes to the hospital.'

'Screw the hospital,' Sudheer said.

'Dekh motay, I love my life. Arjun Bhatia *ki beti ki izzat ka band baj gaya toh* my life won't be worth *chaar* annas.'

'*Izzat to hai hi nahin iski abhi.*' Sudheer spat out. 'And the *randi* is not going to die, she's just been knocked out by her head hitting the table.'

'She is not coming with me. That's final. Now, Rishi ji, just open the shutter slightly, and see if there are people outside. I am afraid we have made quite some noise here already.'

The wooden slats were opened and closed fast. 'No one that I can see.'

'Good that we are in Noida. If this was Lajpat Nagar, we would have had a small crowd outside already.'

'So what do we do?' Rishi asked, doing another quick up–down of the window slats. 'And why the fuck did your man not tell us there was someone inside?'

'People can't be expected to know everything.' Sudheer stood up from the chair, and Chuha cocked his gun against him and he sat down again. '*Jab in logon ko pata nahin ki inki behen kisko chod rahi hai, to behenchod mujhe kaise pata hoga? Aur English main ek kahaawat hai.* To err is human, and to forgive the man holding the loaded gun is divine.'

Chuha snapped his fingers, '*Aye, chhote bhai,* your sister is coming to. Put the tape on her mouth and tie her hands together.' Mohan hesitated and Chuha snapped his fingers again, then threw him a roll of wire he had carried with him. 'I don't want her running around this house, or shouting, we have made too much noise as it is.'

'This is Delhi. No one cares, and even if they do, we can handle them,' Sudheer said, his eyes still on the gun.

'When he learns what you did to his daughter, I am sure your father is going to care and I don't plan to handle him, thank you very much.'

'She fell, it was an accident.' The significance of what had happened was sinking in. Sudheer's voice trembled.

Mohan was still crouched at his sister's side, trying to put on the tape as gently as he could. 'I think he is right. Papa is not going to like this.'

'I am not afraid of him. The old man's gone soft, can't manage his damn business, can't manage his damn house.' Sudheer started to stand up again but looked at the gun still pointed at him and thought better of it. 'Remember, that's why we are here, we are doing what he can't do any more.'

By this time, Arijit had almost crawled his way over to Riti. Chuha strode over, pushed the heel of his boot into Arijit's back, and held it there, as if squashing a cockroach.

'Enough talk,' Chuha said. 'The original plan is out. We aren't taking this *behenchod* to my place. That's decided.'

'She won't,' Sudheer said. 'She won't tell anyone anything.'

Arijit struggled and squirmed under the weight of Chuha's shoe, but with his hands tied behind, and face down, he could do little else.

'Here is how it goes down. Rajkumari here goes to the hospital to get her head checked, and Rajkumar walks free. Our original plan is out. Because once she tells her papa how you two beat her up and some *rakshas* took her *rajkumar* away, *woh bilkul* sentimental *ho jayenge aur* police *ke bade bade lund ko bulayenge. Aur* police *Rohtak se Patna tak sab ki patloon utaarke sabki gaand sookhengi, aur sach batayoon toh, mujhe* police *se apni gaand ko bachana hai*. But if he is safe and sound, Rajkumari will be happy and your papa will be smart enough to let the police stay away. After all, *beti ki rangraliyaan* even he wouldn't want the world to find out.'

'That man is not walking free.' Mohan had stood up after taping Riti's mouth. 'He owes us, and not just for screwing our sister.'

Chuha shook his head. 'I am going to regret this tomorrow but I suppose it's the least entertainment I can provide, given how much you paid me. And I am sorry my man didn't notice the woman inside, yes, that was a mistake.'

'You don't have to do anything,' said Sudheer, 'and as you yourself so kindly said, you have fucked up enough for today. So just give me the gun and let me finish this.'

'*Ranjha ko Heer ke saamne maar doge to* your father may let you live, being as you are his son, but he sure won't spare me.'

'What do you have in mind?' asked Mohan.

'Ten minutes. Tops. We have been pushing our luck. *Aur kismat kunwaari ki choot ki tarah hoti hai, zyada ghusaya toh phaad jayenge.*'

Mohan asked once again, 'What do you have in mind?'

'Rishi ji, hold Rajkumar up, will you, but before that, let me see what's around.' He looked around the room – his man had been right, there was nothing there except big fat books and loads of electronics. 'Not a bat or a hockey stick,' grumbled Chuha.' Which man does not keep a bat and a hockey stick in his house. *Saala, teri behen hijre ko chod rahi hai.*'

Rishi yanked Arijit to his feet, and though he struggled with his hands tied, he was no match for Rishi's gym-made rippling muscles. Everyone saw now, Arijit's eyes glowing with rage, almost leaping out of their sockets, while he strained against his restraints.

'Look Mohan, look at his eyes. He is going all Sunny Deol–Balwant Rai *ke kutte* on us.' Sudheer laughed. 'Which movie was that?'

'I don't know, I don't watch that crap,' Mohan mumbled.

'*Abey yeh sab chutiyapa baad mein karna,*' Chuha said. 'And that dialogue is from *Ghayal*. Every Jat *ka puttar* knows this by heart.' Chuha laughed for a few seconds. Then he gestured towards Sudheer. 'Now that Rajkumar is standing up, punch him in the face. Punch him hard.'

Sudheer did not need to be told twice. He rushed forward and started throwing punches. Left, right, left, till after five, he was panting and doubling over, holding on to his knees.

'Yeh kya hai, mar rahe ho ya chumma de rahe ho?' asked Chuha. 'This kind of punching can throw down your sister, but on a man that's just foreplay. The problem with you, *motay*, is your entire body is jiggling, like a Punjaaban's flabby boobs, and the force is going everywhere. Let me show you how it's done. *Isko Patiala punch kehte hain.*

'See, you don't need to move your body while punching. Just stay steady, move hand back, and boom.' Chuha's fist cracked forward, straight on to the bridge of Arijit's nose, and you could almost see it move as it broke, and blood came streaming out. 'We do it like this, and this, and this. See, my body stays still.' Chuha was pummelling Arijit's face as Rishi struggled to hold him aloft with the impact of the punches, backing up against the wall for support.

'See,' Sudheer screamed at Riti, his eyes gleaming with hate. 'See what we do to your little friend. This is what happens when you fuck with our honour.'

Riti tried to get to her feet, her hands and mouth restrained, but Mohan caught hold of her from the back. She bawled through her restraints, begging them to let him go, and Sudheer just smiled. 'Just see what we do, just see.'

Blood was streaming down in little rivulets from Arijit's broken face. He was barely conscious, as he mumbled slowly into the tape covering his mouth.

Chuha stepped aside and looked towards Mohan. 'You want to take your turn, little brother?'

Mohan shook his head. Sudheer walked up, shoved Chuha to the side and brought out his Berretta. 'I will take his place.'

'*Saale, aankh dikahata hai,*' Sudheer grunted, '*Aankh.*'

He started hitting Arijit's eyes with rapid, overhand strikes using sometimes the barrel, and sometimes the handle. Arijit's eyes were already swollen and shut, a mangled mess of purple-red, and yet Sudheer did not stop.

'Take that *madarchod,* and that, and that. *Aaj se tu Romeo nahin rahega. Likh ke deta hoon.*'

'That's enough. I think we have all made our point. Let's go,' Mohan said, nervously looking out through the window slats.

Sudheer looked at his watch. 'The rat said ten minutes, *choot.* I still got four.'

It was two in the morning, and the house was dark in its silence. Arjun sat quietly outside Riti's bedroom, his face buried in his hands, rocking back and forth.

'Fortunately, Riti did not get a concussion,' the doctor had said, 'a cut on the head and a twisted ankle. Nothing to worry about Mr Bhatia, just get in touch with me if she feels dizzy or loses her balance.' There were two ayahs sleeping in the antechamber, in case she needed to get up, yet Arjun sat outside the room, not wanting to go anywhere far.

How had she come back? What were the men in New York doing? They were supposed to keep watch, to prevent exactly this from happening.

Arijit must have been involved somehow. If he could have gotten into the telephone system, he could have fooled those men in New York.

The poor bastard, Arjun thought, he had paid for all this.

Riti had wept, more than he had ever thought she would have to, when they had brought her in.

'They beat him without mercy,' she had said between sobs. 'They had his hands tied and mouth gagged and Sudheer punched his face again and again. Then they beat him with their guns and rolled him on the ground, and kicked him in the ribs and groin. Then one of them twisted and broke his leg, I could hear the sound, oh the sound, I can still hear it.' Arjun had sat impassively at her side, running his fingers through her hair. 'I cried so much, I told them to stop, I told them it was all my fault, but they had tied my hands and covered my mouth ...'

Arjun had sat similarly impassive when Sudheer and Mohan had come to his room, after the doctor had left. They had told him everything. How they had traced the Vantor leak to Arijit and how they had gone to teach him a lesson and how once inside he had found their sister with him. Through it all, Arjun said not a word.

'I lost my temper, I am sorry,' Sudheer said, 'but it was an accident. I had no intention of hurting her. I got angry, and don't tell me I had no right to, this was about our family's honour.'

Arjun had remained silent, just looking straight at Sudheer.

'I know you are mad at me, papa, but I am not going to bend over asking for your forgiveness. I did what I felt was right. Hell, if it was someone else, they would have killed their sister. For good reason too, because without honour, a woman's life means nothing. That is our culture, and you should know that.'

Preeti was standing there, right next to her sons, and she backed him up. 'We should never have sent her to America. See what she has become. A pervert.'

Arjun looked at Preeti and then back at Sudheer.

'Papa, I know your silent treatment. You want to make me shiver in fear,' said Sudheer. 'I am sorry if this offends you, but I have decided not to be scared of you. So if you take off your belt and beat me, as you had done once for selling your watch, I am ready to take it.'

Preeti moved over to Sudheer, touching his head affectionately. 'No, no ... nothing like that ...'

'I was out there taking care of business,' Sudheer continued. 'I found out who the enemy was, all by myself. Do I hear a thank you for that? No, I do not.'

Preeti said, 'I am sure your father understands how hard you have worked.'

'No, he does not, he never does.' Sudheer sniffled back his tears of anger. 'He will tell me to take responsibility and when I do something, and I do it right too, he clams up as if it were me who shamed the family.'

Mohan stood quietly in the background, looking at his feet. 'This is a big conspiracy, papa – Riti and Vantor, the link with Arijit cannot just be accidental.'

'Forget it, Mohan,' Sudheer said. 'He thinks we are too stupid to make the connection, because only he can. I know why he is angry – he is angry because we figured it out, and he could not. I mean, who will he look at tomorrow, and pity and shake his head? The only one of us that has ever mattered to him is Riti, anyway, forget it ...' Sudheer threw his arms up in disgust. 'I refuse to be your ugly, fat mistake any more, I refuse to stand like a dog outside your door, begging for you to pat my head, to consider me worthy of being your son. So as I said, go ahead, and beat me with a belt or a bat, but I won't apologize, I won't fall at your feet, I won't be scared.'

Finally, Arjun broke his silence.

'Beating you that one time, the way I did, that was wrong of me. I was angry for some other reason and I took it out on you. You were a small child and I should have known better. But my intention was honest. I wanted to teach you a lesson, that you should not steal and talk back to your elders, but maybe I ended up teaching you the wrong thing. That it was all right to hit someone you love, someone who cannot respond to your violence. I accept the responsibility for teaching you that.'

Preeti started to protest but Arjun silenced her with a raised finger.

'Now, about your *responsible* handling of this situation. Riti had told me about Arijit a few months ago, I knew about their relationship, I just hadn't told any of you yet. Because I had misgivings about the boy, about his real intent, and I was trying to find out. I knew he had been behind Vantor, and I was trying to get to his boss, something I don't think I will after the stunt you two pulled today. Because now everyone knows we know. And the ones behind him will cut those strings and go underground. So I hate to tell you this, but you screwed up. Again. As I expected you to.'

It took a few seconds for Preeti to process what Arjun had said. 'You knew your daughter was living in sin?'

'I didn't know she had come back from the US without telling me, and that somehow her calls were being forwarded from the US to here, so every time I was calling her in the US ... never mind ... but yes, I knew the rest.'

'You didn't feel it fit to tell me, her mother?' She was sobbing now.

'That's papa,' Sudheer said. 'He loves his family so much that he likes to keep them in the dark. Because you, me, Mohan, all of us are leeching off papa's money. Do as you want, but as I said, I am not scared of you.'

'As to you not being afraid of me, Sudheer,' Arjun said, 'I am happy that you are not. But, to be honest, I really was not giving what you just called the "silent treatment". I was just thinking to myself, what I will do to you should anything, and I mean anything, happen to Riti.' Arjun gently adjusted the collar of Sudheer's dishevelled shirt. 'What I will do then won't be for your improvement because I have given up on it. I will do what I want to because I will be angry and I will be out for revenge. Since you are all grown up, you can ask around. You can find out what's happened to those who have gotten on my wrong side, the ones who are still alive to tell you, that is. Now you may think I am too old, and too past my prime for you to care, and that may well be true but then you don't know that for sure. Now here is the question I want you to go home and think over. Do you want to find out?'

They had left soon after, and Arjun was sure that Sudheer was scared, in the way a father knows how his son feels, no matter how distant they may have become.

There was one more thing left to do. He put in a call to Dr Raheja, the director of the All India Institute of Medical Science, who he knew would be on duty at the hospital. He had gotten Arijit transferred to AIIMS from the hospital to which he had first been admitted, and Dr Raheja had assured Arjun he would personally look after Arijit. 'The son of a very old friend,' is what Arjun had said, 'Got into some bad company.'

Dr Raheja's voice was grim at the other end.

'His right eye has severe internal bleeding, and there are some lacerations on his skull. One of his ribs is broken and he has a compound fracture on his thigh. The face, I cannot even...'

'Will he live?'

'I think he will.'

'Any permanent damage?' he asked, dreading the answer.

'We don't know that yet. The swelling needs to go down for us to make a better evaluation. But I am afraid for the eye. And his right leg. I will come back tomorrow, and hopefully will have better news.'

He had gotten one of his men to call Nayantara earlier in the night, pretending to be from the hospital, telling her that Arijit had met with an accident. He wondered when she would be in the city, and how she would take the news. Would she come here, to his house, he wondered. Did she even know where he stayed? No, she would not come to him, he knew her well enough, and after today, she definitely never would. It was funny, Arjun thought, all these years they had been apart and he had never ever once thought that what they had between them would ever end. They might never meet each other again or share a cutlet in Mitra Cabin, but that didn't mean it was over.

Today he knew it was.

He dozed off on the chair and dreamt of sun-kissed gardens in Lahore, his mother's voice, and his brothers, in the distance, calling out to him from the wall. There he was, running towards them, when suddenly everything changed. There were now dark clouds like mountains in the sky, and all he could hear was the chug-chug of a hundred trains. He looked to the right, and saw lying on the lawn the old gentleman in the white suit he had seen on the platform, bloodied and battered. Arjun reached down to help, and the old man's face became Bangali's and he said, 'Live a little, *behenchod*,' before breaking into a hideous smile, and it was a corpse, its body buried in the ground, the skull sticking out, worms coming out of the eyes. Arjun kept running away from the corpse, but his brothers were gone, and the wall seemed to have moved further to the horizon, but now to his left was a funeral pyre, the wood crackling and hissing, columns of smoke rising to the sky. There were people standing round the pyre, familiar faces, some he could recognize, some he could not, and then he saw there was another pyre a distance away, and then further beyond, yet another, each with a crowd of silent mourners, all in white, gathered around. He looked at his shirt, there was blood on it, and yet he ran past the pyres, not daring to look too close for fear of discovering who lay on them, till in front of him stood Dr Raheja. He had in his hand a big brown cardboard box and a clipboard, and on seeing Arjun running towards him, struck the package out and said, 'Delivery for Arjun Bhatia.' Arjun tried to dodge him and run past, knowing what was in the package but not wanting to find out, but then everyone, from every pyre, turned around to look at him, and they all started laughing, till it echoed everywhere, the laughter, and he woke up in a cold sweat, his heart galloping, his hands cold, and Arjun felt fear, of the kind he had felt that night in Lahore, stacked up against sweaty bodies, waiting for death. He got up and paced up and down his palatial bungalow the whole night, deep in thought, and only when the sun's rays had broken through the darkness did he finally go to bed and sink into a dreamless sleep.

13

'BABUJI, EVERY TIME I SEE YOU, YOU SEEM TO HAVE GROWN thinner. Are you getting enough sleep?' Arjun liked Nimmi, Sudheer's wife, because even though she had been brought up in London and Geneva, she was still aware of the social graces of a Punjabi family in that she wore a sari at her in-laws' place, kept her eyes appropriately cast downwards, and spoke in a syrupy voice, soaked in concern, that Arjun could not but admire for its modulated correctness.

'What can I say? He doesn't listen to me any more. Stays awake all night, talks to people on the phone, and then all day talks even more,' Preeti said, shaking the golden bangles of her hand with vigour as she put paneer on her plate. 'See if you can talk some sense into him.'

Four months had passed since they had brought Riti home unconscious. Four months it had been since he had spoken to either of his sons. They would call and he would avoid the phone, and when they came, he would leave the house or lock himself in one of the rooms. But today was his birthday and that had always been celebrated with a big party on the lawn and VVIPs and musicians flown in from Pakistan or England, and even though he had begged off the celebrations this year citing poor health, Preeti insisted on having the brothers over for a family dinner.

'How long are you going to be angry at them?' she would keep saying in the weeks leading up to the birthday.

'They beat their sister up like she was an animal. What do you mean *how long am I going to be angry with them*?'

'They made a mistake,' she would say dramatically, 'they have been trying to say that and you won't even talk to them. What do you want them to do? Fall at your feet? Rub their noses in the ground?'

Preeti had gone at it, morning, afternoon and evening, wearing him down as the day came closer, till finally he had relented. And so they were all in the same room once again, the two brothers, sitting next to each other, big smiles pasted on their faces, everyone around trying their best to pretend that the last few months had not happened.

Riti was not at home that evening. She had been staying with Arjun ever since that day. Today she had gone out with a school friend of hers, and even Preeti, who had not stopped letting Riti know exactly how she had felt about her 'living in sin' these last few months, did not stop her from going. It would be best, both the parents realized, if she was not at home when the two brothers came, for even though they say time heals, it does not do so that quickly.

Sudheer said, his mouth full, a bit of curry dribbling down the side, 'She is right, papa. You look miserable. Have you got a check-up done? I mean a full physical, with what-they-call-it...' He looked towards Mohan, hoping for help.

'Yes, I have,' Arjun said dryly, 'the doctor told me I have a condition. It's called growing old.'

'Come on,' Nimmi said, flashing a whitened set of cosmetically improved teeth. 'You are not old.'

'I feel old,' he said, looking back at the reflection on the edge of his plate, which lay untouched, with the food on it. 'When you come to as many forks on the road as I have, the shadows of the paths not taken grow longer, and what you may not realize at your age is that shadows have weight, heavy enough to make you grow tired dragging them along.'

'Can you try to call them to see why they have not sent the cake yet?' Nimmi tried to change the topic, looking at her husband. 'It's almost nine now and I told them repeatedly to have it here by eight. You would think a five-star hotel would have better service than a bakery shop in Fatehnagar.'

Just then, Ramesh, the head of security of the house, a six-foot-something mountain of a man, stumbled heavily into the dining room.

'It's Riti ma'am,' he stammered, and his eyes betrayed panic as he looked nervously over his shoulder towards the passage.

'I thought she was ...' Preeti never completed the sentence.

For there in the doorway stood Riti.

She was in the same salwar kameez that she had had on when she left, except now she had sindoor on her forehead.

Right next to her stood Arijit. He held a cane for support, his right eye was covered with a white patch, and his once-handsome face still bore marks of the savage beating he had received. Sudheer's chair slid back and he stood up, Arjun shot his hand out to stop him, and Sudheer sat down again.

'Happy birthday, papa,' Riti said.

'What have you done? Oh my God, what have you done?' Preeti started moving towards her daughter when she caught Arjun's disapproving shake of the head through the corner of her eye, and stopped.

'I see you have brought a guest,' said Arjun calmly. 'Will you not join us for dinner?'

She shook her head. 'This is a family event.' She looked towards Sudheer. 'We are not welcome here.'

'And yet here you are,' said Arjun. 'So there must be a reason for coming. Not that I can't guess, looking at the sindoor, but please, go ahead, tell us why.'

'I came to tell you, and everyone else, that I am leaving. For good,' she said quietly. 'The black mark on this family, as mummy likes to call me these days, will go away...'

'Go away?' Preeti was crying now. 'What are you saying? You have already smeared our faces with the darkest ink and now you are going to do this? Is this why we brought you up? To see this day, that you would get married like this, like a thief, to some *loafer* from the road?'

Sudheer was trying his best to control himself, what with Nimmi noiselessly urging him to stay silent, but then he lost it. 'I should have killed him. I really should have. Maybe I would be rotting in jail by now but at least we would have had our honour.'

Arjun raised his voice. 'Enough. One more threat out of you, and I will get Ramesh here to throw you and your fake concern out of my house.' Sudheer bowed his head low and Nimmi made an angry face at her husband.

Arjun now looked squarely at Riti. 'I have told you before, I have no problems with who you marry, or the choices you make in life. But I will not accept this man. Because I know why he is doing this and it's not because of love.'

He then turned towards Arijit and folded his hands slowly. 'I am sorry. I am sorry for what my sons did to you. This does not come easy, folding my hands like this, but I know I have to answer for what they did.'

Arijit stayed stooped over his cane, and said nothing.

'But that does not mean I do not understand what you are trying to do.' Arjun pulled his hands back and kept them to the side of the plate. 'I understand your game.'

'That's it?' asked Riti. 'That's all you have to apologize to him for? That's what you have to answer for? Just for Sudheer and Mohan? How about what *you* did to his family?'

Arjun sat silent. No one spoke for a few seconds. Then Sudheer asked, 'What are you saying?'

'Ask papa,' Riti said. 'He knows what I am saying. Don't you?'

Arjun looked down, his head flopping forward to his chest, and Riti continued, 'I think it's only fair that all of us get to know why papa is so afraid of Arijit marrying me. So that before we understand his game, we know what papa's is.'

'Take that tone with your father and I will pull your tongue out, as if you haven't caused us enough shame,' Preeti yelled, and took two threatening steps forward, when Mohan stood up and got in front of his mother.

'Pulling my tongue out or blinding his eye won't change the truth,' Riti said, her voice as low as before, 'of what this family is. Of what papa really is.'

Arjun adjusted his shirt, and stood to his full height. 'Let me tell you what Riti is talking about. Arijit's father was my best friend. We were in the gun business together. He met with an accident many years ago, and his family blames me for what happened.'

'You killed him,' Riti said. 'At least be honest. It's not that anyone will make you pay for your crimes – you have bought out the whole world.'

'Oh my God,' gasped Preeti, clutching the end of her sari to her mouth. 'Oh my God, it's her son. It's their son.'

'Is that all?' Riti asked. 'Or have you still forgotten something?'

'After his father died,' Arjun's voice quivered, 'I had an affair with his mother.'

Nimmi gasped and then looked at everyone, worried that her reaction had been noted.

'Not just that, you left after you got bored of her.'

'Is that what he told you?'

'He does not need to tell me everything. I can figure things out on my own.'

He sighed, suddenly feeling exhausted. 'If it pleases you, if you believe it humiliates me further, I will say that too. Yes, I did kill your father. Because if I hadn't he would have killed me. It had come down to that.'

Riti said, 'Thank you. Thank you for this final bit of honesty.'

'Why, Riti, why are you talking to me like this?' Arjun sank into his chair. 'You have always been the most polite, the most gentle of all my children.'

'I was gentle because that was how I had been raised to be. A little flower. Papa, don't you see that I see it now? I have been living in a bubble. And I would have all my life had not my brothers put a tape on my mouth and made me watch them thrashing nearly to death the man I love, while laughing among themselves. I have thought long and hard over this, and though I will never forgive my brothers for what they did, for taking away Arijit's eye, I realize that they are not all to blame. For they are just the symptoms of an evil that exists in this house. You.'

'Do you want your boyfriend to lose his other eye and then beg in front of Jama Masjid?' asked Sudheer. 'And do you need a few slaps to knock some sense into you? How dare you speak to papa like this?'

Arjun gave Sudheer another withering glance and he once again looked away.

'It is because of you, papa, that Sudheer and Mohan are the way they are. They do not need to stop at murder because they know that in this city nothing will happen to them. They know this is what their father did when he was young and, look how he got away because everyone was scared of him. They were trying to make you happy, and that's what I find so sad, that the only way to earn your love is by being more fearsome than you.'

'I have never expected that of you. Nor from my sons. That they should make people afraid of them.'

'Of course not from me. I am a daughter, the wallflower. Of course I am not expected to punch out eyes and break ribs. That kind of bravery is for the boys. For me, the measuring stick is different. I should nod and obey and carry the tray during Diwali.'

'I never brought you up like that, and you know it.'

'Accept it. You only want obedience. From the world. From your family.'

'He has poisoned your mind against me,' Arjun said sadly. 'As I was sure he would.'

'See, that is precisely the problem. I cannot have an opinion. It has to be someone else planting ideas in my mind, because I do not have a brain of my own. That's what you feel, all of you.'

'This is not about you. It's about him and me. I know him.' He pointed towards Arijit. 'If I was in his place, and I wanted revenge, this is exactly what I would do. I would take out the thing my enemy values the most, the one thing he can never win back.'

Riti raised her voice for the first time, thumping her heel into the ground. 'But he is *not you*. He does not think like you. I know you will never believe me. So from today I have taken the decision not to even try. Whatever he is, or whatever you chose to believe, he is my husband. That's how it is, and that's how it will always be.'

Arjun's lips pursed into a straight line. 'Arijit, this is for you. You have won this round. I concede defeat. You have come into my house, on my birthday no less, taken my daughter from me, and you have shamed me in front of the people I love the most, and this is more than you could have done in years of sniping away at my business interests. So yes, you won this.'

Arijit spoke for the first time. 'I never asked Riti to say what she did. I never wanted to shame you. I would never have told her anything had it not been for what happened that day. She wanted to know why you were so determined that I was here to take revenge, and I told her why you might think so.'

'So, you have nothing against me, right? Absolutely nothing?' Arjun asked. 'The Vantor thing was just...I don't know...you tell me.'

'When did I say I have nothing against you? I do. Not because of what you did to my family, but because of what you have done to this country. Governments change, yet nothing changes for the people because of men like you, who don't play fair, who rule without the responsibility, who sit in their palaces and move their paid pawns.' Arijit hobbled for a moment on his stick. 'It's not you the man that's the problem, uncle, it's what you stand for. '

Arjun mock-clapped slowly. A sharp smile lit up his face. 'That's a nice little monologue. Not Salim–Javed quality nor do you carry it off like Dilip Kumar but still I will give you a few paise for the delivery.' He turned his attention to his daughter, sombre again.

'Riti, I respect your decision, but now I must ask you to respect mine. Never, and I mean never again, as long as you are with this man, come back to this house.'

'Gladly.'

'You have turned your back on this family,' Arjun continued, his voice flat. 'The family will do the same. You have tried to humiliate me in front of those I love. And so the doors of my heart and my house close on you forever.'

'I am sorry you feel that way.'

'In return for that consideration, I will make sure that my sons don't try to go after you or your husband, but if your husband continues taking shots at my business, I will be free to deal with him, in my own way. '

'So what you are saying is you won't let Sudheer and Mohan try to kill him, this time you will do it yourself.'

'Take it as you may,' Arjun said. 'I won't defend my motives nor explain my methods to outsiders. You are an outsider now. That is how it will stay.'

They stood for a while, silent, each holding their positions, except for Preeti who kept weeping, her head perched on Mohan's shoulder. Struggling to turn himself around while balanced on the cane, Arijit patted Riti's shoulder and said, 'Come on, let's go. There's nothing more for us here.' They walked away and the frozen silence stayed behind, till Arjun stood up and said, 'Thank you all for coming. And I hope you don't mind if I don't stay for the cake.'

Much later that night, Arjun sat in his study, his legs propped up on the table while looking out through the window. It was dark in the room, the only light coming from the lawns outside, when Arjun received a visitor. Not really a visitor, for she was his wife, but Preeti rarely came to his study, and definitely not when Arjun had locked it from inside.

'I wanted to say something,' she said, and Arjun could see even in the dim light that her eyes were puffy and swollen. He moved to turn on the light.

'No, let it be.'

They sat together on the couch, not touching, a giant wall of emptiness between their shoulders.

'You told me it was over with her.'

'It was. It is over.'

'Have you met her since?'

He did not reply, not for a while.

'Look, I don't care if you have been with other women. I just want the truth.'

'I might not have been the best of husbands. But I am not like that.'

'Have you met her since?'

He nodded.

'When?'

'Only to tell her to get her to control her son, to tell him not to meet Riti.'

'She didn't listen?'

He shook his head.

'I want you to make some promises. Will you keep them?'

'I need to know what they are first.'

'You trust me, don't you?'

'I still would need to know what you want me to do before I promise.'

'You will not take Riti back. No matter how much she begs and how hard she pleads, no matter what happens to her, you will not let her come back.'

'She won't come back, she is a stubborn girl.'

'I know you want her to. I know you care for her in a way you don't care for our sons.'

'I guess you are right. I care for her the most. She is the kindest and gentlest of all our children.'

'And yet Sudheer and Mohan would never ever dare to talk to you the way she did. They would never sleep with your enemy. They would never have shamed you like this.'

'I don't want to argue with you about them, not today, please.'

'You promise? You will not take her back. Promise me that.'

'I promise,' he said with a grudging nod of his head.

'And I want you to promise that you will finish this viper and his slut of a mother. You will destroy them and you will not show them any mercy.'

'I can't, because he has Riti. Don't you see he has taken her hostage?'

'But Riti means nothing to you, that's what you just said.'

'I never said that.' Arjun raised his finger. 'Don't put words in my mouth. I said I promise not to take her back.'

'She is not our daughter any more.'

'She is mine. And always will be.'

'Then what is the point of the promise?'

'The point is I will do as you asked. She will never be a part of my life again. She will not get a paisa from me, she can never stay in my house, but that doesn't mean I will knowingly put her in danger.'

'Okay then, I want another promise. You will never see that witch again.' Preeti swallowed back a fresh burst of tears. 'It's not because I am jealous. I used to be once, not any more. It's because you visiting her will be seen as approval for this marriage. You may not care for your status any more, but I do, I do care what people say about our family, about you. Because tomorrow people will start talking, all over the city. Because tomorrow you won't be Arjun Bhatia, tomorrow you will be someone whose daughter eloped and married beneath our standing.'

'I promise.'

'On Sudheer's head? You promise?'

'That's silly, I don't do such things.'

'You have to.'

He mumbled something, she stood up to walk away, and then turned around to face him again.

'You wouldn't know this, but the first day I saw you, you were working under a car. Mirwaiz, remember him?'

'Of course I do.'

'He was holding the garage jack, and fooling around, as he usually did.'

'Poor kid, went to Azamgarh during the riots, never came back.'

'I couldn't see your face, just the top of your head and those arms. I remember your arms then. They were lean and muscular, they had sweat and grease all over, and Mirwaiz was saying 'What happens if the car drops on you, Ustaad?' and you said, 'I can hold the car up with my thumb.' There was something in your voice that made me believe that you could really do that, and that a car was nothing or even a truck, you could hold the world up if you wanted to do. You did, for all these years, hold the world up. And

I will not, as long as I live, let anyone bring that world down on us, be it your daughter.' She paused. 'Or even you.'

Sudheer adjusted the plush satin pillows around his lower back and gently shook his bottom from side to side. The heated water-bed responded softly in rhythm and he could not help but smile, despite all the trouble he was in. Ordering this bed from an American mail order catalogue was one of the best decisions he had ever taken – it almost seemed to balance out his choice of wife – and the smooth, satiny and wobbly sensation on his body made him feel sexy, in the way his nights never could. He sighed deeply, rotated his shoulders, reached out to the night table on his left and took the topmost magazine. This will do, he thought with satisfaction, the latest issue. He reached out to the right, took a little squirt from the lubricant bottle, glided his hand down through the opening of the front of his pyjamas, and started leafing through. The images of naked, buxom women in various imaginative contraptions filled the pages. Nimmi didn't mind him doing this in bed, perhaps because it meant she would not have to, her conditions being, as she had put it so joylessly, 'Don't do it when I am in bed and wipe yourself and your thing clean once done, I don't want our bedroom to smell like a hovel on GB Road.' He was getting into a nice rhythm when he heard Nimmi's voice, and he turned soft immediately.

'Will you stop that? We need to talk.'

He looked up and there she was, standing in the doorway, turned slightly to the side, in a nightdress he had not seen her wear before. It was cream and lace, hugging her body, the light silhouetting her curves, and Sudheer could not help his eyes straying to her ample behind, which he admired even more now that she had put on weight. If it were anyone else, he would have thought she was trying to seduce him, the way she stood, but more than a year of marriage had taught him that if there was anything she disliked more than visiting her in-laws, it was having sex with him. Once he had said, in the way of a complaint, 'When we are doing it, you look as excited as if you are watching the 8.40 news on Doordarshan,' to which she had spat back, 'The news at least lasts for 20 minutes. You are more like an advertisement. Twenty seconds and done.' Nimmi had a tongue on her, and not in a good way, and Sudheer resented this rude intrusion into the highlight of his day.

He dutifully put the magazine to the side.

'So how did the meeting with papa go?'

Oh, so that was it, thought Sudheer.

'None of your business,' he said grumpily, reaching for the magazine.

They had met earlier in the day in Ranvijay Pratap Singh's bungalow on Aurangzeb Road, on the green lawns, to a heavy breakfast served by his army of impeccably liveried servants. There was Mohan to the right of the head of the table, and Nimmi's father, Praveen Ahuja, in a Saville Row suit to his left. Also at the table were the finance secretary and Ranvijay Pratap Singh's son whose name Sudheer did not remember because he was known simply as 'Rocky' and, right opposite him, the old man, RP himself, in a long kurta and a brown shawl. That he was down there as the host, pouring tea for his guests, was a sign as big as any that this meeting was important.

'Beta,' he had said, in a gentle cajoling voice. 'We would of course like you to talk about this with your father. I would have asked him myself – we go way back – but as you know, your father has not been very communicative of late. Not that I don't understand, with what your family has been through.' He stirred the milk into his tea. 'But time is so short, I think it's better you do this on your own.'

Ever since Riti had left, Arjun had retreated into a shell. He still ran the business, but he rarely met any of his clients, letting his underlings handle negotiations. Sudheer had tried to suggest that he should hold durbars again, at least for the most important of his clients, because they didn't always appreciate working with hired help but Arjun had brushed the suggestion aside, as he did with more or less everything Sudheer said.

This was a big deal though. The government was conducting a fire-sale of public sector units, disinvesting mostly in iron and steel, and RP had worked hard to undervalue the assets through his people in the ministries. Which meant there were crores to be made by just winning the tenders, and selling the assets in the open market. Mohan had explained to Sudheer that the moneymakers would not be the machinery, but the future contracts the units held. Those future contracts had not even been priced as part of the asset sale, which meant that the government would be handing out millions in free money, and Sudheer knew that Nimmi's father, who had recently bought a number of steel plants in Eastern Europe and the country formerly known as USSR, was the first in line to lap it all up.

There was a problem though. The Mehtas. They were the biggest family business in India, with the power to outspend any opposition, and no businessman worth his name would make a big play without knowing their plans.

'We have to know the Mehtas' position. Do they plan to bid for the public sector undertakings through front companies? Do they want to sit out? If they are planning to bid, would they be open to an agreement, a share? We have to know all this before we put up the money,' RP had said, wrapping the shawl round his shoulders and coughing mildly. 'Now the Mehtas were once my men and I could have handled this myself then. But then your father took them away from me, many years ago, and now they talk only to him. No one else.'

Sudheer had asked, 'So you want me to talk to the Mehtas? Bring them to the table?'

Rocky had been to the point. 'Yes. But without involving your father. We need to move fast, real fast, and Arjun uncle has kind of become like a government department himself.'

'No disrespect to Arjun,' RP had interrupted his son with a mild glance of irritation. 'But we think, *all* of us think, that it would be better if you took the lead on this deal. I mean the Mehtas talk only to Arjun, but in real terms, they talk to the Bhatias. If you know what I am saying.'

The significance of what RP was suggesting was not lost on him. Only Mohan said it aloud first, 'You want us to go behind papa's back and talk to Mehta pretending as if we are speaking for papa.'

The silence from the rest of the table confirmed that.

'But if you want us to do this, we need to know why,' Mohan continued. 'You have to stop this "we need to do this fast" bullshit, because that's a line used by salesmen when they are desperate for a sale.'

It was Praveen Ahuja who spoke. 'We are not lying to you, getting something through Arjun ji does take a lot of time nowadays. And, I don't know how to say this better, given that we are related, but Arjun ji costs a lot of money. A bit too much, and that also people are willing to pay, but then you know...you have to move things fast.'

Sudheer looked angrily at his father-in-law and banged the cup down on the plate forcefully. 'You think we are wholesale cloth suppliers in Chandni Chowk, that we are going to undercut our own father?'

RP caughed softly once again and said, 'It's not money Mr Ahuja is talking about. If we went to your father, no one knows when he would talk to us. Even if he did, he would then bring in other partners, work other angles, and that's all fine for him because that's the way he runs his business but, right now, we don't need all that.' He reached out and gave a loving pat on Rocky's shoulder. 'I don't blame Arjun. He and I are old people, of Hindustani classical and of five-day Test matches, we move to a different rhythm. Your generation, it's all pop music and one-day cricket and I can't tolerate either, but I know better than to stand in front of the stream.'

Sudheer had realized the opportunity this held for him, but his answer had been non-committal. And now his wife was pushing him on that, obviously at her father's insistence.

'Papa said you said nothing,' Nimmi said, looking back at Sudheer. 'Do you want that to be your answer? Nothing?'

'What your father is asking me to do, I can't. I am in enough trouble with the old man from the last time I did something on my own. If he finds out now I went behind his back ...'

'Oh please. You did the right thing. You behaved, for once, like a man. I so wish my husband would do more of that. Be a man.'

'That's not the way papa saw it. I have had enough of "being a man" for some time now.'

Nimmi moved her feet up and rolled on to the waterbed. She bounced slightly, and with it her cleavage did too, revealing even more as she lay on her stomach, the mangalsutra nestling in between.

'This is a bit different from what you did last time, right? You almost killed those two, not that I am saying that would have been a big loss to the world, but I can understand why he would be angry, she being his daughter and all.'

She rolled once again, and playfully kept her hand on Sudheer's chest. 'I hate your sister. I can't go to one party without hearing whispers and rumours about her, and of course they make sure that I get to hear. Do you know anything about where she is now?'

'Don't know and don't care,' Sudheer said with a wheeze, feeling intensely the soft fingers of his wife moving down his chest. 'Well, what are the rumours about her?'

'Leave it, it would make you angry.' Nimmi's long red fingernails seemed to sink into Sudheer's soft, flabby chest.

'Go ahead. You wouldn't have told me if you didn't want to tell me.'

'They say she is a high-class call girl and that her husband pimps her out. One person even claimed ... you know ... that he knows someone who has ... you know ... done her.'

'My sister, working? Even as a call girl? Now that's funny.' Sudheer laughed, a big guttural laugh, shaking the folds of fat on his chest and his stomach like rings of jello. 'She never saw what it means to be poor. I did. Papa had lost all his money and Mohan and I had to be taken out of school because he could not afford to pay our fees. Riti was too small then. She never saw that life. As long as she can remember, life has been Geneva, Monaco or New York, all paid for, and not even the heat of this blasted city. How long has she even been in India?'

'I was just saying what I heard.'

'Riti cannot work a single day in her life, unless you call shopping at Spencer's or Macy's work.'

'You say that but I don't think so, I mean why would she have gone with that man then? He looked like a beggar on a local train.' She touched her palm to her forehead and made the sign of begging. '*Allah ke naam pe kuch de de* types.'

'Hah, he looked like a hero when we found him though. *Saala* Romeo.'

'Well, seeing what you did to him, Aamir Khan and Salman Khan have nothing to fear.'

He grunted and moved a bit closer so that her breasts were pressed against the side of his chest. She seemed to press back.

'He is just a phase in Riti's life, her little rebellion against papa. It's like this. When your life has no problems, you need to invent them, else why are you alive? The moment that idiot asks her to work, which I am pretty sure he will once he realizes she isn't bringing any money from this house, she will come running back with her tail between her legs.'

'It's been more than six months now since your sister ruined that cake I got for your father.'

'Give it a year. Remember what papa had said. *The door of this house closes on you forever*. He was sending a message to her husband. No money from here. Of course papa didn't mean it, papa loves her more than his life. The moment her husband turns her out, papa will take her back. She will be married off somewhere abroad, and her misadventure will be forgotten, unless of course the bastard puts his little seed in her, which I am sure he will want to do as soon as he can, because that will be his insurance.'

'What about putting your seed in me?' Her hand had now gone down to his fly, which he could not see any more, hidden as it was by his surging belly.

He wanted to ask her why she was being so agreeable tonight, and then he didn't because he knew why, so he closed his eyes and felt the motion down below, as her hair fell on his stomach, covering it, and he felt thankful that for a few seconds he mattered.

It was then the decision was taken.

He would do as Nimmi's father wanted. He would talk to the Mehtas.

'*Dada-babu* and *boudi*, they haven't been here for a while?' Sonali asked, her back propped against the big Godrej almirah, as she munched on puffed rice and looked up at the framed picture of Arijit and Riti on the shelf.

'You are distracted today. I have been trying to teach you this song for the past hour, and there you go again,' Nayantara said, her left hand on the harmonium. She could not bear to look at that picture any more, for it reminded her of how her son used to look, once upon a time, handsome and with both eyes that could see, and yet she could not take it down and put it away, like she had the other pictures.

'No, no,' Sonali said, sticking her tongue out and making a face of contrition, 'it's just that I have to go right now to the Haldars and do the dishes. I will be back in half an hour, and then we can start again.'

'I have nothing better to do, so I am going to wait here for you holding my harmonium?' Nayantara asked. 'No, you don't have to come back, I am angry.'

Sonali had a large toothy grin which she now flashed. 'Please, *didimoni*, I will make it up to you with a nice cup of ginger tea.'

'Fine,' said Nayantara, her mock frown dissolving away. 'By the way, they haven't caused any trouble for Rupali, have they?'

'Not after you spoke to them, *didimoni*, you are the goonda of the area,' Sonali said with another titter.

Goonda. Ruffian. Nayantara made a tired gesture with her hand, wondering when she had become an enforcer herself. Perhaps, as they say, when you hang out with the wrong crowd, you become like them.

Rupali was Sonali's sister. They lived in the slum down the road and both worked as maids. A few days ago, Rupali had come back crying, because the man of one of the houses where she worked had tried to pull her on to his bed. She was afraid because he was the local councillor from the ruling party. When Nayantara had come to know of this, she had gone to his party office, where he stayed all day with his bunch of louts playing cards and carrom, and had a few words with them. There must have been something about the way she had given them a piece of her mind, because they stayed quiet all through.

I am not afraid any more and they can sense that. There is nothing they can take from me that has not been taken yet.

Today she felt happy in a loopy sort of way. There was no reason to be happy, not after what had happened to Arijit, but she just did. She had to get up and make something for herself, because the sun was going down and there was nothing in the fridge. But she didn't want to stand in front of the gas stove, at least not before she had the ginger tea that Sonali had promised. Though she knew Sonali hadn't gone to work today because she had seen the Haldars leave in a taxi with suitcases tied to the top of the Ambassador, which meant she was probably flirting around with that Bihari guard from the new multi-storeyed building. It would take her more than half an hour to get back.

Love, Nayantara wondered, what a strange little thing that was. She had seen that Bihari guard walking down the road, checking out every woman that passed by, and he reminded her of Nilendu, the height, the broad shoulders and the roving eye, and could not help but think Sonali would probably end up like her. Or maybe she was a smart girl, though Nayantara was not quite so sure of that, and would take a different path. The girl did have a sweet voice and very good musical memory and she was gifted with a good hand for the sewing machine. But then I had all of that too, Nayantara thought, and look what happened to me.

There was a lovely breeze outside, rustling through the leaves. The sky was painted in a palette of red and yellow, and the birds were flying home for the day. Two kites swayed crazily up above, and there at the corner house, was a boy and his father holding them up. That boy reminded her of Arijit, he always did – there was some similarity though she never could figure out what it was, or maybe she had reached that point where everyone that age reminded her of Arijit. She sat near the window, watching the kite and the birds fly, lifting her legs up so that they were balanced on the sill. She started humming one song after another, some that her mother had taught her, some she had learned herself, tapping her thigh with her palm in rhythm, looking upwards.

Everything was finally perfect.

When Sonali came back, almost two hours had passed.

'Sorry, *didimoni*, it took a bit longer than I expected, let me make the tea for you.' The words had barely tumbled out of her mouth when she noticed Nayantara lying on the ground, slumped over to the side.

'*Didimoni, didimoni*, are you all right?' Sonali bent down, shaking her by the shoulder.

There were two perfect wet lines down Nayantara's cheeks where the tears had rolled down, and yet there was just a hint of a smile still on her lips.

Nayantara Banerjee was no more.

Arjun Bhatia looked to his left, and then to his right. It was eight, and there was a cricket match going on. He could hear the commentary coming from multiple houses, which meant there was little chance that anyone would see him. He bent forward, took something out from his pocket, and popped the lock. The last time he had broken a lock was thirty years ago but it felt just like yesterday. It took him a bit more time though, but then again his hands had never shaken like this before, and when the rusty Godrej lock gave way, he breathed easy, unbolted the door and stepped in. The numbness returned to his arms and legs and he stood there alone in the dark.

He had felt the numbness the day the call had come from Calcutta. It was as if the news was a drug, the type that doctors inject you with before an operation, draining all the sensation away from his arms and legs. At first he could not believe what he heard, and then once he could, he had not been sure what to do. He would not make it to her last rites, he could not, because Arijit and Riti would be there and because he had promised his wife, and yet he had to, just had to, say goodbye, even if it was a hurried visit in the dark, silent like a thief, to the place where they had met for the very last time.

Arijit was selling off this place, Arjun's men had told him, and they were giving Nayantara's stuff away just as she had wanted, so there was not much time left before everything was gone. As he moved his torch around, being careful not to turn the lights on lest he alert the neighbours, he realized he may be too late. The living room was almost empty, the table was gone, so were the shelves and the pictures and the chairs, except one chair whose leg was broken, and no one had wanted to take that. Arjun walked into the bedroom and that too had been emptied, the bed was not there though the steel almirah stood heavy, perhaps too ancient for people's taste. It was open, its contents gone with a few saris still left in the corner. There were boxes packed everywhere, cobwebs on the wall where furniture had been, and Arjun moved the spotlight of his torch around, hoping to recognize something that would trigger a memory, something that held meaning, something of Nayantara that he would recognize.

He felt forlorn, like he was standing at a desolate station after the last train had left. There was nothing remaining of the person who had once been here, nothing to hold on to, nothing to take back.

It was silly of me to come, he thought, as he turned towards the door. In the darkness, his foot hit something hard and he winced in pain. Turning his torch downwards, he saw what it was.

A trunk.

His heart skipped a beat. He recognized that trunk. Even more than the trunk, he recognized the lock.

They had bought the lock together from New Market, and he sank to his knees and ran his fingers over the dials. A number-lock.

Could it still be?

He turned the black dials slowly, scared that it would not open. But it did. She had not changed the combination all these years. It was the numbers of his birthday.

The trunk opened and Arjun felt it then, as if his heart was in the grip of a monstrous vice and someone was turning the lever.

Right on top was his shirt, the one he had left behind the last day, folded and neatly ironed. He took it out and placed it on the ground. Below that, there were piles of saris that they had bought for her together, and between the folds he found the framed picture that used to be on the wall, of him and Bangali. There was another picture, not framed, but he recognized it immediately, from the one time he had taken her to a studio on Park Street. She had hated all her pictures except this, and he looked at it, and there she was, as heart-wrenchingly beautiful as always. Arjun ran his index finger over the picture and then he put the black-and-white photo in his shirt pocket.

The journey had been worth it.

He riffled through the rest of the trunk, hoping to find something there, maybe another picture, just something more he could take back.

Then he felt it. An envelope.

Was there a note in it? Had Nayantara left for him a last message, a goodbye, in a trunk which only he could open?

He quickly opened the flap. There was no letter inside.

Instead there were movie ticket stubs. Ten, twenty, perhaps more. Every movie they had ever gone to together at Roxy, Tiger and Globe.

Arjun recognized them all. He turned the envelope over, and that was all there was. Movie ticket stubs. Little scraps of what had been the best time of his life.

He sat there on his knees for some time, not moving.

And then he curled into a ball on the ground and wept like he never had in his life.

It was late at night, close to two, when he returned to Taj Bengal. The receptionist at the front looked at him with an expression of concern.

'Sir, there were several calls for you from your residence in Delhi in the past thirty minutes. They said it's very urgent.'

Arjun didn't want to talk to anyone back home, not tonight anyway.

'Sir, I insist. Please call home. It is very, very urgent.'

'Did they say what it was about?'

She shook her head.

He dialled the number. It rang and then rang some more.

Strange, he thought, where are the servants? Where is security?

He tried again. This time someone picked up.

'Hello,' he said into the receiver.

From the other end came deep, laboured breathing, and then Preeti spoke.

'Come home, come home, please.'

'Why? What's happened?'

'It's Sudheer... he is... they...' and her voice broke into heavy sobbing.

14

SUDHEER STOOD OUTSIDE, HOLDING ON TO THE PILLAR FOR support, as the driver pulled the red Jaguar out to the front and on to the gravel. He tottered forward towards the door, and yelled, '*Aye*, you at the wheel, get out.'

The driver, a young man with a small moustache, looked back at him alarmed.

'Sahib, you cannot drive now. Let me...'

The other drivers were standing there, all looking at this little scene in amusement, the fat man in the inappropriately tight shirt, wheezing from the excitement and the drink, shouting at the top of his voice at this small driver. They knew who he was and so they stayed back, and they were happy that they did, because Sudheer reached to the side of his trousers and brought out a gun.

'*Madarchod,* now will you let me drive or will you not?'

The driver obediently opened the door and stood to the side.

'Get in,' Sudheer said, still brandishing his gun. 'You are going to sit there.' He pointed to the back seat.

'Sahib, I will go home on my own.' The driver, who had just joined a month ago, wanted no further part in this.

'*Main maalik aur tu naukar. Samjhe? Main jo bolunga, tu woh karega. Agar gadi ki* exhaust pipe *ko apne gaand mein ghusaane ko boluun,* pant *utaarke ghusayega. Samjhe?* Now get in the fucking car.'

The driver obeyed, turning once towards the other drivers and security, hoping for some help. Some looked away, some smiled, some shook their heads.

They sped out of the gates towards the Gurgaon–Mehrauli highway. Despite being drunk, Sudheer felt steady at the wheel, though at this hour of the evening on a weekend, the roads were not crowded, and even the cars that were there were pushed to the side in front of the speeding Jaguar.

'You know why I am driving?' asked Sudheer, his words slurred. 'And why you are sitting in the sahib's seat?'

The driver shook his head. 'No, sahib.'

'Because I will become a driver, that's the only thing I am good for.' He laughed out loud. 'That's all my father thinks I am good for. You, *madarchod,* are my first ride.' He moved one hand from the steering wheel and made a mock salute.

It was only yesterday that he had come to know of it. Arjun had removed him from the big airline deal after all the work he had put in. He had wanted to meet his father, but even that he could not do nowadays without going through his underlings. In desperation, he had called Arjun.

'I am not taking you away from anything. I only want you to go through Mathur. He has his men in the civil aviation ministry, and he has worked there himself,' Arjun had said.

Sudheer had interrupted angrily. 'Stop lying to me, papa. You are giving me a minder.'

'Whatever you want to think,' Arjun had said brusquely, and then paused, as if deliberating on what to say. 'And if you do want the truth, yes, you have screwed this whole thing up so far. But then, what's new?'

'So what can I do to make it up?' asked Sudheer. 'Drive Mathur around? Carry his files? Polish his shoes? Drop his children to school?'

'The problem with you, among a hundred, is that you don't know how to finish a job.'

I will show you, when I pull the deal with the Mehtas and make crores for my father-in-law and RP. I will finish this one good.

Sudheer rolled down the window and took in the night air. Usually a night of drinking helped relieve the pain, but not today. He was already feeling hung over when he should have been feeling high, his stomach churning like a fifteen-year-old's after downing his first Bacardi.

It was the party. He just shouldn't have come. This was the crown jewel of Rocky's farmhouses, the biggest by far in Chhattarpur – a large swimming pool and acres of sprawling lawns with large marble statues of naked Greek gods scattered intermittently along its length. Since this was Rocky's party, Rishi would not be invited. They had a beef from college, something silly about some bet on a cricket match that Rocky had not paid up, and any time their groups met at a club or at a party, there would be words thrown and sometimes fists. Mohan also had backed out with some mumbled excuse, which meant he was screwing one of his girlfriends tonight, the lucky bugger, or staying home with his toy trains and jigsaw puzzles, and Sudheer could never figure out why Mohan did that. The Khanna brothers had gone to London for a wedding, Puneet was on his honeymoon in Pattaya, and Surinder, God knows where he was passed out, because he didn't pick up the phone. So here he had come, without his posse, and the party list was of course mostly Rocky's friends, and the usual hangers-on one gets used to seeing at these parties – the models, the small-time actresses and star-struck college girls, none of whom he cared to know or fuck, which is why he had sat at the bar all evening, drinking and sulking, and looking towards the dance floor at the swaying hips and jiggling boobs from time to time, before sinking back into his glass.

Then the DJ started playing a remixed version of 'Saat Samundar Paar', and it must have been the tequila shots or just that he loved the song, but he had gotten up, slammed the drink on the bar table, and stomped over to the dance floor. Then he had started to dance, and within seconds, his shirt was drenched to the skin with sweat and yet he kept shaking every fold of fat in his body, huffing and panting from the effort. There was a little circle for him now, people were standing around, with Sudheer swaying his arms and his legs every way, which is when 'Saat Samundar Par' melded into 'Tu Cheez Badi Hai Mast'. Sudheer went to do the Akshay Kumar pelvic thrust, when right at that moment a little edge of the whisky hit his head, his legs flew out below him, and he landed on the floor with a heavy thud and rolled ingloriously to the side. He looked up, everyone was smiling, and there was this one man, standing between two girls, holding each of them by their waists, who just exploded with laughter.

'Look at that fat pig. Just look at him.' He slapped one of the girls on her butt. 'Get up, get up, piggie, and shake your tail.' He reached into his wallet, took out some currency notes and circled them around over his head. The two girls seemed to find that very amusing, and all that Sudheer heard, over the music and the giggles, was their laughter, and, just like that, the whole world seemed to be laughing at him at once.

He got up, struggling against the lightness of his head and the slippery floor below his shoe, reached to the side of his trousers, and, still off balance and tottering, fished out his .22, disengaged the safety and pointed it straight.

He saw the man properly now, big eyes bulging out from his forehead, dressed in his fifties like he was in his twenties. The girls were moving away, colour drained from their faces in fear, and the man took a few steps back.

'You know who I am, *behenchod*?' Sudheer waved his gun around unsteadily. 'My name is Sudheer Bhatia and ...' He reached to the side to stop his trousers from sliding down further, held as precariously as they were by the rising slope of his butt.

The man threw his hands up, and the floor was emptying fast now, the shrieks of girls rising above the thump of the music.

'Come on, yaar, *thodi masti kar rahe the.*' The man had raised his hands in surrender. He was scared.

'*Tab,*' Sudheer had said, '*tu mast hi marega.*'

Was he going to press the trigger? Of course he wasn't, he wasn't that far gone, but then that bastard's scaredy-cat face made the charade worth it.

Maybe I would have shot him, thought Sudheer, had not the bouncers gotten to me first. Those bastards had been too strong. Rocky had run in from God knows where he had been, and then they all had led him away to a private room.

Once the door had been closed, Rocky had shouted at him,

without even a bit of respect for who he was. 'Are you out of your mind? Do *you* know who that is?'

'All I know is that *chutiya* is alive whereas he should be dead right now,' Sudheer had slurred.

'Fuck you, man,' Rocky had said in that accent of his, which somehow reminded Sudheer of his sister, not just because it was heavily American but because his voice was like a girl's, which he always found funny coming from the mouth of a man named Rocky. 'That's James Maharaj.'

'What? Who the fuck is that? And what kind of a name is James Maharaj?'

'He is Gulati's daughter's boyfriend, that's who he is.'

'Defence minister Gulati?'

'No. The milkman.' Rocky slapped his forehead. 'Yes. Of course. The defence minister. What were you thinking?'

'Which of those two girls was the defence minister's daughter? *Doodh ki* tanker on the right?' Sudheer cupped his hand in the air over his chest, 'or *registaan* on the left?'

'Neither.'

'Haha, Gulati's daughter would have thanked me for killing him then. Hell, she might as well have licked my ass.'

'You are drunk.' Rocky gestured to his bouncers who had followed him into the room. 'You there, call his driver and get sahib out to the car.'

'Yeah, I should go home.' Sudheer had brushed aside the bouncer who was reaching out for him. 'Your party sucks worse than your mother.'

Sudheer smiled at the memory of having told off Rocky. Maybe the party hadn't been that bad after all.

'Are you all right, sahib?' the driver asked from behind, leaning forward towards the driver's seat. 'If you let me, I can drive the rest of the way.'

'What's your name?' asked Sudheer, lowering the volume of the music system.

The man hesitated.

'Or do you want me to call you sahib?'

'Satyaprakash Jha.'

'So Satyaprakash Jha, what music do you like? I am guessing not what's playing in this car.'

'Sahib, please let me go.'

'*Arre,*' Sudheer said cheerfully. 'What's to let go? Tell me, who is your favourite singer?'

'Sahib, *chodiye na.*'

'I asked you a question.'

'Kumar Sanu.'

'*Waah waah, kya baat hai.* Sing me a song of Kumar Sanu. And in his voice.'

He turned the music system off.

'I can't sing.' Satyaprakash was sitting, hands folded, trying to check where Sudheer's gun was.

'Sing me a sad song of Kumar Sanu.'

'I can't sing... please.'

'Ten thousand rupees.' Sudheer pointed to his wallet. 'One song. *Chal guru ho ja shuru.*'

Satyaprakash Jha coughed once, and then again, clearing his throat nervously.

'*Abey, bahut ho gaya nakhra,*' Sudheer yelled. '*Gaana chaloo kar.*'

'*Ab tere bin jee lenge...*'

That's when it happened. A sharp boom, the sound of breaking glass, and then a warm burst of liquid hit Sudheer on the back of his head. Satyaprakash Jha's body flew forward, his head hit the back of the passenger seat, and there were bits of his brain and skull all around, on the windows and the upholstery and dripping down Sudheer's hair and his shoulder.

Sudheer heard another shot and on instinct, he swerved the car to the right. The bullet hit the door on the driver's side, missing the window. He turned his head in the direction of the shots, and saw that there was a motorcycle on that side, and two men sitting on it, but that's all he could make out in the darkness outside.

The drink was gone, and Sudheer felt surprisingly lucid. He pressed on the accelerator with every ounce of his weight. The road was deserted and the Jaguar sped forward, which is when he heard another shot, and this time the car jagged crazily to the side. Sudheer smelt burning rubber. They had shot out a tyre.

The Jaguar careened forward, driving on metal, and though he could not see them, Sudheer knew they were on his tail. Holding the steering wheel with one hand, he reached to the side to get his gun out, when he realized it was useless. He would never be able to get a shot at the target while it was moving. So he kept the gun near the gear box and moved his hands back to the steering.

He was going to outrun them, Sudheer told himself, this was, after all, a Jaguar. And that bike... God knows what desi shit that was.

The gun fired again and again. The driver's window shattered into small shards of glass and Sudheer felt the bullets sinking into him, like two lead caterpillars burrowing slowly in.

Madarchod. They shot me.

He saw the men clearly, handkerchiefs round their faces, one of them bald, and he turned the wheel sharply to the right to hit them and they shot again and missed, trying to protect themselves from being run off the road.

The Jaguar again raced ahead till they shot out another tyre. In the distance, Sudheer could see the headlights of an oncoming truck.

No, make that three trucks. Right behind each other.

Sudheer felt nothing. Just a creeping sensation of wetness, and he knew it was his blood. The men were now at his side, and the pillion rider extended his arm to get his gun as close and as steady as he could. Sudheer turned his head and, over the roar of the car and the bike and the rumbling of the approaching trucks, picked up the gun and emptied the magazine blindly in the direction of his attackers. '*Ma chode tere. Ma chode.*'

Then he felt the searing pain of another bullet shattering his collarbone, and he clutched hard on to the steering wheel. The Jaguar started turning in a circle, one turn then a half, in a cloud of sparks and fire. He tried to step on the accelerator but the car did not respond. As the truck came straight at him, he could smell petrol and burning metal, and heard the rumbling of the bike moving away. He tried to lunge against the door, but his body, ridden with bullets, refused to budge.

'You amateurs don't know how to finish a job.' Sudheer leaned back into the driver's seat, a little smile on his lips. His voice was now a low murmur, 'As papa would say, you are just like me.'

Arjun sat in the VIP waiting room of the All India Institute of Medical Science, hunched forward on the couch, head in his hands. They had come all through the night and into the morning, ministers and businessmen, and he had thanked them all for standing by the family in this hour, and then had politely sent them their way. Just an hour ago, he had finally convinced Preeti to go home, along with her extended family. She had to look after Nimmi as she was with child and needed special attention, that was what Arjun had said, and after Preeti had left, he had given specific instructions to call the family doctor and get him to prescribe something that would let her get some sleep. Preeti seemed to have aged ten years in these last twelve hours, and when she had left, her eyes were so swollen from crying that she could barely see. Arjun had felt a sense of relief once she agreed to go home for there would be people there to watch over her.

As he watched her go, he remembered what she had asked him to promise – never to go to meet Nayantara. On Sudheer's head.

She was dead when I went. And I never promised on Sudheer's head. And all this is nonsense anyway. Whatever it be, she will never find out. No one will.

Only his security was left, discreetly manning the perimeter and the entrances of AIIMS, and so was Mohan, standing all this while at the door, looking out at the passage. He had not cried, he had not said much. The only difference from his normal behaviour, Arjun observed, was that he was pacing nervously about.

'Mohan, don't hold it in, beta. It doesn't help to keep it inside.'

'Sudheer will pull through. I know that.'

'Then why are you ...'

'Isn't it obvious?' Mohan said with sudden energy. 'Arijit tried to kill Sudheer and we are sitting here, like helpless women, doing nothing.'

'What do you want me to do? Take a gun and start shooting people on mere suspicion while my son is dying here?'

'It could only have been Arijit.' Mohan became calm once again. 'Did Riti come here to the hospital?'

'She called. I let Mathur talk to her. He thanked her for calling and told her that she does not need to come to the hospital, and that she will be informed of any developments. I think she got the message.'

'But of course.'

'If you are trying to suggest my daughter is a part of this, you better have some solid evidence to back it up.' Arjun picked up the small bottle of water next to him and finished it in a gulp. 'I am walking a tightrope here too, don't make me snap.'

'It's Arijit. It could be no one else. Only he would have the, pardon my language, balls to pull this off, now that he has Riti. He is finishing us off, in different ways, don't you see?'

Arjun stayed silent.

'Things are not the same,' Mohan said. 'People aren't as afraid of us as they used to be. There are a lot of things going on that you don't know.'

'Like how you and Sudheer met RP and Simmi's father and they advised Sudheer to go behind my back to Mehta?'

'If you knew why didn't you ...'

'Because I wanted you two boys to learn. The whole deal is doomed, the Mehtas have already made their move from the back, and they are waiting for their rivals to go in and get their legs blown off. That's why I have kept away.'

'Well, then, why didn't you tell Sudheer?' Mohan spluttered. 'He would have lost his leg too.'

'You were very young then ... I don't know if you remember, but we had lost all our money.'

'Of course I do, but how does that have anything to do with ...'

'What scared me the most then, what kept me up at nights, was the thought that I would not be able to bring my children up the way I wanted to. That I would be a poor father, a weak father, like so many, who can do nothing but let their sons and daughters go into the world as they watch from afar, unable to do anything but pray to God. There is nothing in the world worse than being a weak father, no greater failure as a human being than not having the power to protect the ones you love the most. I have tried all my life to protect all three of you, in the way I have felt was the best. I have pulled Sudheer and you from the edge many times, and I know that made you two angry, at least it did Sudheer. I did it because it made me feel powerful, as a father and as a human being. But now I have come to realize I made a mistake. I should have let you fail. All of you. Sudheer, you, Riti. Only through failure and heartbreak would you have learned, would you have known what it means to lose and what it feels like to win it back again. It was my mistake. My arrogance brought you up wrong. I have realized that now, after Riti left, and so I didn't say anything. I let things be. Maybe I would have still pulled Sudheer out, if it looked like it was going to become a disaster, maybe that way I will never change as a father, but still I was going to wait till the very end before I pulled the parachute cord. But then ...'

'So let me do this, papa, let me deal with Arijit,' Mohan pleaded. 'If it is my mistake, so be it. Let me learn.'

'No, not now. Not when one of my sons is dying and my daughter is gone. Not now.'

'Don't be worried for me. Nothing will happen. I have my men, I am not foolish that I will try to do this myself.' Mohan held his father's hand in his. 'I am going to get Arijit picked up and I will question him. No violence, nothing. Just questioning. Then I will have him watched, his phones tapped, and we smoke out whoever is behind him.'

'Don't do that. I am telling you not to.'

'Why? You killed his father and Sudheer bust his face. God knows, he has reason enough to want to send our family to hell.'

'If he is innocent, I don't want him to have to face whatever you are planning, not after what we have already done to him.'

'And what if he is guilty?'

'Then even worse. He is waiting for you to strike back and you are going to walk into his trap.'

'May I come in?' They both looked up to see Abdul Ismail standing at the door. Behind him were two of his men.

Arjun motioned them in. Ismail closed the door and left his men outside.

'When I came to know Sudheer's gun had been fired, I was suspecting or rather praying that he had hit one of them. Well, he did.'

Ismail had a piece of paper with him, which he kept on the table in front of Arjun and Mohan.

'A small government clinic nearby. A man checks in last night with a bullet wound from a .22. He has another man with him. He has a gun. So the doctor does not file a police report. But he does file it in their records.'

'How do we know this is his real name?' Mohan asked.

Ismail smiled. 'Oh, it's his real name, all right. We have already located the shooters. All your men need is for you,' he said, and he looked at Arjun, 'to tell them what to do with these two.'

'Where are they?'

Ismail took a chit of paper out from his blue shirt and kept it on the table.

'Here's the address. They are cousins. Small-time crooks.'

Arjun looked at it for a second. 'Pick them up.'

'They are staying with his family, hiding inside their home. It is going to be difficult for your people to bring them out without... you know... some unpleasantness.'

'Get in touch with Sandeep. Not Ramesh, keep him out of this. Tell Sandeep to have men dressed up as police go and knock on the door.' Arjun thought for a moment. 'If they come quiet, fine. If they try to run, catch them from the back. Make sure at least one of them is alive. Then take them to a safe house, and this is very important, do not do anything till I come.'

Ismail looked surprised. He stayed silent for a moment and then stroked his beard contemplatively. 'Leave the questioning to Sandeep. You stay here.'

'No,' Arjun said. 'I need to go myself. It's time I got my hands dirty again.'

It was late at night, close to three, when the doctors came out of the operating room. Arjun had the best team in the country working on Sudheer, two doctors had flown in from London, and there were three more coming the next morning from the US.

Dr O'Brian gave the news. 'It's a miracle he is alive. Your son has the luck of the Irish, I say.'

The truck had not hit Sudheer's side of the car. The driver had been skilled enough to swerve and hit the tail of the car, sending it rolling down the side of road. Then Sudheer's layers of fat had cushioned his organs from the bullets and withstood most of the damage, and while there was still massive internal bleeding and multiple fractures on his clavicle and limbs, none of his major organs had been ruptured. He was not out of danger yet, Dr O'Brian said, because the internal bleeding had not stopped entirely, but in the next forty-eight hours, things would probably get better if he remained stable.

'If it is okay, may I see him?' Arjun asked.

'In an hour or two, maybe. But only five minutes. And only you. Let's not get the family back here. I don't want his room to become a convention.'

They let Arjun in after three hours. The first sight of Sudheer, lying there on the bed in blue and white and with all sorts of tubes and machines connected to his body, made Arjun tear up, and he stopped and held the wall for support.

This is how Nayantara must have felt when she saw Arijit. This is revenge. The universe's revenge.

Then he entered, small, silent steps and sat near his bed. Sudheer's eyes were closed and he breathed heavily, and Arjun looked intently at the displays and the dials, almost as if he could will them to make his son better.

'Papa, is that you?'

Arjun reached out and held Sudheer by his forearm. That was the only place there was not bandage or needle.

'Yes, it's me. You are going to be all right. Everything is going to be all right.'

'If anything happens to me, promise to look after my son.'

'We don't know if it's a son and stop talking nonsense.'

'On the subject of nonsense, seems like my fat protected me. Heard the doctors talking about that.'

'That's what they say.'

'You always told me to stop eating laddoos. If I had listened to you, I would be dead now.'

'I promise that from now on I will feed you laddoos myself. Now try not to talk, will you?'

'I am sorry I screwed up. I am a failure.' One of the instruments gave two blips and then a small red light came on.

'No, you are not. You are my son.'

A doctor and a nurse came in. Arjun knew he had to leave. He was going to stand up, when Sudheer said, 'Look after Mohan. He needs a lot of looking after.'

'You have looked after him all these years. Get better and look after him yourself.'

'You remember that cat that died, that ayah's son had that cat, remember?'

The doctor silently mouthed the words, 'You should leave, please.'

'What cat?' Arjun asked, showing a bit of irritation.

'That's why you sent me to boarding school, remember? Because I killed that cat.'

'You need to stop talking now. All this can wait.'

'I didn't kill that cat, papa. Mohan did. I took the blame because you would be mad at him. You were always so mad at all of us then.' The effort of speaking turned his cheeks pale but Sudheer went on, 'That's why I said, look after him, in case I don't make it. He needs care.'

'Why did Mohan kill that cat?'

'He just said he didn't like its meow.'

Rishi sat upstairs in his Maharani Bagh duplex, wearing nothing but a pair of briefs. There was a day–night game with Australia this evening, the bets were coming in every minute, and he was in his bedroom, door locked, windows locked, the entrance to the verandah locked, with a number of phones, sheets of papers with bets, a glass of whisky, a muted television with the cricket match on, a half-finished box of biryani and a shiny Glock, fully loaded.

The intercom buzzed and he pressed the button.

'Is she here?'

Over the years, Rishi realized that his tastes had undergone a change. He now preferred single malt over beer, Hollywood over Hindi movies, and older women, in their mid-thirties, to the waif-like twenty-somethings that flitted about in the parties he frequented. There was just more to hold on to with older women, but with young girls, as he liked to say, it was like making love to soda, a bit of fizz and pop, but then ultimately just water and air. This one today would be special – the beautiful wife of a small-time bookie who owed him money, a mother of two – and he could not wait to slip off his briefs and greet her in the nude when she walked through the door for the first time. He always liked to give the ladies that surprise.

'No, it's a gentleman. He said you would be expecting him,' said Madhavan from downstairs.

'Can he hear you?'

'No, sir, I have kept him outside the door.'

'Search him thoroughly.'

'I already have.'

'Do it again.'

'Yes, sir.'

'Once you have done that, bring him up.'

In two minutes, there was a knock on the door. Rishi strode up, opened it, and then quickly went back and sat on the bed, his hand comfortably close to the Glock.

Mohan walked in, dressed in a black suit, a white shirt and a pale blue tie. He looked once around the room and then sat down on the couch next to the television set.

'Want to search some more?' he asked, without a trace of irritation in his voice. 'The only thing left was to pull my foreskin down to see if I had a gun there.'

'Yeah, what to do. These are tough times. People getting shot on the highway.'

'What about that then?'

'I don't know what to say. We fucked up.'

'No, we didn't fuck up. You did.' Mohan lost his cool for just a moment and then he was back to his cold self. 'I told you to get someone good to do the job.'

Rishi took the glass of whisky and took a sip. 'Look, it's not as if I can put an ad in the paper for this sort of stuff. I just got who I felt was the best. Those two came recommended.'

'Oh, so that was the best?' Mohan raised an eyebrow. 'There is an elephant and an ant in a car. They are told to kill the elephant. They kill the ant.'

'What can they do if your brother decides to drive and the driver sits in the back?'

'Maybe take a look before firing. I don't know, does that sound particularly difficult?'

'Fuck it, man. Mistakes happen. They tried their best.' Rishi threw his hands up in frustration. 'What can I do if your brother wears layers of lard like it's a fucking bulletproof vest? The number of bullets they got in would have stopped an elephant in heat.'

'Why didn't you get Chuha to do the job? I paid enough I suppose. Why did you get shooters on the cheap and pocket the difference?'

'Look here.' Rishi pointed his finger menacingly at Mohan. 'I am not a cook that you can slap me around for putting too much salt in your paneer. You know who my papa is, one snap of his fingers and you little pricks will be walking around in Tihar with your hands on your bums. This isn't the '80s any more, okay? Your papa counts for nothing in the city. Nothing. Can't even manage his own family, daughter goes and sleeps with the son of an enemy. Yes, we have all heard that. So take your attitude elsewhere, you little shit-stain.' He looked at the ceiling. 'Fuck me for having even taken this on. That too as a favour.'

'You talked to the shooter yourself, right?'

'Yeah, so what?' Rishi frowned.

'My father knows who the shooters are.'

'So?'

'So? He was going to have his men bring them in and then they would have beaten your name out of them. It's only your good luck that I was there when Ismail brought the names in. Otherwise my father's men would have been knocking on your door right now.'

'So you got the shooters killed. Big deal. Even if they had identified me, who cares? I am protected. No one can touch me.' A call was coming in on one of his phones and Rishi disconnected it without picking it up. 'It would be different for you though, if your father came to know who put the hit on his son. I am guessing there would be an uncomfortable family dinner after that.' He stood up and walked up to the bar to pour himself another peg. 'So stop making it out as if you did me a favour. You saved your own ass.'

'You think my father counts for nothing?'

'Sudheer is my good friend for years now. He is a stupid fat fuck but he is a good friend. And I like you too. You get laid a lot, and I have heard that you are hung like a horse, which means God likes you too. But that doesn't mean I can't tell you the truth. That's what everyone says, and I am sorry if it comes across as blunt. Your dad is finished.'

'Do you know why I wanted Sudheer to die?'

'You want to move up in the inheritance ladder?'

'No, it's because he thinks like you. He thinks my father counts for nothing. Sometimes even I do, but then I am smart enough to realize I am wrong.'

Rishi gave a sarcastic grunt.

'My brother was going to go behind his back to the Mehtas. Thought that would get him in the good books of his wife and father-in-law.'

'Good for him. He should have.'

'What he didn't know was that papa knew. He is always a step ahead.'

'Now I don't get you. Why do you want to kill your brother again?'

'Because Sudheer wanted to rebel against papa, he wanted to be the bad boy. He had, as the Americans like to say, daddy issues. And the way he was going on, papa would have lost his patience and cut us off, sooner or later, just as he did with Riti. And even if papa had done nothing, we would have destroyed ourselves, because doing what papa does not do himself is doing something that's not right.'

'You are his sons. Everyone loves their sons. He wouldn't have cut you off for a few bad business decisions. Daughters, different things.'

'Sons or daughters, whatever they may be, papa does not tolerate fools. Because, as he says, fools get themselves and others killed. Sudheer is a fool. That's why he had to go. Otherwise he would have gotten me killed. And now thanks to you, I have lost the opportunity and I can't take another shot because papa will start suspecting me, if he hasn't already.'

'Give me a break. Your father isn't God.'

'I wouldn't be so afraid of him if he was.'

'Then?'

'I am afraid he is the devil.'

'And what are you then? The son-of-the-devil?'

The intercom buzzed again. Rishi pressed it.

'Sir, the lady is here.'

'Search her but don't get too frisky, okay? I would not want you to come before I do.' Cutting off the intercom, he looked at Mohan and shook his head in the direction of the door. 'Now if you will excuse me, I have to let off some steam.'

Mohan adjusted his jacket and tie and walked towards the exit. 'I like the sound of that.' A small smile darted across his face. 'The son-of-the-devil.'

Rishi gave a contemptuous wave of his hand as the door closed behind Mohan. As it clicked shut, he eagerly worked his boxers off and waited for his guest, already rock hard. In a minute, there was a soft knock, he leapt to open the door, telling himself to catch her expression when she first laid eyes on his gym-toned body.

But instead of a lady in a sari and a sleeveless blouse, which is what he had imagined she would be wearing, the round tube of a silencer was aimed at his face. Before he could move or get a word out, Rishi's body flew back, and hit the ground with a dull dead thud.

'Rishi ji, if only you had given me the job, *motay* would have been dead,' Chuha said, looking at the blood splatter on the wall and on the TV with a sad smile face on his face, 'and you would have been alive.'

Sudheer had come home. They had transported him in a special emergency vehicle. Then he had to be carried up to his bedroom, swathed in bandages as he was, held up by six people, and put down on a bed specially imported from the US. He would stay there for a while but, as Nimmi kept saying to one and all, he had come home. She was the host of the party, walking around proudly, aglow with motherhood, more happy than Arjun had ever seen her. The whole mansion was full of people, relatives from every side of the family, friends and business partners, outnumbered only by the balloons, some spelling out 'Welcome home' and some with the line 'We love you Sudheer' and some just dancing around in the breeze. Arjun had walked about shaking hands, thanking guest and was looking to slip away into a quiet corner when Preeti caught him by his arm.

'What's the matter with you?'

'Me?'

'Yes, God has given our son a second life, we are going to have a grandchild soon, we are a family again, and there you are, walking about with that expression on your face. What's the matter?'

'Nothing. Why do you think there is something the matter?'

'It's Riti, isn't it? You are missing her today.'

Arjun stayed quiet, looking out of the large French window.

'She has made her choice,' Preeti said firmly.

Arjun looked down at his shoes, shook his head, and took a sip of wine.

'Yes, she has. As have Sudheer and Mohan. They have all made their choices.'

'For once, I approve. I very much approve.' Preeti looked across the hall, her eyes finding Mohan and his companion, a girl in a black cocktail dress. Arjun had never seen her before, but someone said she was one of India's top models. Preeti leaned towards Arjun and whispered, 'He's never brought a girlfriend of his to a family event.' She giggled. 'I think he is serious about her. She is so beautiful. Don't you think so?'

'There is something I want to tell you before I tell the boys.'

'What's that?'

'I have decided to split the business between them. Sudheer

will get what he wants, Mohan will get his share, and they will have what they've always wanted. Independence.'

Preeti's eyes twinkled. 'Seriously?'

'Yes,' he said. 'The whole business has become too big for me. And the boys are old enough to move into the real world by themselves.'

'I want to tell them this! I want to see the expressions on their faces.' Preeti could barely control her excitement. 'You don't know how much Sudheer has wanted this. You have no idea.'

'I think I do,' Arjun said slowly.

'So you will be at home more frequently now?'

'I guess.'

'I am so happy. We all worry about your health, you know. You are growing old and yet you do not want to slow down.'

Arjun smiled, and then someone called out her name and Preeti hurried away, and the moment he knew she could not see him any more, the smile on Arjun's face slowly vanished.

He looked out of the window again. He thought of Lahore and his brothers, their faces now blurred in his memory; of Bangali, driving and singing; of Arijit repairing transistors in his oversized shorts; of Sudheer and Mohan playing cricket with him and Sudheer hitting a ball so hard that it broke the glass of a second-floor window; of Preeti bringing him halwa in her father's garage; of Riti walking with him in Central Park; and of Nayantara, and the ever-shining stars in her eyes.

All of these memories, like old ticket stubs in a dusty trunk.

Wiping his eyes with his sleeve, Arjun looked down at the wine.

All he saw was his own shadow, black reflected on shimmering red.